A MAIDEN'S KISS

"Please don't cry, Cicely. I didn't mean you didn't please me." He reached for her hands and held them tightly in his own. "I think you look . . . glorious."

She tilted her face up to his. "Truly, Simon?"

He couldn't help himself. Her sweet, tempting lips were so close. He leaned down and kissed her. A tender kiss, meant to do no more than reassure this innocent maid that he found her desirable. But when his lips met hers, his noble resolve faded. She tasted as delectable as honey, and her body, now pressed against his, felt so soft and supple. He let his mouth linger, savoring the taste and scent and feel of her.

His body trembled with the strain of holding back as he deepened the kiss. The way she welcomed him, reaching up to tangle her fingers in his hair, it was as if she would hold him against her forever. Finally, she drew away.

"Dear Cicely, forgive me," he whispered.

"There is naught to forgive. I liked it, very much." Her expression grew impish. "I want more, Simon. . . ."

BOOK YOUR PLACE ON OUR WEBSITE AND MAKE THE READING CONNECTION!

We've created a customized website just for our very special readers, where you can get the inside scoop on everything that's going on with Zebra, Pinnacle and Kensington books.

When you come online, you'll have the exciting opportunity to:

- View covers of upcoming books
- Read sample chapters
- Learn about our future publishing schedule (listed by publication month *and author*)
- Find out when your favorite authors will be visiting a city near you
- Search for and order backlist books from our online catalog
- Check out author bios and background information
- Send e-mail to your favorite authors
- Meet the Kensington staff online
- Join us in weekly chats with authors, readers and other guests
- Get writing guidelines
- AND MUCH MORE!

**Visit our website at
http://www.zebrabooks.com**

MY GALLANT KNIGHT

TARA O'DELL

Zebra Books
Kensington Publishing Corp.

http://www.zebrabooks.com

ZEBRA BOOKS are published by

Kensington Publishing Corp.
850 Third Avenue
New York, NY 10022

Zebra, the Z logo Splendor Reg. U.S. Pat. & TM Off.

First Printing: October, 1999
10 9 8 7 6 5 4 3 2 1

Printed in the United States of America

*To my own darling young knight, Thomas, and to my mother,
Helen Marquardt, whose support and sacrifice taught
me the essence of love.*

CHAPTER 1

"Nay! 'Tis not God's will!" Lady Adela de Valois raised her hands in an imploring gesture. "Our daughter has not the compliant, pious nature to be a bride of Christ. She will be miserable at Montreau."

"Then you have failed in your duty, madam!" The bitter lines which etched Robert de Valois's face deepened. "As her mother, you are charged with the task of molding her character. If you had not indulged her foolish whims, she would have learned meekness and obedience instead of willfulness. I vow you have ruined her with your cosseting!"

Adela approached her husband and gently touched his shoulder. "You are overwrought, milord. The strain of these past months . . ."

He drew away from her. "I am well enough. The worst is over. We did not lose everything, as I feared. We have Tathwick and the lands. Hugh's inheritance remains intact."

"Then why . . . ?"

"I have told you. I made a vow, a solemn vow to God. If we did not lose all, if King John's wrath passed us by, I promised I would give my daughter to the Holy Church."

"Then you have promised what you had no right to." Adela's eyes filled with tears. "Think of Cicely, love. How can you look at her and imagine her as a quiet, dutiful nun? Though she be but eight years, her character is plain. If you must promise one of them to the Church, then let it be Hugh . . ."

"Hugh! He is the heir! He will rule Tathwick after me!"

"And he has not half of Cicely's spirit. Already he favors ciphering with the priest over battle practice. I do not believe he would be unhappy at the prospect of taking holy orders."

Robert's dark eyes grew incredulous. "What nonsense! Certainly the boy will be a knight, as were his father and grandfather before him. The lineage of Valois warriors stretches back to the days of the Conqueror himself!"

Adela closed her eyes, praying for guidance, for the right words to sway her husband. Although what she suggested went against all the precepts of society, she knew she spoke rightly. Cicely might be a maid, but she was the one with the strength to hold Tathwick. Adela could feel it in her bones.

"Enough!" Robert strode toward the door. "I am finished discussing the matter. A vow is a vow. 'Twill be as I have said!"

Adela followed him. "Then you may have the pleasure of telling her your decision, milord!" she snapped. " 'Tis none of my doing!"

Some of the sternness left Robert's face as he quit his wife's solar. The thought of explaining his plans to his daughter unsettled him. He had hoped Adela would take on the task.

* * *

"Daughter, I'm giving you to the Church." The words sounded harsh in the sunlit autumn garden, as cruel and stunning as a bowshot.

As soon as they were out, Robert sought to soften them. " 'Tis a great honor. I will bequeath a substantial sum to the priory at Montreau. You will be well treated always. If you serve obediently and diligently, there are opportunities to rise in the order . . ."

His words trailed off, silenced by the bewilderment in Cicely's brown eyes. With her heart-shaped face and dark blond curls, she was a striking child, as exquisite as a flower. To see her in such turmoil was like a dagger in his gut.

Her pink lips trembled. "You're sending me away? Why, Papa?"

The dagger twisted. "Because I have no choice. I have no lands left to dower you. Tathwick goes to Hugh, and there is nothing else."

The girl's ivory-skinned brow puckered. "Surely we are still a great Norman family. Are we not, Papa?"

He took a deep breath. The years had not been kind to the Valois family. Little by little, the vast lands they had once ruled had slipped away. First, the rich demesne in Angoulême, then pieces of the English property. Some was lost in disputes with other landlords, some used to fund the Lionheart's crusades. Lately, they had been helpless victims of King John's greed.

"You can always be proud of your name, Cicely. Your great-great grandsire arrived in England with the Conqueror himself and was much rewarded. And before that, the title of Valois was one to be reckoned with in Normandy. But we are no longer rich, child. There are things you cannot understand, evil in this world that you cannot know . . ." He groped for words as the impotent anger welled up inside him. Cicely was much too young to understand the treacheries of kings. "All I hold now is Tathwick," he said softly, "and that must go to Hugh."

"But why? Because he is the elder? 'Tis only by a twelve-month!"

"Nay, child. Because he will grow up to be a man, and you a maid."

"Why does that matter?"

"Ladies do not rule, Cicely. They have babies and tend households."

She frowned again. "You are sending me away to have babies and tend a household?"

"Nay. You will be a nun. A holy sister. 'Tis a great honor," he repeated. Exasperation rose in him. Cicely had never appeared simpleminded before. Did she deliberately provoke him?

Her delicate jaw jutted forward. "I don't think I would like being a nun."

"You will do as I bid."

"Maman will not make me!"

"She will. She obeys me, and you will also!"

The tone of his voice silenced her, but he could see the rebellion in her eyes. A new uneasiness gripped him. Would she shame him before the prioress when he took her to Montreau? Cicely had always been an impulsive, outspoken child. He should have tried to beat the stubbornness from her, but her fragile beauty made it impossible for him to lay a hand on her.

"You must understand, daughter. I have no choice. A high-born maid can only marry or take the veil. Since I have no land with which to dower you, the priory is the only way I can assure your safety."

The perplexed frown was back, stealing the sunshine from her features. "Why can I not marry without lands? Edgar and Asa married, and Asa had no property at all."

"Edgar and Asa are baseborn. They marry where they will, with my permission, of course. But you can wed only a man with property, and none will want you without lands of your own."

"I would not care if he were a lord," Cicely said earnestly. " 'Twould be enough if he were kind and good, like Edgar."

"No daughter of mine will wed beneath her. I will not have it!"

" 'Tis not you who will be wed! I do not see that it is your right to decide for me."

The uneasy feeling inside him deepened. Would Cicely dare to argue right and wrong with the nuns and priests? They would count him a sinful man for raising such an intransigent child, and doubly wicked for sending her to the Church.

He raised his hand reflexively. "Curb your tongue, demoiselle, or I will still it with my fist. You will do as I bid."

Hurt welled in her eyes. They were an unusual shade, almost purplish brown, the hue of a velvety alder catkin. Now they brightened with the glitter of tears.

He hardened his heart. 'Twas his weakness which had encouraged her scandalously forthright nature. "There now. You will not cry. I forbid it. You will hold your head high, remembering you are a Valois, and you will do your duty. As we all have."

Robert turned on his heel and strode from the garden. As his steel-shod boots thudded on the flagstones of the walkway, he became aware that he gripped something in his hand. He opened his fingers and watched a crushed flower flutter to the ground to lie in a smear of pink. A campion, one of the latest flowers of the season. He had absentmindedly picked it while he waited for Cicely.

A lump started in his throat. He had condemned his lovely, vibrant daughter to the same fate as the flower. Life in the convent would press the passion and vitality from her. All that beauty and exuberance would be lost.

A tear rose to his eye. Never again to hear Cicely's bell-like laugh, to smile at her childish antics . . .

She sat a better horse than his son, was utterly fearless of hounds and hawks, liked to climb trees and race through the courtyard like a wild village child. Yet she was not unfeminine. When she bobbed a curtsy and twirled her skirts in a display of miniature womanhood, he always felt a glow of pride—and a touch of astonishment—that he had sired such an irresistible maid.

He reminded himself that there was little place in life for innocent beauty. If he could not keep her safe, his sweet flower would eventually be plucked by some unscrupulous lord, mayhap King John himself. Then the sparkle in her eyes would turn to the bitter glow of hatred; her impish charm fade to despair and shame.

Nay, that loss he would not endure. Better that she live the barren life of a nun and keep a hint of her loveliness.

He set his jaw and pushed through the garden gate.

The hooves of the horses of the small traveling party sounded loud on the frost-hardened ground. Cicely sat rigid on her palfrey, aware of every nuance of her surroundings—the soft kiss of the mist against her skin, the way the muscles of her mount coiled and stretched, the reek of wet wool and oiled armor from the armed knights on either side of her.

Soon she would be shut off from these things, and she knew she would miss them desperately. The freedom and exhilaration of riding, the passing of the seasons in the familiar landscape around Tathwick, even the feel of her own clothes and the sounds and scents of the castle, all of these would be lost to her.

She had asked her mother what life would be like in the priory, and her mother, sighing, had told her. Lots of prayers and quiet time, mayhap music if the prioress were lenient. With the endowment her father was providing, Cicely would not be expected to do the hard labor of a regular novice. She would have a life of leisure and ease.

When Cicely inquired as to what she would do when she was not praying, her mother's face had grown worried and grim. There would be sewing of course, her mother said, the perpetual task of all women of gentle breeding. And if she expressed an avocation for ciphering or healing, she might possibly assist in the scriptorium or infirmary.

A muffled sob escaped Cicely. Didn't her parents realize what they had done to her? 'Twas torture for her to be still during Mass, and that was only once a week and on holy days. How would she endure hours, days, weeks, months, *years* of quiet prayer?

The thought of it filled her with a panic so great, it took all her will to keep from kicking the sedate palfrey into a gallop and racing off.

But that would be witless. She had no idea of where she was or of how to get home. And even if she reached the safety of Tathwick, they would not let her stay. She had no choice but to accept her father's decision.

The tears began to flow, streaming down her cheeks. How could this awful thing happen to her?

"We're very near," announced the knight riding on her right. "I can hear the bells calling them to prayers."

"The priory is built on a rise. As soon as we clear the valley, we should see it."

Cicely recognized the answering voice as that of her father. The familiar tones enlarged the lump in her throat.

She closed her eyes, knowing that her mount would keep pace with the others without her guidance. Then, realizing that the next few moments would be her last of freedom, she opened her eyes and strained to see.

Her father had spoken true. As the track climbed, the fog lifted, and Montreau appeared in the distance.

Low stone walls, built for shelter rather than defense. Buildings of a variety of shapes and sizes. The chapel in the center, its tall spire rising gracefully toward the slate-colored sky.

The sight sharpened Cicely's distress. Already she could imagine the wooden doorway in the stone wall closing behind her.

Before they left Tathwick, she had asked her mother if she would be able to come home for visits. A pained look had crossed Lady Adela's face, although her voice had been steady and soft as she'd answered that novices did not usually leave the priory. Then she had suggested that when Cicely was older she might make a pilgrimage or visit another order.

But they would come to see her, her mother went on to assure her. She would not break off all ties with her daughter, no matter what the prioress thought. Thankfully, Montreau was not far from Tathwick. There would be visits, as well as frequent letters.

Letters. Visits. As if she were a prisoner—which she would be. Like Maud the Fair, locked in the Tower of London because she had displeased the king. Cicely had overheard her parents talking about the poor lady, pitying her.

Why could they not see that they were doing the same thing to their daughter?

A new spasm of despair seized Cicely, and she sobbed aloud. Her father eased his mount beside hers. "There now, child. Do not do that." His voice was coaxing, desperate. Cicely knew he feared she would embarrass him by openly expressing her unhappiness.

At the thought, her grief turned to anger. How dare he worry about himself when she was the one to suffer!

"I will not shame you!" she told him bitterly. "But this I

vow: Someday I will leave Montreau. I will not live there when I am grown! I will not!''

Her father opened his mouth, but did not speak.

Cicely looked away, wiping her tears with the sleeve of her undertunic. Although she was not clear on the matter, she knew one of the reasons she was being sent to Montreau was that her father had made a vow to God. She would do the same. Although she had no holy relics to swear upon, her promise would be as binding as his.

"I will not live all my days at Montreau," she repeated. "I vow that someday I *will* escape."

She turned defiantly to face him. Beneath the nasal of his helmet, her father's face looked stricken.

CHAPTER 2

As the bells sounded for matins, Cicely carefully closed the vellum pages of the book on her lap. She cast a furtive glance at the door of her cell, then returned the leather-bound tome to the hiding place under her pallet and blew out the tallow candle propped on the edge of the *prie-Dieu* next to the bed.

After pausing to listen to the sounds in the hallway, she crawled beneath the fur-lined coverlet and sighed. She had reached a particularly stirring portion of the tale she was reading, and it was utter frustration to have to put it away. But she dare not stay up later. If found out, she would be subjected to a tongue-lashing from Sister Matilda and the certainty of once more being called in to see the prioress.

Cicely fidgeted. She could not sleep until she knew how things turned out in the story, if the sad lady of Brittany, locked in a tower by her selfish husband, would ever be rescued.

Sighing again, she turned on her side. Surely the tale would end happily. The story of Yonec had been written by Marie of

France, and a woman author would never curse a member of her own sex to a lifetime of imprisonment. A gallant knight would come to the lady's aid, Cicely was certain of it. But how would he get into the tower? How would he accomplish his bold rescue?

She squirmed on the hard pallet and fought the temptation to retrieve the book from its hiding place. There was a tiny square of moonlight filtering into the cell through a window. If she carried the book to the spot, she might be able to make out the words.

She held still and listened. Everyone must be at midnight prayers or asleep, as she was supposed to be.

Emboldened by the quiet, Cicely slid her legs from beneath the coverlet and shivered at the chill which attacked her bare flesh beneath the brown serge gown. She counted herself fortunate that her family's bequests kept her from the worst hardships of priory life. She was not required to attend prayers at matins, but could sleep until prime. She had a private cell, tiny though it was; a warm, fur-lined coverlet; and a cushioned *prie-Dieu* so she could kneel to pray in comfort rather than on the cold stone floor. These were luxuries most of the other inhabitants of Montreau did without.

Her prison was not unbearably harsh, yet it was still a prison, Cicely thought as she eased the book from beneath the pallet. She was no better off than the lady of Brittany, locked in a tower.

She tiptoed to the sliver of moonlight, wincing at the coldness of the floor beneath her bare feet. Once in the light, she opened the book with shaking fingers. The small piece of silk she used to protect the precious pages fluttered to the floor. Helpless to retrieve it, she used the tips of her nails to delicately turn to her place.

She had barely found the last line she had read when the

sliver of light vanished. Cicely let out a moan. The clouds might not pass for hours.

Admitting defeat, she closed the book and returned to her pallet. She stowed the book away, then again lay down and wriggled to warm herself. If she could not read the written story, she would make up her own. In her tale, a knight in the guise of an owl would come to rescue the lady. The owl would fly up into the window of the tower room. At the moment she kissed him, the owl would turn back into a man.

But why would a woman kiss an owl? she pondered. How would the lady know that her rescuer had arrived?

A knock at the door startled Cicely from her speculations. "Sister Cicely—are you well?" someone called.

"Of course," Cicely answered in a muffled voice.

"I heard noises," the woman said. "I thought you might be ill."

"Nay, I . . . I had an unpleasant dream."

"Ah. I will pray that your peace will not be disturbed further this night."

"Thank you, Sister Clotilde."

Exhaling deeply, Cicely sank back on the pallet. She tried to retrain her thoughts on the lady in the tower, but her mind would not obey. 'Twas a silly tale. Knights did not turn into owls and back again. In life, ladies locked in towers by their husbands languished and died there. The exciting stories she read, the beautifully illustrated books her mother sent her, were no more than fanciful dreams.

Yet she needed them. Needed their hope and promise to keep her own dream alive. Ten long years she had lived at Montreau. Although she had refused the final step of taking vows, anyone sensible would say that she was destined to die there.

She doubted anyone remembered the impassioned vow she had made at the priory gates—that someday she would leave, that she would not accept this life as her destiny. She had been a child when she made that vow, a foolish, spoiled child. What could she have known of the world outside the cloister walls, the world she so desperately craved?

Many of the nuns who had joined the order as grown women cautioned her about the horrors of the secular world. The realm of men was evil and dangerous, they said, a godless place where women were abused or ignored, their bodies bartered by king and lord in senseless power struggles. She was fortunate, they told Cicely. She would never have to endure the unpleasantness of the marriage bed, the trials of childbirth, the grief of losing a child to disease or a husband to war.

They praised the peace, the order, the sanctuary of holy life. Some of them, in truth, did find happiness. Sister Clotilde appeared content to fuss in her herb garden, decoct medicines in the stillroom, and devotedly tend the sick in the infirmary. Others knew true religious calling.

But not Cicely. If not for her books, she did not know how she would have survived.

Thank the Blessed Virgin that no one else at Montreau was able to read French! If any one at Montreau had guessed that the books Cicely's mother sent were not religious tomes but scandalous *romans* from France, even Cicely's noble background would not be enough to save her from punishment. The prioress and subprioress would feel impelled to discipline her sins with forced fasting and prayer.

But books could not satisfy her yearning for a different life. The venturous tales and fanciful stories did not bring her any closer to leaving Montreau.

"Blessed Jesu," Cicely whispered softly. "Mother of God, aid me. Give me a sign that my vow is true, that it not be divine will I die in this place."

A foolish prayer, she thought. Anyone who heard her and knew what she asked would be shocked. Of course, it was God's will that she become a nun. She had been given to the church by her family; their will must be guided by the hand of God.

But she did not believe it. She had never believed it. It was her *father's* will that she go to Montreau, not her Holy Father's!

Cicely gave another exasperated sigh. What torments she suffered, always arguing with herself. Better that she should turn her thoughts back to the story.

The owl's eyes, she decided suddenly, his eyes would reveal who he was to the lady. They would be tender and full of feeling, and the poor woman would know at once that her rescuer had come.

But how would they escape the tower? The owl could not carry a full-grown woman in his beak. Nor could a man fly back down to the ground.

Mayhap instead of the owl transforming himself back into a knight, the woman could turn into a bird, a linnet or nightingale, a creature lovely and delicate. Then they could float down together on the soft wind and live in peace ever after . . .

Cicely woke with an aching head from lying awake too late thinking about the story of the lady and the owl. The lack of noise coming from the common sleeping room told her that it must be well past prime. She jumped up from the pallet and hurriedly smoothed her gown, fearing she would be severely chastised for missing the first prayers of the day.

Odd that Sister Clotilde had not awakened her. The older nun always looked after her, attempting, often futilely, to keep her from getting into trouble.

After taking time to use the chamber pot and splash water on her face, Cicely hurriedly fastened the white wimple over her braids and went out.

As soon as she left the dorter where the novices slept, she knew something was amiss. There was none of the usual bustle of sisters going about their duties in the courtyard. No one carrying water from the well or firewood from the woodpile. No smell of porridge from the refectory.

Where was everyone? Cicely's heartbeat quickened as she hurried toward the chapel. When she peered inside and saw only a handful of the older nuns at prayers, her excitement increased. The routine of the priory was seldom interrupted. What could have happened?

Cicely began to run, her leather shoes slapping against the frost-covered ground. As she rounded the corner of the main convent building, she slowed in astonishment. Inside the gate of the priory was a troop of knights, and one of the men was talking to the prioress, his helm pushed back to reveal his grizzled, dirt-streaked face. He looked angry, as if he were arguing with Prioress Elena.

The delicately built woman faced him boldly, her erect, unyielding posture betraying a complete disregard for the discrepancy in size between herself and the massive knight. Prioress Elena was clearly determined to deny the visitor his request.

Cicely felt a stir of pride in her own sex. What right did these crude soldiers have to intrude on the peace of Montreau and demand to have their way?

But what did they want? she wondered. Had they been sent to escort someone from the priory? Mayhap even Cicely herself!

Her heart almost stopped at the thought. After all these years, her prayers had been answered! Her father had finally relented!

Mayhap her mother was ill and needed her. Nay, she did not want that to be the reason.

Had her brother decided to take holy vows himself and now she was an heiress? Improbable. Even if Hugh decided to do such a thing, her father would never let him.

Cicely's spirits dampened as she failed to find a plausible reason for her release. The knights were likely there regarding some uninteresting matter such as a dispute over rights to grazing lands or honey collection.

Cicely crept closer. Several of the other novices had gathered around, looking like a flock of sparrows in their brown habits as they eyed the group of knights with a mixture of curiosity and fear.

Cicely also drank in the sight of the visitors, their brightly colored surcotes muddied from travel, the cold gray sheen of their mail and helmets, the huge, dangerous-looking horses they rode . . .

Her eyes alighted on a wain at the back of the troop. Something or someone was bundled in the back of the vehicle. Cicely moved forward for a closer look. At the same moment, the prioress discovered the watching nuns and said in a calm, carrying voice, "All of you—return to your work and prayers."

The women scattered like a frightened flock. Cicely stood her ground a moment longer, until the prioress' disapproving stare penetrated to her very bones. Then she followed the others.

Curiosity burned in Cicely as she hurried to find Sister Clotilde to tell her the news. She searched for her friend in the herb garden and the stillroom. Finally, she went back to the gate. The knights were gone.

Puzzled, Cicely went down to the root cellar, where Clotilde kept some of her herbs, and came upon Sister Hawise filling a basket with cabbages and leeks for the evening meal.

"Sister, have you seen Clotilde?"

The old nun shook her head. "A shameful thing. An outrage."

"What is?"

"Allowing knights into the priory. I can scarce believe the prioress would allow it."

"You know why they are here?" Cicely asked excitedly.

Hawise shook her head again. "Men's business," she said. "'Tis not right that they intrude. If one of their own ails, an army surgeon or some other should tend him. This burden should not be forced upon us."

"What burden?"

Hawise's rheumy eyes met Cicely's. "The prioress sent for Clotilde to tend an ailing knight. They took him to the infirmary."

"Sister Clotilde is tending a knight?"

"She is the most skilled among us."

Cicely did not know what to think of this extraordinary circumstance. There was a man within the cloister walls, an actual knight!

"I daresay Sister Clotilde will do her best to be rid of him quickly," Hawise said. "She has no liking for men."

"You mean she will not aid him? Even if he is sick or injured?" It was well-known that Clotilde despised men; she said the very sight of them made the gorge rise in her throat, reminding her of having been brutally used by one of her father's soldiers before she came to Montreau.

"Nay, she will not refuse him." The old nun sighed mournfully. "She is bound to give aid to the sick, as we all are. 'Tis one of Christ's teachings."

"Then, what do you mean she will 'be rid of him'?"

Hawise shrugged. "If she can, she will mend him and send him on his way. Or, if his trouble is mortal, she will ease his passing."

Cicely did not wait to hear more, but turned and dashed toward the infirmary. A strange fear gnawed at her. Would Clotilde allow the knight to die? Would her hatred of men cause her to neglect someone sick and helpless?

By the time she reached the low building, Cicely's worry had eased. It was inconceivable that Clotilde would turn away

an ailing man. Old Hawise was merely being odd and peevish,
Cicely told herself as she pushed open the door to the infirmary.

The sharp smell of herbs and medicines tickled her nose.
The place was dark, as always. Windows were thought to let
in ill humors which might impede healing.

The glow of a lamp at the far end alerted Cicely to Clotilde's
location. She wondered if the older nun would send her away.
Although she sometimes helped Clotilde prepare decoctions
and tinctures, Cicely's actual knowledge of the healing arts
was limited. She suspected Clotilde tolerated her presence
because she liked her company rather than because she believed
her to have a true vocation.

Clotilde looked up as Cicely neared, her gray eyes full of
warmth. "Child, what do you here?"

"I . . . I heard you had been ordered to tend a knight. I
thought you might need help."

The older woman nodded. "Come closer."

As Cicely approached the cot on which the man lay, her first
thought was that he was dead. Verily, he looked like a carved
effigy lying there, his upper body clad in mail.

But his head was bare, and she could see that his face was
too flushed to belong to a marble statue.

As she neared, the odor almost made her gag. The man
smelled as foul as the penitents who came to beg for alms at
the gate, yet this was not the reek of stale, unwashed flesh, but
sickness.

"Does he have a wound which has putrefied?" Cicely had
heard that sometimes an injured arm or leg had to be cut off
lest the corruption spread. She wondered if she could bear to
watch if Clotilde were forced to do such a thing.

"Nay. 'Tis merely a fever."

"But he seems so ill." The man appeared insensible, his
breathing shallow. Beneath the flush of fever, there was a

grayish cast to his skin. To Cicely, his condition appeared grave indeed.

"Not a fever as we know it," Clotilde said. "The knight who brought him said it is a strange sickness which he contracted in the land of the Saracens. The fever comes and goes. When he is in the throes of it, he is very ill. But always before he has recovered completely."

"The Saracens? You mean he is a crusader?" Cicely asked in awe. Crusaders were the most valiant of warriors. When they took a vow to free the holy city of Jerusalem, all their sins were instantly remitted. If they died fighting for the Christian cause, they were transported directly to heaven.

"He is said to have taken the cross," Clotilde's voice sounded skeptical. "But he was struck down by the fever before he reached Antioch." Her eyes met Cicely's meaningfully. "I do not believe God would so afflict a truly pious man."

Cicely glanced again at the unconscious knight. Whether he was a saintly crusader or a greedy mercenary, she felt a compelling need to aid him. "What shall we do?" she asked. "Should we not take off his mail?"

"Aye, I suppose so."

Clotilde's offhand answer unsettled Cicely. "Is there nothing else we can do for him?" she asked. "Would not meadowsweet lower his fever?"

"Mayhap. Why don't you fetch some while I remove his mail?"

Cicely hurried to the little storeroom where the medicines were kept, then, realizing that she needed a candle or lamp to find the right jar, returned to the main room. She paused as she saw Clotilde standing motionless, staring down at the man on the pallet. A chill went down Cicely's spine. As much as Clotilde despised men, it must be distasteful for her to have to touch the knight. Would she let her revulsion keep her from doing all she could for him?

At last, Clotilde leaned over and began to ease the man's arm out of the mail shirt. Cicely let out a sigh of relief and approached the cot. "Can I help?" she asked.

Clotilde nodded. "Jesu, how do men wear such things? 'Tis as heavy as lead."

Cicely joined in the other woman's struggle, and they finally freed his arm. They gradually worked his other arm out of the mail sleeve, then, after pausing for breath, tugged the shirt over his head and dropped it with a crash to the floor.

Cicely winced as she saw they had caught the man's face with the garment's metal rings. A long scratch inscribed his cheek. "Poor thing," she muttered. She reached out to finger the wound, thinking she would bring some salve to put on it, then jerked her hand back. "He burns with fever!" she cried. "I will get the meadowsweet without delay."

She grabbed a candle, hurried to the storeroom and found the mixture, and ran back to the sickbed. As she approached, Clotilde gingerly held up a mass of yellowish linen. "We'll have to burn it. No amount of laundering could salvage something which stinks so foully."

"What is it?" Cicely asked, eyeing the strange garment.

"I believe it's called a gambeson. A padded shirt that men wear to protect their skin from their mail."

"We cannot burn it," Cicely protested. "What will he wear when he leaves here?"

Clotilde shot Cicely a strange look, then threw the gambeson to the floor. "If you can find someone willing to wash it, by all means save it for him."

Cicely remembered the medicine she had brought. She leaned over the man, intending to pour some of the mixture into his mouth. The sight of his bare chest made her pause. She had never seen an unclothed man before, at least not since she was a child. Were all men built so massively? Did they all have such coarse hair on their chests? Yet, the rest of his skin looked smooth, silken almost . . .

Clotilde cleared her throat, and Cicely remembered herself. She placed her hand behind the man's neck and lifted his head. She dribbled a little of the meadowsweet tea into his mouth. To her relief, he swallowed. She gave him more.

By the time she was done, her hands were shaking. It was so odd to touch him, to feel his fevered flesh, his solid form. She stared at his face, at the golden stubble on his cheeks, the pale scar near his right eye, the dusky amber of his eyelashes and eyebrows. With his fair coloring, he might have Saxon blood.

"We should cover him up," Clotilde said, "lest he grow chilled. When his fever lessens, we will have to bathe him." The disgust in her voice was evident.

They covered him with blankets.

"Go then," Clotilde said. "I will sit with him."

Cicely nodded. "I'll bring you food."

She hurried off and obtained what she needed from Hawise. The cellarer was very sympathetic to Clotilde's circumstances, and she thought nothing odd in Cicely's caring for the other woman's needs.

Cicely hurried back to the infirmary and found Clotilde sitting on a stool beside the comatose knight. She handed her the basket containing some bread and cheese. "Would you like to go outside?" she asked, acutely aware of the closeness of the sickroom. "You could get some fresh air."

"I would be most grateful." Clotilde rose and walked toward the door. Before she reached it, Cicely called out, "Wait! Do you think I should be alone with him?"

Clotilde turned slowly. "He is too weak to do more than raise his head."

"What I mean is . . . do you think it fitting that I tend him?" The words stumbled out, sounding foolish, but Cicely could not quite believe that the prioress would wish a novice to be alone with a man, even an unconscious one.

"You've taken more interest in healing than anyone else," was Clotilde's reply. "I think you are well qualified to tend him." With those words, she went out.

Cicely stared after her, then slowly turned her gaze to the stone-still man on the pallet. The very sight of him made her heart beat faster, her palms sweat. Could Clotilde not see how their patient unsettled her? Or, was it that he distressed Clotilde so much she could not bear to be near him either?

Nay, their reactions were very different. Clotilde seemed repulsed by the knight, while Cicely was fascinated. True, he smelled rank, but already she was growing used to the odor. He was odd to look at, but not in a displeasing way.

She reached out to feel his forehead. His fever had abated some. His skin was not so dry and hot. She touched his hair. 'Twas not the flaxen hue true Saxons possessed, but a deep gold shade, like autumn leaves.

She wondered what color his eyes were. Blue mayhap. She thought blue eyes the comeliest. Whenever she pictured the knights in the *romans* she read, she always gave them blue eyes.

The thought snapped Cicely from her dreamy mood. A knight! There was a real knight lying not inches away from her!

All these years she had dreamed of a strong, gallant knight coming to rescue her, and now he was here!

Her gaze took in his long shape beneath the coverlet. He was tall and strong-looking, as her rescuer should be. One of his hands had slipped from beneath the blankets. Cicely studied it, noting the size of his fingers, the pale scars which marked the tanned flesh. This was a hand which wielded a sword, a hand used to fight and kill.

Gingerly, she reached out to touch him, marveling at how different his fingers were from her own. He had blunt, square nails. Tiny golden hairs sprouted from his knuckles. She ran a fingertip along the underside of his hand, feeling the rough calluses, the potential strength.

Without warning, his fingers suddenly closed, gripping hers tightly. Cicely gasped and tried to pull away. His fingers flexed once and he groaned; then he released her.

Cicely watched his face, her heart pounding. She could still feel the heat and power of his grip. What had it meant? Some reflex from his fevered dreams? Or was he trying to communicate with her? Asking her to stay. To help him.

Something akin to panic flooded Cicely. Was this knight the answer to her prayers? Had he come for her?

What if he died before she found out the truth?

Frantically, she again felt his forehead. The fever remained, although it did not burn as hot. She moved her hand down to touch the scratch along his cheek, thinking that she should get some healing salve.

Her hand touched his jaw, feeling the roughness of his whiskers. Then his dry, cracked mouth. The shape of his lips absorbed her. So altogether different than a woman's. Not that she had ever felt a woman's lips, except for a dry sisterly kiss on the cheek.

"Water," the man suddenly croaked, the word coming out as a vibration against her fingers. Cicely jerked away and went to do his bidding.

Her hands shook as she found the pitcher Clotilde kept by the door and poured some water into a pewter cup. When she returned to his side, he was still and mute once more. She tipped his head back and dripped the water into his mouth. He drank, messily this time, pausing once to mutter something else, something she could not understand.

She watched him some more, feeling helpless.

Clotilde finally came back.

"I gave him some water," Cicely said.

Clotilde nodded. "We should bathe him."

Cicely gave her a startled look.

" 'Twill bring down his fever."

Cicely tried to think how to respond. If she pointed out the impropriety of her helping to bathe a man, Clotilde might think better of allowing her in the sickroom at all.

Clotilde reached out and touched the man's forehead. "His fever is better. Mayhap we do not need to bathe him. If you can tolerate the stench."

"I've grown used to it," Cicely said.

Clotilde nodded. "If you could stay with him a few hours longer, it would be a great kindness for me. I shall have to sit up with him this night, I fear."

"Of course."

"If he rouses, give him more water," Clotilde instructed. "If his fever worsens, the meadowsweet. I won't be gone long."

Cicely watched the other woman leave. There were butterflies in her stomach. She had never tended a patient by herself before. She could not imagine why Clotilde kept leaving her alone.

But the older woman scarce seemed to care if the man lived or died. Cicely set her jaw. He would not die, not while he was in her care.

She reached out and stroked his forehead. A man. Big and muscular and sweaty. As strange to her as if he were a wild beast from the woods. The few monks and holy men who came to the priory looked nothing like this. There was power in him. She could feel it.

Why had God sent him? It was too extraordinary to be mere chance. That he should fall sick and be given to Clotilde to tend. Clotilde who hated men, who would rather nurse a rat or other vermin than a warrior.

"Why are you here?" Cicely whispered to the knight. "Have you come for me?"

The man opened his eyes. Blue eyes.

CHAPTER 3

An angel leaned over him, her expression tender, her fingers soothing on his cheek.

Nay, this could not be heaven. A wretch like him would never know God's grace.

'Twas a cruel trick of the devil instead. And she, a sweet-faced beauty sent to torture him. A nun, with white wimple and plain robe, sent to entice his soul farther into hell.

Ah, but it was fine to look at her. Such smooth skin, a dainty mouth and slightly pointed chin. Those melting doe eyes.

He had not the strength to defile her, that was the irony. Even if she tempted him beyond endurance, he could scarce muster the will to caress her silken cheek. The bitter thought made him grimace.

"Do not fret, I pray," she whispered. "You will mend, I promise." Her voice was soft and musical, as lovely as her face.

Where was he? Did his soul hover somewhere between the pleasures of heaven and the torments of hell?

He tried to raise his head to look around, but the woman placed her hand on his shoulder and gently pushed him back. "Shhhhh. Do not exert yourself. If there is anything you need, tell me and I will fetch it."

His strength faded. He gave in and closed his eyes, but not before he caught a glimpse of a darkened room and the nearby lamp that gave the angel her halo.

He was not dead. The suffering of his body remained with him, the grinding ache in his bones, the dryness of his mouth, the thin dizziness of his thoughts. He burned not with the fires of eternal damnation but with the cursed fever.

Despair swept over him. Better that he should die than suffer this humiliating weakness. A knight he was, a man who earned his bread by the strength of his sword arm. And, once again, he lay feeble and helpless. What terrible wickedness had he done to deserve such a fate?

Ah, but he remembered now.

He had seen murder done and been unable to prevent it. He was a failure, a weak, useless fraud.

With effort, he pushed away the images of violence and death and let out a rasping sigh. Almost at once, he felt a cool hand on his cheek. "Oh, please don't die, sir! Please!"

The anguished words startled him. He opened his eyes, remembering the woman, the angel.

"You can't die," she said. "I won't let you. I may never have another chance."

The determination on her face puzzled him. What did she want? Why did she care if he died?

He vaguely recalled Engelard saying that they rode near a convent. Some French name the place had. But why had he been put in the care of this sweet-faced novice?

He opened his mouth to ask where he was. Nothing came out but a dry croak.

"Water!" she cried in a panicked voice. "I will get you water!"

When she returned with the water, he got a good look at her. Such beauty was wasted on a nun. He could lose himself in the warm depths of her brown eyes.

And her gentleness. 'Twas like balm to his spirit after the jarring motion of the wain. She raised his head carefully, touching him as if he were made of spun glass. The water tasted good, cool and fresh.

"Sleep now," she said. Her hand stroked his brow.

Obediently, Simon closed his eyes.

"How does he?" another woman's voice called.

The hand on his forehead stilled. "He is better. I gave him some water."

"Mmmm," the voice answered. "Don't make a pet of him. He is a knight and unused to kind treatment."

With a flutter, the hand went away. Simon wondered vaguely about the other woman. Who was she to the pretty one?

There was a puzzle here. He would use his wits to solve it. If only he could keep his thoughts from drifting away.

Again, he felt a hand on his forehead. "Did he speak?" the other woman asked.

"Nay, he tried but . . . I fear his throat was too dry."

"You did well. He needs rest most of all."

This one would be the true healer, Simon decided. She would send the little nun away. A sense of loss assailed him. For a brief time, an angel had tended him. Truly she must have a kind spirit or she would not endure the unpleasantness of his sickness. He could smell his own rank odor, guess at the stubble on his cheeks. Under the blankets, his chest was indecently bare. He was not fit for the eyes of a gentle maid.

Yet, she had pleaded for his life, willed him to recover.

Don't go, he beseeched her silently. *Stay with me, let me hear your voice and look upon your face and I will recover ten times as rapidly.*

"I should be at prayers. I missed sext and none both."

"Your aid has been most helpful, Sister Cicely."

"I will bring you supper, Sister Clotilde. And I will spell you tomorrow if you wish to leave his side."

Footsteps. Light, graceful.

Simon struggled to open his eyes. The woman standing by the bed was fairly young and not displeasing to look at. As she watched the angel leave, a wistfulness came into her face.

Simon recognized the look. The healer loved the little nun. And not in a sisterly way.

He had a rival.

The healer's capable fingers touched his throat, feeling for his pulse. Simon allowed himself to sink back into the torpor of fever. Before the waves of unconsciousness washed over him, one word filled his mind. Cicely.

Cicely knelt at the chapel rail and bowed her head. Behind her, she could hear the soft murmur of prayers from the other nuns. "Blessed Jesu, hear my prayer," she whispered. "Heal the knight who has come to Montreau. He is a worthy man. A crusader. Restore to him his health and strength . . ."

Her words trailed off. 'Twas wrong to pray for selfish reasons. Did she truly care for the knight? Or did she only see him as a means of escaping Montreau? Her petition must be sincere or God would not answer it.

Nay, she did not want the knight to die, even if he should refuse to aid her. She would feel a loss to think of any man dying, especially one so magnificently wrought.

She recalled the knight's naked torso. What power was there in the corded muscles of his arms, the sleek expanse of his chest! He was like a beautiful animal. For that reason alone she did not want him to die, the sheer waste of it.

She stood up from her place near the rail and crossed herself. The conviction that God had sent the knight would not leave her. Though the thought defied everything she had been taught, she could not let go of it. Her escape was at hand, if only she would reach out and seize it.

And if only the knight recovered.

She knelt down and began to pray again.

"His fever has worsened," Clotilde said when Cicely went to the infirmary the next morning.

"Can you do anything?" Cicely asked anxiously.

Clotilde rose from the stool, looking weary. "I've given him meadowsweet, and I also had two men from the village come and bathe him, to see if that would bring his fever down. But nothing seems to help. I fear his body must win this battle on its own."

The older nun moved as if to go.

"You're leaving me alone with him?" Cicely fought a sense of panic.

"I am very weary, and there is nothing I have done that you cannot do. If you could spell me for a few hours, I would be most grateful."

Clotilde left and Cicely took a seat on the stool. Time dragged by. She spent it praying silently, willing the knight to get better. From time to time, she got up and felt his forehead, assessing the terrible heat which seemed to be burning up his body.

Soon after none, he began to rave. His words were garbled, indistinct, and she could make out almost nothing. She tried to calm him, to stroke his face and reassure him. Abruptly, he sat up. His eyes were wide open but unseeing. "In the name of Christ, don't kill them!" he shouted.

She grabbed his arm and tried to push him back to a reclining position. He moaned and flailed about, and his thrashing movements made the blankets fall away, revealing his nakedness. The men who had washed him had not even put his chausses back on.

With horrified fascination, Cicely perused his lean belly, his long, muscular legs, the thatch of dark gold hair at his crotch, his pink, wrinkled-looking privates. Then she averted her gaze, thinking of how rude it was to look upon a man who was insensible. Quickly picking up the blanket, she covered him.

He continued to moan and writhe. Cicely cast an anxious glance toward the door. Should she fetch Clotilde? What if something happened to him while she was gone?

She tried to stroke his arm to soothe him. He struck out, as if wielding a sword, and hit her hard on the cheek. She pulled back, wincing, then decided she would not be deterred. Moving to stand at the end of the cot above his head, she put her hands on his temples and gently caressed him.

His thrashing gradually eased. He stopped jerking his head back and forth, and his limbs went still.

Cicely began to hum, a simple melody from her childhood. She heard him mumble something, then sigh. A sense of relief and an aching tenderness went through her. She let her fingers glide through his hair, massaging his scalp, and it seemed she could almost see the terrible tension and anguish leave his face.

His expression grew peaceful, and she thought how unearthly handsome he was, how pleasing his features, despite his rough beard and the pallor of his skin. She could stand there for hours, soothing him. But what about when Clotilde returned? She might think it very strange for Cicely to stroke their patient as if he were a fretful child.

Regretfully, Cicely ceased her caressing and went back to the stool. The knight was calm now; there was no reason for her to hover over him.

Clotilde returned a short time later. "There's been no change?" she asked.

"He grew quite agitated. I was afraid he would fall off the cot. Then his turmoil gradually subsided."

Clotilde looked at her and frowned. "What happened to your face?"

Cicely touched her cheek; it was still sore. "He was delirious. He did not mean to strike me."

"I should not have left you alone with him," Clotilde said angrily. "Next time I do so, I will give him poppy to make him insensible."

" 'Tis nothing. I should have kept clear of him when he began to toss and turn."

Clotilde turned back to their patient and felt his forehead. "He seems cooler. Mayhap the worst of the fever has passed."

Cicely nodded, wondering if her care of him had somehow helped fight the sickness.

The next day the knight seemed better still. When Cicely arrived in the infirmary, Clotilde reported that he had actually been lucid for a short time during the night.

"I gave him some broth," she said, "and also helped him put on a monk's robe. Getting him back into his hose and tunic was beyond both of us."

Cicely approached the cot, wondering if the other nun guessed that she knew the knight had been naked beneath the blankets.

"When he wakes, you should give him some more broth." Clotilde pointed to a pot on a nearby table. "If he does not rouse soon, you might have to take it back to the kitchen to be reheated. Now that his fever is gone, we must take pains to see that he does not get chilled. I have thought of having a fire built here at night. Winter is not far away."

"How long do you think it will be before he is well?" Cicely asked.

Clotilde sighed. "I don't know. He is very weak. But I hope 'tis soon. I will be relieved to have this burden pass from me."

"Where will he go when he is well?"

"Back to his troop, I suppose. Prioress Elena said the other knights were traveling to Bedford. 'Tis only a day's journey to the north. He still has his horse and a sumpter pony. They were left in the care of the ostler in the village."

A horse and a pack animal—that was exactly what they would need if the knight were to take her away from Montreau! Cicely's excitement grew. It had been her dream so long, she could scarce believe the possibility of escape was at hand. As to what she would do once she was outside the priory walls, that was rather vague. But she would not worry. Something would come to her. It must be God's will that she leave Montreau. Otherwise, He would not have sent the knight.

Cicely sat down by the cot as Clotilde left and began to contemplate her journey. Although she could not sneak out with a large bundle, she must take her books and a few things her mother had sent her . . .

"Cicely?"

Her gaze flew to the knight's face as he spoke her name. His blue eyes bored into her, making her insides flutter. She licked her dry lips. "Aye. I am Cicely."

"Cicely." His tongue caressed the word, turning it into something she had never heard before. "An odd name for an angel," he said. "But you are not an angel, are you? You are a nun."

"I have not taken vows yet. I am but a novice."

A faint smile touched his mouth. "I wonder that they leave you alone with me. I would imagine they would find some ugly, wart-faced sister to tend me."

"Clotilde is not ugly," Cicely said indignantly.

"Nay, she is not. But she does not like men either. While you . . ."

Cicely stood up. The way the man looked at her made her heart pound.

His smile broadened. A breathtaking smile. "Come back, little lamb. I am no danger to you." He lifted his hand. "See the way my muscles tremble? The fever leaves me like this. 'Twill be some days before I can hold a sword or sit a horse." He raised his eyes to hers again. "Or molest a maid either."

"The broth." She eased away from the cot. "Clotilde said you must have it when you awake. Before it grows cold."

"You will feed me?"

Intent blue eyes froze her in place. "Of course," she said, picking up the bowl. "I have tended you three days now. You were insensible and have not known I was here."

"Are you certain?"

Her bones threatened to turn to jelly. She held the bowl in a death grip to keep from dropping it. "You were out of your head with fever, sir. You raved and shouted. You even struck me."

His eyes widened. "Nay, I would not."

Cicely turned her head so he could see the bruise on her cheek.

"Christ's blood!" he swore. "Many pardons, lady. I did not mean to be such a brute."

"Think naught of it. You were out of your wits."

The knight looked away, and a look of terrible grief crossed his face. "Each time it is worse. My thoughts wander more. My body weakens. Someday, it will destroy me altogether."

Cicely approached him urgently. "Please, you must drink now. It grows cold."

He allowed her to lift his head, to tilt the earthenware bowl to his lips. He gulped the broth down.

As she turned to put the bowl aside, he reached out and

grasped her hand. "I am grateful, sister. Your kindness overwhelms me."

"Nay, 'twas naught." She could hardly speak. He was touching her; she could feel his flesh burn hers, though he was not fevered.

"Yea, it was. When I was deep in the torments of the sickness, you gave me something to live for."

"That is nonsense." She pulled her hand away. "I am nothing to you."

He shook his head. "You are a dream, Cicely. A dream of light and beauty, shining in the darkness of my life."

The intensity of his voice, his strange words, embarrassed her.

"If there is anything else you need, I will get it," she said.

"The other woman, the healer. Will you fetch her for me?"

Cicely nodded, disappointed that he trusted Clotilde more than her.

"I must make water," the man said, seemingly guessing her thoughts. "I would not shame a maiden with my crude needs."

Blushing, she went to get Clotilde.

She returned the next morning. Clotilde was not there, and the knight was asleep. Out of habit, Cicely touched the patient's forehead. His skin was cool, his color better. She breathed a sigh of relief at finding him so improved.

She sat on the stool and waited. Finally, he opened his eyes. He smiled when he saw her, and Cicely felt a thrill travel down her body. She struggled to find her voice. "You are better today."

He nodded, and his smile faded. "For now. Until the next time."

"Will the fever ... do you think it will return to afflict you?"

His face grew grim. "There is no way of knowing. Many men die when they first fall ill. But even for those, like me, who survive, there is always the chance the sickness will recur. 'Tis my curse, my punishment."

"Punishment for what?"

He shook his head and did not answer.

She felt his unhappiness. It made her heart ache. "But you did not die," she said brightly. "Many men do, as you said. That God saw fit to spare you is a sign of his favor, a sign that He has a purpose for you."

His gaze jerked to hers. She saw a faint hope flare in his eyes; then it was gone. He shook his head. "I live only so that I may do penance for my sins. That is the only purpose I have."

His words distressed her. She wanted to reassure him, to tell him that God had sent him to aid her. But it seemed too soon. He scarce knew her, or she, him.

She stood and smoothed the blankets over him. "What are you called, sir?"

"Simon," he said. When he offered nothing more, she knew a twinge of puzzlement. Most knights gave the place of their birth or their father's surname along with their Christian name.

"Have you no family?" she asked.

A bleak look came over his face. "When I went on Crusade, 'twas against their wishes," he said. "I cannot go back there. I *cannot.*"

Cicely nodded. She knew what it was like to be cut off from the comfort and support of family. If she succeeded in leaving Montreau, 'twas likely she would never be able to return to Tathwick.

The thought grieved her, but it did not dissuade her from her plan. Her family had abandoned her to Montreau. She could go on without them if she had to.

She glanced again at Simon, and a fierce need to comfort him came over her. "You must have faith, sir. Although your life has been difficult so far, that does not mean you have no hope of finding happiness. You must persevere.''

His smile was back, transforming his face. He did not look ill or weary, but so comely Cicely's breath caught.

''How could I lose faith when God has sent such an entrancing angel to tend me?'' He reached out and took her hand in his. Cicely smiled back at him, and a sense of triumph sang through her. God *did* favor her plan to leave Montreau. She could feel it.

The infirmary door creaked open. Cicely quickly pulled her hand away.

By the time the nun had reached them, Cicely was arranging Simon's blankets and discussing whether he felt well enough to eat some bread along with his broth.

Cicely paused outside the infirmary door and adjusted her wimple. At last she had a chance to speak to Simon alone. Several of the sisters had acquired coughs as the weather changed, and Clotilde had wanted to keep them in the infirmary, so she could doctor them with coltsfoot and hyssop. To maintain their privacy, a screen had been put up around Simon's cot, but Cicely had not felt that she could speak freely when she visited the knight the past two days.

But just this morning, Clotilde had told her that the nuns' coughs had improved enough that she had sent them back to the dorter. As for Clotilde, she had said that she meant to spend some time in the garden, gathering the last of the herbs.

This was it—the moment she had waited for.

Taking a breath for courage, Cicely entered the infirmary and approached the screened-off area.

''Good day, sister,'' Simon said as she rounded the screen. He was sitting up, dressed in a monk's robe. It was much too small for him, barely reaching his shins and hanging a little past his elbows. It made him seem even larger than he usually appeared.

"You look quite well," she said.

He nodded. "I expect to be able to leave soon."

Cicely took a seat on the stool and tried to hide her trembling hands in the folds of her habit. "Where will you go?"

"I will try to catch up with Engelard and see if he will hire me on again. 'Tis not likely, but I must try." There was a harsh note in his voice.

"Do you fear he will refuse you because of your illness?"

"No commander desires a sickly knight in his train."

She cleared her throat and said, "Mayhap I could hire you, Sir Simon."

"You? What task could I possibly perform for a fair, gentle maid like you? Tell me now, and I will do it gladly."

"I would not be able to pay you much."

"Pay me?" He smiled. "I vow that if the thing you ask is possible, I would *beg* you for the honor of doing it."

"I want you to take me with you when you leave."

His expression grew astonished, then wary. "Where would you go?"

"To Pembroke Castle. My godfather holds it." Until this moment, she had not thought of the possibility that her godfather might offer her refuge. But she knew she must give some destination or Simon would think her mad.

"The mighty Earl Marshal? If you wish to visit his keep, I would advise that you write and ask for an escort. It is many days from here."

Cicely took a deep breath. "I cannot ask for an escort. He does not know I am coming."

This puzzled him, she could see it. In another moment he would grasp the truth, that she did not want him as an escort, but as a means of escape. There was no help for it. She could not explain her need for secrecy without revealing that she acted against her family's will.

"You go there unannounced?" he asked.

"I . . . I mean to ask for Lord William's aid in something, but I cannot do it in a letter. I must speak to him personally." She stood and moved closer to Simon, praying that he cared for her enough to overlook the unseemliness of her plan. "I want to leave Montreau. I am not suited to the holy life. I wish to leave here and never return. I beg you for your assistance. I will pay you what I can."

"Demoiselle," he said softly, "you do not know what you ask."

"Aye, I do!" she cried. "I have had years to think on it. Years and years!"

"How old are you?"

"I was eight when I came here, and I have spent ten years within these walls. I ask you, nay, I beg of you, deliver me from this prison!"

He reached out, as if to soothe her, then thought better of it and withdrew his hand. But his voice was gentle when he spoke. "My little flower, you cannot guess at how gilded and lovely your prison is. The world outside these walls is harsh and wicked; believe me when I say that a maiden like you is better off—"

"Nay, I will not listen!" She was close to shouting. Quickly, she lowered her voice, fearing someone might come in and overhear. "Nay, I will not. I know in my heart that I do not belong here. 'Twas not meant to be. Only my father's foolish vow has wrought this hell for me."

"He vowed to give you to the Church?"

She nodded.

"He could afford to dower you, but he chose not to?"

"He said he could not dower me well enough to attract a

man of my own station, and he would not have me marry beneath it.''

'Twould seem he was a wise man,'' Simon said. "I have seen what happens when a gentlewoman is wed to a man who cannot care for her. 'Tis an ugly thing.''

"That may be, but it should still be the woman's choice.''

"Few women are competent to judge men as husbands. I vow your father did you a favor.''

Anger flared in Cicely. How dare he imply that she was too witless to choose her own husband! "I know my own heart,'' she retorted. "I would not choose foolishly. There are men who are not of noble blood, men who are kind and good and who might well make worthy husbands.''

"And what do you know of men, my lovely maid?'' Simon stood up suddenly. He grasped her about the waist and pulled her to him. "You trust me, don't you, Cicely? You think my heart is kind, that I would not betray you. But I could forget my vow at any time. It might only take a whiff of the scent of you, a glimpse of one of your dainty ankles. Without your habit to remind me that you are a nun, I could easily turn into a beast and ravish you.''

She was squashed against him, her breasts pressed to his hard chest, her groin proximate to his thighs. She could feel his strength, his maleness. Slowly, carefully, she lifted her face, expecting him to kiss her.

He pushed her away so roughly that she nearly fell over the stool. When she raised her tear-filled eyes to his face, she saw that he watched her with look of utter anguish. "Be gone from me,'' he whispered. "Please, Cicely, do not tempt my black soul even deeper into hell. I cannot help you. If I tried, I would only destroy what I have vowed to protect.''

She straightened her shoulders, fighting to deal with the shock of his refusal. Her dreams were shattered, but that was not the worst of it. The harshest pain was knowing that she would never experience his kiss.

Smoothing her habit, she moved toward the opening in the screen.

CHAPTER 4

He was cursed, Simon thought bitterly, staring at the ceiling of the infirmary. There was no other answer for the circumstance he found himself in. Bad enough that his future was a hollow jest; now a sweet-faced innocent sought to lure him into utter folly.

Jesu, what was the little wench thinking of? What man did she mistake him for that she thought him foolish enough to steal a noblewoman from a convent and attempt to cross half of England? If her father found them, he would be killed, and likely drawn and quartered first!

He might owe her a debt for her kindness, but it did not extend so far as risking his neck and balls. God's teeth! He was already beset by difficulties on every side. He had little coin, scarce enough to feed himself until he found Engelard and asked, nay begged, for a position in the garrison at Bedford.

And if the man refused him, what then?

Tightness gathered in Simon's throat as he rose to a sitting position. His affliction had once more destroyed his hopes. Was it his punishment for failing those who cared for him?

The sickening images filled his mind. Swords raised over terror-filled faces. Screams and cries, edged with the mysteries of a foreign tongue. But the voices were familiar. He'd heard them often from the depths of his fevered dreams.

His gut twisted, and nausea threatened to bring up the meager meal of gruel and bread he'd recently eaten. He stood and forced himself to breathe through his mouth, trying to calm himself.

What a cruel streak God had. To smite him with fever and render him so helpless that he could not defend those who had saved him!

With effort, he sought to shake off the almost palpable weight of his despair. 'Twas the most craven and wicked of sins to long for death. He must not give in to the yearning to be free of this terrible pain. Once again, he had survived an attack of tertian fever, an affliction which had killed many men before him. If God had let him live, there must be some reason he was spared.

He took a long shuddering breath. The little nun had said as much. With her sparkling smile and gentle voice she had eased his anguish, had almost made him hope . . .

Hope for what? His future was grim indeed. Why would any commander want to hire him? Twice already he had failed.

As a mercenary in Poitou, the fever had prevented him from participating in a crucial battle. And here in England, after Brian of Engelard had engaged him for the garrison at Colchester, he'd fallen ill on the way to Bedford and delayed the whole troop for two days.

He clenched his jaw, struggling for control. He knew no other life than being a knight. If no man would hire him, what would happen to him? Would he be forced to beg his bread?

He thought of the soldiers he'd seen in the streets of London.

Men on crutches, missing arms or eyes. They were often abused by the beggars who were whole, taunted and spat upon and beaten. A miserable existence, almost worse than death.

He forced the hopeless thoughts away. There must be some purpose for him. Mayhap he was meant to go back to Valmar, to beg for forgiveness.

Nay, he could not! He could not!

Returning there would only remind him of his other failure, the dark blot upon his soul. How could he ever find redemption? How would he ever atone?

He closed his eyes, and suddenly the image of Cicely appeared before him. A smile tugged his lips as he considered the absurd request she'd broached to him. She was having some sort of crisis of faith. Likely it was common for younger nuns and monks to doubt their calling. Mayhap his being here at Montreau had brought it on.

His smile faded. Once again he had wrought grief on a kind, generous soul. It seemed that all who tried to aid him must suffer. He groaned. "Sweet Cicely, I'm sorry. I did not mean to cause you distress."

"Sir, did you speak?" Sister Clotilde peered around the screen, her face stiff and disapproving as always.

"I was mumbling, 'tis naught."

"For a moment, I thought you had spoken Sister Cicely's name."

"A dear child," Simon said, composing his features. "I owe her much. I would that you took care of her after I leave."

Sister Clotilde gave him the first sincere smile she had bestowed on him. "Aye, she is a joy. Montreau would not be the same without her."

Simon wondered if the older nun had any inkling of how desperately the little novice wanted to escape the convent. Likely not. Love was often blind. For that matter, was fleeing Clotilde's affections part of Cicely's scheme? Nay, he did not think so. The little maid seemed completely unaware of Clotilde's feelings.

Simon met the nun's eyes meaningfully. "I have wondered a little that you allow Cicely to spend time with me. A hardened knight alone with a kindhearted maid?"

"You were very ill, sir," Clotilde answered in a cool voice. "I doubted you had the strength for improper behavior. I also thought that spending time with you might enlighten her on the nature of men. Innocent young women sometimes nurture silly notions about crusaders . . . that they are somehow especially brave and noble because they fight for God's cause."

"And you trusted that time in my company would disabuse her of such nonsense?"

Sister Clotilde smiled. "You are most perceptive, sir knight."

Simon had the urge to tell the sister that she could scarcely be more mistaken, but he restrained himself. It served no purpose to alert Sister Clotilde to her favorite's true nature. If the older nun could not see Cicely's very obvious attraction to him, she was indeed blind.

Jesu, what a fool she is! he thought with some heat as Sister Clotilde left. If he had truly been a villain, he could have easily bedded Cicely. He was not so ill that he did not recognize a woman eager for a man's touch.

Another reason to refuse her. There was no way he could travel with Cicely. The first time they were alone and she looked at him with those melting brown eyes, he'd have her on the ground with her skirts up!

He took a deep breath. Nay, he would not think such thoughts. Not when there was a chance she might come to say good-bye to him. He must remember that she was a nun, a virgin, a noblewoman. To touch her not only meant probable death at the hands of her father, but another unforgivable sin on his soul.

God had already turned His face away from him. He would not risk further damnation for a woman, no matter how fetching she might be.

How much should she put in? Sweet Mary, why had she not paid more attention when she watched Clotilde?

Taking a deep breath, Cicely steadied her hands and poured a spoonful of the poppy juice into the wine. Surely that amount would not kill him. And if it was not enough to put him to sleep, then she would know God did not favor her plan.

Of course God did not favor her plan! What an asinine thing to imagine! She schemed to drug a man and then seduce him— hardly holy acts!

Cicely took another deep breath. Then again, they said God helped those who helped themselves. If she truly believed in her heart that God wanted her to leave Montreau, then she must trust that He would forgive the things she did to realize her vow.

She wiped her hands on her habit before picking up the cup and gently stirring the drug into the wine. This was the test. If the sleeping mixture did not work and she failed in her final effort to convince Simon to help her, she would give up her dream and live out her days at Montreau.

"Blessed Jesu, I vow it," she whispered. "If Your will does not favor my plan, I will accept Your decree."

Decisively, she walked out of the stillroom.

Her heartbeat quickened as she approached the screen in the corner of the infirmary. What would Simon think of her bringing him wine? She had never brought him anything but water and broth before. Would he suspect what she planned?

Nay, of course not. He would take it as a gift. Then she would say good-bye to him. He was leaving on the morrow before prime. If her plan failed, she would never see him again.

Tears gathered in Cicely's eyes. What would she do without Simon to talk to, to look at? In only a few days, he had become her sun. His existence made her own bearable. Without him, she would be plunged into despair and loneliness.

Was this love? This harsh pain in the depths of her body at the thought of never seeing him again?

It was so much more intense than she imagined. Not like the lovely tales she read about in books. This was real, and heartrending.

She paused outside the screen and said a silent prayer, then called softly, "Simon, are you awake?"

She heard sounds of movement. He came around the screen. "Cicely," he said.

As always, the sound of her name on his lips made her heart turn over. Could that breathy, passionate endearment really be her name?

"I . . . I brought you some wine." Her voice shook. Her hands shook. She feared she would dissolve on the spot.

As he reached out and took the cup, she realized he was wearing his normal clothing. The sight of him in tunic and hose set her back another measure. Somehow the simple garments made him appear even larger and more intimidating than she remembered. Were his shoulders truly so broad? His thighs so long and lean?

St. Botolph help her, what was she doing looking at his thighs!

"Cicely. Sit down." His voice was firm, commanding. He sought to help her, to keep her from making an utter fool of herself.

She followed him behind the screen and sat down on the stool. He seated himself on the cot a respectable distance away. Without taking his eyes from her, he took a sip of the wine. He frowned, but took another swallow.

"I've come to say good-bye," she said.

He nodded.

"I'll probably never see you again."

"Mayhap not." He smiled. "But I will cherish the memory of our friendship the rest of my life."

It was too much. She sat not three feet from Simon. But she could not touch him. Dare not touch him.

Nor could she tell him that she no longer cared what happened to her after she left Montreau, as long as she could be with him. He was the only hope in her empty life. Without him, she would know despair.

"Would you like some?" Abruptly, he offered her the wine goblet.

Cicely hesitated. To drink from the same cup that his lips had touched was almost like kissing him. But she dare not risk it. If the poppy put her to sleep, her plan would be spoiled. She shook her head.

It was agony to look at him and think of his leaving her. Never to look into his deep blue eyes again, to watch his mouth, to lay her hand on his brow and smooth his wavy, dark gold hair away from his face.

He stood up. "Don't cry, Cicely." He gulped down the rest of the wine, then looked at the cup as if he did not know what to do with it.

Cicely reached out to take the vessel. She must leave. The sooner she left, the sooner he would sleep. "Good-bye, Simon."

"Good-bye." He made no move to touch her. His manner was formal, distant. Doubts nagged at Cicely. What if he felt nothing for her? What if he said kind things only out of politeness?

If her instincts were wrong, then her plan was not only indecent, but cruel. She sought to bind a man to her against his will, to entrap him into helping her.

"Simon."

It took a moment, but finally he looked at her. Triumph sang

through Cicely. The sheen of moisture in his eyes could not
be mistaken. He did care! 'Twas his honor which held him
back. Her plan would dispose of that nonsense. Once he bedded
her, there would be no impediment to their being together. If
he fell ill again, she would nurse him. Always, she would be
there for him. She would make him happy. And she would be
free!

Simon stared glumly into the darkness. Why had she made
it so difficult? Why could she not have said good-bye quickly
and then left?

It had near unmanned him to see the tears rolling down her
cheeks. Thinking of it now, he wanted to weep. Such a sweet
angel, and he could not help her. He could not even help
himself.

He exhaled a heavy sigh. Strange, but he felt tired. After
days of rest, he could not fathom why he suddenly craved sleep.
His body seemed heavy and awkward, his thoughts distracted.
'Twas as if he were fevered again.

With another sigh, he gave into his deepening lethargy.

The floor of the infirmary was cold on Cicely's bare feet as
she tiptoed across it, pausing every other step to listen. It had
not been easy to sneak out of the dorter. She'd had to wait
until after matins to be certain she did not run into anyone
returning from midnight prayers. Now she worried that the
drug had worn off. What would she say to a wide-awake Simon?

She paused outside the screen to gather her courage, and
listened to his slow, even breathing. The sound of a man deeply
asleep. But were his wits confused enough for her purposes?

Resolutely, Cicely moved behind the screen. She'd made a
vow. She would keep to it.

"Simon," she whispered, "Simon."

He gave no indication that he had heard her. No hitch in his breathing, no movement, nothing.

With shaking hands, Cicely unfastened the girdle at her waist and laid it on the stool. Her habit came off next, slipping to the floor with a rustling sound. Her shift followed. She stood naked and listened to the breathing of the man inches away from her.

Now was the final test. Would he shout and reach for his sword when he felt her climb into bed with him? Her heart hammered in her chest. Her muscles seemed to go rigid.

It was the cold which finally forced her to act. She groped for the blankets and pulled them aside, then slid her body next to the sleeping man's.

There was scarce room for both of them on the narrow cot. Cicely wriggled closer to Simon. He'd slept in his clothes, and she could feel the rough wool of his hose against her legs. But he did not seem to be aware of her. What next?

She must entice him. How did you seduce a sleeping man? Mayhap she should have gotten him drunk instead. Clotilde said that drunken men were the worst, ready to rut with any woman who got near them. But how could she have convinced Simon to drink so much wine that it addled his wits?

This was a better plan. If only she could rouse him enough to perform the act.

She reached out and touched his face. Her fingers found his lips, and she recalled how entranced she had been when she'd first explored his features. A pity she could not see him. She reminded herself that there would be other times.

But not if she did not manage this one. If she could not get him to take her maidenhead, her plan was ruined. She must convince Simon that she was not meant to be a nun; only then would he agree to help her escape.

She moved her hand to his chest. So warm, so solid. It was a delight to snuggle against him.

Her hand crept lower. All she had to do was find his male member and press it inside her. She knew where it went from having explored the night before. Although on occasion she had experienced throbbing, restless sensations between her legs, she had never connected those feelings to being with a man. But after spending time in Simon's company, the throbbing there had been very strong. Strong enough that she had gone to her cell and touched herself to soothe it.

When she did, she found that she was wet. Not like her courses, but milky and slippery.

The opening inside her scarce seemed large enough for a man's member to fit within, but she knew the act was said to be unpleasant for the woman, especially the first time. She could endure it. With Simon anyway. All knew that the act gave a man pleasure. And she truly wanted to give Simon pleasure. He had known so much suffering.

She struggled with the cord to his hose. How did a man endure fussing with a knot every time he needed to make water? Mayhap he did not. Since he did not need to crouch to relieve himself, a man might simply pull down the garment.

Cicely tried that approach, working the waist of the hose over Simon's hips. It would have been easier if he could have aided her, but he lay inert.

Exquisite heat seeped through her as her fingers touched his buttocks. His skin was coarser than hers, faintly rough. The muscles beneath felt firm and strong.

Cicely was suddenly breathless and very warm. She could feel the aching heat of her own flesh as she touched his. Aye, she was ready. More than ready. Even her breasts tingled.

She pressed one of them against the bare skin of Simon's belly and almost gasped at the sharp sensation which sang through her. "Oh, Simon, if only you were awake. This is sublime."

She pushed up his tunic and rubbed herself against his chest. By now, she was half-lying, half-crouching over him. Lowering her body against his, she let out a moan of delight. The sound froze in her throat as the man beneath her stirred. She waited, wondering if he would wake. Part of her longed for him to be fully aware, while another reminded her that it was too soon. She was still a maid.

Remembering her intent, Cicely supported herself on one elbow and slid her free hand down Simon's belly. Her fingers closed around silky, loose flesh. This, then, was his sex. Somehow she must get it inside her.

She shifted over him, trying to position her body so that she could grip his member and push it between her legs.

"Sweet heaven, this is difficult," she muttered. Despite the wetness, her opening seemed too small. His shaft, on the other hand, seemed not only too big, but extremely difficult to manuever. " 'Tis like threading a needle with a worm," she groused. "I cannot do it."

Frustrated, she released his shaft. She had some fear of hurting him. Men were said to very sensitive in their privates, and she knew soldiers wore codpieces to protect themselves from injury. It could not be good to batter him around like a lump of gristle.

Sliding down next to him, Cicely snuggled against Simon and sighed. She was sorely fatigued and near the end of her endurance. The delicious sensations were fading away. All she felt now were tired muscles and eyes gritty from lack of sleep. She had heard that carnal relations were unpleasant, but never that they were such hard work!

She would lay there awhile, she decided, then try again. Tears of frustration filled her eyes. Why did she pretend? 'Twould be no easier later. Eventually, she would have to face the truth.

She had failed, and the message was clear. Simon was not her rescuer. She was not meant to leave Montreau.

A sob choked her. Had she not promised to abide by the outcome of this night? That if her plan failed she would resign herself to her fate?

The thought filled her with stark despair. Then tears began to flow freely. She gave in to her grief and wept.

Such strange dreams he had. Devils tormented him, poking and pinching. He wanted to push them away, but he could not move.

Later, there came a sound by his ear. A woman weeping. It must be part of his dream. But he could feel her tears.

He turned toward her, wanting to comfort her. She was soft and warm. So very real.

The crying stopped. He sighed and slipped back into the darkness again.

Something was wrong. He knew as soon as he woke. His flesh quivered, the hair along his nape prickled. It was as if he were awakened from a dead sleep by a call to arms.

But there was no battle.

He was in a bed, warm and comfortable. And beside him was a woman.

He sat bolt upright. The priory. He was in a damned priory! There should not be a woman in bed with him!

Groaning aloud, he reached out to touch her. Even before his fingers grazed smooth, delicate features, he knew. Cicely!

He jerked his hand away and gulped air. Was there not some way to save them? If he got her back to the dorter and left immediately . . .

She sat up. "Simon?"

He groaned again. "Jesu, wench, what have you done to me!"

"Simon ... I ..." There was a muffled sob. He heard her climb from the bed. Rustling noises. She was putting on her clothes.

"Good God, Cicely. You were naked!"

She began to cry in earnest.

Fear coursed through Simon. This was the end for him. He'd bedded a virgin, a nun. He'd be strung up. His struggle to find a position as a mercenary seemed laughable now. He would not live long enough to worry about being a beggar!

"I'm sorry, Simon," she moaned. "I'm sorry."

"Oh, Cicely, don't cry." He stood up and was surprised to find that he was clothed. His hose was bunched around his hips. He'd been naked enough to accomplish the deed. Only, a tiny voice nagged, why didn't he remember?

He reached out for her. She was crying uncontrollably. "What happened?" he asked. "Did you come to see me in the night, and I attacked you?"

"No, no," she whimpered.

"What happened?"

There was no answer but great racking sobs.

"It doesn't matter," he said. "I'm responsible. I've ruined you. I will make it better somehow. I swear it."

"Take ... me ... away. Take me ... with you."

He'd thought her plan mad when she first suggested it, but now it seemed like the only course. If they disappeared, if her father never found them ... For a moment Simon contemplated a life with Cicely. He'd never dreamed of having a woman so lovely, so sweet ... so helpless.

He groaned. "It won't work, Cicely. I can't care for you or protect you. I've nothing to offer."

"Please, Simon. All I ask is that you take me with you. You don't have to wed me or protect me or anything else."

"Jesu, you are a stubborn wench."

She sniffled. "I have no one else to turn to. You must help me."

She sounded so pathetic. A true damsel in distress. If he refused her, he'd be committing an even fouler sin than taking her maidenhead. "Dear God," he whispered, "if I aid this angel, will You come back to me? If I save her, will I finally regain Your favor?"

"Are you praying, Simon?"

"Yea, I'm asking for strength for the task ahead of me."

"Then, you will help me?" There was a jubilant tone to her voice which irritated him.

He sighed. "I have no choice."

CHAPTER 5

She was free! Cicely's hands trembled with anticipation as she placed the last few books in the bundle and tied it securely. Simon had gone to the village to fetch his horses. She was to meet him at the postern gate at prime.

When the chapel bell rang, Cicely jumped. She was late! If she were not there as promised, Simon might decide to leave without her.

She opened the door to her cell and peered out, then crept down the hall of the dorter past the main room where the poorer novices slept on rows of pallets. Most of them were still abed, delaying rising until the last possible moment.

Reaching the doorway, she slipped out into the dark and cold. Only a faint gray in the east gave a hint of the coming dawn.

She hurried across the yard, past the garden and the infirmary. Seeing a light in the window, she hesitated. Clotilde was obviously up and about. A sudden pang went through Cicely. The older nun had always been so kind; it did not seem right to leave without saying good-bye. But Clotilde would never understand, especially about Simon.

Hearing a door open, she moved back into the shadows. A hooded figure left the infirmary and moved toward the main buildings of the priory. Cicely held her breath. If Clotilde saw her, everything would be ruined.

The figure disappeared into the dorter. Cicely exhaled deeply, then began to run.

When she reached the back entrance, she opened the gate with shaking fingers and went out. A tall shape loomed out of the morning mist. "Simon," she whispered.

"Aye."

The familiar sound of his voice sent a shiver through her. She hurried toward him, eager and yet shy at the same time. "I'm pleased to see you. I feared you would leave without me."

He gave a harsh exclamation, then grasped her arm with gloved fingers. " 'Tis not too late to turn back, Cicely. We could say our farewells now."

"But you said . . . you would take me . . ."

"I have few supplies and little coin." His voice was grim. "The weather worsens day by day. I cannot promise I will be able to keep you safe. I cannot promise anything."

Cicely tilted her head up so she could see his face in the faint illumination of the growing dawn. She marked the fine symmetry of his features, the soft gold of his hair. How big and strong he seemed, so fierce and imposing in his tattered surcote and gray chain mail. If ever there was a gallant knight capable of rescuing a maiden, this was he.

"I'll not turn back," she whispered. "I have made a vow, and I will keep to it."

He sighed; then she saw him close his eyes and move his

lips as if praying. "Give me your pack," he said after a moment. "I'll tie it on the sumpter pony. Can you ride?"

"Of course. I learned as a small child."

"That is a relief, although you'll have to ride pillion and Lucifer has a jarring gait."

"Your horse is named Lucifer?"

"Aye, for his temper. But he is a fine warhorse. Even if I collapsed in the saddle from wounds or fatigue, Lucifer would continue to fight."

She handed him her bundle. "Blessed Jesu, what have you in this?" he asked. " 'Tis heavy as if filled with stones."

"Clothes. Some personal items." Instinct warned her not to tell him about her books.

He shook his head. "I know naught of traveling with a woman, but I pray that you have brought some warmer garments. 'Tis a season of uncertain weather, and I cannot afford to pay for lodging."

As the last bells of prime sounded, Cicely suddenly remembered the need for haste. "Let us go. I fear I will be missed." She touched his arm.

He guided her to the warhorse and lifted her into the saddle. "Will they send someone after you?"

"There is no one to send." Cicely glanced toward the low wall separating them from the priory. "But I . . . I do not wish to explain . . ." Her voice trailed off.

"Ah, Sister Clotilde," Simon said.

He went to get the lead for the sumpter pony, then climbed up in front of her. The feel of his body—solid and strong— helped quell the butterflies which formed in Cicely's stomach as the huge horse began to move.

"What do you know of Sister Clotilde?" she asked.

"That she does not like me."

" 'Tis not only you. She has no liking for knights."

"Or any man."

"She cannot help it. Before she came to Montreau, she was . . . hurt by a man. One of her father's knights." She had almost said "raped," then realized it was not the kind of thing a maiden spoke of with a man. As if she had not tried to entice him to perform the same act with her.

"I am sorry for her," Simon said, "but 'tis not right for her to judge all by the actions of one man."

"Still, she did her best to heal you."

"She tended me as duty required, but no more. And it was not *she* who brought me back from the depths of the fever."

The intensity of his voice made Cicely recall when Simon first came out of his delirium. The way he spoke her name. Like a blessing. A benediction. She remembered the first time he'd looked at her with his beautiful blue eyes and she'd felt his gaze touch something deep inside her. The memory made her shiver.

"Are you cold?"

"Nay." She tightened her grip around his chest, glad he could not see her face. Could he recall any of it? How she had pressed her naked flesh against his? Touched him?

When he woke with her lying naked against him, he'd acted as if he had defiled her. Did he guess that he had done nothing? That it was she who had tried to seduce *him?*

"If you grow chilled, tell me and I will give you my cloak to wrap around you."

"I thank you, Simon, for your consideration."

He sighed again, and Cicely wondered what he was thinking. Their bodies were close, separated only by their clothes, his mail. What would happen when night came? Would they lie together? If he believed that he had taken her maidenhead, why should he not perform the act again?

Nay, he would not. This Simon was all duty and honor. The fierce hunger she had sensed in him before was now carefully guarded.

An aching melancholy seeped through Cicely. The price for her freedom might well be her rescuer's disdain. Such urges he had awakened in her, and now she must ignore them.

He was mad, Simon decided. The fever had burned his wits to ashes. Why else would he have agreed to this ridiculous task? To steal a gentlewoman from a priory and escort her across England. 'Twas foolish and dangerous and mayhap even blasphemous.

But, nay, she had not taken vows, so that sin did not weigh upon him. She was not truly a nun—merely an innocent maiden, whom he had dishonored.

But *how much* had he dishonored her? It did not seem that such a question should arise, but he found that it did. They had been naked in bed together, and that, in itself, was enough. He had pursued this rash course because he owed her a boon to compensate for what he had done. But what had he done? He did not remember initiating the act. If he lay with her unaware, was it still a sin?

Nay, he should not pursue such reasoning. The man was always at fault in such things. Cicely could not possibly have known what she was doing. 'Twas up to him—being older, more experienced, and a man—to control his carnal urges and keep them both from disaster. Obviously, he had failed.

If only he could remember more of the night. The thought nagged at him. Had the effects of the fever momentarily dulled his wits? Why else did he have no memory of the details? Surely they had kissed. And she had removed her clothing. Why could he not remember looking upon her nakedness? How her body had felt close to his?

What wretched luck, that he must suffer penance for his lust and yet not remember the pleasure of it! He could not recall if her lips tasted as sweet as his imaginings . . . If her breasts were as high, firm, and lovely as his fevered dreams had promised . . .

Jesu, he was a monster! Even as he castigated himself for his sin, he hungered after the wicked details. Mayhap that was why God had charged him with this duty. 'Twas a test, his last chance to prove himself worthy.

Simon gripped the reins with determination. He would not fail. *He would not.*

He cleared his throat. "Cicely, have you by chance written ahead to warn the Earl of Pembroke of your arrival?"

"Nay, I . . . I . . ." He felt her tense. "I had no means of sending him a message, lest the prioress learn of it and inform my father. As I told you, I must keep this journey a secret."

Guilt nagged Simon. Was it right for him to aid this woman when her plans went against her father's will? Yet, he had done the same, following what he believed was his calling despite his family's vehement opposition. Was that the sin which damned him, the fateful decision which doomed all his plans to failure?

At the time, it had seemed so right, as if God Himself was urging him to choose the crusader cause, despite the pain it caused his loved ones. Even his mother's tears had not swayed him. What was her claim upon him compared to God's? A man grown could not linger at his mother's hearth, coddled and protected. He must go out in the world and prove himself.

And so he had . . . proved himself a sinner and a failure.

The despair settled on Simon's shoulders like a weight. Somehow he must redeem himself—and this sweet, naive woman riding behind him seemed the means. If he could take her safely to William Marshal, he would have at least performed one noble service in his life.

Whether Cicely's goal was right and true need not concern him. His duty was only to keep her from harm, including the evil which lingered in his own heart.

Even as he contemplated his sinful, lustful nature, the woman behind him pressed her delicate body closer against his. It seemed not even the heavy barrier of his mail could block out the feel of her, small and warm and finely made.

For a split second, Simon could not help but close his eyes and savor her provocative closeness. It was heaven and it was hell. He would suffer the torments of the damned on this journey, but he could no more take her back to Montreau than he could plunge a dagger into his breast.

Reluctantly, he forced his eyes open. He would not forget his duty. They would face many dangers, of that he had no doubt. God would test him, and not all the trials would involve his moral worthiness. Nay, it seemed likely that the most difficult task would be keeping them alive. King John's England was a dangerous place. In the disorder caused by the conflict between the great lords and the king, lawless men had risen to power in every corner of the land, preying upon travelers who did not have the means to defend themselves.

Simon's grip tightened on the reins once more as he considered their perilous circumstances. His horses and armor were a wealthy prize in themselves, although few outlaw bands would risk attacking a knight unless their numbers were substantial or they had the advantage of ambush. Traveling alone, he would have had to be wary. With the burden of a woman to care for, he faced even greater odds.

The weight of an additional rider would slow down Lucifer and ruin his effectiveness in fighting on horseback. The need to protect Cicely would distract him. Worst of all, her comeliness made her an enticing target for the basest sort of ruffian. Most men would be deterred by her habit, thinking that the possible pleasures of a tumble with a beautiful nun were outweighed by the certain damnation it would bring upon their souls.

But there were godless beasts to whom no depravity was

taboo; indeed, true villains might find the very forbiddenness of raping a bride of Christ too tantalizing to resist.

Simon shuddered at the thought. Traveling with Cicely was like parading a banquet before a row of starving, desperate men and hoping he could hold them off.

They would have to keep to the well-traveled roads. If what Cicely said was true, they were in little danger of pursuit. Better they should remain in the open and risk being seen than endure the dangers of the lawless countryside.

But nights would be difficult. As he had told her, he had insufficent coin to afford lodging for them and the animals. They would have to camp along the roadways. Building a fire could draw outlaws; they would have to do without. Yet, he could hardly imagine how Cicely would fare. He hoped her pack contained much warm clothing. Certainly it was heavy enough.

He sighed. Night was some hours away. He would concentrate on one thing at a time. His task for now was to put as much distance between them and Montreau Priory as possible—in case Cicely was mistaken and someone did come after them.

Cicely turned as much as her precarious position on the horse allowed. A slow smile spread across her face as she realized she could not see the priory behind them. Free. She was finally free of that stultifying prison.

Sudden giddiness enveloped her. She wanted to hug Simon, to whirl around in circles.

Of course, she could not. If she let go of his broad back for even a moment, she would go tumbling to the ground. She would have to celebrate the moment quietly, secretly—as she had experienced so much of her life these past years.

But the exhilaration continued to bubble up inside her. The sunrise was spectacular. The muted violets and pinks which trailed off into the flat gray of the November morning appeared almost unearthly in their loveliness. And the harvested fields around them—surely they were the most beautiful sight she had ever seen. Although they might be brown and barren, they beckoned, reminding her of the heedless, open landscapes she'd raced across as a child.

Oh, to ride headlong over the land. To feel the cold wind in her face and arrive breathless and frozen-cheeked in the castle bailey. Such vivid, potent memories she had of that other life.

The actual experiencing of it would have to wait. She did not think Simon would allow her to take his destrier for a wild, purposeless ride.

Not that that she actually *could.* The huge warhorse was a far cry from the gentle-natured ponies of her girlhood, and it had been so long since she'd ridden, her skills were very rusty. The muscles in her thighs seemed tight and unyielding; the ease of sitting astride had obviously left her. She was uncomfortably aware of the horse's rump forcing her legs apart. *A most unlady-like position,* she thought as the animal's broad haunch bounced against her privates. A sudden blush warmed her face. No wonder ladies did not normally ride astride, but endured the awkwardness of the sidesaddle.

Her embarrassment deepened as more sensations radiated out from between her thighs. That part of herself seemed to have come alive since she'd met Simon. She had only to think of him, and the tingling would start there. Now it was happening and she wasn't even thinking of him, merely riding a horse!

How odd it was. As if Simon had awakened something inside her and now it would not go away.

She would not think about it. If she did, she would want to squirm, and she knew enough of riding to know that squirming would be unsettling to the horse. Probably to Simon as well. He might even guess why she was doing it.

A shocking thought, and thinking it seemed to make her

more uncomfortable. Now she was actually wet. She was certain of it. The wetness which had been there when she'd tried to force Simon's member inside her. The remembered image made her breasts throb. She was immediately aware of the fact that her nipples were squashed against Simon's back.

They tightened, seemed to grow hard. Could he feel them? Jesu, certainly not. He had on a mail shirt and that padded garment underneath. Her cloak and habit were also between them. There was no way Simon could tell what she felt.

Bless the saints for that, at least. Bad enough that she should be bedeviled by these yearnings, she did not want Simon to guess how crude her thoughts were. He believed her to be an innocent. And she had been, until she met him. With his intoxicating maleness, his awe-inspiring body . . .

No! She would not think these thoughts; she would not. Instead, she would concentrate on the scenery, and the buoyant sense of liberation with which the morning had infused her. They were riding along a road. From the location of the sun in the sky, it appeared they headed west. There would be a town soon, Easton.

Cicely herself had never traveled there, but she had heard two of the older nuns—Lisette and Maude—describe it. They had gone there while a fair was in progress, and they spoke of the many merchants' stalls they had seen, selling every sort of ware imaginable—gloves and farm implements, ribbons and weapons, glassware from Flanders, furs from Catraith, wine from Aquitaine and Brittany.

The sisters had spent most of the day at the stall selling holy relics, including John the Baptist's tooth, and attending the passion play performed in the village common. But what faint glimpses they'd provided of the rest of the fair had inflamed Cicely's imagination and caused her to recall attending a similar event as a young child. It all came back to her—the exotic smells, the many people, the dazzling array of merchants' goods. Though barely old enough to walk beside her mother, she had drunk in the magical sights, determined not to miss a moment.

By the end of the day, she had made herself sick on sweetmeats and vomited on her new calfskin shoes. Yet the luster of the experience remained undiminished in her mind.

There would be no fair in Easton at this time of year, she realized sadly. But there would be other sights. She longed to see a great castle, to watch the knights patrol the walls and the lord's banner snap in the breeze. Mayhap they could find some excuse to go inside the bailey, and she could watch the squires practice in the lists and observe the coming and going of servants in the yard.

And when they reached Pembroke Castle, she would have reason to enter the donjon itself, to feast in the banquet hall and watch the musicians and jongleurs perform. 'Twould be like the old days, except she was a woman now. A woman who—as her father had made clear—had no place outside the cloister walls.

A frisson of ill ease traveled down her spine. She had not thought much beyond her passion to be away from Montreau. Petitioning her godfather for a place in his household sounded like a plausible plan, but 'twas by no means certain that he would agree. What if he decided to send her back to the priory instead?

Her anxiety turned to dread . . . and then stubbornness. She would not let anyone send her back to the priory, not even the formidable Earl Marshal. She would run away first!

There must be some other means of making her way in the world. A pity she had no skills with which to earn a place in a noble household. Despite her years assisting Clotilde, she could not claim to be a healer. Her needlework skills were only tolerable, her singing voice ordinary, and she played no instruments. The only unusual attributes she had were the ability to read and write both Latin and French.

Could she convince some nobleman to hire her as a scribe or clerk? If she were a man, that would be likely enough. But she had never heard of any woman engaged to read and write for a lord. Most men, especially in the Church, argued that females were not fit for anything but bearing children and sewing!

A lie if there ever was one, Cicely thought hotly. She knew many women at Montreau who, out of necessity, performed tasks typically thought of as "man's work." Cicely had no doubt that Clotilde was as fine a healer as any nobleman's leech. That Sister Hawise kept her accounts as meticulously as any abbey's cellarer. Sister Maude's skills in animal husbandry would be the envy of any herdsman, and she had heard the bishop himself admire Prioress Elena's ability in administering Montreau as a prosperous, peaceful holy house.

Certainly women were the equal of men in every aspect except size, strength, and fighting ability! 'Twas only men who persisted in arguing otherwise.

For a moment, Cicely regarded the outrageous nature of her thoughts. Where did such defiant, rebellious convictions come from? No one had ever told her these things; indeed, she had had the opposite reasoning forced upon her all her life. Yet, she *knew* these things to be true.

Exactly as she knew she did not belong at Montreau.

The thought made Cicely's earlier excitement return. She had done it! She had left Montreau, exactly as she had vowed nearly ten years before. And nothing and no one could make her go back!

Suddenly, the image of her father's face—his features set in rigid lines beneath his helmet—flashed into her mind. He had sworn to beat her if she did not do his will. And that was when she was a young child. How much harsher would he be now that she was a woman grown?

A shudder traveled down Cicely's spine. She dare not let her father find her, at least until she had spoken to Earl Marshal and knew if he would support her cause.

She cast an uneasy glance behind them. "Simon," she said, "mayhap we should take the forest trackway rather than traveling through the town. I do not want to be seen."

Simon turned his head. "I thought you said that no one would come after you."

"Not now, but mayhap later. And a knight and a nun *riding pillion*—we make too unusual a sight. We will be remembered, if we are seen."

She heard Simon sigh again and felt another pang of guilt. He had not wanted this duty. She had tricked him into aiding her. Somehow she must see that he did not suffer for helping her. "I vow, Sir Simon," she told him, "I will see that you are not punished for your part in this. I will tell my godfather that I forced you to take me."

Simon gave a harsh, humorless chuckle. "And of course he will believe that."

"He will!" Cicely insisted. "I was always a difficult child. He will not be surprised to find that I . . . that I . . ." She paused, suddenly realizing that she was not ready to tell Simon the truth of what she had done. If he knew the extent of her unmaidenly scheming, he might be disgusted—disgusted enough to set her down on the roadway and ride off. The only hold she had upon him was that he believed he had dishonored her and owed her a boon.

"You could have left the priory without me," she began haltingly. "My sin in the thing is as great as yours, and yet I have let you feel beholden to me. I owe you a debt as much as you . . . owe me. And it is to discharge that debt for which

I make this vow. I say it again, Sir Simon, I will not see you suffer for your kindness. I vow it upon my immortal soul.''

Simon could not repress a grim smile. What an odd way of looking at things the little wench had. As if she could vow to protect him and see it through. As if she did not know how powerless and vulnerable she was in the world outside the cloister. Her gentle innocence touched him. No wonder she had stolen Clotilde's heart. Cicely of Montreau was an intriguing mixture of naivete and stubbornness. No matter what happened on this journey, at least he would not be bored.

He guided the horse off the trackway into the barren forest, and a kind of wary determination swept him. 'Twas not his role to question the nature of the trial ahead. He had been anointed as God's warrior, and this time he would not fail.

CHAPTER 6

Cicely closed her eyes and pressed her forehead against Simon's broad back, trying not to think about how miserable she was. The muscles in her legs quivered and ached, her bottom felt as if it had been pummeled, her arms were numb. But the worst of it was her terrible need to relieve herself.

She knew she should say something, but it seemed so awkward. Even if Simon did stop, she would have to walk some distance for privacy. The winter-bare forest offered little cover.

The sense of intimacy and ease she had felt between them at Montreau had vanished. She was embarrassed and uncomfortable with this silent, serious Simon.

Clearly, she was to blame for the change. When she had sought to seduce him, she had altered things forever. No longer could she see Simon as a perfect, idealized knight come to rescue her. He had became a flesh-and-blood man, a man she desired in a very unholy way.

He, too, must see her differently. No longer the innocent

angel who had called him out of his fever, but a manipulative, willful woman who had used his sense of duty and responsibility to compel him onto this difficult course.

She did not want to bring him more trouble. And so, she would not ask him to stop, though she gritted her teeth with her misery.

Jesu, the woman wriggled around a lot. With every movement Simon imagined he could feel her breasts pressed against his back, her legs rubbing against his hips. 'Twas witless, given his armor and layers of clothing. But the provocative images would not leave him. Her sweet body so tantalizingly close . . . The secret core of her womanhood so very near . . .

Simon clenched his jaw and tried to will the wicked thoughts away. Never had he had so much trouble controlling his carnal urges. But this time he was tortured by the knowledge that he had been naked with this woman. His flesh had touched her flesh. And every sinuous movement she made behind him on the horse brought the scintillating memories rushing back.

Except, there were few memories—a bare glimpse of her in the darkness of the infirmary, enough to make him realize what must have transpired between them. But the rest of it was a mystery. Try as he might, he could not summon up even how her skin had felt against his.

And it was sinful to try. He castigated himself for his lustful musings, yet it was next to impossible to keep from thinking such things. He needed to be away from her for a time. To regain control over himself.

Abruptly, he reined the horse to a stop. "Let me help you down. 'Tis time for a rest."

He heard her sigh and wondered if she was also plagued with restless longings. Impossible. She was a pure, gentle maiden. Or had been until he defiled her.

"Hold my hand and slide down," he told her.

She took his hand and gave a muffled groan. "I can't," she whispered.

"Don't be afraid. I won't let go until you're safe on the ground. Lucifer won't step on you. He knows I won't tolerate bad manners toward someone I've allowed to ride him."

" 'Tis not that. I . . . I . . . cannot seem to get my legs to move."

Simon frowned, then turned so he could grab Cicely by the arm and ease her off the horse. He tried to set her on her feet, but she crumpled to the ground.

"Cicely!" He dismounted rapidly, and after pulling her out of range of the destrier's huge hooves, knelt beside her. "What's wrong?"

She raised a flushed face to his. "My legs . . . they don't seem to work. It's been years and years since I rode a horse."

Simon exhaled a sigh. Riding came so naturally to him that he had not considered how difficult it would be for her for the first few days or so. "I'm sorry, Cicely. Let me help you up."

She rose stiffly. The sight of tears of pain glistening in her eyes filled him with concern. "Rest awhile," he urged.

After a moment, she started to hobble away. "Can I aid you?" he asked.

She turned and spoke in a muffled voice. "I must seek a moment of privacy."

Awareness dawned on him. Traveling with her would be rife with these awkward moments.

He moved to the other side of the destrier to wait. Jesu, he felt ill at ease with this woman. Every word they spoke, even the simplest, most natural matters, seemed edged with tension. And he must endure days of this.

And nights. The thought caused an almost unbearable hunger to well up inside him. To have Cicely so near and yet be unable to taste and explore her as he yearned to do—'twould be the undoing of him. And how was he to protect her when his wits were so addled by lust that he could scarce see straight?

Yet he must. 'Twas his duty. A hellish test of his worthiness.

He heard her approach, panting slightly. "Simon?" she called tentatively.

He moved so she could see him. "I am here."

Her face was flushed, heightening her beauty. Doe-soft eyes. Rosebud mouth. The perfection of her delicate, heart-shaped face. For a moment, Simon felt as if he were struck dumb.

She stared back at him, and the childlike innocence of her face subtly changed to reflect a beguiling womanliness. Was it not desire which shone in her melting brown eyes? She must have wanted him last night. She had been willing . . . was still willing.

Simon's breath caught. God demanded too much. If he had never lain with her, he could endure the torment. But now . . .

"Should we not continue on?" She gestured. "If someone should come after us . . . I would like ·to be well away from Montreau ere we stop for the night."

He gave a jerky nod. Bless her for her restraint, for reminding him of his duty. He had almost been lost.

He went to help her on the horse, clenching his teeth at the waves of longing which swept through him at the feel of her slender body. Though he settled her on the destrier as quickly as possible, her warmth seemed to penetrate his gloves and ripple through his flesh. He walked away and began to adjust the burdens on the sumpter pony's back.

By the time he'd collected the pack animal's lead and mounted Lucifer, some of the dizzying yearning had subsided. He could once again concentrate on the pathway ahead of them. As he searched their surroundings for any sign of danger, he released a long sigh. The first real test, and he had passed.

* * *

Cicely clutched Simon's broad back, her emotions in turmoil. She had seen the desire in his eyes. But instead of meeting his hunger with an affirmation of her own, she had babbled on about someone coming after them. She'd had a chance to experience passionate love, and she had shunned it. Why?

The question troubled her as they continued on through the forest. Was it fear that made her turn away from the promise she had seen in his beautiful blue eyes? Was she a coward after all?

For ten years she had heard tales of the crudeness and cruelty of men. Although she vowed she did not believe them, mayhap in her heart she did. For why else had she called up the barrier between her and Simon?

She could feel the stiffness in his body, the careful way he helped her on the horse. 'Twas as if he dare not touch her. As if her flesh might burn him. Condemn him. Destroy him.

For a moment there had been none of that. The fire between them was bright and warm, urging her nearer. Then, suddenly, she was afraid.

It was fine to dream of true love, of a knight who would rescue her and carry her away to freedom. It was an altogether different matter to be alone in the forest with a man and to realize how strong and powerful he was. How raw and crude his maleness made him. No halo-crowned Gabriel, but a flesh-and-blood warrior.

He fascinated her. He also frightened her. Last night, safely drugged, he had not seemed threatening. She could pet him and stroke him and urge him to her will. Like a silky, docile lapdog.

But with him wide-awake, outside the security of her priory prison, some part of her had second thoughts. What if he took her roughly, without kisses or endearments? How would she endure it if he shattered her childish dreams of love?

Coward, she thought silently. If he took her, it would be because she had offered herself. Blatantly, outrageously. Why should he not push her to the ground and seize that which she had given freely the night before?

She drew a sharp breath, stiffening at the thought. A part of her yearned for their joining, even as he did. Her body did not fear the act, though she knew there must be pain. 'Twas her mind which hesitated.

Her thoughts were filled with shadowy warnings and insidious doubts. Would he cast her aside once he had what he wished?

Nonsense. 'Twas Simon's honor which had made him aid her. A corrupt man would have bedded her when she first came to ask her boon of him. Made clear his price for helping her and collected it long before setting off.

Instead, Simon had urged her against involving herself with him at all.

And she had tricked him. The shameful memory caused Cicely a new wave of distress. She was the one who was dishonorable. If Simon ravished her and abandoned her, 'twas likely no more than she deserved. But he would not. All she had to do was draw away and never would he touch her.

Was the converse true? she wondered. If she encouraged him, would he take her? Did she want him to?

An endless tangle, but she would have days to ponder it.

Days of riding . . . A groan rose to Cicely's lips. The agony of her thoughts she could endure, but the misery of her body was another matter.

"What is it, Cicely?" Simon asked. "Are you sore from the jostling of the horse?"

"Aye, I . . . I did not think it would be so uncomfortable."

"We could stop soon . . . unless you fear we will be followed."

Cicely weighed her options. Put more miles between them and Montreau or halt now and possibly be able to ride the next day?

"If you see a likely place, let us stop there."

They traveled on. The sun reached its meager apex in the sky, then sank rapidly into a tangle of trees. The pale gold light, which had provided some warmth, waned even more. A chill rose from the muddy, half-bare earth and assaulted Cicely's aching limbs. By the time Simon called a halt among a stand of oak and beech, she was near to shivering.

Awkwardly swinging his leg over the horse's withers, Simon climbed down first this time. He reached for her waist and pulled her off the horse in an iron grip, then balanced her against his body so she wouldn't fall.

If she had been able to block out the pain, she might have enjoyed the proximity of his hard strength. As it was, she was distracted by the effort of ascertaining which of her muscles were less sore.

He released her. "Walk it off a bit," he said.

She took a step, then her legs crumpled, tumbling her into a pile of damp leaves.

Once again, Simon knelt beside her. "Here, let me aid you."

He grasped her arm and helped her up, then kept a grip upon her as she took a few shaky steps. " 'Tis not merely the riding," she told him, "I'm cold as well."

"So you are," he said, taking off his gloves and rubbing her chill fingers with his own warm, callused hands. "I think it is time to fetch heavier clothing from your pack."

Cicely watched nervously as he went to the packhorse and untied her bundle. He carried it to her and and held it out. She hesitated, then reached for the pack. "Simon, I . . ."

"Of course. Let me allow you some privacy." He started to walk away.

"Simon," she called, "I must tell you something."

He turned and she saw the rekindled hunger in his eyes. He was thinking of her being naked as she changed her garments.

She licked her lips, thoroughly unsettled. "I have a confession to make. There is no clothing in my pack. I . . . I have nothing warmer to wear."

His expression grew puzzled. "What is in there, then? What have you seen fit to bring on this journey, rather than sensible goods?"

He moved nearer, and Cicely began to tremble. Would he be angry at her? Would he force her to leave her beloved *romans* behind?

His face grew stern. "Answer me, Cicely. If I am charged with your care, I must know if you carry holy relics or other valuables you have stolen from Montreau. If so, it is much more likely that they will come after—"

"Stolen?" she interrupted with a gasp. "You think I would steal from the Holy Church?"

His brow creased. "Mayhap you only meant to borrow the things, but I vow, 'twill seem the same to them. Even if you intend to return the goods or pay their value, 'tis still trouble you have brought us."

Cicely felt her face flame and her muscles go rigid with anger. "What sort of wicked creature do you think I am?" she demanded. "I would never steal from anyone. Nor 'borrow' things, as you put it. The books are mine own! All gifts from my mother, bless her soul! They have kept me sound in my mind these past ten years, and I vow I will not be parted from them!"

"Books?" Simon looked stunned. "Your pack is full of books?"

"Aye!" She repressed the urge to throw the heavy bundle

at him. Although she had wrapped them well, the fragile tomes might be damaged by such treatment. Instead, she knelt and placed the pack carefully on the ground, then untied the ends of the linen bedcloth which held the bundle secure. Reaching inside, she unwrapped one of the leather-bound volumes and held it out. "This one is my favorite. 'Twas written by a woman named Marie of France."

Simon knelt and took the book from her. He examined the workmanship of the binding, then gingerly opened it.

"Can you read?" Cicely asked eagerly. How wonderful it would be to find someone she could share the beloved stories with!

His eyes scanned the script and a puzzled look came over his face. " 'Tis not Latin."

"Nay, it is written in *langue d'oil,* the language of common speech."

He raised his gaze to hers. "How come you to have the skill of ciphering this? Did one of the nuns teach you?"

Cicely shook her head. "Most of them would be appalled if they knew of my books. For these not holy works, but tales of ladies and knights—real people, not saints and bishops. I learned to read French when I was a child, before I was banished to Montreau. My mother had a serving woman from the court of Louis in Paris."

"And you retained the skill all these years?"

"Every year my mother sent me a new book. I know it cost her dear to obtain them, but she knew what joy they brought me, and I think it helped assuage her guilt."

"Guilt?"

Cicely sighed. "She knew I did not belong at Montreau, and she sorrowed over my unhappiness. I would dearly like to see her, but I cannot go back until I . . ." She shook her head. She might never see her mother again. If she returned to Tathwick, her father would insist that she be sent back to the priory, even if she had convinced William Marshal to aid her cause.

"You are fortunate that you had at least one parent who understood what was in your heart."

Cicely looked up and saw Simon's handsome features etched with sadness. "Did they disown you?" she asked gently. "Force you to leave your home?"

"Nay, nothing like that." He handed her the book and stood.

Cicely watched him walk back to the packhorse; then she returned the volume to its wrapping and secured the bundle. She rose awkwardly and approached him. "May I bring them?" she asked. "They are very valuable. If things get difficult, I might be able to sell some of them for hard coin." Pain shafted through her at the thought, but she knew she had to be practical. If Simon took her to Pembroke, she must have some means of paying him for his trouble.

Simon didn't answer, but after a moment he seemed to find what he was looking for in his saddle pack. He approached her, holding out a heavy tunic of deep blue samite. "Put this on, else you will freeze this night."

She took it, not knowing what to say.

Then he looked down at her sandals and shook his head. " 'Tis not possible. Even if we tied them tight, my shoes would never serve. Your feet are half the size of mine."

He returned to the packhorse while Cicely examined the tunic. It was beautifully made, embroidered at the sleeves and neck with golden thread. "I cannot wear this," she said. " 'Tis much too fine for traveling."

"You will wear it. I've carried it with me for six years and put it on only once. Better that my mother's handiwork should go to keep you warm than rot away in my saddlebag."

"Your mother made this?" Cicely held the garment at a distance, more determined than ever that she could not wear it.

"Aye. Many years ago. So I would look fine and proud when I went to the king's court."

"You were large even then."

"Aye. Growing up tall and broad-shouldered, I could choose no other destiny than knighthood."

There was a touch of bitterness in his voice. Cicely wondered if he had not wanted to be a knight. "Did your father insist that you take up arms?" she asked.

"Aye, although, to his credit, he believed I had no choice. As I said, my size sealed my fate." He turned suddenly. "Have you seen any priests or monks who look like me?"

"Nay, but I thought that was because . . ." Cicely frowned, thinking of her brother. Hugh had wanted to take holy orders, but her father had insisted he earn his spurs so he could defend Tathwick. It seemed men did not always have choices in life either.

Simon held out his hands—big, long-fingered, scarred, and callused. "These are not the hands of a scholar or clerk. So, being that I am of noble blood, they must be used to kill. There is no other way."

"I'm sorry, Simon." Cicely clutched at the tunic, feeling the pain which radiated from her rescuer. Like her, he had endured the misery of a life which was not his by choice.

He looked at her, and a smile softened his features. "Put on the tunic, Cicely, and I will try to find some chausses and stockings for you to wear under your nun's garb."

Cicely's gaze returned to the rich garment. She held it out to him. "You said it would be a hard, rough journey. I cannot risk ruining a gift from your mother."

"I vow she would want you to have it. She would rather the garment be ruined than risk a little maid like you freezing."

He went back to the packhorse. Cicely took off her cloak

and hung it over a branch while she wriggled into the tunic. It came down past her knees, and she had to roll up the sleeves thrice to free her hands. "Bless the saints, your mother did not make you a long court robe," she called out. "I would be tripping over it."

Simon walked over to her, holding out a pair of heavy wool chausses. "Try these on. Mayhap if we . . ." He paused, and a look of mirth danced in his eyes. "God's blood, if you don't look odd—with a man's tunic and that nun's coif."

Cicely's fingers went to the linen headdress. "I will take it off. That way if someone sees us, they will be less likely to guess where I have come from."

She unfastened the pins at her ears, then pulled off the wimple. Her braids uncoiled and fell to her hips. She smoothed them out and asked, "Is that better?"

Simon did not answer, and when she looked up, his face wore that hungry, wolfish expression once more. "How long your hair is."

"In truth, it's a bother," she said nervously. "It has such a stubborn curl, which makes it very hard to braid. Sister Clotilde usually has to help me."

Simon's mind was flooded with the image of Cicely's lovely face surrounded with silky curls. Of lush waves swirling over her bare breasts. 'Twould be something to see the maid with her hair down. To wrap his fingers in those sleek, honey-colored strands and feel their softness against his bare skin.

He swallowed, then said. "Mayhap you should wear some sort of head covering. For warmth. Let me see if I have something you could use."

He moved back to the packhorse and busied himself rummaging through the saddlebag, not trusting himself to look at her any longer. The heavy tunic only served to emphasize the delicacy of her fine-boned wrists and slender neck, while the blue heightened the ivory perfection of her skin. He did not need these unbearable reminders of her femininity.

He found a strip of wool and handed it to her, then walked off.

There was much to do in setting up their camp. The horses must be tended. He must find water. Dig out the food he'd bartered for with the ostler in the village. Scout the area to make certain they would be safe for the night. A dozen things to distract him from the bewitching little novice who was his charge.

Cicely watched Simon bustling around and wondered if he was angry with her. "What can I do?" she asked him. "How can I help you?"

He spared her one glance and said, "Tie up your braids and put on the hose, as I've told you."

Chastened, Cicely went behind a clump of bushes to re-arrange her garments.

She pulled the chausses on and tied the drawstring tight around her waist, then rolled up the legs. They hung loose and awkward under her skirts, but she could feel their added warmth. 'Twas going to be very difficult for her to relieve herself now, but she could not discuss such things with a man, to point out that she would not only have to lift her skirts, but also undo the drawstring and roll down the chausses to accomplish the matter.

For a moment she wondered how men endured the trouble, then realized that a man would not have to bother undressing. He could simply pull down the garment in front and be about his business.

The reminder of the physiological differences between the sexes caused the familiar aching heat to fill her body. She was wearing Simon's clothing. Though the chausses had clearly been laundered since he last wore them, that did not entirely alter the intimacy of the situation. The cloth that had rested against his private parts was now warm against hers.

The thought made her restless. It made her want to go watch Simon as he unsaddled the destrier and unpacked their supplies. To enjoy the sight of his strong, graceful body, to think of his long legs encased in the chausses she was now wearing.

She closed her eyes. Outrageous thoughts, sinful and yet delicious. Blessed Jesu, it was well she was no longer bound to be a nun, for what sort would she make with such lewd images filling her mind at every turn!

She went back to where Simon was arranging things in the clearing. He pointed to a blanket spread out beneath one of the oaks. "You will sleep there. I will remain near the horses and keep watch."

Cicely regarded the ten paces between the blanket and where Simon would rest. 'Twas clear he wanted to keep plenty of distance between them.

"I will not build a fire this night," he said. "Mayhap later in our journey we can risk it." He held out a leather pouch. "Are you hungry? I bartered for some cheese and bread in the village."

Cicely took the pouch. A pang of guilt went through her as she contemplated how she would ever repay him. If they came upon a peddler, she must try to sell one of her books. They would need coin to buy supplies, and if there was any money left, it would go a little ways toward discharging her debt to the knight. But which of her precious books could she bear to part with?

"Here is some wine as well. The last of my soldier rations." Simon offered her the skin, then went back to his place near the tethered horses.

Retrieving her cloak from the branch where she had left it, Cicely spread it out on the ground and sat down with the pouch and wineskin. "Would you not come join me?" she asked.

He came and squatted by her. She took out the hunk of bread and the round cheese. Without a word, Simon drew a knife from his belt and handed it to her. Cicely cut a slice of cheese and bread and offered it to Simon. He took the food and ate, his eyes scanning the woods around them.

She opened her mouth to tell him that his belly would ail if he did not relax while he dined; then she realized that he must be accustomed to eating under such circumstances. Still, it made her unsettled to have him crouched nearby like a restless animal.

"Are you so fearful we have been followed that you must keep watch every moment?" she asked.

" 'Tis not trackers I fear, but bandits. I do not know these woods, and many wild places are now infested with wolfsheads and ruffians who prey on travelers."

"But you cannot keep watch every moment. You need to sleep. I can tell by the strain on your face that you are weary. It has only been a few days since the fever left you, and you must not push yourself too hard. I am not sleepy. Why can I not stay awake and watch while you rest? Later you can take your turn."

He looked at her, his face soft with amusement in the fading light. "And what could you do, *ma petite,* if some bandits did come? Would you charm them with tales from your books?"

"I would wake you, of course." Cicely felt a twinge of aggravation. She was not *quite* as helpless as he thought! "If you should fall sick again because you do not rest, what use will you be to either of us?"

The glint of humor vanished from his face, and he looked bleak and hopeless. Cicely wished she had held her tongue.

She held out the wineskin. "Have a drink and then take your rest. You have done all so far. I would do something to help our cause, if I could. My eyesight is sharp. My hearing excellent. I will keep as careful a watch as you would."

He took a drink, and his smile flickered again. ''With an angel to watch over me, mayhap I will find my rest after all.''

Angel. The tender word seemed to cause a quivering in her chest, as if a tiny, sharp arrow had lodged there.

CHAPTER 7

He woke suddenly and scanned his surroundings to orient himself. Faint moonlight filtered through shifting clouds above, and he made out the shape of a small figure seated nearby.

"Cicely?"

"Aye." The tremor in her voice unsettled him. He rose and moved toward her. She was huddled over, shivering.

"Cicely, are you cold?"

"A lll . . . litttttle."

He went to her and wrapped his arms around her. Despite the layers of clothing she wore, her teeth chattered violently.

"I'mmmmm ssssorry." She was shaking. "I am not used to sllll . . . eeping outside. It is so dddd . . . amppp."

"What part of you is the coldest?"

"My ffff . . . eeet."

Simon searched out her sandaled feet. They were indeed as cold as ice. He rubbed them vigorously. "We must get you some warm stockings."

"I nnnn . . . ever nnnn . . . eeded stockings before. When the snows were deep, I had only to walk to the chhhh . . . apel and back and Clotilde always let me warm myself by the brazier in the infirmary on the wwwway."

"Why did you not get up when you felt yourself growing chilled? If you had walked or moved around, 'twould have eased you."

"I ppppr . . . omised to keep watch."

"Silly wench," he said tenderly.

He finally got her feet unthawed, but she continued to tremble. He started to pull her close, then realized the cold metal of his mail would draw heat away from her body.

He removed his cloak and heavy mail shirt. Then, clad in his bulky gambeson, he draped his cloak over both of them and pulled her down to the ground, encircling her with his arms.

"Better?" he whispered.

She nodded. "But I fear you will have difficulty keeping watch this way."

Not true, he thought. *I am as alert as I've ever been in my life!* She lay with her back to his chest, his arms tight around her slender shoulders, her silky, fragrant hair brushing against his chin and the unmistakable softness of her bottom pressed against his groin. When she squirmed, trying to warm herself, he was instantly aroused.

Sweet torment. To have her so close and not pursue greater intimacy. But there was an undeniable pleasure in simply holding her. Comfort in the feel of her lithe, yielding form. And the scent which rose from her skin—sweet herbs and femininity. It filled his senses, soothing and enflaming him at the same time. Long-ago memories of nurses and servants cuddling him. His own mother, fragrant with attar of roses as she held him to her breast.

Aye, better he should think of Cicely as some sort of saintly madonna he must protect.

But his body was not fooled. This was no untouchable symbol of womanhood. As she warmed in his arms, he was reminded of Cicely's sensual vitality, and of the fact that they had lain together the previous night. Unclothed.

His shaft rose hard and insistent. His testicles ached. As if it had been many months since he found release.

Which, clearly, it had. The puzzle resolved itself in his mind. Whatever had happened between them the night before, he had not taken Cicely's maidenhead. Of that he was certain.

Either she was so innocent that she did not know he had not completed the act, or she wanted him to think that they had been joined and use his guilt to make him aid her.

In truth, it did not matter. Even if she believed he had deflowered her, he knew he had not. And that awareness meant he must continue to restrain himself. What agony. To be alone with her, to hold her close and not act upon his potent urges. How he longed to know her as a man knows a woman! To explore her secret curves and hollows. To taste her skin and suckle her breasts. To bury himself deep within her . . .

Nay, he would not think of it. He would go mad if he did!

How was he to endure the constant temptation? There would be many cold nights on their journey. Either he would have to make a fire, or sleep next to her. Which prospect endangered them more? One way, he feared for their lives. The other, their souls.

As Simon's breathing grew even and deep, Cicely relaxed. She was warm. And safe. With his big body surrounding hers, she felt as if no danger could reach her.

Her knight. His breath wafted against her hair. His strong arms encircled her waist. Never had she felt so safe, so cherished. 'Twas like being a little girl again and snuggling in the comfort of her father's embrace, before her father had turned against her and sent her away.

The memory brought a shaft of pain, and she clutched Simon's arms more tightly. Would this knight betray her as her father had? Once he had fulfilled his promise and taken her to her destination, would he abandon her?

'Twas all she asked of him, all she had charged him with. But she could see how difficult it would be to say good-bye.

And all the more so if she indulged in her fantasy of giving herself to him. As tempting as it was to think of offering her body to Simon, she knew it was not right. Such an act would bind him to her with guilt and duty, and he had already given more to her than he owed. Once already she had played upon his sense of honor. She could not do so again.

And there was the matter of her own heart. If Simon left her after she allowed her yearning fantasies to blossom, she would be overwhelmed with despair.

Nay. She must allow things to go no further than this. Simon was an honorable knight, and he would not attempt intimacies with her unless she made it clear she desired them. But that was a pathway she could not follow. For her own sake, and for his.

Still, there was this delicious closeness, this sharing. She meant to savor every moment.

A mist crept over the forest in the night, and they woke to find a silvery frost covering the ground. It glistened in the golden glow of the sunrise as they untangled their clothing and got to their feet.

"A good day for traveling," Simon said.

Cicely nodded. She was not looking at the sky but at him. Bareheaded and clad only in his linen gambeson, he reminded her of an angel. His wavy, tousled hair shone golden, and the way his broad shoulders filled out the heavy, cream-colored garment gave the illusion of wings. Only when he turned to her and she saw the stubble on his jaw did she recall how very mortal he was.

Mortal and *male*. She was suddenly uncomfortable. "I must seek a moment alone," she said.

She walked into the woods, brushing dry leaves off her clothing. In the darkness, cuddled next to him, she had felt at ease and content. By daylight, her nervousness returned. She could not quite relax with this man. Every time she looked at him, her heart seemed to beat faster, her breath to rise like a bubble in her chest.

After finishing her business, she walked back to their camp. "Is there a stream nearby?" she asked him.

"Aye." He pointed. "Down that ravine. I thought I would water the horses there after we ate."

"I need to wash. Do you have a cloth I could use?"

He went to a saddle pack and returned with a strip of clean linen.

"I'm sorry I am unprepared for our journey. I was so anxious to be off that I did not think clearly of what I might need."

He shrugged. "I have lived out of a pack so long, 'tis second nature to me. Indeed, 'twas strange to sleep on a cot and have a roof over my head when I was at Montreau."

She took the cloth.

"Go and wash," he said. "We must set off soon."

Simon watched her walk away. She looked so slight and fragile, her slender shape near lost in the heavy tunic. But never could he forget she was a woman, no matter how naive and childlike she sometimes appeared. He longed to watch her as she washed, to feast his eyes on her graceful form as she performed the simple act. He wondered if she would remove the tunic and unlace her habit so she could wash more thoroughly.

The image of ivory-skinned breasts filled his mind. Of rose-tipped nipples puckering with the cold. Jesu, even if he was so crude as to invade her privacy, he dare not come upon her when she was half-naked! If she should turn and look at him, he would be lost. He would fall to his knees at her feet and worship her. He would suckle each nipple with such tenderness, such reverence. Lay her down upon the stream's bank and kiss every curve and contour of her body.

A deep shudder racked the length of him. Imagining the sin was near as bad as doing it. But he could not help himself. She had beguiled him. Made a mockery of his vow to protect her and aid her.

He jerked around and went to see to the horses.

The little stream was half-frozen. A crust of ice glazed the edges, and when Cicely bent and dipped her hand in the water, her fingers immediately went numb. She splashed her face and neck, then straightened, shivering. 'Twas too cold to wash more.

She dried herself with the cloth, then smoothed her braids with frozen fingers, thinking she should replait her hair. But she had forgotten her comb, and such a task would take longer than she dared be away.

She walked back up the ravine, keeping a careful eye on her surroundings. Blue tits and sparrows pecked among the bracken. A wren sat in a bush feeding upon some red berries. Above her, the dark silhouettes of blackbirds shone in the bare tree branches. Their caws sounded around her. In the distance she heard a song thrush calling.

But otherwise it was quiet. No bells ringing to call her to prayers. No voices echoing through stone walls. None of the noises of daily life at the priory: the chop of an axe cutting firewood, the clatter of a milk pail, the low of cattle in the fields. Naught but the gentle soughing of the wind in the trees and the twittering of the birds.

After so many years surrounded by people and noise, there was something lonely in the quiet. A kind of relief came over her as she reached the top of the slope and saw Simon saddling the destrier.

"There are some oatcakes in my saddle pack if you are hungry," he said, scarcely looking at her. "Did you take a drink at the stream?"

"Nay, I did not."

"I will fill a skin when I go down to water the horses."

She watched him roll up the blankets and store them in the pack, then retrieve the wineskin and put it away. "Is there anything I can do to help, Simon?"

He shook his head. "I'll see to the horses; then we will set off."

Cicely's muscles protested bitterly as Simon lifted her onto the destrier a short time later. "Ohhhhh," she moaned.

" 'Twill get better as the day wears on," he promised as he mounted in front of her. "Your muscles will loosen and the discomfort will ease."

Gritting her teeth, she prayed that he was right. How would she endure days and days of this? She felt achy and stiff from sleeping on the ground, her thighs and buttocks were miserably sore, and despite her attempts to wash, she still felt dirty.

You must get through this, she told herself. If she meant to fulfill her vow, she had to tolerate some unpleasantness. What was a few days or weeks of being uncomfortable compared to years of freedom?

"How long do you think it will take to reach Pembroke?" she asked.

"If we do not encounter bad weather or other difficulty, we might be there in a less than a fortnight."

Cicely gave a sigh of relief. Surely she could bear up that long.

But the riding and the distresses afflicting her body seemed endless. Cicely tried to distract herself by observing the scenery around them and reminding herself how long it had been since she had seen anything outside the sheltered world of Montreau. She sought to relish the sight of rolling hills, russet and brown in the distance. Of forests dark against the smoke gray sky. Of birds darting among the pale birches and the tawny shadow of a fox streaking through the tall, dun-colored grass. The elegant grace of a doe as she warily dipped her head to drink from a moss-edged pool.

When they returned to the road, Cicely spent time observing the inhabitants of the hamlets they passed. Legs bare beneath their long, rust-colored smocks, serfs spread lime and dung on the fallow fields, and grubby children tended pigs rooting for acorn and beechnut mast at the edges of the woods. The women of the small settlements went about their endless tasks of gathering firewood and carrying water for cooking and washing.

The peasants seemed more careworn than Cicely remembered from her father's lands. The adults' faces were thinner and more pinched, the children more spindly legged. And she saw few babies or nursing youngsters carried on their mothers' hips.

When she remarked on the matter to Simon, he shook his head. "The king squeezes the lords for taxes to pay for his war in France. They, in turn, demand more work from their villeins. 'Tis a harsh time, when only the most greedy and ruthless thrive."

"But their lord"—Cicely pointed to the towers of a castle in the distance—"can he not see that if he works them too hard, they will sicken and die and his fields lie untended?"

"Not all men see the reason of such thinking. They imagine

that their serfs are like the forests and the hills, that they will always be there.''

Cicely frowned. Mayhap she did not want to meet the lord of the lands they traversed if he were so foolish. Still, when they left the road as it veered toward the distant stronghold, she asked, ''Why do we turn into the forest?''

''I know naught of the man who controls these lands. I thought it safer to avoid the main road.''

''What do you think he might do to us?''

''Capture us and hold us for ransom.''

Cicely stiffened in outrage. ''How could he dare? Are there not laws to protect travelers?''

''Aye, but such laws are enforced by the sheriff of the shire, and we cannot presume he is a man of good character. Most sheriffs have purchased their power from the king, and often as not, their goal is personal profit rather than upholding the law. It may well be that the sheriff is in league with the local lord to extort and steal from passing travelers.''

''Does the king not care that men violate his laws?''

''The king has troubles aplenty, and little time to spare on justice for people like us. With the great barons on the verge of revolt, and his campaign on the continent a near disaster, John is fighting to survive.''

''Survive? What do you mean?''

''Oh, they would not kill him, though I suspect many think he deserves to die. Merely strip him of some of his power.''

''But what men are these who dare take up arms against a king anointed by God?''

''Men like any others. Some greedy and evil. Some genuinely outraged that the king has allowed graft and corruption to rule the land.''

''Will they succeed?''

Simon shook his head. ''I know not. Nor do I know on which side of the matter the weight of truth lies. Many of the men who would seize the king's power would govern no better themselves; indeed, they might serve us more ill than John.''

''I have heard none of this,'' Cicely mused. ''Little news comes to the priory, and of that which does, I never thought to pay much attention. But it seems I should have.''

A shiver ran down her spine. If the king's laws could not protect them, they were like lambs passing through a countryside full of wolves.

She could not help gripping Simon's waist more tightly as she remembered the older nuns whispering of the cruelties and depravities of men. In the priory, she had been protected and safe. Now Simon's strong body might be all that stood between her and brutalization. What if he should lose his life defending her? What a terrible blot upon her soul that would leave.

And a crushing weight upon her heart. Simon was more than her protector, her savior. He was very dear to her, and she dreaded that she might bring him further misfortune.

They camped that night in a little glen. Simon snared a hare and roasted it to eat with their bread. While their supper cooked, Cicely warmed her hands over the fire, enjoying the delicious heat.

But when their meal was finished, Simon scuffed dirt over the coals and put out the flames.

''Do you still fear bandits?'' she asked.

He nodded as he sat down on the ground. There was a weariness to his movements which worried her.

''You seem tired,'' she said.

He did not answer.

''Is it because of the fever?''

He sighed. ''Mayhap.''

''Clotilde said that you caught the sickness on the way to

the Holy Land. I have wondered how you survived it then. Did an army physician tend you?''

He did not answer for a long time, and Cicely began to wonder if she should have held her tongue. But she was curious; she knew so little about him.

Finally, he spoke, tracing patterns in the dirt with his eating knife as he did so. ''When I fell ill in Constantinople, a Muslim family took me in.''

She gave a gasp. ''You were tended by infidels?''

His mouth twisted in bitterness. ''Did you think they were all evil monsters who spitted Christian babies on their swords?''

She shook her head. ''I . . . I don't know what to think.''

''Of course, you have been taught, as I was, that the Saracens are Godless, wicked people.'' He raised his gaze to hers, and his voice was impassioned. '' 'Tis not true. Many of them are as moral and righteous as any Christian. They even believe in God.''

''But they don't believe in Christ,'' Cicely said softly. ''That is what damns them.''

''They believe he was a prophet, a wise man. But nay, they do not think he was the Son of God.'' He closed his eyes, looking pained. ''Does that mean their souls are unworthy of God's grace? That they deserve to be treated as less than men?''

Cicely took a deep breath. She did not know how to answer him. He seemed so tortured by his thoughts. Somehow she must distract him. ''Do you not know what causes you to grow ill?'' she asked.

He stood suddenly, moving away from her. ''Only that it seems to smite me at the most inopportune times. Before a battle or as my companions prepare for march. 'Tis almost as if God wishes me to fail as a soldier.''

''Mayhap He does. Mayhap being a knight is not your true calling.''

He turned to look at her. "I told you. There is no other way for a man like me. I am not trained to be a clerk or a priest."

"But there must be something else you could do." Cicely tried to recall what other duties noblemen performed. "You might be a steward or a castellan for another lord. You would not always have to travel then, but would stay and guard a fief and oversee its operation and defense. I vow you would be good at that, for you seem to have a practical bent to your thinking. You would be able to foresee and plan for the needs of the castle inhabitants, as you have done for me."

An idea came to Cicely. What if she could convince William Marshal to make Simon castellan of one of his many castles? It would be a way to repay Simon for his aid, and it would save him from the hardships of the life of a hired knight. But she could not mention the idea, not until she arrived at Pembroke and discovered if she had the influence to sway the earl to her own cause, let alone Simon's.

She stood and approached him. "I believe God must have some noble purpose for a fine, brave knight like you. I cannot believe He would abandon you after you have strived so hard to do His will. The Pope himself said that all who wear the crusader's cross are blessed."

Simon shook his head. "I have lost all faith in that cause. 'Twas not a grand, glorious dream, but an evil, corrupt undertaking by men who sought not God's glory, but the elevation of their own wealth and power."

"But surely some of them, men like you . . ."

His blue eyes grew as hard as shards of ice. "Men like me are the greatest fools of all."

She put a hand on his arm. "I cannot believe that God has turned from you, that your affliction is His punishment."

He shook off her hand. "You cannot know how I have failed . . . the terrible things that weigh upon my conscience."

The despair on his face pierced her like a lance. What sins did he carry in his heart?

"I doubt that you have done anything so awful," she soothed. "We are sinners, all of us. If you are sincerely repentant, God can forgive anything."

But even as she spoke, the familiar doubts assailed her. Were there not many things she had done for which she felt no regret? There were those who would say her flight from Montreau was a wicked act, in defiance of her father and of God's plan for her, yet she experienced no guilt, only relief and elation. What if Simon had also done something for which he could not seek penance?

She moved nearer to him, longing to touch him, to ease his unhappiness. "Simon, whatever it is that grieves you, I cannot believe that it means God has turned His face from you. Ill things often befall good and virtuous people."

He looked at her, smiling faintly. "You are as balm to my spirit, Cicely." He reached out and fingered one of her braids. "Mayhap your innocence and childlike spirit will heal me."

"I am not as pure hearted as you think." She looked down, suddenly embarrassed. "I have done selfish, wicked things."

Was lying naked with him one of those things? Simon wondered. Had he coaxed her into allowing liberties, or had *she* tried to entice him?

From the faint blush coloring her cheeks he could almost guess the latter. Mayhap his sweet angel was not so virginal after all. Mayhap she experienced the temptations of the flesh as excruciatingly as he did.

An unbearably arousing thought. Why was it that every moment of closeness between them inevitably reminded him of his intense desire?

He released her braid and moved to the packhorse to get blankets for their bed.

* * *

In the morning, they ate the last of the cheese and coarse bread, washing it down with water since the wine was gone. "We need to purchase more food," Simon said as he stowed the waterskin in the saddlepack. "We will have to stop in the next village, despite the risks."

Cicely felt under her habit for the gold-and-onyx cross which hung between her breasts. "I have a few things of value. Some jewelry which we could use to barter with."

"The people in these villages have no use for coin or valuables. In turn for food, I will work. It is much easier for me to haul firewood with the horses than for the peasants to gather it by hand. And there are other tasks I can perform."

"I could help," Cicely offered eagerly. She searched her mind, trying to think of something she could do to earn food. Gloomily, she realized she was no more fit to work for her keep in a rustic village than in a large castle.

Simon shook his head. "I would not have you mar your soft hands nor risk getting hurt performing harsh labor. You are born and bred a gentlewoman. 'Tis not right for you to toil like some village goodwife."

"What of you, Simon? Are you not also of noble blood? Why is it right that you should hire yourself out like a stableboy so that I may eat?"

"I am used to it. Though 'tis thought to be a fine and heroic calling, in truth, except for kings and great barons, most knights perform many ignoble tasks. Digging tunnels to undermine a castle, butchering animals for food, polishing and preparing weapons—there are many rude chores in a knight's life."

"Do not most of them have a squire or other retainers for such tasks?"

He gave a weary sigh. "Aye, I had a squire once, and two

other companions who traveled with me. But they are all dead now. Perished of the fever."

"Oh, Simon, I am sorry."

"Don't be. I have often thought that such an end is more blessed than the one I have come to."

There it was again, the dark shadow of despair which seemed to hover over this strong, brave knight. How would she ever convince him that he was not cursed by God and fate?

He helped her on the horse and mounted in front of her. Cicely pressed her face against his broad back, though the links of his mail felt sharp and cold against her skin. Closing her eyes, she whispered a prayer. God had granted her the fulfillment of her dream; she would ask Him to aid Simon in finding a purpose for his life.

Blessed saints, don't let it storm! Simon scanned the threatening sky, tension coiling in his gut. If an early winter squall came upon them, they would have to seek shelter. On his own, he could weather a night of sleet and ice. But poor Cicely would freeze.

He eased the destrier off the forest track, intending to return to the roadway. Despite his instincts that danger awaited them there, he would not risk getting caught in the wilds with no protection from the weather.

His sense of unease grew as the underbrush grew heavier. He felt as if eyes watched them from the surrounding thickets of hawthorn and rowan. His right hand left the saddle pommel where the pack pony's lead was tied and reached for the scabbard of his sword. He drew it out and used it to slash at low-hanging branches which blocked their way. But his real purpose was otherwise. If they were ambushed here, where the thick growth greatly hampered the destrier's movements, the only advantage he had was to have his weapon at the ready.

Behind him, Cicely dozed. Her slight weight pressed against his back, and the soft sound of her breathing reached his ears above the crackle of dried leaves beneath the horses' hooves. He thought of waking her, then decided to let her rest. She would get little repose this night if they were forced to take shelter in a crowded castle bailey or to bed down in some villein's cottage.

Besides, his vague disquietude was likely for naught. His nerves had been on edge the entire journey. He was unused to traveling alone and unaccustomed to being responsible for the safety of a woman. The vulnerability of his charge weighed heavy on his mind, the obligation to keep her safe honing his normally wary temperament to knife-edge keenness.

A branch cracked behind him, and Simon pulled hard on the reins to turn his mount. A figure rushed forward and cut the sumpter pony's lead, while another man jumped down from a nearby tree. "Ahhheehhhh," the man shouted, waving his arms at the terrified packhorse while the other bandit pulled hard on the pony's lead.

Simon thrust the destrier's reins into the hands of a now wide-awake Cicely and leaped to the ground. "Ride!" he shouted, then slapped the destrier's flank. The big warhouse snorted, jerked forward a few paces and stopped. Simon spared a second to curse himself for training the horse to always stay close in battle, then rushed after the fleeing men and the pony.

The bandits were clearly terrified to see him racing after them, sword in hand. But they did not release the pony's lead, nor slow their wild pace. Not only did they obviously know the twisting forest pathways better than he, they were fleet of foot and unhampered by the burden of mail and heavy weapons. They negotiated the thick, choking underbrush much more easily than Simon and finally left him behind, panting heavily, the sound of his own labored breathing echoing dismally in his ears.

He turned back, fury and despair near choking him. All his traveling gear, what little food and drink they had left, extra clothing, blankets, all the provisions they needed to survive—everything was gone.

How could he face Cicely and tell her that he had no choice but to return her to the priory? That he had enough on his conscience and could not bear the additional burden of being responsible for her perishing in the wilds of England?

So distraught he was, so anxious to return and make certain that Cicely was unharmed, Simon almost did not see the bundle lying among the trampled hawthorn canes. But the white fabric stood out clearly from the browns and grays of the underbrush. He knelt and picked up the bundle. Had his irritation at having to transport Cicely's useless books caused him to be careless in how he tied the bundle to the sumpter pony? Why else had they been saved when all else was lost to the thieves?

He pressed the bundle to his chest and again broke into a run. Cicely had been out of his sight too long, and there might be more robbers besides the two he had chased. If they tried to grab Cicely, Lucifer would fight to the death to protect his rider, but there was significant danger that Cicely would be thrown in the process.

Relief swept through him as he glimpsed the gray of Cicely's cloak and the dark haunches of the warhorse through the trees. She was still astride and presumably unhurt.

"Simon!" she gasped as she saw him. Her face was pale with fright, her eyes wild.

He gentled the stamping horse, then dropped the bundle of books and reached for her. Her body trembled as he lifted her down, and she hugged him close, as if she would never let go. "Oh, Simon, thank God you are safe!"

He rested his face against the fabric covering her hair and said his own silent prayer of thankfulness.

For long seconds, they clutched each other; then Simon

abruptly realized their circumstances. Her face was pressed against his neck, her body near melded to his. Except for the barrier of his mail, they were as close as lovers.

As he gently disengaged her arms from around his neck, she looked up at him. Embarrassment colored her features, but the expression in her eyes revealed a longing that shame had no part in. She wanted him. There was hunger in her wine-dark eyes, yearning in the way she parted her lips.

Simon felt the answering need rise up in him. 'Twould be so easy, so natural to lay her down upon the bed of fallen leaves and love her. Every throb of his heart, every pulse of blood through his veins, made him ache to do so. But the threat of danger still tingled against his taut nerves. The thieves might try to steal the remaining horse and the rest of their possessions. They must keep moving.

He guided her back to the destrier and helped her up. "The pack pony is gone," he told her.

Her eyes widened in alarm. "My books?"

With his loins tight with unrelieved lust and worries about their survival gnawing at his thoughts, irritation quickly replaced his tender mood.

"As luck would have it," he snapped, retrieving the cloth-covered bundle, "*this* is all we are left with. A pity you did not pack more wisely, else we might have salvaged enough to continue our journey. As it is, we must turn back. I'll not have the blame for your death weighing upon my already sin-blackened soul. I am returning you to Montreau."

CHAPTER 8

"Nay!" Cicely cried. "I won't go back! I'll freeze to death in the woods ere I return to Montreau!"

"And well might that happen!" Simon retorted. "We have no blankets, no food, no flint for making a fire. I'll not have your death upon my conscience! I have failures and sins aplenty. I'll not add to them, even for your sake."

"Simon, please! There must be some way!" Cicely held out her hands beseechingly. "I'll absolve you of all blame for anything that happens to me."

He jerked off his helmet and threw it to the ground. "*I* will know I failed. And *I* will never forget how foolish I was to even begin this journey! What was I thinking of, to let things come to such a pass? On my own, I might have had a chance to find a place in some lord's garrison. Now I will be fortunate if I don't starve in the woods myself!"

Guilt lanced through Cicely. Had her selfishness destroyed

Simon's life? Heaven forfend! She could not bear to live with that upon her conscience.

She remembered her plan to ask William Marshal to reward Simon with a position at one of his castles, and fierce dermination again flared in her breast. They *must* finish this journey. It was the only hope, for both of them.

She reached beneath her clothing and pulled out the gold-and-onyx cross. ''We can use this to barter for supplies. If we find no villagers willing to part with the things we need, we'll go to the next castle we come upon. 'Tis a risk, aye, but we have no choice. Without food nor fire, we'll not manage the journey back either.''

''And what will we tell the steward or whomever we barter with? That you are fleeing a convent, and I am aiding you?''

''We'll tell them that ... that you are a knight seeking service and that I am ... your wife.'' The words tumbled out thoughtlessly. Only as she heard them did Cicely realize how presumptuous they sounded.

Simon turned so she could not see his face, and Cicely closed her eyes. He meant to refuse her, to tell her that he could not endure the thought of being wed to her, even in pretense. That she was a willful, stubborn shrew, and he meant to be rid of her.

''It might serve,'' he said. ''But what of your nun's habit? That gives the lie to the tale.''

She touched the brown wool of her skirts. The fabric was warm and soft, but the design too easily gave away her circumstances. ''Mayhap I can trade my habit for another garment before we reach the castle. There must be some peasant woman with an old kirtle she would part with.''

''I will have to leave that business to you,'' Simon said shortly. ''I know naught of women's garments.''

Cicely's despair lifted. It seemed that her plan might work, and that Simon might accept it, despite the gloomy, black-tempered expression he wore.

"Come," she urged, "let us ride on to the next village."

He retrieved his helmet and thrust it on. "There are many difficulties ahead of us," he said as he climbed into the saddle in front of her. "We might yet be taken for ransom if the local lord is unscrupulous, although with naught but a sword and one horse, he likely will think me too poor to bother with."

His words ended with a sigh, and Cicely breathed her own exhalation of relief as Simon settled his big body in front of hers. She would not allow herself to lose hope. She did not believe God would abandon her now, not after so miraculously bringing Simon to her rescue. Her brave, strong knight. If only she could convince him that things would work out for him. That, someday, he would find his calling and be happy.

Daily, he compounded his foolishness, Simon thought bitterly as he guided the destrier through the forest. 'Twas not enough that he undertook such a ridiculous mission, but now—when he had a chance to turn back, to right his mistake—he allowed this morsel of a wench to lead him deeper into disaster.

What was her hold upon him? It could not be guilt over what had passed between them that fateful night at Montreau, nor even that he had made a vow to aid her. Now that he knew the risks, the sheer hopelessness of her cause, there would be no disgrace in changing his course. Indeed, if he truly cared for her welfare, he *should* take her back to Montreau immediately.

That he did not had nothing to do with chivalry or honor. It had to do with some part of him which could not bear to disappoint her, to destroy her touching faith. Faith in him. In goodness. In the absurd notion that there was some chance for happiness in this life.

All the things which he had long since despaired of, she still held dear and precious. That touching innocence, that faith, was such a rare magical thing, he could not bear to be the one to shatter it.

But someone would. It might be the lord at the nearby castle. He might have his men rob them of all they possessed and turn them out to freeze. Or, put them in a dungeon and demand some absurdly high ransom for their freedom.

At worst, the local lord might allow his men to make sport of them. Kill him and rape Cicely.

A shudder traveled down Simon's spine. She would not survive such treatment, and although he would fight to the death to prevent it, one man was nothing against a whole castle garrison. In the end, he would go to his Maker with another terrible failure upon his conscience.

The guilt settled like a stone in his gut, and all that eased his sense of doom was the feel of Cicely's arms around his chest. Though it must be his imagination, it seemed she held him not merely to secure herself on the saddle, but with tenderness. As if she cherished him and wanted to hold him close to her heart.

That was her fateful power over him, that she reached inside him and made a spark of memory bloom into life once again. The memory of being loved.

Cicely's stomach lurched uneasily as they approached the castle on the hill. She told herself that it was the lack of proper food which caused this queasy feeling in her belly. There was nothing to fear, after all. God would protect them.

As He had protected them from the bandits in the wood? The worrisome thought nagged at her. Nay, surely that was part of His plan. That they would be forced to go to this castle. Mayhap she was meant to meet someone there, someone who would help Simon.

Gray walls rose up in front of them, high and forbidding. It scarcely seemed possible to Cicely that she had once dwelled in one of these ominous edifices.

But Tathwick had been home, filled with people who loved her and indulged her. Its oppressiveness had been mitigated by the familiar refuges within—the garden, with its nose-tickling fragrance of herbs and flowers, the lazy sound of bees among the blooms, the lingering heat of sun-warmed walls. Her mother's solar, acrid with the odor of dyed wools, the neatly wound spools stacked in a rainbow of hues in a chest by the big loom. The spicy sweet scent of mulled wine heating on the hearth on a winter evening. Warmth from the fire and from the sunlight flooding in through the green glass of the one glazed window in the castle on rare bright winter days.

All the memories came back to her. Of the stables, redolent with earthy odors. The day her pony foaled and she watched the still-damp little chestnut filly struggle to stand on unsteady legs. Her father's hunting bitch sprawled in the straw with a dozen squirming puppies as Cicely begged her father to let her name the mewling bundle cradled in her arms.

Blackberry, she'd called the pup. An absurd name, but she'd picked it because of the dog's glossy black coat, such a startling contrast to the tan and rust brindled fur which marked the rest of litter.

The hound would be dead by now, these nearly twelve years later, but the memory was still bright and vivid in her mind. It reminded her of all she had lost, and spurred her on in her plan. The lord of this castle would agree to help them, she knew it!

The guards scarcely took note of them as Simon guided Lucifer across the bridge over the ditch. They did not make a very prepossessing sight, one lone knight riding pillion with a heavily garbed woman behind him. Only the destrier drew the interest of the guard at the portcullis. Cicely saw him examine the huge warhorse, then raise his gaze to take the measure of Simon.

A well armed knight, he saw, bigger and broader shouldered than many, but with armor so battered and rent, 'twas clear its owner no longer was a man of means. A crusader, the knight had once been, but now he was reduced to carrying his wife or leman—whichever she is, the guard thought—behind him on his own mount.

"Ho, there, sir knight. State your business," the guard called.

She felt Simon tense, then take a breath. "I would speak to your lord."

"What business have you with Geoffrey of Blackhurst?"

"We would like to barter for supplies so we might continue our journey."

The guard's eyes narrowed beneath his helm. "And what do you carry that would interest my lord?" He motioned with his head toward Cicely. "Does your lady have jewels hidden beneath that wrapping of rags?"

Cicely became flushed. The only garment she'd been able to procure in exchange for her habit was a thin, well-worn kirtle, and to keep warm, she had been forced to wrap herself up with strips of wool. She feared she looked like little more than a beggar.

The guard's question hung in the air, and Cicely could sense Simon's indecision. If the soldier thought they carried nothing of value, he might refuse them entrance. But if he believed they truly possessed some wealth, there was always the chance he would try to seize it by force.

"Holy relics!" she blurted out. "We carry holy relics!"

The guard gazed at her in surprise, then perused Simon and his tattered surcote marked with the crusader's cross. "From the Holy Land?" he asked.

Simon nodded.

"My lord is not an overly pious man but his lady . . . she

might have an interest in such things. For her sake, I'll let you into the castle.'' His voice, which had softened for a moment, grew hard and forbidding once again. ''But, I warn you, if you trouble or distress Lady Blackhurst, 'twill go hard with you. Her husband dotes on her, and she has been sore grieved by misfortune this past year.''

''We would not trouble her at all,'' Simon said, ''but speak directly to your lord.''

The guard gestured that they might pass by. Simon rode Lucifer through the gate and into the bailey. He guided the horse to an area for stabling livestock. Dismounting, he handed the reins to a grimy-faced squire, then reached up for Cicely.

''In the name of Mary, I hope you have a plan,'' he mumbled as he helped her down.

Cicely saw the squire start to lead the destrier away. She halted him so she could reach up to untie her bundle of books from the stallion's saddle, then cradled them against her chest as they started across the bailey.

Simon shook his head. ''You promise them holy relics, then offer books that not one man or woman out of a thousand in England can read. I vow, that clever tongue of yours will be the death of us.''

''I thought it the safest thing to offer,'' she shot back at him. ''The guard did not look like so ruthless a man that he would dare steal saints' bones. And if we did not tell him we carried something of real worth, he meant to turn us away. Once we are in the hall and able to speak privately with Lord Blackhurst, we will admit the ruse and bring out my jewelry for his eyes alone.''

Simon shook his head again and did not answer. Cicely felt a bubble of fear form in her chest. The words ''holy relics'' had risen to her lips without conscious thought, and she had immediately taken it as a sign that the Almighty had guided her in what to say. But now she had doubts. Would God condone a lie—no matter how desperate their circumstances?

The hall was near empty. Simon approached a female servant and asked to be conducted to Lord Blackhurst. The wench stared at him, frowning. "He's in the solar with milady."

"I would not disturb him," Simon said. "We will wait here until the evening meal." He gestured to Cicely. "All I ask is something to drink for my wife and a place by the fire to warm ourselves."

The woman nodded toward the hearth. "I'll bring ye some ale."

"Wine would be better. My wife's condition . . ."

The serving woman examined Cicely's midsection with sharp eyes, then, apparently satisfied that the bulky rags concealed a swelling belly, nodded and hurried off.

"You compound our falsehoods," Cicely said.

"I would not have you forced to drink ale. 'Twill make your stomach ail after the little food you have had this day."

"There were times I fasted at the priory. I swear to you, Simon, I am well enough. I would not have you lie to protect me."

"To say you are my wife is a greater lie, and you condoned that."

His voice was harsh, disapproving. Cicely's mood sank further. Even if they came through this journey unscathed, she feared Simon might come to despise her.

They approached the fire, and Simon shooed away the dogs sleeping there so Cicely could take a seat on a stool near the flames.

She sighed in gratification as the blessed warmth seeped through her. When the wine came—a rich, sweet vintage—it contributed even more to her lassitude. She vowed not to think about their objective for a time, but to simply enjoy the bliss of being comfortable for the first time in days.

Time passed. Gradually the hall came to life around them as servants came to prepare for the evening meal. Simon observed their activities carefully. He noted that the bread trenchers were cut thick and the jugs of ale on the tables were plentiful—a sign that the lord of the castle was not miserly with his men. But the goblets at the lord's and lady's places at the table on the dais were pewter rather than silver. Either this lord was a man of modest means, or he kept the fine plate stored away for when guests visited.

Simon also examined the clothing and physical condition of the servants he saw. They were not starved-looking, and their garments were fashioned of stout fabric, though it might be patched and mended. Had the lord once known greater prosperity and fallen lately on hard times? Had he chosen the wrong side in this business with the king?

Simon's concentration on the puzzle of Lord Blackhurst continued as the hall filled. The soldiers went to their places with little ribaldry or jesting and immediately began to eat.

Beside him, Cicely sighed, and Simon turned his attention to her. Seeing how wistfully she gazed at the food, he had almost made up his mind to ask at the nearby table if they could spare anything when the serving woman who had brought them wine appeared with a hunk of bread and a cup of pottage. "For your woman," she whispered, then hurried away.

So, Lord Blackhurst did not terrorize his servants, Simon reflected, but neither were they easy with him. Indeed, there was a sense of tension vibrating through the hall. The anxious mood deepened as the lord and lady appeared and took their seats at the high table.

Geoffrey of Blackhurst was older than Simon had expected. Once he had likely been a handsome man, but years of worry had taken their toll, etching his face with harsh lines and frosting his black hair with streaks of silver. Dark, shrewd eyes burned beneath scowling brows. Simon's hopes sank. A hard man, and a clever one.

Simon was so preoccupied with Lord Blackhurst—the decider of their fate—he scarce noted the lady of the household until her husband turned toward her and spoke. The contrast between the two was startling. If Lord Geoffrey was past his prime, his wife had scarce left girlhood. Her pale skin had the smooth perfection of a child's and her reddish brown hair a bright, rich luster. She was thin to the point of unhealthiness, her wrists like sticks poking out from the sleeves of her heavy samite gown.

To a man like Simon, who well knew the terrible trials of childbearing, she was a sight to inspire pity—and a twinge of anger. What right did this hard, ruthless-looking man have to wed this frail woman-child and risk her life in begetting his heir?

Then Simon saw how Lord Blackhurst looked at his wife, and his resentment eased. As the hawklike gaze softened and the weary mouth curved into a tender smile, the years seemed to drop away from Geoffrey of Blackhurst. His affection for his wife was plain to see.

"When, Simon?" Cicely whispered beside him. "When do we speak to him?"

"After they have supped, I will approach the high table."

"What of me? Do you mean to leave me here?" she complained.

"Lord Geoffrey strikes me as a man who would rather barter with a knight than a maid."

"But I am the one who carries the crucifix. And I thought up the tale of the holy relics. Besides, how do you know seeing me won't inspire their sympathy?"

Simon shook his head. Though Cicely's argument had merit, he would not risk her safety. If Lord Blackhurst had him seized and thrown into the dungeon, he wanted her to have some chance to escape.

The lord and lady of the household began to eat. The man's appetite was hearty; his wife's, nonexistent. She used her eating knife to cut and poke at her food, but never brought the utensil to her lips. Several times, Simon saw Lord Blackhurst offer her a bite from his own knife, as if coaxing her to eat. Although she accepted the offered morsels, 'twas all she consumed during the meal.

For a moment, Simon considered that she might be ill and unable to tolerate much food, then discarded the notion. She had none of the other telltale signs of disease. Indeed, she did not look unhealthy, merely very sad, as if she suffered from an affliction of the spirit rather than the body.

Did she hate her husband and despise his affection for her? She did not pull away from Lord Blackhurst when he tried to feed her, nor recoil when he put his hand on her shoulder. She seemed almost indifferent to him. And to the rest of the activity in the hall.

At last, Lord Blackhurst pushed his wine goblet away. Saying a silent prayer, Simon got to his feet and walked toward the dais.

Cicely tensed with frustration as she watched Simon cross the hall. She wanted to help him, to do her part to improve their circumstances. After all, was it not her fault that they came to be here? If she had not been traveling with him, Simon would not have been in the woods where the bandits waited. And without the encumbrance of a passenger, he might have been able to turn the destrier in time to prevent the theft of the packhorse. 'Twas her responsibility to right the wrong she had done this brave, noble knight—if only he would let her.

Cicely stood and began to walk toward the high table. She made her way along the side of the hall, determined not to anger Simon by interrupting him as he bargained with Lord

Blackhurst, but to wait in the shadows to see if he needed her aid.

As Simon bowed low before the high table, Cicely thought again of the impressive sight he made. His hair shone gold in the rushlight, and when he straightened, he held his formidable body as proud and erect as a gleaming blade. How could any deny that this was a man to be reckoned with?

Simon spoke and their host answered, but Cicely was too far away to hear their words. She chafed impatiently at her passive role. She wanted to have some say in her destiny, not bide her time while men decided things.

Slowly, she edged nearer to Simon. How was she to aid him if she could not discern what was said?

"The guard said that you carried holy relics." Lord Blackhurst's gaze assessed Simon coolly.

Simon cleared his throat. "In truth, 'tis not a holy relic, although the object we offer for trade has religious significance. My wife possesses a crucifix, fashioned of gold and inlaid with onyx, which we propose to sell to you in exchange for supplies and a packhorse."

"A crucifix? Not some saint's knucklebone or a piece of the true cross?" Lord Blackhurst sat back in his chair, looking disgusted. "My sentry said you were a crusader. That you had brought back some precious items from the Holy Land."

"I did attempt a crusade, but ill health forced me to turn back at Constantinople. I had no opportunity to acquire sacred objects. But the crucifix—'tis truly of fine workmanship, I thought mayhap your lady . . ."

"My wife does not need jewels or gold! What she needs is a miracle!"

Simon drew a deep breath. *Now what?* a voice inside asked in dread.

Blackhurst's chair scraped harshly against the wooden dais as he stood, and his voice echoed low and sinister in the now quiet room. "What my wife does *not* need is a mountebank pretending to be a crusader. A lying bastard who disturbs her peace of mind! After your other false words, I would not be surprised if the crucifix is fashioned of dross and paint!"

"Nay, 'tis real! I vow it!"

Simon cringed as Cicely rushed forward and confronted their host. " 'Tis my fault," she declared heatedly. " 'Twas I who spoke of holy relics. I was afraid you would turn us away, and we are desperate. Thieves stole our packhorse and all of our supplies. I beg you, milord, please consider what we offer!"

"Who is this beggar woman?" Blackhurst demanded. His face grew red, and the muscles in his neck stood out like ropes. "Guards! Guards! Have these two charlatans removed from the hall!"

"Nay!" Lady Blackhurst who had been watching events unfold with the same listless, weary expression she wore during the meal, suddenly sat forward and laid a pale hand upon her husband's arm. "I would see the crucifix, milord. Please."

At his wife's words, Blackhurst's demeanor altered from blazing anger to an expression of tender concern. "Are you certain that is what you wish, Bella?" he asked her quietly.

His wife nodded, and Simon released his indrawn breath and sent a silent prayer of thanks to the Blessed Virgin Mary.

At Blackhurst's curt gesture, Cicely drew near to the dais. She pulled the crucifix from beneath her clothing and slid the gold chain over her head. With trembling fingers, she held out the cross. Lord Blackhurst leaned over the table and retrieved it, then handed it to his wife.

For a long moment, the young woman examined the piece, her bloodless lips pursing. Then her gaze met Cicely's. " 'Tis very fine. Was it a gift?"

Cicely nodded. "From my mother."

Lady Blackhurst frowned. "I do not feel right about this transaction. 'Tis not fitting that I should take from you a gift from your mother."

"Oh, please," Cicely implored, "we truly need the supplies, else we cannot continue our journey!"

"Where do you travel to?"

"To Pembroke Castle. The great Earl Marshal is my godfather. We intend to ask him to take Simon into his service."

Lady Blackhurst's gaze shifted to Simon. "Is your husband a skilled knight, with much battle experience?"

"He is the bravest and most valiant of soldiers!"

Simon winced at Cicely's extravagant words. Did she not realize the toll his sickness had taken? How many commanders he had already disappointed?

"Mayhap milord could take him into service." Lady Blackhurst turned toward her husband. "I've often heard you speak of your need for good men for the castle garrison. Why not offer this knight a place at Blackhurst?"

"But we know naught of him. He might be a liar or a thief. Or run at the first sight of an army. I cannot hire a man who brings with him no recommendation beyond his doting wife's praise!"

"But he appears so proud and stalwart." Lady Blackhurst's wistful gaze examined Simon. "His brow is high and noble. His eyes honest and kind. And I can tell from the way he looks at his wife that he truly loves her. Surely such a man would not disappoint you, milord."

Simon opened his mouth to protest, determined that the lie regarding his relationship to Cicely could not continue. But Cicely forestalled him by dropping to her knees and holding out her hands in a beseeching gesture. "Oh, please, Lord Blackhurst, give Simon a chance. 'Twould mean so much to us."

Lady Blackhurst's tremulous voice immediately echoed Cicely's. "Please, milord. For my sake."

Lord Blackhurst's gaze met Simon's. There was wariness and warning there, but also a faint measure of sympathy, as if to say, *You, too? You also endure having your life ordered by a little slip of a wench?*

Simon hesitated, thinking that there was still time to set things right. But Cicely was on her feet and at his side in a second. She hugged him tightly, her arms around his waist, her dainty flower face pressed to his chest as she spoke low and imploringly. "You see, Simon, everything will work out. God has not forsaken you after all."

He looked at her helplessly, then gently set her aside and went to one knee before the dais, bowing his head in the traditional gesture accorded one's lord. "I, Simon of Valmar, vow to serve you, Lord Blackhurst, to the best of my ability. God be willing."

CHAPTER 9

"What have you done?" Simon demanded of Cicely as they stood in the middle of the bathing chamber, watching the steam rise from the newly filled tub. "We came here to barter for supplies. Nothing was said about my seeking a position in the garrison."

He began to pace across the damp stone floor. "I'm not even certain I wish to take service with this man. I know naught of his loyalties, whether he sides with John or the rebel barons. He might be an unscrupulous, power-mad fiend, for all we know of him!"

"Oh, surely not!" Cicely exclaimed. "Any man so attentive to his wife's wishes could not be lacking in honor."

"And what do you know of men, Cicely? You've been locked away in a convent these past ten years!"

"But Lady Blackhurst has been so kind to us. She saw that we were fed, offered us an opportunity to bathe, even said she would try to find us a private chamber so we would not have

to bed down in the hall. I cannot think anyone so generous
would have an evil husband . . .''

Simon whirled to face her. ''By the saints, you are naive,
Cicely! Very few women have a choice in whom they wed.
Blackhurst might be the devil himself, yet if her father gave
her to him, Lady Blackhurst would have to make the best of
it. Though *she* appears to be a veritable angel—at least in
regard to you—'tis her husband who worries me. Furthermore,
I thought you wanted to go to Pembroke Castle. How do you
propose to do that now? Do you imagine Lord Blackhurst will
give me leave to take you there? And what excuse will I give
when I return here without you? They think we are man and
wife!''

Simon ran a hand through his hair, feeling his anger and
frustration grow by the moment. Of all the things which distressed him, 'twas the thought of being forced into close proximity with Cicely which was most unbearable. *A private
chamber*—blessed Jesu, he'd rather sleep in the pig sty than
share a bed with this impossibly alluring woman!

''But I thought . . .''—her lovely face crumpled, and she
gave a little hiccuplike sob—''. . . I thought this was what you
wanted, Simon. That because of me you despaired of ever
finding a lord to take you into service. And I wanted to . . . to
make up for . . . that . . . and the loss of your horse . . . the
trouble I've caused . . . you . . .'' Her gasping breaths grew
closer together, until her voice gave out completely.

Simon stared at her stricken face and felt his anger fade. Oh,
sweet silly wench—what was he ever to do with her?

He drew near and pulled her against his chest, gently cradling
her delicate form. ''Shhhhh, shhhh. You *have* made up for all
of it. Your debt is paid in full. And I *am* grateful. 'Tis only
that . . .''

He sighed heavily. How was he to explain how unsettling
he found their circumstances? Blackhurst saw him as a lying

scoundrel. Though he might agree to offer Simon a place in his guard, he did not trust him, nor likely mean to give him any real responsibility. Blackhurst could bide his time until his wife lost interest in their cause, then see that they were sent on their way—minus the crucifix and any other of their possessions he might think to take as payment for his trouble.

"I should not have . . . 'Twas wicked of me . . ." Cicely was still babbling words of apology. Simon gave her a shake, at a loss as to how to stop her tears. With every sob, he felt as if his own heart were being torn apart.

"Hush, now," he said desperately. "What if Lady Blackhurst comes in and sees you crying? She will think very poorly of me, I vow. For my sake, you must quiet yourself."

At his words, she nodded against his chest, then pulled away and sniffled. Though her cheeks might be tear streaked, her soft brown eyes slightly red, she still appeared miraculously fetching to Simon. 'Twas all he could do to keep from kissing her.

"Whist now, you must bathe before the water cools," he told her. "I will turn my back and wait for you to finish."

She nodded again, then gave another delicate sniffle. Simon walked to the farthest corner of the small room and faced the fire. Under his breath, he muttered prayers to every saint he could think of, asking for the strength to endure the long, torturous moments ahead.

Another hiccup rose in Cicely's throat, and she struggled to smother it down.

Holy Mother, what a nuisance she had made of herself to poor Simon! Certes, he must hate her now. Because of her impulsive tongue, he was chained to a lord he did not wish to serve. And chained to her as well. The whole castle thought

they were wed. They would be expected to sleep together.
Bathe together.

A tantalized shiver went through her as she realized the intimacy of their circumstances. She was in a small, well-lit room, removing every stitch of her clothing. All that protected her modesty was Simon averting his eyes.

Of course, he would not look. 'Twould not be honorable.

Besides, he would not want to bed her now. He was probably so angry with her that he no longer found her comely.

Jesu, how had she misread him so badly? She had thought this place in Lord Blackhurst's garrison was exactly what he wished for. Had he not told her he despaired of finding a lord who would take him into service?

She still could not see what distressed him. Lord Blackhurst seemed like a decent man, if a little impatient and hot-tempered. And were not those also Simon's faults? Mayhap that was why he seemed to mislike their host—he could not abide that which he abhorred in himself.

So prickly Simon was, so eager to think the worst of everyone, especially himself. A wave of tenderness went through her. She would do near anything to make him happy. But how was she to do so if she could not fathom his thoughts? There must be some way . . .

"Cicely! Why are you not yet in the tub?" His harsh words made her jump.

She hurried to resume undressing. "A moment, please. I am wearing so many layers . . . 'tis truly a trial."

She was breathing hard by the time she got down to her chemise, yet even so, she was chilled. The heat from the fire did not seem to reach her. She wanted to move near and warm herself, but dare not. If she did not get into the tub soon, Simon would shout at her once more.

She went to the tub and stuck one foot into the water. It had grown tepid while they argued. With a shiver she climbed in and sat down. The water reached almost to her shoulders, but cold air swirled around the parts of her which were exposed.

She sank in deeper, then realized she had forgotten to undo her braids. Frantically, she unpinned her head covering and began to work the plaits free.

Once they were undone, she dunked her head in the water and came up sputtering. Now she was truly freezing. Her hands shook as she soaped her hair. 'Twas not an easy task to wash waist-length tresses. Especially when they were as stubbornly curly and prone to tangling as hers were. Try as she might, she could not seem to get all the soap out. At the priory, she always had someone help her rinse.

"Simon," she called. "I cannot do this. I need help."

"Help? Help with what?" He sounded as if he were gritting his teeth.

"I need you to pour water over my head. Over near the fire, there are some buckets." Soap ran down her face and seeped into her eyes. "Hurry, Simon," she begged.

Heavy footsteps sounded on the flagstones. He dipped a bucket into the tub and doused her head.

"Oh, thank you," she gasped. "Mayhap another one . . . If I don't get all the soap out, 'twill be sticky and impossible to braid."

He did as she bid. Cicely pushed the wet hair out of her face and opened her eyes. Simon stood next to the tub, his face turned away from her. She could not help hoping that he had peeked a little. Then she realized how selfish the thought was. She had demanded enough of this man without seducing him into something he clearly did not want.

"Thank you, Simon. I'll try to hurry."

He moved back to the fire. Indeed, she feared he would roast alive, so close he stood to the hearth.

She no longer felt cold as she finished bathing. The thought that Simon possibly could have—for one tiny moment—seen her naked seemed to warm her. A warmth that came from inside her body.

As she soaped her breasts, she saw that the nipples were taut and erect, and a tingling throb started between her legs. Jesu, she was wicked! But why should he not see her naked? She had once pressed her unclothed body against his. How was this any worse?

"Simon, can you bring me a drying cloth? Please?"

She stood as he neared the tub. For one split second, his rigid gaze met hers; then he tossed her the drying cloth and whirled away.

Cicely felt a stab of disappointment. His glance had never crept below her neck. Either his will was stronger than she imagined, or he truly did not desire her.

Probably the latter. He might never forgive her for binding him in service to Blackhurst Castle.

Another chill afflicted her as she dressed. And like the odd warmth that had affected her previously, this cold came from inside her.

Simon closed his eyes, and the provocative image flashed upon his consciousness. Only a moment had he weakened, but such were Cicely's charms that it was enough. Enough to drive him to madness. He would never forget the vision of her pert, pink-tipped breasts cresting the water as she held her hair out of her face and waited for him to rinse it.

A glimpse, no more, but it led his mind down delicious pathways of sin. Knowing the power that one glance had over him was the only thing that gave him the strength not to peek again when he gave her the towel. For that time she had been facing him, eyes open; she would have known if his gaze had wandered.

And that he could not bear. For if she knew how desperately

he lusted for her, Cicely—generous, tenderhearted Cicely—would probably want to make a gift of herself to him.

"I am done." Her soft voice rang out, disturbing his thoughts. Simon opened his eyes. His turn to bathe. To wonder how he would endure days of this. Weeks.

He moved toward the tub, intending to take the quickest bath of his life.

He had asked one of the squires to help him remove his armor, but there were his boots and the rest of his clothes to remove. And he had no squire or serving wench to aid him. Lady Blackhurst obviously assumed his "wife" would be only too pleased to do the honors.

And Cicely would, he had no doubt of that. She would jump to help him in any way she could.

The thought of her slim fingers touching any part of him was intolerable.

He sat down heavily on the bench near the door and bent to remove his spurs.

"May I help you?" Cicely's wistful voice, coming from the other side of the room, rubbed his raw nerves to the quick.

"Nay! I would appreciate being allowed the same privacy I gave you!"

He heard her retreat to the fire. Damnation! He had not meant to shout at her.

Still ... anything to keep her away. To keep those soulful brown eyes from regarding his body with the innocent curiosity that so aroused him. From searching his face for something ... some saintly virtue he did not possess. If only she knew what a wretch he was, how many people had suffered because of him.

But he could not bear for her to know, so he kept up this pretense. A gallant knight, she thought he was. Her salvation. And never did he tell her how he would fail her in the end.

He removed his boots and crossgarters and cast them aside, then struggled with the drawstring of his hose. As he jerked them down, he realized it was not so warm here away from the fire. He shivered as he pulled his tunic over his head and crossed to the tub.

He scrubbed himself rapidly, trying not to think about Cicely sitting in this same tub, the water swirling around her breasts. Those beautiful breasts, as sweet and perfect as her face.

At the thought, his shaft rose. It could not have come at a more inopportune time, for a soft, feminine voice suddenly called from outside the door. "Simon? Cicely? Are you finished?"

"No, milady," Cicely answered.

"I have brought some more hot water. It cools so quickly."

Simon ducked further down into the water as the door opened and petite Lady Blackhurst entered, followed by two squires carrying steaming buckets. She glanced at Cicely by the fire, then at Simon in the tub. "You do not bathe your husband?" she asked.

Cicely went bright red. "I . . . I . . ." she stuttered.

A puzzled frown marred Lady Blackhurst's face. "Forgive me," she said sharply. "I did not mean to intrude."

She turned to go, motioning that the squires should follow her. Cicely crossed the room. "Please. Don't be distressed. 'Tis merely that . . . we were quarreling."

"Of course." Lady Blackhurst's voice drifted back to them from the hallway; then the squires went out and the door shut behind them.

Cicely looked at Simon. "Do you think I should go after her?"

"Mayhap you should give her time to collect herself. Obviously, she was embarrassed."

Cicely nodded. "Besides, what else can I say? That we are quarreling is a reasonable excuse. Isn't it?"

She looked at him again, and slowly her face changed. He

could tell when her thoughts shifted from Lady Blackhurst to him. When she became aware of his nakedness.

And he was aware that she was aware. His shaft swelled even further, threatening to rise out of the water. He thought to remind her about his privacy, but his mouth was too dry.

She was staring at his chest. He wondered if she recalled bathing him when he was sick. Then, unconsciously, she brought the tip of her tongue to her upper lip, and he knew that her thoughts were not innocent.

The air in the room seemed heavy, stifling. Simon waited for her to close the space between them. To come close enough to touch him.

Her face was rapt, but pained-looking. She also struggled with her urges, shyness warring with desire. Or was it virtue fighting wantonness?

But it was her battle, and if he failed in all else he would not influence her. His own control was tenuous. With every moment that passed, he was on the verge of exploding. Of taking the choice out of her hands.

He was letting her look at him, and he was not snapping at her about privacy. The realization filled Cicely with excitement.

He was so beautiful. Water droplets glistened on his broad chest, catching in the swirls of dark gold hair and highlighting the powerful muscles beneath his heat-flushed skin. The sight made her want to lick him, to lap up the shimmering water like a cat, then rub her lips over the tantalizing texture of his chest hair.

She knew exactly how he felt, how he smelled, from that night at the priory. The night she had tried to seduce him.

Guilt shattered her exquisitely sensual mood. It had been wrong of her to trick him, to take away his choices. And now she was on the verge of doing so again. If she touched him, she would be provoking him to do something which was against the code he lived by. They were not wed, no matter what lies they told others. And Simon obviously did not believe in bedding a woman who was not his wife.

At least a gentlewoman. Certainly he had enjoyed whores and serving wenches in his years of soldiering. All men did that.

For a second, Cicely felt a pang of jealousy for all those lowborn, common women who had been allowed to touch him, love him . . .

Then Simon suddenly cleared his throat, and she was jerked from her contemplations. "I must finish," he said.

"Of course." She turned her back and moved near the fire. What had she been thinking, to stare at him so? He must imagine her a wanton. If he remembered any of that night at the priory, then he knew that she was one.

Blood rushed hotly into Cicely's cheeks. What a wretched muddle she'd gotten them into. They would be expected to share a bedchamber. If there was only one bed or pallet—which was likely—they would have to sleep next to each other. To endure this endless wanting and denial.

No wonder he was angry with her. She had disrupted his life, forced him into this unfortunate situation. Somehow she must make it up to him. Somehow . . .

She heard Simon get out of the tub. He made the rustling sounds of dressing when the door opened once more.

"Sir Simon," a squire announced, "milady has sent me to escort you and your wife to your bedchamber."

The squire led them down a maze of hallways to a tiny room near the kitchen. "Milady says that she knows 'tis small, but 'tis warmer than other places in the castle. And if you need to light the brazier, the cooking fires are not far away."

Simon bowed. "Express our gratitude to Lady Blackhurst. She is most generous."

The squire left them, and Cicely examined their new quarters. Used as she was to a tiny priory cell, the room seemed very cozy and comfortable. But what of Simon? He was a big man; he might feel trapped and uneasy in such a small place. "What think you?" she asked.

" 'Twas very kind of Lady Blackhurst to think of your comfort. As for myself, I will be spending so little time here, my needs hardly matter. A garrison knight does not have time to lie abed. I will be busy on guard duty much of the time, or training in the lists."

"Of course," Cicely answered.

He had made it clear that he would endure as little time in her company as possible. So, he did despise her.

She saw Simon look at the narrow pallet. "I will sleep on the floor," he announced.

"But you will freeze!"

"Nay, I have endured worse. See, there is an extra blanket here. 'Twill be no worse than sleeping on the ground, and I have endured much of that these past years."

Cicely sighed. She knew she could not dissuade him, but it was not right that he deferred his every comfort to hers. What a burden she had become to him.

And what a wicked creature she was, Cicely decided as she blew out the lamp and lay down on the pallet. She had cruelly tricked Simon into aiding her. 'Twas not God's will that he help her escape from Montreau, but her own selfish fancy.

Never had she considered the consequences for Simon. He had tried to tell her that he had no desire to entangle his life with hers, but she had refused to listen.

Now they were in a fine mess. The whole castle thought they were man and wife. Simon could not be rid of her even if he wanted to. Mayhap she should try to think of a way to continue her journey without him and set him free from the responsibility of caring for her.

But the thought of leaving him made her feel so sad, so terrible, 'twas like a bleeding wound inside her. Nay, she did not have the strength of will for that. She was too weak. And sinful. And heartless.

The tears began to flow as she considered her awful flaws. She quickly pressed her face into the scratchy pallet to smother her sobs. At the very least, she would not add to Simon's troubles by weeping aloud.

She was crying. Simon stared into the darkness, his stomach clenching with each muffled sob. Poor little maid. What a day she had endured. First, the fright of the bandit's stealing their packhorse, the turmoil of deciding what to do next, the trip to the village to barter her nun's habit, then the scene in the great hall. 'Twas enough to shatter the composure of a much stronger woman than she.

In truth, she had persevered valiantly. Never had she let their circumstances defeat her. If he was not overjoyed to find himself in Lord Blackhurst's garrison, he was alive, with a roof over his head and a warm meal in his belly. This morning, all those things had been in doubt.

And he had Cicely to thank for their favorable circumstances. She had refused to admit defeat, and in the end, she had had her way.

So, why did she weep? Was it simply the relief of finally being safe? Simon had known knights who bore up fearlessly during a battle, then cried like a babe after the fray was finished. He could allow her the same.

If only it did not tear so at his heart. He longed to comfort her, to hold her close and whisper soothing words.

But he dare not. For he knew from the banked fire inside

him that succor would turn quickly enough to passion, tender words to heated caresses. The fine edge of his control depended on his keeping his distance. Without the barrier of cold space between them, his resolve would waver.

For how was he to forget that glimpse he'd had of her in the bathing chamber? The ivory and pink glow of her skin, the alluring symmetry of her breasts, the graceful curve of her arms and shoulders, the slender column of her neck—all of it engraved upon his senses, tormenting him as soon as he closed his eyes.

Aye, this was hell. And heaven, too. Though he might never know her intimately, he would have that image of her to carry with him when they parted.

For somehow, he must find a way to set her free. To gain the means necessary to continue their journey. He had promised to see Cicely safely to Pembroke Castle, and he would do so.

And then, when he was alone again, enduring the lonely existence of a hired knight, he would lie in the darkness and remember that splendid moment of her beauty.

She had quieted at last. Simon breathed deep in the silence and let his own thoughts drift away.

"Madam? Madam?" the soft voice pierced Cicely's dreams, but she kept her eyes shut tight. They could not be calling for her.

Then came a gentle touch on her shoulder, and Cicely could no longer maintain her hold on unconsciousness. She opened her eyes to see Lady Blackhurst bending over her.

"I'm sorry to wake you, but 'tis near sext. When you did not rouse, I feared you might be ill."

Cicely sat up and rubbed her eyes sleepily. "I am well enough. Merely very tired." She glanced around the room. "Where is Simon?"

"The steward is showing him around the castle. He appeared in the hall early this morn, eager to begin his duties. He seems like a fine, zealous knight—I told my husband we are very fortunate in having him at Blackhurst."

"Oh, he is an exceptional warrior, I am certain." Cicely stood and stretched.

Lady Blackhurst's eyes lit with curiosity. "Have you never seen him practice in the lists? You cannot have been married very long."

Cicely turned away, pretending to search for her clothes. She must remember not to let down her guard, to forget the tangle of lies she had woven. "Nay, we have not been wed long at all."

"Tell me more of yourself," Lady Blackhurst urged. "Where are you and Sir Simon from?"

Cicely could not help smiling at her hostess' frank curiosity. "My husband and I are traveling from . . . a place called Tathwick. Southeast of London. Not far from the coast."

"Was your husband employed as a knight at Tathwick?"

"No . . . I mean, aye." Cicely hesitated. Her knowledge of the world outside the cloister was so limited, 'twas difficult to conjure a tale which explained their circumstances. "Simon did serve at Tathwick, but only for a short time."

As Lady Blackhurst's gaze searched hers, Cicely felt herself flush. Then a knowing look spread over her hostess' features. "Ah, I think I understand." She drew nearer, smiling conspiratorially. "Could it be that the two of you were wed against your father's wishes? Is that why you left Tathwick?"

Cicely nodded. It seemed like a reasonable explanation, and one which might discourage Lady Blackhurst from probing too closely into Cicely's background.

Lady Blackhurst clapped her hands in delight. "How charming! Two young lovers who defied the sanctions of their families and fled alone across England. I vow, 'tis a tale like that which the jongleurs sing. Tell me, was your father lord of Tathwick? Did he dismiss Simon when he learned of your *tendre* for him?''

"Nay, my father is the . . . the steward there.'' Lady Blackhurst's guess was too accurate for Cicely's comfort. 'Twould be easy for someone at Blackhurst to have heard of Robert of Tathwick and to recall that he only had one daughter, and that she had been in a convent these past ten years.

Lady Blackhurst gave a satisfied sigh. "I knew it. I knew that you had come to such dire circumstances through no fault of your own. Geoffrey was worried that Simon had been dismissed from service for some sinister reason like theft or treachery. He'll be so relieved to learn that Simon did nothing worse than fall in love with the steward's daughter!''

"Milady, I must beg you, do not tell your husband this story. 'Twill embarrass Simon most terribly.''

"But''—Lady Blackhurst frowned—"I must tell him something. To clear your husband's name. Else Geoffrey will never give Simon a fair chance to prove himself worthy.''

"Tell him . . . tell him the gist of the story, then, but do not mention Tathwick. I still fear that . . . that my father might send someone after us.''

"That would be very cruel of him. Now that you are wed, what purpose would it serve to tear you from your husband's side? As the Scriptures say, 'What God has joined, let no man tear asunder.' ''

Cicely shook her head. "I still fear my father might try to separate us. Please, milady, if you could honor this request.''

"I will keep your secret.'' Lady Blackhurst smiled shyly. "I do so want us to be friends. You must call me Bella and feel free to confide in me.''

Her wistful words tugged at Cicely's heart. Lady Blackhurst must be very lonely to offer such familiarities to a stranger, especially one she believed to be of no higher status than a landless knight's wife. "Have you been married long, Lady Blackhurst?" she asked.

"Please call me Bella, I beg you. I cannot get used to everyone calling me 'mistress' and 'milady.' " She made a face. "It makes me feel as if I am a hundred years."

"And how old are you, Bella?"

"Fifteen. I was wed to Geoffrey at thirteen, so I have been here near two full turns of the seasons." Her gray eyes suddenly glistened with tears, and Cicely was struck by the tragic expression on her face. Some great sadness weighed on this young woman's heart.

"What's wrong?" she asked softly. "Don't you like it here? Is your husband unkind to you?"

"Geoffrey? Oh, no, he is the very essence of kindness to me, although sometimes I wish he would not be. He treats me like a beloved daughter, rather than a wife. I don't want to always be pampered and cosseted, as if I might break into pieces at a sharp word!"

It crossed Cicely's mind that Bella looked very much as if that were true, as if she were so fragile that she could be crushed by any hint of adversity. One could hardly blame Lord Blackhurst for trying to protect this delicate woman-child.

"Has he always treated you so?" she asked.

Bella shook her head as tears welled up and coursed down her cheeks. "Before the babe, he would sometimes . . ." A pitiful sob escaped from the young woman's throat, and she turned her face away.

Cicely wrapped her arms around Bella. They were nearly the same height, although Bella was so slender, 'twas more like holding a child than a grown woman. "The babe," Cicely whispered, "what happened to the babe?"

"He only lived . . . a few days . . . and I did not even see him . . ." Her voice broke. "I . . . I was too sick . . . Geoffrey thought I would die, and now ... now he will not touch me ... for fear ... for fear there will be another ..."

The last words came out in a wail of pain. Cicely tightened her arms around the sobbing woman. "I am sorry, Bella, I am."

Gradually, Bella quieted. After a moment, she pulled from Cicely's embrace and rubbed at her flushed cheeks. " 'Tis unseemly of me, to burden you with this, especially when you are so newly wed yourself. But there is no one at Blackhurst I can talk to. My maid is a flighty creature, much too busy flirting with the knights to care for my troubles. And the older women I've spoken to, they only tell me that I should be grateful for my husband's forbearance."

She walked the few paces across the tiny room, then turned to face Cicely, composed and calm now. "But I am not grateful. I *want* a babe. And I am more than willing to risk childbed again."

"Have you told your husband that?"

She nodded. "He holds me tenderly and tells me I must wait until I am stronger. That he would grieve terribly if I died bringing his heir into the world."

"I'm sorry. I cannot advise you. In truth, I know little of such matters."

Bella approached, her face pleading. "But I had thought ... You seem a few years older than me, but not too old. And you clearly love your husband. I thought you could tell me ..."

Cicely went rigid at the word "husband." Bella saw and sighed heavily. "I should not have troubled you."

" 'Tis not that, Bella. I would be happy to aid you, if I could, but ... my mother died when I was young and I lack knowledge of childbearing matters." Another lie. Jesu, her soul was growing black with them. "Mayhap if you consulted a midwife ..."

Bella shook her head. "Nay, she is the worst of all, forever telling me that I am blessed in having such an understanding lord. But they don't understand, 'tis not only the babe, I miss my husband's caresses, his presence in my bed.''

"He sleeps in a separate chamber?"

"Aye. He says I will rest better if I am not disturbed by his snoring, but 'tis not true. He only snores a little, and the sound of it soothes me. 'Tis lonely to live as I do. I have no one to talk to. No one to share my solar and gossip with." She gave Cicely a tremulous smile. "That is why I begged my husband to take your husband into service. 'Twas not kindness, but selfishness. Despite your poor clothing, you seem like a gentlewoman, and near enough to my own age that you might understand my circumstances."

"I will be your friend, Bella, I promise."

Bella nodded. "I think you will. You and Sir Simon are not thieves nor charlatans, I could tell as soon as I saw you. Why is it that men are so suspicious? My husband trusts no one, it seems, not even his own soldiers."

"The world of men is treacherous. They must learn to be wary and always on their guard. Or, so I have been told."

" 'Tis glad I am that we are women." Bella's smile broadened. "I would have us keep no secrets from each other."

Cicely returned Bella's fond look, but her insides felt tight with anxiety. What a mess of lies she had created in her new life!

CHAPTER 10

"So, what think ye o' Blackhurst?" the seneschal asked Simon as the two climbed down the steep stairway which led from the outer ramparts of the castle.

" 'Tis well fortified and maintained. And situated as it is, with the river forming a natural moat at the entrance and the steep hills to the rear, few armies could take it, except with siege engines."

The seneschal, who was called Black Robert because of his thick mane of soot-colored hair, grinned broadly. "Aye, ye're a seasoned soldier, ye are. Lord Geoffrey could have done worse. Though if it'd not been for his little slip of a wife, he'd not have taken ye on. Blackhurst is ever wary of strangers."

"Has he reason to be so?"

Black Robert shrugged. "No more so than most men, I be thinking. 'Tis an evil time, what with John fightin' in France instead o' ruling the land like a proper king. Not like his father was, certes. Old Henry would never have allowed such lawlessness. He'd have ruffians like what attacked ye rounded up and hung before they'd o' had a chance to sell their booty. But John's been too busy in France to see to the welfare o' honest English folk. And he'll pay for that mistake, by and by. Few lords care a mouse's arse for what goes on across the channel. They'll set old Johnny down right and proper.''

''You think the barons will win?''

The seneschal grinned again. ''I'd wager on it. But Blackhurst, now he's not one for choosing sides until he has to. If his liege, Richard de Claire, decides for the barons, he'll have to come down off the fence. 'Til then, he'll sit tight here with his wife.''

The hint of derision in Black Robert's words aroused Simon's curiosity. ''Blackhurst does seem unusually devoted to his wife.''

Black Robert rolled his eyes. ''Been wed near two years, but ye'd not know it. He's yet like a green boy mooning over a maid. She lost a babe some months back, and since then he's coddled the wench like a newborn lamb.'' The seneschal turned to face Simon, his onyx eyes gleaming. ''When I heard her speak out for ye, I knew Blackhurst would take ye on. Won't deny her a thing, he won't.''

''I have something of an understanding of his lot,'' Simon answered dryly.

''Oh, aye, ye do at that.'' Black Robert guffawed. ''Yer wife, though, she's not so melancholy and moonsick as Lady Blackhurst. She even appears to have a mite of sense. How long have ye been wed?''

Simon hesitated. Instead of lusting after her last night in the bathing room, he should have insisted that he and Cicely attend to the matter of getting their stories straight. 'Twould be disastrous if they contradicted each other on simple questions. ''Not long,'' he answered.

''Long enough to plant a babe in her, I hear.''

Simon remembered the lie he'd told the serving woman when they'd first arrived. She'd obviously gossiped with the other servants and the news had traveled to the ears of the knights.

This lie he could not let continue. They might be able to pretend they were wed, but they could not conjure a babe where there was not one, especially with their current sleeping arrangements.

" 'Twas a false alarm." He shook his head, trying to look grieved. "The strain of the journey must have delayed her courses."

"Ah, a pity. If yer wife was to have a babe here, mayhap 'twould ease milady's heartache. She's fair mad to get with child again. But Blackhurst won't hear o' it. He even sleeps in a different chamber, lest he be tempted to try and start one."

"Is it so dangerous for her to conceive?"

"The old women say nay. They say she could bear again safely." Black Robert shook his head. "Did ye ever hear such nonsense? A man so dotes on his wife that he won't risk her to childbed? 'Tis the only way to get an heir, and Lord Blackhurst fair needs one. He's older than me, he is, and a fightin' man must always look to the future."

"Are you wed, Black Robert?"

"Meself? Nay, I'm satisfied with the serving wenches, and I'd not have the worry." He met Simon's gaze. "Ye cannot tell me that yer pretty little wife is not a weight upon yer thoughts every moment of the day."

Simon sighed in answer. *If Black Robert only knew,* he thought. *If he only knew.*

"Sir Simon, you're to go to the solar before you sup. Milady commands it." The young serving maid flashed him a dimpling smile, then bobbed a curtsy and ran off.

"Lady Blackhurst's own maid, she is," Black Robert said. "Ye'd best heed her."

They had entered the hall after washing up at the well near the stables. Simon nodded to his companion. "I'll do as she bids. Thank you for taking me around."

"Ye're welcome. 'Tis pleased I am to have ye here, Simon."

Simon crossed the hall, following the direction the lady's maid had gone. When he entered a hallway and heard feminine giggles, he knew he neared his destination.

Entering the solar, he halted in stunned amazement. In the center of the room stood Cicely, garbed in a wine red gown trimmed with gold. Her bare neck shone creamy white against the rich color, and the luxuriant fabric stretched tightly over her breasts. Her hair hung in thick honey-colored curls down to her waist.

Simon stared at her, utterly dazzled. Could this be the innocent, childish novice he'd rescued from Montreau? She looked every inch the elegant lady. A lady any man would want for his bed. At the thought, his loins stirred hungrily.

Lady Blackhurst turned and saw him staring. Her thin face lit with color as she enthused, "Does she not look a vision? For shame, sir, to allow all this beauty to languish beneath rough rags. I know your journey was difficult, but you could have found her some finer garments, surely."

" 'Twas not his fault." Cicely took a step toward Simon. "He could not help that our packhorse was stolen. If not for me, he would have fared much better. I fear I have been a sore burden to him."

"Is a wife a burden to her husband? I think not. 'Tis his duty to care for her."

Seeing the displeased expression on Lady Blackhurst's face, Simon spoke quickly. "Of course, my wife is not a burden, but a delight. And you have made her appear even more delightful. I vow, I was struck dumb with awe when I first entered." He hesitated. "But I cannot think it would be practical for her to wear such attire outside the solar. If we could impose further on your kindness, I would ask that you furnish her with more ordinary garments."

"Can she not at least wear the gown for the meal this even? She looks so lovely. I vow her very presence would add light to that dank, dark hall."

Simon jerked his gaze back to Cicely. "She'd freeze, uncovered like she is. And 'tis not appropriate for a married woman to wear her hair unplaited."

Cicely looked down at herself. "You did admit, Bella, that the bodice was rather tight. I don't want to make a spectacle of myself." She glanced at Simon. "I really should defer to my husband's wishes."

"Just one night." Lady Blackhurst crossed her arms and gave Simon a petulant look. "For one night I want to pretend I am in some great castle dining with fine lords and ladies." Her pouting expression turned beseeching. "Please, Sir Simon. You owe me a boon after I took your part last even."

Simon glanced again at Cicely and wondered how he would endure sitting beside her while she looked so delectable, not to mention later when he must share that tiny room with her. "Of course, milady." He bowed. "As long as your husband approves, I would not withhold my permission."

Lady Blackhurst beamed at him. "Of course Geoffrey will agree. He seldom denies me anything. And now, if you are not to spoil the mood of my banquet, we must find you some finery as well."

Did Geoffrey of Blackhurst feel as much the fool as he did, Simon wondered as he sat at the lord's table with his employer and his wife and Cicely, all of them dressed in court attire. The servants had been giving them astonished looks all evening, while many of the fighting men were hard pressed to smother their snickers. They must think their lord had gone mad.

Better that than they imagine that he and Cicely had truly risen so high in Blackhurst's favor in one day. Uneasily, Simon searched the room for Black Robert. The seneschal might be put off by seeing Simon seated in the place reserved for noble visitors. Simon did not want anything to damage the friendship growing between them.

Failing to catch sight of Black Robert, Simon allowed himself one lingering look at Cicely. Instantly, his heartbeat quickened and his body responded. The way the upper curves of her breasts showed alabaster above the gown's low neckline; the wanton splendor of her thick hair trailing down her back; the rosy gleam of her lips, echoing the deep color of her dress— every sensual detail reminded him that she was not a nun, a forbidden virgin that he dare not touch, but a passionate earthy woman who appeared to desire him as much as he did her.

The thought made him shudder, and he quickly looked away, thanking the saints that he had not been seated beside her. Court manners dictated that she should share a trencher with Lord Blackhurst, while Simon dined next to their hostess.

But not being tortured by her provocative beauty every moment of the meal was small comfort when he considered that she sat in full view of the rest of the hall. If one of the men even dared cast a lewd glance Cicely's way, he was prepared to challenge him!

Simon took a deep breath. They would survive this, and in the end, it might benefit them. The people of Blackhurst would interpret his jealousy as the normal reaction of a fond husband, and he would gain goodwill from his employer by honoring Lady Blackhurst's wishes.

Milady looked much more animated this night, and she'd eaten more from their shared trencher than he'd expected. Cicely was obviously good for her.

Cicely. As Lady Blackhurst had said, she seemed to light up the room with her beauty. And 'twas not merely the grand clothes nor the excitement which made her so radiant. 'Twas her spirit, her marvelous sense of life.

A shudder of longing went through him. Cicely seemed to warm his cold, weary soul by her very presence. Her glowing, innocent hope, her unflagging belief in the possibilities of life renewed him and healed him.

But, eventually, he must leave her.

The thought came to him, wrenching and cruel. Whether Cicely found a place in Blackhurst Castle as a companion to its mistress or he took her to Pembroke and delivered her into the guardianship of her godfather—either way he would have to give her up.

She was not for him. A flawed sinner such as he did not deserve such perfection. Once, mayhap, when he'd been young and dreamy-eyed and optimistic he might have sought her as his wife. But now he knew that dream could never be. She needed a man who was strong and healthy. Someone who would never fail her. Never hurt her.

The gloom closed around him, and for a moment Simon was in another great hall, facing another woman of spirit and beauty. She was crying, begging him. He turned away and left her, his heart stubborn and bitter, so set upon his course that he could leave his own mother weeping in despair.

A shaft of guilt burst through him, like an arrow shattering his heart. He had failed her, and now he could never go back. Never face what he had done. His father must despise him. And she . . .

Dreadful visions filled his mind. That his mother was dead, that she had died grieving for him.

He did not want to know. Could not face the terrible truth. So, he would not go back there. Never claim his heritage, his name . . .

"I vow, Sir Simon, what is wrong? You look so distressed."

He jerked to awareness. His hostess was staring at him. "Madam, I . . ." He sought to smile reassuringly. "Forgive me. I was remembering a long-ago incident. It has naught to do with you or your kind hospitality."

Her eyes were cold, offended. " 'Tis most strange, sir, that this memory should come to you now."

"I have been too long out of the company of fair ladies like yourself. I have grown morose and foul humored."

"Too long out of the company of ladies? But what of your wife, sir?"

Simon felt his attempt at a smile grow strained. "I meant ladies I am not familiar with. Cicely and I have . . . we have grown so comfortable with each other, I fear I no longer endeavor to make convivial conversation with her at meals."

"But I thought you were newly wed." Lady Blackhurst cast a glance toward Cicely, then looked back at him. "You are scarcely an old married couple yet. Indeed, I do not sense you are at ease with each other at all."

Simon inwardly cringed. Jesu, how was he to manage this subterfuge? Any more mistakes and their whole story would be suspect.

He met Lady Blackhurst's suspicious gaze. "I vow, lady, you have found me out. The truth is, I quarreled with my wife ere we arrived here. 'Twas my fault, but I have not yet had the courage to beg her pardon. Mayhap that is why you sense tension between us.

"As for the other, my argument with Cicely reminds me painfully of a disagreement I had with my mother years ago. That incident weighs upon my mind and has made it difficult for me to enjoy this fine meal and lovely company." He met her gaze beseechingly. "I do, indeed, beg your forgiveness for my lapses."

His hostess' face softened. "Of course, Sir Simon. But it

seems to me it is not my absolution you crave, but that of your sweet wife. I give you leave to go to her. Take her to your room and settle this matter between you."

Simon nodded and rose, eager to make an escape before he muddled things further. Lady Blackhurst caught his hand, and her eyes seemed to shimmer with tears. "Make her happy, Simon, and I vow I will forgive all your social lapses. Tonight and in the future."

He bowed low, then, breathing a sigh of relief, went to get Cicely.

"The saints aid us, we are going to be found out!" Simon took two steps to the wall of the tiny chamber, then whirled around. " 'Tis one thing to lie to a knight like Black Robert, or even to tell a tale to a Blackhurst, but his wife is another matter. She sees beyond the facts we have given her, and senses something amiss. I vow, she will keep meddling between us and catch us in lies. Eventually she will go to her husband and tell him that we are not what we said, and he will have us thrown out into the snow!"

"She would not do that," Cicely said, aggravatingly calm in the face of his turmoil. "She cares for me. Even if she knew the truth, she would try to aid me, I know it."

Simon shook his head. "You are ever naive, Cicely. Lady Blackhurst is like a spoiled child. If you disappoint her, she will forsake you faster than milk turns sour on a summer's day."

"And you are a miserable scold who sees naught but the worst in people!"

"Mayhap that is because they have so many times proven my worst suspicions true! Listen to me, Cicely. We have to compare the facts we have given our hosts. What have you told Lady Blackhurst?"

''I said that we have been wed but a short time. That we are from Tathwick, where my father is steward.''

''Tathwick! If anyone discovers that your father is not the steward there, but the lord, we are caught!''

''I left there ten years ago. I can't think anyone remembers me.''

''Mayhap not, but it is too close for comfort.'' Simon ran his fingers through his hair. ''What else did you say? How did you explain that we left Tathwick?''

''I said my father did not approve of the marriage, and we were fleeing his wrath.''

Simon groaned. ''Jesu, that is all we need, for Blackhurst to believe we are running away from an enraged father.''

''Bella thought it a touching tale. She means to help us.''

''That is well and good, but if she tells her husband, he may see the matter differently.''

''I tell you, she won't! She will keep our secret.''

''Why? Because she cares for you so dearly?'' Simon could not keep the sarcasm from his voice. Jesu, Cicely was like a babe in the woods when it came to guessing another's character!

''Aye, she cares for me. Why should she not? She is ever so lonely. Her husband treats her like a child. Did you know he will not even share her bed? He so fears he will get her with a babe and she will die, he scarce touches her except with the most chaste caresses.''

''Mayhap she should be grateful for his forbearance,'' Simon said coldly. ''Plenty of women die in childbirth, especially when they are as sickly and frail as Lady Blackhurst.''

''That is because she is so lonely and unhappy!'' Cicely's voice trembled with intensity. ''She desperately craves a child, and she would risk her life to have one. But her husband is too dense to see that she wastes away from longing for what he will not give her!''

"If she starves herself out of unhappiness, then she *is* a foolish child who deserves her lot!"

"You don't like her. We are safe and warm because of her kindness, but you still speak cruelly of her."

" 'Tis not that." Simon paced across the room. " 'Tis more that I don't trust her. I don't believe she can be counted on to save us if our lies are exposed. Which is the real matter we should be speaking of—we must compare the tales we have told." He turned to her. "I explained to the seneschal that we thought you were with child when we first arrived, but now we know otherwise. Have you said anything to contradict my words?"

Cicely shook her head. "I said naught of the matter at all."

"Good. At least we'll not be tripped up by that lie. I also told Lady Blackhurst that we had quarreled before we arrived and that was why we were tense and uneasy each other."

"That part is not an untruth." Cicely gave him an injured look, then moved away and faced the unlit brazier. He saw that her body was racked by a tremor, and a pang went through him. By the saints, he did not want to hurt her!

"I'm sorry," he said. "I do not mean to be so harsh with you. But you must agree that 'twould be disastrous if Lord Blackhurst discovered our true circumstances."

"Why? Because you would lose your position here?" She gave a sniffle.

"Mayhap. Or, he might tell us to be gone, lest he should have to deal with your father if he comes after us."

Her shoulders shuddered again, and Simon's heart sank. He should not have shouted at her. Nor been so ruthless in his questioning. She was a sweet, kind maid; 'twas not right of him to force her to become suspicious and cynical.

He went to her and turned her to face him. "Cicely, I'm sorry to be angry with you. 'Tis only that I fear for your safety."

She raised her great brown eyes to meet his, and her full

underlip quivered. "I know you mean well, Simon. I'm sorry I am such a trial for you."

"Hush now." He cupped her dainty chin in his hand. "You're not a trial to me. Because of your quick thinking and determination, we are safe here at Blackhurst. You even secured me a position in the garrison with your eloquence. I owe you for that, Cicely."

"Truly, Simon? You mean that?" Her eyes shone with unshed tears. He thought again that she was one of the few women he knew who looked beautiful even when tearful.

"Of course." He removed his hand from her face, suddenly aware of how near she stood and of the way the upper curves of her breasts gleamed like ivory above the neckline of the ruby-colored gown.

She saw the direction of his gaze and said, "What do you think of the gown, Simon? Was it not gracious of Bella to loan it to me?"

" 'Tis too small for you." His voice sounded strained and breathless in his own ears.

"Aye, I am larger than Bella, but she thinks the seams can be taken out. We did not have time to do that today; she promised she would have her maid attempt it. But what of the color? Do you think it pleasing? She had a blue gown that she offered me as well; I favored this one. In truth, I have not worn anything so fine since I was a girl."

She lovingly stroked one of the long, flowing sleeves while Simon forced himself to answer. "I like the color, aye, but mayhap you should wear the blue next time. 'Tis a more subtle hue."

"Subtle?"

"Aye. Mayhap in the blue you would not stand out so much, and every man in the hall would not stare at you."

"They were not staring at me."

"Of course they were! Did you not see them?"

"I was sitting at the high table, and I am a stranger. 'Twas natural for them to glance at me now and again."

"Huh! 'Twas not curiosity which made them gape at you. 'Twas the sight of your half-naked breasts!"

Cicely looked down, as if seeing her opulent cleavage for the first time. "I thought you would be pleased," she whispered. "I thought you would think I was comely. Is this not how the royal court in London dresses? Bella told me that I was all the fashion in this gown."

"Queen Isabella may dress that way, mayhap, but she is from Angoulême, and the customs there are near as scandalous as those in Sicily and Andalusia. Truly, Cicely, you cannot think I would be pleased to have you flaunt your body before a hall of rough knights!"

"But Bella told me . . ." The tears Cicely had managed to suppress earlier now broke free and trickled down her cheeks. "I only wanted to please you . . . I didn't know . . ."

Simon exhaled a sigh of mingled frustration and remorse. *You fool! Of course she didn't know the effect she'd have on men—she's been living in a convent since she was a little girl!* "Please don't cry, Cicely. I didn't mean you didn't please me." He reached for her hands and held them tightly in his own. "I think you look . . . glorious."

She tilted her face up to his. "Truly, Simon?"

He couldn't help himself. Her sweet, tempting lips were so close. He leaned down and kissed her. A tender kiss, meant to do no more than reassure this innocent maid that he found her desirable. But when his lips met hers, his noble resolves faded. She tasted as delectable as honey, and her body, now pressed against his, felt so soft and supple. He let his mouth linger, savoring the taste and scent and feel of her.

Then, she opened her mouth, inviting him to explore even further, and he was lost.

His body trembled with the strain of holding back as he

deepened the pressure of the kiss. The way she welcomed him, tilting her head so her mouth moved against his, reaching up to tangle her fingers in his hair, it was as if she would hold him against her forever.

Her mouth was greedy for his, open and wet, enticing him, provoking him. It seemed as if she knew instinctively that there could be more to a kiss, that tongues could touch and tease, caress and mate.

With a groan, he gave her what she sought. His tongue stroked the sensitive silk of her inner lips, then found her tongue. Tentative at first, then assured and sensual, she met his movements with a delicate quest of her own.

Excited beyond control, he filled her mouth with his tongue, thrusting with a rhythm innate to all males. This, finally, seemed to shock her. She drew away.

Horrified by his boldness, he whispered, "Dear Cicely, forgive me."

She licked her lips, as if tasting him upon herself, then looked up at him. "There is naught to forgive. I liked it, very much." Her expression grew impish. "I want more, Simon."

"Nay, 'tis wrong!"

"It does not feel wrong to me, but rather, very right."

" 'Tis sinful!"

"To touch our mouths together? Why? I do not recall any commandment forbidding that."

"Because . . . because it leads to other things. I am not made of stone, Cicely!"

She smiled. "Nay, you are not. You are made of skin, muscle and bone. And I have felt how warm and strong you are."

A shudder of longing traveled down his body. "I vow, you tempt me to madness. But I will not relent. We are not wed, and we dare not share such intimacies as are reserved for husband and wife."

"You will not kiss me again?" Cicely's voice rose plaintively.

"Nay. I have been too forward already. I will not allow my crude animal urges to lead me further into sin."

"But I discern no sin in kissing. 'Tis only a sharing of pleasure between . . . friends."

She gazed at him hopefully, and he repressed a groan of exasperation. What sort of doctrine did they teach at Montreau? Had she never been cautioned regarding the temptations of the flesh?

"I cannot, Cicely. Your innocence makes you blind to the wickedness that dwells in my heart. You cannot realize that every moment I am alone with you, I know the tortures of hell. My body longs for yours, but I dare not give in lest I lose the struggle to defeat the corrupt, foul demon of sin."

"Have you taken a vow of chastity?"

Simon felt the blood rush to his face, and he looked away from her. "Nay. Although many who went on Crusade did so, I was not one of them. I feared I could not honor such a vow, and I thought it the greater evil to promise what I could not keep."

"So, you have lain with a woman before?"

Jesu, this was worse than confession! "Aye," he growled. "I have said as much."

"But you would not lie with me. Why, Simon? Do you not care for me?"

He groaned. "Of course I do. Do you not understand that it is because I care for you that I struggle to keep you safe from my lustful urges?"

"I don't want to be safe," she whispered. She drew near him and tilted up her lovely, flowerlike face, waiting for him to kiss her.

All the promise and beauty in the world seemed to glow in her soft brown eyes. Why could he not have this woman, this moment, to make up for all the loneliness and despair he had known?

He placed his hands on either side of her precious heart-shaped face and lowered his head.

Paradise. To kiss her and hold her. To experience her soft, womanly form as she melded herself to him. He felt as if all his life he had waited for this moment, this woman. His beloved Cicely.

"Oh, Simon," she gasped between kisses. "I have wanted you to kiss me for so long . . . ever since I first saw you. You were sick and weak . . . and yet I knew. You are my knight . . . so gallant . . . and strong."

Gallant. The word pierced the erotic haze surrounding Simon. How gallant was this, to deflower a maid who trusted him to care for her? And he *would* end up deflowering her if they continued like this. Already he fought desperately to control the ruthless hunger of his body. If he did not end things now, he would lose the battle.

With a terrible groan, he pushed her away. "Nay, Cicely, I cannot! Don't ask this of me! I am not as strong and noble as you believe. I am not!"

He fought to control his breathing, to regain rational thought. When he looked up, he saw that she watched him with a desolate expression. Her pain clawed at his heart, but he hardened himself against it. What he did was best. *Sometimes to protect those he loves, a man must do things which seem cruel.*

"I'm sorry." Her lovely mouth quivered. "I did not mean to entice you against your will. I know you value your honor, Simon, and I would never do anything to hurt you."

She turned away. "I must undress for bed now, lest I ruin this beautiful gown. Mayhap you should leave until I have finished."

He took a deep breath and adjusted his own clothing, then went out.

CHAPTER 11

Tears trickled from beneath Cicely's closed eyelids as she shifted her body on the straw pallet. She was cold, but she had not the will to find a servant to fetch coals for the brazier. The terrible ache inside her felt much worse than the chill. Simon had not returned to the chamber, and she well knew why. He did not trust himself around her. He saw her as a wicked Eve who had tried to entice him into sin.

And it was true. She would have seduced him if she could. But clearly, it was not what he wanted. If it came to a choice, he would always choose his honor over her.

Honor—how she hated his notion of what it meant to be a worthy knight. Oh, she was a depraved, horrid creature. She would choose love over honor every time. Simon was well advised to stay clear of her.

Already she had done such despicable things. She had tricked him into rescuing her from Montreau, and because of her, he had lost his packhorse and supplies. Even if she had secured him a position in Lord Blackhurst's garrison, 'twas clearly not an arrangement which satisfied him. He had been troubled and unhappy from the moment they left Montreau, and things had not improved at Blackhurst. He hated the lies which bound them together.

And why should he not? He was burdened with a woman who embroiled him in difficult situations and tormented him with her wantonness.

Somehow she must find a way to free him. If she truly cared for him, she owed him that. But how? The lie that they were married complicated everything.

She burrowed deeper into the blankets, trying to think of a plan. Although her heart bled from his rejection, she knew Simon was right. For his own sake, he should stay away from her.

" '. . . Guigemar led away his mistress with great rejoicing; all his pain was now at an end.' "

Bella heaved a blissful sigh as Cicely finished the *lai* and reverently closed the leather-bound book. "That was so beautiful. I never knew that words could create a world so magical and lovely."

Cicely smiled across the solar at her companion. She had been reading while Lady Blackhurst sorted colored threads and prepared her embroidery frame. " 'Tis one of my favorite tales," Cicely said. "As many times as I have read it, it never ceases to enchant me."

"And you said you had many more, didn't you?" Bella gazed eagerly at Cicely, her work forgotten.

"Aye, my mother sent me a book near every year on my birth day. I must have near ten, I think."

"Where was your mother? Why did you not live with her?"

"She . . . she did not dwell at Tathwick, but another manor."

Cicely felt her heartbeat quicken. Another slip—what lie could she conjure to explain away this one?

"Your parents, they were not wed?"

Cicely shook her head, but inside she felt like a traitor to her beloved mother. She had made her less than a lady in Bella's eyes.

"Ah, mayhap that explains why your father is so protective of you. He feared you would end up like your mother. He must have loved her." Bella gazed soulfully at Cicely, waiting for another romantic tale, this one of her parents.

Cicely did not want to disappoint her, but it was awkward spinning lies about those she cared about. "I'm certain he did," she said. "But my father is a practical man. He does not let his heart rule his head." That much was true. Why else had he condemned her to a life at Montreau, knowing she would be miserable?

"I think mayhap your husband is also a practical man." Bella's voice grew biting. "He seems little enough concerned with *your* happiness."

"Oh, that is not true! Simon is ever so considerate of me!"

"And yet, he allows a quarrel between you to fester. I know, Cicely. The servants tell me that he does not share the bedchamber where you sleep, but finds his own place with the other knights. So far, he has not dallied with any of the maids in the castle, but 'tis only a matter of time. Few men are as disciplined as Lord Blackhurst. I vow, if your husband does not share your bed, he'll go to another woman's soon enough."

"Nay! He would not!" As soon as the words were spoken, Cicely began to doubt them. Why shouldn't Simon seek out a serving wench? He had said he was not celibate, that he had not given up the pleasures of the flesh.

Bella put aside her embroidery things and approached Cicely, who was seated in the window where there was light for reading. "I fear your father has sheltered you overmuch, and you know little of men. 'Tis not agreeableness which wins their hearts. To make them care for you, you must make some demands upon them. Get them to demonstrate that they love you, and test their devotion regularly. In seeking to prove to you that they care, they are convinced themselves.''

''I don't think that is the trouble between Simon and me,'' Cicely protested.

''Well, I think otherwise. I have spoken with your husband, and I believe he loves you, but does not know how to show it. Give him the means to demonstrate his *tendre,* Cicely. Think of something you would like, your heart's desire, and ask, nay, *demand* that he obtain it for you.''

Cicely repressed a sigh of frustration. If only she could tell Bella the truth. Simon would seek to fetch the sun, moon and stars for her if she asked him. But the only thing she sought of him was that which he would not give—his love, his passion. He chose honor over her, and it was not a choice she dare try to sway. If she took his honor, she feared she would destroy him.

''Think, Cicely, think.'' Bella sat beside her, her gray eyes impassioned. ''What is it that you desire? What can Simon do to make you happy?''

''I am happy here, Bella.'' She gestured to the cozy solar, hoping to distract her hostess. ''You have opened your home to me. Treated me like a sister. I cannot thank you enough for your generosity.''

Bella frowned, clearly displeased that Cicely had changed the subject. She stood. ''I am pleased to offer you what I can. Indeed, it is I who owe you. You have eased my loneliness.'' She gestured to the book on Cicely's lap. ''And you have entertained and enlightened me. I vow, I do think *I* would be happy if only . . .''

Bella sighed heavily, and Cicely knew at once what troubled her. She wanted a child and nothing else would satisfy her.

''Have you spoken to your husband recently?'' she asked.

"You seem stronger than when I arrived. And your face has more color. Mayhap he will realize that you are now able to endure the risks of childbearing."

Bella shook her head. "He says we must wait until spring. By then, I will be fifteen years, and there will be plenty of milk and eggs to fatten me." She gave a shrill laugh. "Months I must wait, then another long while as I carry the child. And, what if I do not conceive right away? There is no telling how many years 'twill be until I can have a babe."

Thinking of the ten years she had waited to be freed from Montreau, Cicely could not help feeling that Bella complained overmuch. "Mayhap the time will go faster than you think," she suggested. "If I read one of my books to you each month, by the time I have finished, you might be carrying a babe. Better yet, I could spend the time teaching you to read. Then, you might enjoy the tales whenever you wished."

"Truly? That is possible?" Bella touched one of the leather-bound tomes reverently.

"I vow, 'twas easier for me, because I was a small child when I learned from my mother's serving woman. But my brother was older when the priest came to teach us, and he managed to master Latin and ciphering, although he did not learn French."

"If you could do this"—Bella's eyes shone with excitement—"I would be so grateful. I would repay you handsomely . . . give you anything you wished . . . jewels, fine garments . . ."

Cicely shook her head. "There is no need. I would do this for the simple pleasure of having someone to share my knowledge with. 'Tis a delight to find someone who enjoys *romans* as much as I do."

When Simon arrived to escort Cicely down to the evening meal, he found Cicely and Bella sitting side by side on the window seat, their heads bent industriously over one of Cicely's books. "See, that is an *a*," Cicely said. "It makes a sound as in the beginning of *amande* or *amour*."

" 'Tis hard." Bella shook her head. "I thought I would be able to read some words by now."

"Once you learn the letters, you'll be surprised how quickly it comes. If we could have the wheeler fashion a frame of wood and fill it with beeswax, we could make a tablet to teach you the letters one by one. That is how I learned."

Cicely started to show her pupil something else, and Simon decided it was time to interrupt. He cleared his throat. Both women looked up. Bella appeared annoyed, while Cicely gave him one of her enchanting smiles. "Oh, Simon, look what we are doing. I'm teaching Bella to read!"

"That's very kind of you. I'm certain she will make a most apt pupil."

Bella raised her brows at this, then rose and gave him an insincere smile. "I suppose I must relinquish you to your husband, Cicely. We'll plan to meet here again tomorrow. And I will see the wheeler about a tablet of wax."

Cicely stood and gave Bella a sisterly kiss on the cheek, then followed Simon out.

"I meant my words, Cicely," Simon said when they were alone in the hall. " 'Tis most generous of you to share your books with Lady Blackhurst."

Cicely gave a little sigh. "I am trying to distract her from her endless pining for a child. And also to find a way to keep her from asking difficult questions. I fear, Simon, that I must ask a favor of you."

Simon stopped in the hallway and turned to face her. "What is it? What's wrong?"

"I . . . I don't know quite how to say this . . ." She glanced nervously at his face, then down at the floor. "Do you think you could bear to sleep in the bedchamber with me, at least sometimes? I'm afraid Bella is . . . she misunderstands things, and it has grown awkward to ignore her well-meaning suggestions.''

''Of course. I understand. She is a persistent, rather manipulative woman.''

''But very dear,'' Cicely said. ''She only wants me to be happy.''

Simon nodded, although he doubted very much that Lady Blackhurst's intentions were completely unselfish. He sensed that the lady was not above manipulating Cicely in ways that would cause him grief.

''I think that is enough for today. Why don't we go outside for a time?'' Once again, Cicely and Bella had spent the whole day struggling over letters scraped in the wax, and Cicely could sense that her pupil grew frustrated.

''Outside?'' Bella frowned. ''What would we do there?''

''We could go for a walk in the garden or to the lists to watch the knights practice. And someday I would like to ride outside the bailey.''

''I hate riding,'' Bella said petulantly. ''And it's winter. We'll be cold.''

''Nay, we will not. See, the sun shines brightly.'' Cicely gestured to the golden glow filtering through the glass panes. ''If we dress warmly, we'll be most comfortable.''

''I don't know. Milord always warns me not to risk a chill.''

''Then, if you go outside with no ill effect, you will prove to him that you are stronger than he thinks!'' Cicely argued. She was desperate. Weeks spent within the confines of the hall and solar had reawakened her restlessness. She felt she would go mad if she did not breathe some fresh air and have a view of something other than tapestries and stone walls.

''Well, if you insist. I suppose since you have been so patient in teaching me to read, I must go along with your wishes this time. But, if I grow cold, I'm coming in immediately.''

Bella dug out two fur-trimmed cloaks and warm gloves from one of her innumerable chests, and the two women bundled up. Cicely could hardly contain her excitement as they walked through the stuffy hall. To be outside, to breathe fresh air and observe the colorful activities of castle life—it seemed like the rarest of treats. She could not imagine how Bella endured her narrow existence. The noblewoman spent nearly all her time in solar, bedchamber, or chapel. Going to the hall for the evening meal was the most exciting thing she did in a day.

Cicely could not help contrasting Bella's life with that of her own mother. As she remembered it, Lady Adela had gone everywhere in the keep. She was constantly in the kitchen, supervising the preparation of the food, or roaming the castle, scolding and advising servants. She oversaw the laundry in the shed off the kitchen, the butter churning in the buttery, the soap or candle-making in the yard. The only time she went to her solar during the day was to make certain her women were not neglecting their work of spinning, weaving, and sewing.

At night, after the meal, her mother might retire to the solar for a few quiet moments with her husband. But even then, Lady Adela's hands would be occupied with embroidering an altar cloth or a new tunic for her son or husband. Cicely could not remember her mother ever being idle, although she must have put aside her work to sleep.

But Bella did not trouble herself with the everyday actitivies of the castle. She expected the steward, the cook, and the serving women to maintain things, and they looked to Lord Blackhurst for their orders. It appeared that before Cicely arrived, Bella's days had consisted of a few hours of sewing— Cicely was shocked to find that Bella's skills were actually inferior to her own poor ability—and many hours moping.

No wonder Bella was so unhappy, Cicely thought. She

needed a purpose in her life, some work to occupy her mind and hands. Lord Blackhurst's plan to shelter his young wife from all the toil and demands of life had gone very much awry. He'd made her into a bird in a gilded cage, singing her heart out over her empty life. 'Twas possible, Cicely knew, that Bella might never bear a living child, nor be fortunate enough to keep a babe alive. Such were the trials of birth and the diseases of childhood that many a man died with no live issue to carry on his name. If Bella's dream never came to pass, how would she endure it?

Cicely decided she must find a way to make her friend take an interest in the world outside her solar. If Bella could forget for a time her obsession with having a child, she might learn to know some pleasure in the rest of her life.

They went out into the yard, and Cicely drank in the smells and sounds—some rude and unpleasant, others not, but all of them like music to her ears and sustenance to her soul. This was life, full of tang and energy. She embraced it.

Beside her, Bella immediately made a face. "What is that terrible odor?"

Cicely laughed. "Honestly, Bella, has it been so long since you left your spice-scented solar? To me, it smells of horses and livestock, with mayhap a few harsher smells mixed in." She inhaled deeply. "The women are boiling herbs for dyeing, I would say. And the smith is burning hickory wood to make charcoal for his forge. But in deference to you, we'll go to the garden. Though there may be no sweet blossoms to perfume the air, we might find a few leftover herbs to please your finicky nose."

The garden was walled to protect the plants from harsh weather, and it seemed to Cicely that Bella breathed a sigh of relief as soon as they were inside. Herself, she disliked the trapped feeling the high walls gave her, pleasant though the garden was.

As she expected, the flower beds were not all barren and brown; holly and privet had been planted near one end of the herb patch, and their bright berries and shiny green leaves formed a splash of color against the gray of the wall. Ivy crawled up the wall by the gate, and the remainders of dried asters and seed pods of willow herb, parsley, and dock shivered in the slight breeze.

"Oh, look!" Bella called out, and Cicely went to see what had pleased her.

Bella held out her hands, cupping a single pale yellow blossom. "A winter rose. Somehow it has managed to bloom even in the cold."

"That bush must get the sun all year round," Cicely said. " 'Tis lovely. Are there any more?"

They both looked in vain for other blooms, but found none. "I'm going to take it to the solar," Bella said. "I'll keep it to remind me that winter can't last forever."

" 'Twill wilt in a day or two," Cicely said. "It might be wiser to press it. That way you would be able to enjoy its beauty longer."

Bella sighed. "By the time it is pressed, 'twill be spring and the garden will be full of dozens of blossoms. I don't wish to wait that long." She sat down on one of the stone benches and stared mournfully at the flower in her hands.

Cicely grew impatient. "Let's go to the lists now. The sun is still high, and it won't be cold."

"Whatever would we do there?" Bella asked pettishly. "Who wants to watch a gathering of knights fight."

"But there is much skill involved, timing and discipline. I've always liked to watch battle practice. It's rather like watching a good dancer or an acrobat."

"Of course you would like to see men fighting, being a castellan's daughter." Bella sighed again, then rose reluctantly from the bench. "Very well. I will accompany you."

They walked across the yard to the practice field near the armory. Bella made a huge fuss about the mud ruining her slippers. Cicely had to bite her tongue to keep from mentioning the dozens of pairs Bella had stuffed in a chest back at the castle.

It was cooler out in the open, Cicely had to admit. She drew the fur-trimmed cloak more tightly around her and glanced at her companion, but Bella was apparently too busy grousing about her footwear to notice the sharpness of the air.

Then they saw the knights, and Cicely's concerns vanished in the thrill of this glimpse into the world of men. Simon was instructing two squires as they squared off with blunted swords. They had apparently been at it some time, as both young men were red-faced and panting, their hose blotched with mud.

Simon was also disheveled and dirty, but Cicely hardly noticed. Her eyes were focused on his bare torso. Dark gold hair swirled slick against the skin of his upper chest, and the rounded muscles of his arms bunched and flexed as Simon took the sword from one of the squires and demonstrated a defensive move. As he made a lunge, the lines of his body reminded her of a galloping horse, grace and taut energy suddenly unleashed.

A harsh longing swept through Cicely. He was so beautiful . . . so male. After years of living in the cloistered world of women, she was desperate for the coarse vitality, the primal essence of men. And Simon was the most consummate specimen she had ever seen. His golden hair and cold-ruddied skin made him seem as striking as an image illuminating a holy book. But the raw animal aspect was there too. He was no perfect, unblemished saint; he was flesh and blood. Dirty, real . . . and potentially violent. Those sleek muscles she admired had been used to kill. The power inherent in his impressive form could be used to preserve life, or destroy it.

Cicely repressed a shiver of excitement. 'Twas partly the

sense of danger which drew her. The wild, untamed part of Simon, that even he denied. She wanted it. She wanted *him*.

Beside her, Bella made a noise of disgust. "Ugh! You must insist that your husband bathe thoroughly before he enters the keep. At this moment, he looks like a filthy swine!"

Cicely fought a smile. How could it be that what attracted her disgusted Bella? But it had been the same way with Clotilde. The older nun had found tending the ill knight repellent, while she had not only reveled in the experience, but had fallen in love with the object of Clotilde's dislike.

"I could have a serving maid bathe him, if you would rather not endure the unpleasantness," Bella said, "but no, I don't think that would do . . ."

Cicely forced her attentions back to her companion. "What were you saying, Bella?"

"I was considering having one of the kitchen wenches bathe your husband, but I've changed my mind. If there is any hope of the two of you resolving your differences, we should not tempt Sir Simon into dishonoring his vows."

"But things are better between us," Cicely said brightly. "He has shared the bedchamber with me this past sennight."

"Still, he appears moody and distant in your company. I do not think you have won his heart completely. Have you considered . . ." Bella paused and made a little *moue* of distaste. "I know you may find the idea repugnant—I certainly would— but I have heard that there are ways to secure a man's affections by pleasuring him"—Bella lowered her voice to a near whisper—"carnally."

Cicely nearly choked. *By the saints, if Bella only knew!*

"Lord Blackhurst would never ask such a thing of me, to be certain, but your husband has been on Crusade, spent months solely in the company of men, been exposed to infidel women. Why, they say there are Saracen whores who will do near anything, and not just with one man, but several at the same time!''

"Goodness! How do you know this, Bella?" Cicely asked in amusement. "Surely Lord Blackhurst . . ."

"Oh, heaven forfend, no! He would never speak thus with me." Bella lowered her voice again. " 'Twas Anna. I overheard her talking to one of the other serving women. She was speaking about Simon and how he was a crusader. She was speculating on whether he . . . that is"—Bella gave her a pitying look—"she desires your husband, and I think she would perform any service for him which he might ask of her."

Hot jealousy rushed through Cicely. "Which one is Anna?" she asked tightly.

"The buxom one with the wavy brown hair and dark eyes. I don't think her comely myself, but there is no accounting for what men favor in a woman. If your husband has developed a taste for the dusky-skinned harlots of the East, she might well please him."

Cicely glanced back at Simon. The practice was over, and he had donned his tunic once more, hiding his spectacular masculine charms. But the hot edge of desire coursing through her had not faded. Why was it acceptable for him to lie with a serving wench, but not with her? Why did his honor demand that he shun a woman he said he cared for, yet allow him to have carnal relations with a woman with whom he had no ties of affection?

She would ask him, she decided. And she would not forgo the opportunity to bathe Simon, no matter how uncomfortable she made him.

"Of course I will assist my husband at his bath. Tell him I will meet him in the bathing chamber. I will go now and ask the pages to heat the water."

With those words, Cicely strode from the practice field.

* * *

Simon approached Lady Blackhurst and bowed. "Milady, how fare you today?"

"Well enough." She smiled at him, looking as contented as a cat who has discovered a puddle of spilled milk.

CHAPTER 12

Steam filled the air as the pages poured bucket after bucket of hot water into the huge wooden tub. Cicely thought the turmoil inside her might burn even hotter than Simon's bathwater. Jealousy, anger, and long-repressed desire simmered in her breast.

She feigned calm as Simon entered the chamber, closely shepherded by Lady Blackhurst. "Here he is," Bella announced. "I would not listen to his protests that he was too dirty to enter the keep, nor that he would have the squires rinse him with buckets from the watering trough. I told him that his wife awaited him, and he would not disappoint her."

Bella gave Simon a sly, provocative smile, and Cicely saw his jaw clench in aggravation. Too bad, she thought acerbically. He had played the saintly martyr long enough. If he found it acceptable to seek satisfaction with other women, he could learn to set aside his reluctance with her.

"Now, undress your husband and get him into the tub."

Bella crossed her arms and waited. She apparently meant to be very sure of Simon's compliance.

Cicely went to Simon and tried to tug his tunic upward. He pushed her away. "I would not have my wife soil her hands on my dirty garments," he told Bella defensively. "I am well able to undress myself."

He pulled off his tunic with such violent energy that Cicely quickly moved away. She'd never seen Simon so angry.

He sat on the bench to remove his boots and crossgarters. Cicely watched, too nervous to do otherwise. Bella stood by, resolute, determined.

Divested of his boots and crossgarters, he yanked down his hose and stepped out of them. Stark naked, he strode boldly to the bathing tub. Cicely's attention was inexorably drawn to the parts of Simon she'd seen only once before. The pendulous organ dangling from the golden thatch, his long, muscular thighs, a glimpse of taut, enticingly shaped buttocks as he turned away to climb into the tub.

Mouth dry, she glanced at Bella and saw a look of appalled fascination on her face.

"Well, then," Bella said breathily. "I'll leave the two of you alone." With a swish of skirts she was gone. Cicely found herself alone with an utterly naked and furious Simon.

Sitting in the tub, he fixed her with a glare. "Are you satisfied, Cicely? I dare you to tell me now that Lady Blackhurst is not a meddling, tactless *bitch!*"

Cicely licked her dry lips. She wanted to defend her friend, to explain that the bath had been her idea. But the thought of turning Simon's fury toward herself kept the words unspoken. She had schemed to bring him here so she could seduce him, but she did not want Simon to know her ignoble intent.

Now that he was here, she was not at all certain she could go through with it. "I'm sorry, Simon. I did not think that she would . . . that she would be so . . . so insistent."

Simon made a sound of disgust. "Well, I am here now, and I can certainly use a bath. Bring me the soap. I'll be done in only a few moments."

She took him the soap, feeling as if she approached an angry bear. He snatched the wooden bowl away from her and, balancing it on the side of the tub, began to lather himself with fierce vigor.

Cicely walked back to the hearth, then turned and watched, unable to keep her eyes away. Everything about him enraptured her. The way the hair on his chest made the soap lather white and bubbly. The patches of tawny hair revealed as he lifted his arms to wash his armpits. The play of gleaming water on his golden, rosy skin . . .

He leaned over and sluiced water over his scalp. Sputtering, he dashed the droplets from his eyes, then glanced over and caught her staring.

"Jesu," he grumbled. "You're as bad as she is. Do you wish me to stand up and parade before you like a horse at market so you can get your fill of looking?"

"I'm sorry," she mumbled. " 'Tis only that . . . you are so beautiful."

Her wistful words altered the mood between them. As his vivid blue eyes met hers, she felt his anger fade, the yearning hunger that was always between them spring to life.

"Oh, Cicely"—he groaned—"if you knew how much I want you."

"Why, then, don't you . . . take me?" She approached the tub. "You've said you've sworn no oath of chastity. If you will lie with other women, why not me?"

"Because . . . because you are a gentlewoman, a lady. As a knight, I took a vow to honor and protect everything you are."

She sighed. "I tire of being a sheltered, protected *lady*. I wish sometimes that I were naught but a crude serving wench who could love whomever she wanted."

"You don't mean that!" Simon said harshly. "Though it may not seem valuable to you, your feminine grace and refinement is precious to me. There is little enough in life that is rare and true. Your sweet beauty is like a shining light that warms my soul."

"If only you would let my body warm you as my spirit does." Cicely stood beside the tub and gazed longingly into his face. "Love me, Simon. Love me as a man loves a woman."

She could see the turmoil in eyes. He grimaced, as if in pain. She waited, breathless. Would he heed her plea? If not, then she would know he loved his dream of chivalry more than her.

He exhaled raggedly, then said, "Nay, Cicely. I will not take what I have no right to."

She turned away, the despair breaking over her. "I will leave now," she said. "I would not distress you with my presence any longer."

She let herself out of the bathing chamber, feeling bleak. But no tears coursed down her cheeks. Simon had made his decision, and she must accept it, somehow.

She walked slowly toward her small chamber by the kitchen. 'Twas unlikely Simon would be willing to share it with her any longer. And what would Bella think? She would assume that Simon had hurt her feelings, and Bella, her staunch defender, would berate him for his lack of consideration.

Nay, she did not want Simon to be harassed when he was only doing what he thought was right. She would have to think of a way to protect him from Bella's wrath.

In a sudden flash of insight, it came to Cicely. She would tell Bella the truth!

She paused in the narrow hallway, considering. The truth would benefit everyone. Simon would no longer have to endure the lie that she was his wife, and Bella would be relieved to learn that they were not lovers torn apart by quarrels and con-

Take advantage of this offer to enjoy Zebra's newest line of historical romance novels....Splendor Romances (formerly Lovegrams Historical Romances)- Take our introductory shipment of 4 romance novels -Absolutely Free! (a $19.96 value)

Now you'll be able to savor today's best romance novels without even leaving your home with our convenient and inexpensive home subscription service. Here's what you get for joining:

- 4 BRAND NEW bestselling Splendor Romances delivered to your doorstep every month

- 20% off every title (or almost $4.00 off) with your home subscription

- A **FREE** monthly newsletter, *Zebra/Pinnacle Romance News* filled with author interviews, member benefits, book previews and more!

- No risks or obligations…you're free to cancel whenever you wish…no questions asked

To get started with your own home subscription, simply complete and return the card provided. You'll receive your FREE introductory shipment of 4 Splendor Romances and then you'll begin to receive monthly shipments of new Zebra Splendor titles. Each shipment will be yours to examine for 10 days and then if you decide to keep the books, you'll pay the preferred home subscriber's price of just $4.00 per title plus $1.50 shipping and handling. That's $16 for all 4 books plus $1.50 for home delivery! And if you want us to stop sending books, just say the word…it's that simple.

Check out our website at www.kensingtonbooks.com.

4 FREE books are waiting for you!
Just mail in the certificate below!

If the certificate is missing below, write to:
Splendor Romances, Zebra Home Subscription Service, Inc.,
P.O. Box 5214, Clifton, New Jersey 07015-5214
or call TOLL-FREE 1-888-345-BOOK

FREE BOOK CERTIFICATE

Yes! Please send me 4 Splendor Romances (formerly Zebra Lovegram Historical Romances). ABSOLUTELY FREE! After my introductory shipment, I will be able to preview 4 new Splendor Romances each month FREE for 10 days. Then if I decide to keep them, I will pay the money-saving preferred publisher's price of just $4.00 each... a total of $16.00 plus $1.50 shipping and handling. That's 20% off the regular publisher's price plus $1.50 for shipping and handling. I may return any shipment within 10 days and owe nothing, and I may cancel my subscription at any time. The 4 FREE books will be mine to keep in any case.

Name _____

Address _____ Apt. _____

City _____ State _____ Zip _____

Telephone ( ) _____

Signature _____
(If under 18, parent or guardian must sign.)

Terms and prices subject to change. Orders subject to acceptance by Zebra Home Subscription Service, Inc. .
Zebra Home Subscription Service, Inc. reserves the right to reject or cancel any subscription.

SP10A9

SPLENDOR ROMANCES
ZEBRA HOME SUBSCRIPTION SERVICE, INC.
120 BRIGHTON ROAD
P.O. BOX 5214
CLIFTON, NEW JERSEY 07015-5214

AFFIX
STAMP
HERE

‖‖··‖‖·····‖‖‖‖‖‖‖‖‖‖‖‖‖‖‖‖‖‖‖

flicts. And she—well, 'twould certainly be easier not to guard her tongue every moment.

She knew a twinge of doubt, wondering whether Lord Blackhurst would insist on sending her back to the priory. Then she decided that Bella would not allow it. Bella would not want to give up her newfound friend, and her husband was unlikely to override her wishes. Cicely could likely make her home at Blackhurst indefinitely, if she wished. And Simon, he would also be allowed to choose his own destiny. If he desired to seek a position at another castle, he would be free to do so. No longer would he have the burden of remaining with his unwelcome "wife."

Another wave of grief went through her. Simon would leave, and she would never see him again. How would she bear it?

But she must. If she loved him, she must allow him to do what he felt was right, no matter that he doomed himself to a cold, empty shell of a life which would never bring him happiness.

Oh, to be able to make Simon see that joy and satisfaction were there waiting for him, if only he would dare to reach out for them. But something had wounded his spirit so badly that he could not. He remained locked in the prison of his own making.

Cicely shook her head as she changed direction and headed toward the solar. She remembered a story Clotilde had told her of trying to mend a fox that had been caught in a snare. Although the nun repaired the beast's broken leg, she had not been able to persuade it to eat. And so, for fear of the human who tended it, the animal had starved to death.

Simon was like that. He would not take the love she would give him, and yet she could see him wasting away for the want of it.

Sighing heavily, she entered the solar.

Bella looked up expectantly from her sewing. "Finished so

soon? I thought to leave you alone until the evening meal.'' Her face grew thoughtful as she observed Cicely's expression. "What went wrong this time? Don't tell me you quarreled again!''

Cicely shook her head. "Nay, we are in agreement at last. I understand now how he sees things.'' Despite her resolve, her voice shook. "I understand that I must set him free.''

"Free?'' Bella put her work aside and stood. A frown creased her forehead. "What sort of talk it this? What nonsense has he said to you?''

Cicely put up a hand. "Before you grow angry at Simon, I have to tell you the truth of our ... our relationship. You see, he is not my husband.''

"Not your husband?'' Bella gasped. "But why ... ?''

" 'Twas I who convinced him to tell that tale. He was opposed to the lie from the beginning.''

"But why did you need to lie? Why were you traveling alone with a man not your husband?''

Cicely took a deep breath and began to explain. She left out nothing, not even the shameful means she had used to convince Simon to take her from Montreau. "So, you see,'' she finished. "I made him help me. And now that he has done what I asked, 'tis his right to be free of me.''

Bella stared at her, obviously incredulous. "And you mean to say that despite all those nights you spent with him, on the journey and here, he never touched you?''

"Well, there was one time that we kissed.''

"But naught else?''

"Nay.''

Bella heaved a sigh of relief. "Thank the heavens. You are still a maid. You are not ruined.''

"Oh, but I wish I were. I wish that at least once Simon would have lost control and ...'' Cicely shook her head. " 'Tis a selfish wish. I seek to bind him to me when he does not want me.''

Bella did not respond. Then, suddenly, she said, ''I have treated you very ill. I did not know you were a lady. I have given you a servant's chamber and behaved as if you were bound to do my bidding.''

''You have treated me like a friend,'' Cicely protested.

''Aye, a friend. I am that.'' Bella nodded resolutely; then her gaze met Cicely's. ''You look fair worn out, my sweet. Let me take you to my chamber. You will share my room from now on, like a beloved sister.''

''That is not necessary. Truly.''

''But you do look sickly. 'Twould give me pleasure to coddle and pamper you.''

Cicely sighed. '' 'Tis naught but a broken heart that ails me.''

''Nevertheless, there are means to ease such things. I will fetch something to make you sleep.''

Cicely could only nod lethargically. She wanted to find relief from the pain, at least for a time.

''You wished to see me?'' Simon tensed as Lady Blackhurst left her seat in the window and approached him as he entered the solar. He did not like this summons. What trouble did she intend to cause him this time? Whatever it was, he would have to bear it. Mayhap he deserved to suffer after what he had done to Cicely. The poor little maid had looked sore grieved when she'd left him. But better that he should hurt her a little now and save her future pain.

Lady Blackhurst neared him, looking like a viper poised to strike. ''Sir Simon, you have lied to me!''

He flinched at her vehemence. By the saints, what had Cicely told her?

"You said that you and Lady Cicely were wed, but you are not. All this time you have bided at Blackhurst under false pretenses!"

Simon almost sighed with relief. Mayhap the truth was best after all. "I do not deny it, lady. I allowed the falsehood because I wished to protect Cicely."

"And whom did you mean your lie to protect her from?"

"I feared that Lord Blackhurst would turn us away if he knew"—Simon paused, wondering if Cicely had told Lady Blackhurst of her flight from Montreau, from what he knew of Cicely, she had probably done so—"if he knew that Cicely was running away from a convent. There was the possibility that her father would send someone after her. I thought your husband might not want to harbor us here if he knew our true circumstances."

"Fortunately, the lie also protected *you.*"

The woman's sneering words aroused Simon's anger. "What do you mean?" he demanded.

"Easy enough it would be under the circumstances to take advantage of Cicely's naivete."

"I have not touched her! Ask her! Ask her, you conniving, lewd-minded . . ." With effort, Simon reined in his temper. For his own sake, he must control his anger. All his instincts told him that this woman was dangerous. A spoiled, selfish creature capable of ordering his death if he offended her too deeply.

Bella smiled coldly, as if guessing his thoughts. "I am satisfied that you did not take her maidenhead. Nor shall you have the opportunity to do so. I have asked my husband to dismiss you. I want you gone from Blackhurst ere the chapel bell rings for vespers."

Simon did not trust himself to speak. He'd thought often

enough of leaving, especially once he'd realized how devoted Lady Blackhurst was to Cicely. But being dismissed still stung. He'd done his best for Cicely and Lord Blackhurst, yet he was being sent away in near disgrace.

"My husband insists that you be allowed to take your horse and all the possessions you arrived with. He also maintains that you must be paid for your services these past two months. I think his generosity is misdirected, but I must defer to him and his soldier's code. If naught else, I will be able to face Cicely with a clear conscience when I tell her that you are well supplied for your journey."

Simon gave a curt nod. He was incensed by Lady Blackhurst's attitude, but he knew there was nothing he could do. Arguing with her would only cause him more trouble in the end. He turned to go.

"Sir Simon." Lady Blackhurst's voice was like a claw in his flesh. He turned, resignedly, to hear what new injustice she meant to accuse him of. "What would you like me to tell Cicely when she learns of your departure?"

Simon scanned his hostess' countenance. Was she mocking him? Seeking to goad him into doing something which would turn her husband against him? He could not discern her motives. "Tell her," he said, "tell her that I wish her great happiness."

Tell her that I love her. That I will never forget her. That I will hold her memory close to my heart for all my days. The agonizing words echoed through Simon's mind as he left the solar. 'Twas true. He did love Cicely. Which was why he must leave, and quickly. Before she discovered what was happening and tried to prevent his departure. He had no doubt that Lady Blackhurst had some means of distracting Cicely so she would not know of his leaving until it was too late.

Unless Cicely wanted him gone. The thought made his insides clench. But he had rejected her, and for the dozenth time. She must see how frustrating this arrangement was for both of them. 'Twas better this way.

And yet, he did not want her to forget him entirely. He had that much pride. He wanted her to remember these past weeks, their adventures on the journey. To recall him with fondness, and for that soft, tender look to come into her beautiful doe eyes when she thought of him.

Out in the yard, he walked slowly toward the stables. He would have liked to have said good-bye to Cicely. To have some last words between them besides the cold, rejecting ones he'd given her in the bathing chamber.

He turned and glanced back at the keep, wondering where she was, what she was thinking.

"Spiteful wench, isn't she?" A weathered hand clapped him on the shoulder, and Simon turned to meet Black Robert's sympathetic gaze. "She will have ye go, no matter the lord's protests nor the little maid's neither. I wonder what ill she sees in ye. A rival mayhap?" Black Robert cocked a bushy brow.

"Could be." Simon released a pent-up sigh. "She would not be the first woman to mislike me because I caught Cicely's fancy."

"Ye should have wed her while ye could," the seneschal said. " 'Tis clear Lady Cicely fair dotes on you. She'd not have a problem with the differences in yer stations."

Simon was shocked. So, *that* was the reason for Lady Blackhurst's contemptuous manner. She thought him a landless churl who had no right to Cicely. Sunk as he was in his own self-pity, he'd allowed everyone at Blackhurst to think he was a poor knight who must earn his bread with his sword. What would they think, he wondered, if they learned that he was heir to not one castle but three—if only he could work up the courage to go home and claim them?

But he could not bring himself to do that, not yet. Although he did feel less hopeless than when he'd first returned to England.

Cicely had given him the courage to believe he might have a future.

"Is it true?" Black Robert asked as they walked toward the stables. "Did ye really not touch the little maid, even though ye shared a bedchamber?"

"Her maidenhead is intact, aye," Simon answered stiffly.

"Ye are a saint then! Or did ye lose some vital part in the Holy Land? I've heard that the Saracens like to maim their captives in gruesome ways." His companion chortled.

Simon could only shake his head. He had been maimed; it was not a wound of his body, but his soul. "I would not see Cicely hurt," he said. "Which is why I would ask a boon of you."

Black Robert's face grew serious. "Ask away. I'm bound I'll help ye, if I can."

Simon reached beneath his tunic and drew out a small leather pouch.

Inside was a small gold and ruby ring. He held it in his hand a moment, then transferred it to his companion's grimy fingers. "Give her this and tell her ... tell her that I hope and pray she discovers what she is looking for."

Robert nodded solemnly. "She's a fine little wench. A pity ye couldn't wed with her. But such is the way o' life."

"Please make certain that Lady Blackhurst does not know of the gift."

"Mum's the word." Black Robert made a dramatic show of sealing his lips.

The two men continued on to the stables, and Simon collected the destrier and secured his possessions on the beast. Mounting, he rode toward the gate. Black Robert followed him on foot, offering advice on the best route to take in traveling west. As Lucifer pranced and stamped, eager to be gone, Simon took his final farewell of the seneschal. "Mayhap we'll meet again someday, Sir Robert, God willing."

"Godspeed, Sir Simon. I'll not forget ye."

Simon rode across the bridge. He tried to tell himself that he was finally free of an unwelcome duty, but the words rang hollow. The rest of his life stretched ahead of him, as empty and barren as the winter sky above.

Cicely awoke to the unexpected comfort of a feather-filled mattress and fine linen sheets. She sighed, then remembered the heartache of the day before. *Simon. Dear Simon.*

The dull ache inside her deepened. There had been a time when to be away from Montreau would have been enough to make her happy. But that time was gone. The key to her freedom was also the key to her eternal enslavement. She would never stop loving him.

She climbed from the bed and began to dress. How could she face him at the evening meal? How would she bear the sight of his beautiful face, knowing that he didn't love her?

She had to endure it. For his sake.

With sluggish, clumsy fingers, she donned her gown, then splashed water on her face. She left the lavish chamber and headed for the hall.

Halfway there, she realized that it was late. Very late. Torches guttered in their brackets, and the castle was deathly quiet. The sleeping potion Bella had given her must have made her sleep the whole afternoon and evening through.

Cicely changed direction and started toward the small chamber near the kitchen. She found it empty and a deep sadness went through her. *Simon, Simon, oh, please, Simon, don't hate me!*

She passed by the kitchen, where the serving boys slept, muttering and snuffling in their sleep, then went to the hall.

It, too, was quiet. Cicely examined the sleeping forms

stretched on benches, searching for Simon's lanky form and fair hair. She did not find him, and a kind of panic went through her. Where was he? Where did he sleep?

She ventured out into the yard and listened to the sounds of the fortress at night. Guards manned the walls, even in the depths of midnight. Simon had taken his turn a few nights ago, she remembered. Was it his turn again?

She climbed the stairs to the ramparts, shivering in the cold night air. There was beauty in the blue-black sky dusted with sparkling stars. And this castle, grand and solid—it made her remember the things she had yearned for at Montreau. The view here would be spectacular, if she could see it. But the moon was a bare sliver, not enough to illuminate the lands of Blackhurst, stretching far and wide.

Her teeth began to chatter, and she wished desperately that she had thought to bring her cloak. She would have to go back.

She started down the stairs, then gave a squeak as a tall shape surprised her.

"God's balls, wench! What do ye here?"

"I . . . I . . . came searching for . . . Sir Simon."

She heard his sigh, a hiss in the darkness. " 'Tis sorry I am, Lady Cicely, to give this news to ye. Sir Simon has gone."

"Gone." Her voice was a muffled sob. She wrapped her arms around herself, lest she shatter into pieces.

"Whist, now, lass. He meant to do right by leaving. He couldn't wed ye, so he left ye to Lady Blackhurst's care. She'll find ye a husband, don't ye fret."

Cicely shook her head, mute with grief.

"But he left ye this, he did." Black Robert pressed something small and cold into her palm.

Cicely searched for a hint of moonlight to view the object by. Her heart twisted in anguish as she beheld the gold filigree and ruby ring. She knew it had belonged to Simon's mother. He'd shown it to her once, when they were discussing what they could use to barter for supplies. Seeing the look on his face as he'd gazed at it, she'd insisted that they sell the crucifix first.

"Did . . . did he say where he was going?"

The seneschal shook his head. "I don't think he'd considered that yet. I won't lie to ye, 'twas not all his choice. The Lady Bella fair tossed him out once she knew ye weren't wed to him."

"He went . . . unwillingly?" A faint hope flared to life.

"Aye. He said naught, but I could see by the set o' his jaw that he was sore grieved to leave. Mayhap 'tis better this way, lady. You could not wed, so he set ye free."

Free. Aye, she was free. Free to mourn her loss for the rest of her days. She stifled a sob.

A warm hand pressed her shoulder. "There now, lass."

She sensed the seneschal's sympathetic gaze in the darkness. "I want to go after him," she said. "Will you help me?"

The comforting hand left her. "Well, now. 'Tis not a thing that maids do, traveling unescorted. There are brigands and robbers in the woods."

"I could keep to the road," Cicely said breathlessly.

"I can hardly in good conscience . . ." She heard him sigh again. "Were it not for the pleasure of thwartin' the lord's shrewish wife, I'd not do it. But ye must wait 'til morning, ye hear?"

"Aye."

"I'll send someone out with ye. If ye don't find him by yon far valley, ye'll have to turn back. Go now, and get yer things. If we are to manage this, ye must leave at first light."

Cicely raced down the stairway and dashed across the yard. As she entered the keep, a stab of guilt struck her. Lady Blackhurst had been so kind to her. How could she abandon her rescuer?

But desperate longing overrode her regret. If naught else,

she must say good-bye to Simon properly. If he told her to go back, she would obey. But if he showed any sign of relenting . . . She took a ragged breath. She would not lose Simon if she could help it.

CHAPTER 13

God help her! She'd added theft to her long list of sins. Cicely wrapped the borrowed cloak more tightly around her, seeking to ward off the chill of the morning mist. The rags she'd worn when she had arrived at Blackhurst were long gone. She'd been forced to take the cloak as well as many other things Bella had loaned her.

I'll return everything or pay for it, I vow. The pledge eased her guilt, but an anxious turmoil lingered. Once again she was running away, leaving behind those who had cared for her and tried to make her happy. And what sort of future did she run toward? Simon might well order her to return to Blackhurst. He might turn her away for the final time.

"There's a cotter's croft ahead, milady. Mayhap we should inquire there." The young squire accompanying her reined in his horse and waited for Cicely's palfrey to catch up.

"I'll go ask if they've seen Simon," she said.

The squire dismounted and secured his horse, then came to help her down. "Do you wish me to speak with them?"

"Nay, I'll do it. I think they'll speak more freely with me than you, Edward."

Cicely's apprehension increased as she walked resolutely toward the small dwelling. They'd been traveling all morning; if there were no word that Simon had passed by here, she feared her escort would suggest they turn back.

Smoke rose from a smoke-hole in the roof and mingled with the fading mist. *Please,* Cicely prayed silently, *let them have seen him.*

There was the sound of an ax striking wood. Cicely paused, then walked toward the outbuildings behind the croft, where the ax blows rang out loudly and rhythmically.

She reached the edge of the clearing and froze. Simon, his chest bare, was chopping up a deadfall tree. The sight of his beloved form sent a thrill through her, but before she could call out, a woman appeared from behind him. Simon stopped his exertions as she neared him. She said something, too low for Cicely to hear, then handed Simon a cloth. He wiped his brow and smiled at her—his glorious angel's smile.

Cicely took a step back, jealousy and anger rushing through her. Then she turned and ran to where Edward waited.

"Milady?" he said questioningly as she approached.

Shaking her head, she hurried to her horse. She pressed her face against the palfrey's withers, sick with despair.

"Milady?" the squire said again.

Tears blinded her as she groped for the saddle. In her distress, she unloosened the pack containing her possessions. The bundle tumbled to the ground. Clothing and books flew everywhere. Cicely paused in her anguish and stared at the mess. Her precious *romans* lay scattered on the frost-covered earth, but she did not care. Nothing mattered but that Simon did not love her. He had scarce left Blackhurst before finding another woman.

Fury beat through her, and she felt an urge to stomp the books into the dirt. Lies, all lies. The French *lais* promised love and happy endings, but Simon was right. There was no such thing as happiness. 'Twas an illusion. A cruel fantasy.

Edward stooped to retrieve one of the books. He turned it over in his big, bony hands. "Are these the tales you read to Lady Blackhurst? I listened one time . . . when I brought milady a basket of tarts from the kitchen. I always wanted to hear more. 'Tis wonderful that you can read."

He held out the book. Marie of France. Her favorite.

Cicely took it, thinking that a dozen years from now, she might well be sitting in the Blackhurst solar, reading to Bella or listening to her read. A lonely, empty life, no less so than what she had left behind at Montreau.

Glancing toward the croft, a sudden resolve came over her. She could not give up. She had not told Simon that she loved him. Until he faced her eye-to-eye and said that he wished to be rid of her, there was always hope.

She gathered up her belongings. As the squire refastened the bundle, she said, "I'll be back anon. There is something I must do."

Simon was still chopping wood. The woman sat on the ground watching him. But this time, she heard Cicely's approach. She came to her feet, a startled expression on her face.

Cicely ignored her. "Simon," she called.

He halted the ax in midair and turned to face her. An intense expression came over his face. "Cicely."

"Black Robert told me that Lady Blackhurst ordered you to leave. But I could not let you go without saying farewell."

He put down the ax and approached her. Cicely waited until he was only a pace away, then rushed to him. She wrapped her arms around his shoulders and pulled him down so their lips met. His arms cradled her against him, gently at first, then more urgently.

She put everything into the kiss. The aching yearning of the weeks since she'd first seen him ... a whole lifetime. They were melded together, joined as one. And it felt utterly perfect, complete.

At last they were forced to draw away for breath. She looked up at Simon, saw her own need and hunger mirrored in his eyes. "I'm coming with you," she said. "If you cannot stay at Blackhurst, I will not either."

"What of Lady Bella?"

Cicely shook her head. "She doesn't understand about love. Despite all the *romans* I have read her, she cannot comprehend what it is like to love someone more than your own soul."

"You speak blasphemy," Simon whispered, but his eyes were tender.

"I care not. 'Tis true!" Cicely reached for him again. This kiss was even longer, more impassioned. They only broke apart at the sound of the woman clearing her throat.

"I am a widow and well acquainted with lovemaking, but that young man does not look old enough to witness this." The crofter woman gestured.

They both turned to see Edward standing by the croft. A deep flush colored his face. "Milady," he said. "It appears we have succeeded in our quest. What do you bid me do now?"

"Return to Blackhurst and give Black Robert our thanks," Simon answered for her. "Cicely is coming with me."

"What of milady's horse?" the squire asked. "You'd be able to travel swifter with another mount."

"I have no means of paying for it," Simon said. "And I will not be more indebted to Black Robert than I already am."

"But we do have the means," Cicely put in. "I have thought of a way to clear all our debts." She started back toward the waiting horses, and motioned that they should follow. Once more removing the bundle from the horse, she opened it and began to hand the bound tomes to Edward. "They are worth a great deal. Mayhap someday Bella may even learn to read them."

"I cannot let you give up your books!" Simon cried. "They are all you have left to remind you of your mother."

She turned sharply to face him. "And why should you be allowed to outdo me, Simon? You left me your mother's ring when you quit Blackhurst. Surely 'tis as valuable to you as my books are to me." She held out her hand where the jewel shone blood red in the pale light glimmering through the mist. Simon placed his scarred, callused fingers over her outstretched hand. He said nothing, but the look in his eyes made Cicely's insides bubble with joy.

"Take the books, Edward," she said to the squire. "Give them to Lady Blackhurst with my blessing."

The youth began to pack them in the saddlebags of his mount.

"Sir Simon, I suppose this means I must find another man to chop my firewood and clean out my well," the crofter woman said, a rueful smile on her face.

Simon nodded. "We must depart, and quickly. Though I think Lord Blackhurst would be disinclined to pursue us, there is no certainty his wife might not force the matter."

"Bella would not do that," Cicely said.

"Oh, sweet Cicely, you will never learn." Simon shook his head. "I vow, it seems I must go through life wresting you away from jealous *women.*"

Cicely gave him a puzzled look. But she did not protest. If Simon thought they should be away, she was only more than happy to go with him.

They said their farewells to Edward and the crofter's widow, then rode off. As they followed the trackway past a little hamlet, the sun broke through the clouds in golden glory. Cicely wondered if she could be happier.

Aye, if she were alone with Simon in a bedchamber, that would be utter bliss!

She glanced at him, riding beside her, and love and desire crested over her. How would she wait for night? Would he finally love her then?

She prayed he would. If not, she feared she might ravish him!

He turned and saw her looking at him. "You are a vision, Cicely."

"I doubt that. I have scarce had any sleep, at least since last even."

He smiled. "Is that when you decided to chase me down?"

She blushed. "Do you think me overbold?"

His smiled deepened. "Always, Cicely. 'Tis one of the things I like about you." He guided the destrier nearer. "You are no meek, timid maid, despite your sweet face and gentle manner. You reach out with both hands to seize your dreams."

Cicely pretended an interest in the trackway ahead. "And, verily, I did *seize* you, Simon. 'Twas shameless of me to kiss you so, and in front of a stranger."

"I would that you would do it again and again." His words ended with a rumbling laugh. Cicely could not help looking at him.

"Oh, Simon," she said, "how much farther must we ride before we stop?"

"Why? Have you designs upon my person?" He winked, and Cicely felt her breath catch. This was a Simon she had never seen before. Playful, teasing . . . and so breathtakingly handsome as he gave her a provocative grin.

"Oh, aye, I do," she breathed out. "I cannot wait to kiss you again."

Abruptly, Simon reined in his mount. "I am yours, Cicely."

He dismounted, then came to help her off the palfrey. Cicely felt so weak and breathless, she wondered if she would be able to stand. It scarcely mattered; Simon did not allow her feet to even touch the ground. He clasped her against his body and rained kisses upon her face and neck.

Cicely shuddered and moaned. She could not seem to get enough of him, of his inflaming mouth, his warm, solid body. Her whole being ached. Her breasts seemed to be on fire, her nipples taut, throbbing points. And deep within her body, the blood pulsed urgently. She craved something more. She feared she would die of it!

"Come, sweet," he whispered, drawing back from another heated kiss. He lowered her to her trembling legs, then took her hand and led her to a sheltered spot among the brush and bracken. Spreading out his cloak, he gestured for her to lie down. She did so, feeling shy. This was the moment she had waited for, but it was so awkward. There were all these layers of clothing between them.

He bent over her and eyed her clothing with a dubious look that reflected her thoughts. Meeting her gaze, he said, "I cannot bed you here. You'd be too cold, and my mail shirt would tear your skin. But I can give you a taste." He lowered his mouth to her neck, then trailed kisses along her jaw.

As hot tremors shook her, she moaned, "Oh, please! I'll go mad!"

"Hush, my love," he whispered. "I'll not disappoint you."

She closed her eyes and took a wrenching breath. As she did so, she felt him pulling up her skirts. She gasped as the cold air met her flesh, then cried out as his warm fingers traced the sensitive skin above her stocking.

"Beautiful," he whispered.

Cicely opened her eyes for a second. Seeing Simon's reverent gaze fixed upon her naked hips and thighs, she squeezed her eyes shut once again. She longed fervently for the privacy of a candlelit chamber. Despite the desire coursing through her, she was not certain she was ready for such shocking intimacy.

But then Simon moved his hand upward, stroking gently, and her thoughts seemed to dissolve. In seconds, her lower body no longer seemed to belong to her. Her thighs splayed wantonly, begging for his silky touch. As his fingers provided the divine, soothing pressure she sought, a harsh cry erupted from her lips, and deep inside her, some tumult burst forth.

Spirals of sensation took her higher and higher, until she floated to the very clouds.

Slowly, she sank back to earth, and found Simon leaning over her, his hand still pressed against her private parts. He bent to kiss her fevered cheek. "Did you like that?"

She nodded helplessly, dizzy with a mixture of euphoria and embarrassment.

"I said I would not disappoint you."

"What of you?" she asked. "You have not yet found release."

"I am used to burning."

She tried to sit up, disconcerted by the wetness between her thighs. His fingers remained tight against her. She felt the heat building inside her once again.

His eyes, heavy-lidded, the pupils dark pools, searched her face. "Do you want to please me?"

She nodded.

"Let me pleasure you again."

"Is that . . . possible?"

He smiled, his nostrils flared in an expression that made him look less than angelic. "Aye. 'Tis a gift of women. Mayhap to make up for all they must suffer otherwise."

The intensity of his gaze took her breath away. "What . . . what should I do?"

"Lie back and let me do what I will."

With a shaky breath she obeyed. It did not seem possible that she could reach the heights she had the first time. But she could not imagine what he would do next. His arousing fingers released her, and he used both hands to gently spread her thighs even wider. He gave her a sleek bedeviling smile, then bent his head to press his lips against her tender, trembling core. At the touch of his mouth, she closed her eyes and gave in to the waves of pleasure lapping over her.

She sensed his skill as he varied pressure and rhythm. Teeth and tongue and lips played upon her as if she were a harp or shepherd's pipe, and the music swelled and soared inside her. She forgot the shock of what he did, and reveled in the magic he worked.

Sliding down the last spiraling current, she found herself face-to-face with her lover. His mouth and chin glistened with wetness, his eyes were like gleaming jewels. "My precious flower," he whispered.

He gently smoothed her skirts, then sprawled down beside her.

"That was wonderful," she said.

"Aye, wasn't it? But it will be even better when we can"—he wiped his mouth with his hand and grinned at her—"do it the proper way."

She felt herself blushing. 'Twas all so new, so intimate. Her nerves were raw and jangling. A few hours before, she'd thought she'd lost him forever. Now here they were, lying together. And Simon—she'd never seen him appear so jovial and lighthearted.

"I must ask you," she said, "why did you change your mind and decide to . . . be with me." She looked away.

He put his hand on her chin and turned her face toward his. "When I rode away from Blackhurst, believing I'd lost you forever, I knew such an unbearable grief I was not certain I could go on living. Then, when I saw you again, it made my heart swell with joy. I could not let you go."

The words he spoke were those she had waited near all her life to hear. Her beloved Simon, could he really be hers at last?

"What will we do now?" she asked. "Do you intend to seek a position in another garrison?"

"Eventually. First, we must go to Pembroke Castle. I mean to convince the Earl Marshal to let me wed with you."

Cicely stared at him. "But I thought you said we could not wed."

His mouth quirked into a smile. "Nothing ventured, nothing gained. Now that I have debauched you, I imagine he will either let me wed you or have me hanged."

"Don't say such things, even in jest!" She searched his face. "You are jesting, aren't you?"

"Since you know the earl better than I, mayhap you can tell me what my chances are."

"But I have not seen him in years. I was but a little child when last we met."

"Yet your memories of him made you think to go to him and ask for his aid. He cannot have been an ogre."

"Nay, he was not. I recall him indulging me with sweetmeats and bouncing me upon his knee."

"Then mayhap he will indulge you in this."

Cicely nodded, but she felt unsettled inside. Lady Blackhurst had believed Simon much beneath her. Would her powerful, wealthy godfather also scorn the man she loved?

"Will you tell him that I am . . . that I am no longer a maid?" she asked.

Simon's face grew serious again. "Of course you are a maid. I did not breach your maidenhead. I was careful of that."

"But what we did . . ." She regarded him uncertainly.

"Oh, aye, 'tis a sin, no doubt of that. But a lesser one than if we had carnal relations."

Some troubling doubt nagged at her. Why had he been careful to leave her maidenhead intact? Was he not going to finish things as soon as they found a bed and some privacy?

She sat up. "Simon, I must know, do you mean to . . . to lie with me?"

His blue eyes shone bright and hot. "I scarce think of anything else."

"But . . . when?"

He sat up and took her hands in his. "When you are my lawful wife, I will lie with you anytime you wish."

"Lawful wife? But when will that be?" She let out a cry of dismay. "What if my godfather refuses you? What if he decides to send me back to Montreau?"

He patted her arm. "We will deal with that when the time comes."

When she continued to regard him unhappily, he took her in his arms. "If we do not tarry here all day, mayhap we can stay at an inn tonight. There are many other pleasures I can show you."

"But 'tis not the same!"

"Not the same as what?" He nuzzled her temple.

"As if you . . ." She took a deep breath. "I want to pleasure *you.*"

"I can teach you that as well."

She leaned back in his arms and sighed. Why did it matter so much that he would not . . . mate with her? Should she not trust his judgment? If her godfather refused to give them permission to wed, it might go better for Simon if she could say she was a virgin.

But what sort of maid was she? She had allowed Simon to do the most intimate things to her, and she meant to continue sinning. Yet somehow his forbearance aroused her fear. Mayhap he thought if he did not bed her, he could leave her more easily.

Simon's kisses grew more fervent, but she could not make herself return them with enthusiasm. The hard knot was back inside her. She did not possess the man she loved. They could still be parted.

He sensed her reluctance and released her so she could sit up. "You are right. We cannot tarry here." He rose, then helped her to her feet.

They did not find an inn, so they spent the night much as they had on their previous journey. Simon held her in his arms, his voluminous cloak spread over both of them. In the morning, she woke suddenly, sensing that something was wrong. She turned to face him, and as her body brushed against his, he groaned. She examined his tense, set expression, and sudden awareness came to her.

" 'Tis painful for you, isn't it?"

He gave her a tormented smile. "Aye, 'tis difficult, especially in the mornings. To go for months without . . ." He sighed.

"You mean you did not dally with any of the wenches at Blackhurst?"

He gave her an aghast look. "Why would I bed another woman when you are the only one I want?"

A sense of relief went through her. She should have known Simon would not betray their love. "Let me ease you," she whispered. "Please."

When he started to rise, she clutched at his tunic. "Please, Simon. It would give me pleasure. Can you deny me that which I've freely given you?"

He sank back down. "Very well, then, my persistent little wench. Have at me."

She gazed at him in consternation. "But you must tell me what to do. I might . . . hurt you."

He quirked an amused brow at her, but said nothing. Then he reached for her hand and pulled it against his groin.

Cicely was startled to feel a hard ridge straining against his hose. 'Twas nothing like the silky flesh she had caressed that night in the priory. He seemed much bigger.

He saw her astonished look and pulled her hand away. "I should not have agreed to this." He sounded as if he were gritting his teeth.

"Nay, nay," she protested. She reached out to touch him again. " 'Tis only that . . . I did not think it would be like this. You are so . . . big."

He smiled grimly. "A dubious endowment with a gentle virgin like you."

Cicely moved nearer, so she could caress him more easily. Then, clumsily, she began to undo the drawstring of his hose. "I want to touch your skin," she whispered.

He groaned again, and his eyes narrowed to fevered slits.

She freed him, and his engorged shaft seemed to jump into her fingers. She stroked him lovingly, fascinated by the smooth, velvet skin and rigid heat beneath. Then she pushed aside his tunic so she could see what she was doing.

"Dear God, Cicely!" She saw him squeeze his eyes shut tight; his fingers clutched desperately at the blanket beneath them.

"Am I hurting you?"

He shook his head, but his features remained contorted.

"What should I do?" she asked.

"Merely . . . touch me . . . 'tis enough."

She took a deep breath and did as he bid. Her fingers traced the length of him, then back. She found the silky, tender tip and stroked it. His whole body shuddered, and he gave a gasp. A pale, moon-colored secretion spurted over her fingers.

"Oh, my," she said.

He caught his breath, then sat up quickly. He pulled a cloth from the pack beside them and gently cleaned her fingers, then himself.

" 'Tis a sin to spill your seed like that, isn't it?"

He nodded. "But it seems I can't help sinning. Sometimes I wake up and find that I . . ." His gaze met hers helplessly.

"It happens while you sleep?"

"Aye." He smiled. "Especially if I dream of you."

She blushed, then glanced down at him. His proud shaft had shriveled back to a soft, innocent-looking thing. "I did not think it would be like that."

"So you said. Did you never see animals, Cicely?"

"I suppose so, but I did not think it would be the same with a man."

"How did you think a man managed it?" he asked, obviously amused. "I would be of little use to you like this. Although, if you keep staring at me, I vow, I will become like an aroused beast again. Big and randy."

She tore her gaze away. "I am happy that I was able to please you."

"Oh, aye." He reached up and drew her down beside him. He kissed her tenderly. "You please me very much, Cicely."

She sighed with satisfaction. He kissed her more deeply, and his fingers fondled her breasts through her clothes.

"Mmmm," he muttered. "We must keep our minds on our destination. If we do not find an inn tonight, I'll not be able to do the things I wish to do to you."

A wave of desire shivered over her. She could still feel a dull heaviness between her legs from his enthralling ministrations of the day before. "Do you not fear that we will burn in hell for this?" she asked.

He shook his head. "My faith, which has been battered and strained greatly these past years, has now encountered an even greater obstacle. I find that if I cannot have you, I care nothing at all for this life. I cannot live without you, Cicely. I find I would gladly burn in hell for these moments with you in my arms."

"It cannot be so great a sin," she said thoughtfully. "God would not make us capable of such delight and then forbid us to enjoy it. He made our bodies to feel pleasure. It cannot be an evil thing.'' She looked at him in wonder. "When you touch me, Simon, I feel as if I have reached another realm, if not heaven, then something very like. How can that be wrong?"

He sighed. "I have asked myself questions like that one as long as I can remember. The Church teaches one thing, but my spirit finds truth in another. I have been raised to kill in the name of God, and yet our Blessed Savior taught that we should love other men as our brothers. 'Tis all a mystery.'' He rose to his feet and adjusted his clothing. "But not one we can unravel at this moment."

After a day of riding, they found an inn and secured a private room. While Simon saw to the horses, Cicely hurriedly bathed herself. The innkeeper had provided a basin of water and a bowl of rather rancid-smelling soap. The water was cold, and she had to use her chemise to dry herself, but beneath her fingers, her skin seemed hot and alive, pulsing with anticipation. All these weeks of waiting, and tonight she and Simon would finally share a bed.

She glanced toward the object of her interest. The straw-filled mattress appeared slightly superior to the pallet in their chamber at Blackhurst, although it could hardly match the comfort of Bella's massive bed with its cloudlike feather mattress. But it mattered not. To be with Simon and to have him touch her with love and tenderness, that was what made her heartbeat quicken. What startling secrets of pleasure would she discover this time? They had both touched each other intimately, what could be more wonderful than that?

Her mind told her that to be joined as one would be more transcendent and perfect than anything she had experienced. Simon said they could not do that, but might there not be a way to make him change his mind?

Nay, she must obey his wishes, she told herself firmly. She

must not allow her weak, sinful nature to urge him into doing something he thought was wrong. She had coerced him too many times already.

Sighing, she pulled her kirtle over her damp shift. Her nipples felt raw against the thin fabric. Her mouth was dry, but the tender place between her thighs, where she had washed, was slippery wet. Eagerness made her shiver, and she paced to the fire and added some kindling. She hoped he would hurry.

In a few moments, there was a knock on the door. Simon entered carrying a cloth-wrapped bundle and a wineskin. "Here are provisions from the innkeeper's wife." He glanced at Cicely and smiled. "In the event you do not yet have an appetite for *food*, the roasted capon and bread will keep."

The way he emphasized "food" made it clear that he alluded to her appetite for something else. She felt almost dizzy with desire.

He put the food and drink on the table, then approached her. Grasping her arms, he pulled her close and kissed her. Cicely melded her body against his, overcome and helpless.

After a moment, he drew away. "This damned mail shirt has come between us long enough. Help me out of it, Cicely."

Between the two of them, they labored to undress him. The pungent odor of male sweat wafted to her nose as the cumbersome garments were removed one by one and pitched to the floor—the heavy surcote, mail, gambeson, and tunic.

"By the saints, I reek," he said. "I need a bath ere I touch you."

"Nay, 'tis not so bad. I rather like it." She raised her gaze to his. " 'Tis your scent, Simon. That's why it doesn't offend me."

"Even so, I must wash."

He strode to the basin on the table and began to pour fresh water from a bucket on the floor.

She went to him. "Let me bathe you. Please. I want to."

His mouth quirked. "Whatever you desire, my sweet. Although, I'll warn you, I'm very ticklish."

She wet the cloth and drew it over the matted hair on his chest.

He flinched. "Cold," he said.

With a sigh of satisfaction, Cicely stroked the cloth over his torso, exploring the firm, rounded muscles, the coarse gilt hair, the smooth, pinkish gold skin. "I never thought a man could be beautiful," she said.

"I vow, you've spent too long in a priory." He laughed.

"Nay, 'tis true. Like a fine, lovely wild beast you are."

"Did you think the same when you tended me at Montreau?"

She nodded. "I could scarce touch you like this, but I wanted to."

"And here I thought you were a saint, tending me though my sickly flesh repelled you."

"You could never repel me, Simon." She raised her eyes shyly to his.

Love and longing shimmered between them, making them both breathless.

Then, Cicely drew the cloth near his underarms and the serious mood shattered. "God's bones!" he yelped, jerking away, "I warned you I was ticklish."

"Hold still, I'm trying to wash you!"

He flinched so badly she finally had to give up and let him rinse his underarms himself.

"Why does it not tickle when you touch yourself?" she asked.

"Mayhap because I know when I am going to do it. 'Tis the surprise that unsettles me. Are you not ticklish, Cicely? Anywhere?" His gaze roved over her. "I vow, I mean to find out."

Cicely fought the urge to back away. His wicked smile turned her insides to quivering mush, but she held her ground, waiting.

Simon approached her and put his hand on her neck. He stroked lightly along the curve of her jaw, then slid his fingers inside the neckline of her kirtle, brushing them over the swells of her breasts. "Take off your clothes, Cicely," he whispered.

She pulled the kirtle over her head and let it fall to the floor. Before she could remove her chemise, Simon pulled her close and examined her with a heavy-lidded, intent gaze. "Such a fine linen—I can see the outline of your breasts and the pinkness of your nipples beneath it." He pulled the fabric of the chemise tight and teased a rigid peak with his mouth and tongue. Cicely gasped and swayed against him.

With a smooth motion, he released the breast he was suckling and picked her up. He carried her to the bed and laid her down, then kneeled next to her. Again, he mouthed her nipple, drawing it, fabric and all, into his mouth. Cicely's body went rigid with pleasure. Her hips jerked and she shuddered as he tongued the linen to transparent wetness and then sucked harder. She moaned, tantalized beyond endurance.

He sampled the other breast, licking circles around the areola, then finally flicking his tongue over the swollen peak.

She clutched his hair. "Such torture, Simon."

"Don't you like it?" he murmured, his mouth still busy suckling.

"Aye, but . . . It makes me want . . ."

He raised his head, blue eyes gleaming. "So many times you have tormented me, Cicely, 'tis only fair."

"When? When?" she moaned.

"In the bathing chamber. Both times. And when you wore that indecent gown Lady Blackhurst gave you. I could see the tops of your breasts"—he interrupted his words to suck hard on her nipple—"and imagine the rest of the bounty of your body. You did not know what you did to me. How I wanted you . . ." His voice trailed off in a groan.

"Then have me, Simon." She slid from beneath him and

sat up to drag the chemise over her head. Fully naked, she faced him. A wild urge came over her, and she cupped her breasts with her fingers, so the rosy, engorged nipples thrust out even farther. "Devour me, love me . . . fill me!"

He took a deep breath and a desperate, longing look came over his face. Then he shook his head. "Nay, I will not take your maidenhead. That is for your husband."

"But *you* will be my husband!" Cicely released her breasts. She felt the heat of desire turn to anger. "All we have to do is plight troth with each other, and in the eyes of the Church, we are as good as wed!"

"And if Marshal or your father should dispute my right to you, what do we do then? Live like wolfsheads in the woods the rest of our days? That might be our only choice, lest they take you away from me and return you to the convent!"

"But if we are not allowed to wed, and we do not take this chance to . . . be together, we will never know"—she reached out for him, imploring—"the glory, the wonder of being as one. I am weak and sinful, Simon. I admit it. I want to experience lovemaking with you. All of it. I want you to be the man who comes into my body and makes me his."

He stared at her, his eyes stricken, his jaw working. "I . . . I cannot take what I have no right to. Once I . . . did that, I would never be able to give you up."

"Then, don't give me up! Fight for me!"

For a long time, there was silence between them; then he sighed heavily. "You are right about one thing. 'Tis wrong to keep doing what we have been doing—sharing intimacy, pleasuring each other, yet not completing the act."

He rose from the bed and picked up his discarded tunic. As he started to pull it over his head, Cicely rushed to stop him. "What are you doing?" she demanded.

"I mean to sleep in the stables. I cannot remain here with you."

He pulled his tunic on, then faced her, his eyes sorrowful.

She wanted to strike him, she was so furious. "You, you . . . said . . . you said that I could come with you . . . that you could not bear to go on living without me!" Her voice came out half-shriek, half-sob. "You are a coward! You will not fight for what you believe in, for what you desire above all else!"

"Mayhap I am," he said wearily. "Mayhap that is my greatest sin of all."

She watched as he gathered together his possessions and left the room.

CHAPTER 14

Simon tossed uncomfortably on the pile of moldy straw which made up his bed. He could not sleep. His eyes felt gritty, as if he had been weeping. His chest ached. Fighting against his distress, he began to pray.

He started to ask for forgiveness, but the penitent words stuck in his throat. How could he say he was sorry for the things he had done with Cicely? He could not regret having availed himself of that irresistible closeness. The warmth and beauty of her body. The life and love she seemed to pour into his soul with each kiss.

He could no more prevent what he had done than a starving man could keep from gorging on food set before him. From the moment he had seen Cicely in the clearing and known she had come after him, he was lost. What he'd told her was true, that he had despaired when he thought he would never see her again. His life had stretched ahead of him, lonely, desolate, unbearable.

And when he saw her again, his heart had leaped with joy. He had acted on that giddiness, that wild euphoria, and, for a time, forgotten the practical realities of their lives. That she was a lady, and deserved better than to be tumbled in the woods or on a well-used mattress in an inn. That he might never have the right to call her "wife" or have her children bear his name.

His madness had faded when she'd stripped herself naked and offered herself to him. He'd remembered then how utterly naive and tempestuous she was. With Cicely, there was no cautious, prudent course. Everything was "here and now," immediate. He supposed her sheltered upbringing had made her that way, allowing her to maintain that quality of seizing what she wanted like a heedless, carefree child.

But there were always ramifications, practical considerations for every action. He had learned that the hard way. Once he had been as impulsive as Cicely. He had followed his heart and pursued his dreams . . . and nearly been destroyed in the end. Worse yet, he had deeply hurt those who loved him.

Never again would he be so heedless. He would not take Cicely's maidenhead because she wished it, nor because he desired to love her more than he wanted anything else in the world. He would wait and win her as his wife . . . somehow.

He sighed heavily. Although he had vowed not to claim his inheritance, knowing that he did not deserve it, he no longer had much choice. William Marshal would not give his pampered goddaughter to a landless mercenary. The earl would only favor his suit if he knew Simon was heir to property.

Valmar, Westham, Rosebrook—were they rich demesnes still, or had the strife of King John's reign devalued them as it had so many other estates? The earl would want to know the condition of Simon's inheritance. But how could he go back there and face his parents?

Anguish tore through Simon, and he threw off his cloak and got to his feet. He stumbled through the stables, causing the horses to snort and shift uneasily as he passed their stalls. Outside, he drew a deep draught of icy air. The sky was murky and overcast, nothing like the depthless black and glittering stars of the Eastern firmament. A man felt closer to God there. Here in England, his homeland, everything seemed so confused.

Restless and cold, Simon began to pace. Dare he dream that he could have it all—a life as a whole man, a wife, a family? He had given up all thought of happiness many months ago, abandoning the seemingly ridiculous notion that he might once more know God's favor. He told himself that he did not deserve it anyway. His sickness and failure were penance for what he had done, what he had allowed to happen. He merited no better.

But Cicely, curse her exuberant spirit, had tempted him into believing that life need not be all despair and suffering. She had forced him to live again. He felt like a newborn babe taking its first breath. Life was painful, harsh and cold, but also dazzlingly beautiful.

He glanced at the inn, a black shape huddled in the darkness. He wanted to wake her and hold her, to tell her what she meant to him. But, he could not. They had parted in anger.

Beautiful, sweet Cicely. He would possess her yet, and when he did so, it would be perfect. And forever.

"These wild lands are called the Marches." Simon gestured to the hilly, deeply forested terrain around them. "Your godfather, the Earl Marshal, rules over a large part of this region."

Cicely gazed with interest at the forbidding landscape. It was much different than the gentle green beauty of the England she knew. "How long until we arrive at Pembroke?" she asked.

Simon shook his head. "A few more days. We have much rugged country to cross. 'Tis glad I am that we have two horses. The going would be even slower if Lucifer had to bear us both."

Cicely, too, was grateful for her sturdy, docile palfrey. 'Twas hard enough having to sleep curled next to Simon each night without also enduring the enforced intimacy of riding pillion. The small number of coins which made up Simon's payment for service at Blackhurst had to be hoarded for food, and since the weather had been clear the last two nights, they'd slept outside, warmed by a small fire.

There was a certain tension between them now, and she felt especially awkward when she lay in Simon's arms at night. She could not forget the deeper intimacies they had shared. They had never spoken of that disastrous night at the inn, and Cicely was not certain why Simon had changed his mind about their pleasuring each other. But she had accepted his decision. He was a stubborn, aggravatingly high-minded idealist, but mayhap that was what she loved about him.

The thought made her sigh, but she quickly suppressed it, fearing that Simon would think she was tired and suggest they stop and rest. She was most anxious to reach Pembroke and resolve the uncertainty of their future. So much depended on whether her godfather would heed their pleas. If he would not let them wed, what would happen? Would Simon leave her at Pembroke, to live out her days in loneliness and grief? For surely she would die of unhappiness then.

A new wave of frustration rose up inside her at the thought. They had come so close to perfect bliss. How could she ever bear to give Simon up?

Simon broke the silence between them. "My chief concern is whether the earl will even be in residence."

"Why would he not?"

"Because he is the king's man, and the king has trouble aplenty these days. John may have sent the earl to gain support for him in the eastern part of England, or to command forces to put down rebel uprisings."

"Will there be war?" Cicely asked. She could still recall

her father and another baron discussing the terrible days of King Stephen and the Empress Maude, when England had known the devastation and chaos of civil war. The Valois family had lost much of their land and power in that long-ago conflict.

Simon shook his head. "I don't think it will come to all-out battle. But there will be a reckoning of some sort, and from what I know of his power and authority as the marshal of England, Lord William will be a part of it."

"And meanwhile we shall have to wait at Pembroke, wondering whether my godfather will condone our marriage."

"You are too impatient." Simon gave her one of his rare smiles. "Think of it, Cicely, if he does allow us to wed, we will be together the rest of our lives."

She smiled back, feeling a slight lightening of her mood. Surely her godfather would not refuse them. Surely he would realize how wonderful Simon was.

As Bella had? Cicely's optimism faded. Bella had not thought Simon worthy of her. What if her godfather also failed to look beyond her beloved's humble circumstances and see the glorious, noble man he really was?

Two days later, Simon drew rein and took off his helm. He sniffed the air, then gave a sigh of satisfaction. "We're getting near. I can smell the sea."

Cicely inhaled deeply, savoring the fresh, exhilarating tang in the air. "How far we have traveled," she said. "I feel as if I were a thousand leagues from Montreau."

"Well, you wanted to escape the boredom and monotony of the priory," he said. "And so you have."

She smiled back at him. "In truth, I cannot regret this journey, no matter what the future holds. So many things I have seen. The only thing that troubles me is Bella. I feel badly that I left her the way I did. Without even saying good-bye."

"If she truly cared for you, she will understand." Even as he spoke, Simon wondered if his words were true. He feared that Bella would have imprisoned Cicely at Blackhurst if she had known that her companion meant to desert her. But he could not tell Cicely that.

"But she was very lonely. I hope she is able to convince her husband to share her bed again. She wants a child so desperately. Although I know he loves her, it seems to me that Lord Blackhurst is most foolish regarding his wife. 'Tis her body and her life she risks in getting with child. It should be her right to choose to take that chance."

"Mayhap he feels that he is older and wiser than she, and better fit to make the decision as to when she is ready for childbearing."

"Oh, you would think so." A defiant expression came over Cicely's face, and she raised her dainty chin a notch. "Like all men, you seem to think your sex possesses the better portion of wisdom."

"I see now why your father put you in a convent," Simon said, grinning. "With your forthright nature, I imagine you were quite a handful as a little maid."

"What a rude, knavish thing to say! My father did not send me to Montreau because he wearied of my rebellious tongue, but because he wanted to protect me!" Cicely rode her palfrey dangerously close to his mount, her eyes flashing.

"You see, you've proven my point!" he laughed. "You look as if you wish to knock me down and pummel me into the dirt."

She glared at him, then gradually her fierce mood eased and she returned his mirth. "I vow you are right. I am no meek, timid creature. Which is why I was so unsuited to convent life. They tried sorely to bend my character to gentleness and propriety, but it could not be done. I fear I am the same as when I was a little girl and I *did* knock my brother into the dirt and pummel his face.''

''How old were you then?''

''Oh, six or seven years at most. And he a year older and half a head taller. But I was so ferocious, he gave in.''

''What did you quarrel over?''

She shrugged. ''I don't remember, but I cannot think it was anything of much importance. Mayhap he teased me, as you have been doing.''

''Are you so certain that I am teasing?'' He fought to make his face look sober. ''Mayhap I really do find you insufferable.''

She gasped with shock, then gave a little bell-like laugh. ''You are not nearly so good at it as my brother was, Simon. Your mouth twitches and gives you away.''

''I have not had so much practice as he did. 'Tis likely I will master it in time.''

Her brown eyes shone with yearning. ''Do you think we will have years together, Simon? A lifetime to jest and tease with each other?''

Simon drew his horse to a halt and drew his sword. Holding it pommel up, so it formed a cross, he said, ''Upon my honor as a knight, I swear that I will do my utmost to make you my wife.''

They stared at each other, and Simon felt the familiar hunger grow between them. The last few days had required all the restraint he could muster. Now he cleared his throat and said, ''Mayhap we should continue on. 'Twould be best we arrived during daylight.''

That afternoon they reached the coast and beheld their destination—Pembroke Castle.

Cicely gave an audible gasp. ''By the saints, 'tis large!''

''And so it must be to house the troops necessary to defend

these untamed lands. The Welsh are cunning fighters. When they are not killing each other, they conduct raids and seek to weaken the English hold upon these lands.''

Cicely glanced around uneasily. ''You do not think we are in danger, do you?''

''Although I would not put it past the Welsh to kidnap a fair English flower such as you, I doubt they would risk it within sight of Pembroke Castle.''

''You are teasing again,'' Cicely complained.

Simon shook his head. ''In truth, the main reason we have been able to travel safely these past days is because of William Marshal. Ruffians and Welshmen alike, they wisely fear to arouse the Earl of Pembroke's wrath.''

''I didn't realize my godfather had such a fearsome reputation.''

''He's a great warrior, and since he is married to Isabel de Clare, he is also one of the richest and most powerful lords in the land. I think John would rather he were not quite so powerful, but the marriage was arranged by Richard ere he died, and there was naught John could do to stop it. Still, John could have fared worse. William is loyal to the king. Although I doubt he has always desired to do so, he has served the interests of the Plantagenet family many times.''

''How do you know so much of him?'' Cicely asked. ''Though he is an old friend of my family's, I know little of his fame. I remember him as a gruff, bearlike man, but with a twinkling smile which made it impossible for me to fear him.''

''Soldiers always talk, comparing battle prowess and skill. I have heard men argue that William Marshal is the greatest fighter in the land, that his skill when he was in his prime outshone that of the glorious Lionheart himself.''

'' 'Tis a wonder that King Richard favored him enough to give him such an heiress. I've always heard that Richard was a vain, proud man.''

Simon snorted. "All the Plantagenets are vain, and mayhap all kings as well. I think Richard favored William Marshal's request for Isabel because he needed William's support. The earl is a favorite with soldiers, and in the early days of his kingship, Richard was still struggling to rally men to his cause."

Cicely repressed a shiver. "One of the greatest men in the land, and we go to him begging a boon. What should I say to my godfather, Simon? What if he does not remember me?"

"Be yourself, 'twill be enough. I vow no man, having seen your sweet smile and glowing brown eyes, could ever forget you."

Cicely took a deep breath and tried to quell the butterflies fluttering in her stomach as they approached the massive keep, which appeared as harsh and forbidding as the ancient hills they had recently traveled through.

But they were cordially welcomed by the sentries and barely questioned before being allowed inside the gate. When Cicely raised a brow, Simon leaned nearer and assured her, "They are used to visitors coming and going and have no fear of a lone knight. 'Twould take a huge army to conquer this fortress, even with help from inside."

As they entered the yard, Cicely gave a gasp. She had never seen so many people and buildings in one place before. It seemed as if several villages were crowded inside the castle ramparts, with an endless number of shops and storehouses and dwellings tucked up against the massive stone walls. The yard was alive with servants and soldiers. Cicely experienced another wave of doubt. How dare she bother such an important man with her petty troubles?

But Simon did not seem intimidated. Dismounting, he told her to wait and went off to speak to a group of knights milling near the foregate. Cicely watched him anxiously. He returned shortly, his face expressionless.

"Well?" Cicely demanded.

"As I suspected, the earl is not here. The knight I spoke to suggested that we speak to Lady Pembroke. He said she is a gracious hostess, and will likely allow us to stay here until the earl returns."

Cicely nodded. "When will we see her?"

"The man I spoke to offered to conduct us to her solar."

"That is most generous. Why does he favor us? We are but humble strangers."

Simon gestured to his tattered surcote which marked him as a crusader. "God forgive me, but I have once again used His holy cause to aid ours. The soldier I spoke to had an older brother who took the Cross. Last he knew, his brother was in Sicily. I think he wishes for me to tell him a little of my experiences."

They found an ostler to take their horses, then followed the knight toward the towering castle. There were so many turrets crowning the keep that Cicely could scarce count them. Simply looking up at the immense structure made her dizzy.

Inside, the building seemed a honeycomb of chambers, one leading to another. Cicely followed Simon and the knight up numerous stairways and down twisting corridors. She was too busy taking in the sights to listen to their conversation, but it did appear that their benefactor was most interested in Simon's exploits among the Saracens. She wondered if it pained Simon to speak of such things. If so, she could not tell by looking at him. His features were composed, his voice calm.

At last they paused in a hallway, high up in the main portion of the castle. Their escort, who was named Anselm, bowed to her. "I will go in and announce you, Lady Valois."

When he left, Cicely licked her lips, then nervously smoothed her gown. Thank goodness she had decent clothes from Blackhurst. She would have been mortified if she'd had to appear before Lady Pembroke in the rags she'd been wearing when she first met Bella!

Anselm returned. "She will be pleased to see you." The knight's eyes sparkled with interest. "Indeed, she said she was most relieved to learn you were here."

Cicely and Simon exchanged a startled glance, then went in.

In the center of the most lavish chamber Cicely had ever seen, sat a fine-featured woman of middle years. Her eyes were dark and keen, and although lines etched the fair skin around them and bracketed her well-shaped lips, 'twas clear Lady Pembroke had once been not only a great heiress, but a great beauty as well.

Cicely dropped into a deep curtsy. "My lady, we are honored," she murmured. Beside her, Simon also knelt.

Lady Pembroke rose, a little stiffly it seemed to Cicely, and moved toward them. "Rise, child."

As Cicely stood, Lady Pembroke clasped her hands. "Thank goodness you are here. One of your father's men, William de Gascon, came to us near a month ago, frantic with worry because you'd disappeared from Montreau."

Cicely stiffened. So, her father had sent men looking for her.

Lady Pembroke smiled. "But come, sit down. You must be very weary from your journey. Would you like some hippocras?"

Cicely followed their hostess to a chair near the fire and soon found herself relaxing, with a silver cup full of hot spiced drink warming her fingers.

"And how many years have you dwelled at Montreau?" Lady Pembroke asked.

Cicely shot a glance at Simon. If this elegant, regal woman ordered her to go back there, what would she do?

She looked again at Lady Pembroke. "I was there ten years, milady."

Lady Pembroke's smooth brow furrowed. "And this young man?" She raised a graceful, beringed hand to gesture to Simon. "How do you come to be traveling with him?"

Cicely took a deep breath. This was the moment of truth. If she could sway Lady Pembroke to her cause, she felt certain that the earl would go along. "This is Sir Simon, a crusader and the most noble and gallant of knights. He came to Montreau when he was sick with a fever, and I convinced him that I . . . I was not suited to be a nun. He has graciously allowed me to travel with him. He has protected me and cared for me on the journey here."

Lady Pembroke's face wore a wary look, and her voice was cool as she spoke. "And why, exactly, have you come here, Cicely?"

Cicely's heart thundered in her chest, and her hands trembled so much she had to set down the hippocras. "Simon and I want to be wed. We have come here to ask for your husband's permission."

Lady Pembroke rose, looking very distressed. " 'Tis not possible that you have been to Tathwick and here in the past few weeks." She turned to face Cicely. "I understand the impatience of youth, but should you not be with your mother at this time? Your first duty is to her. This other matter"— she fixed Simon with a sharp look—"surely that can wait. Indeed, 'twill have to wait. Now that you are heiress to Tathwick, you will require the king's permission to wed."

Cicely's voice came out in a choked whisper. "Heiress to Tathwick? What do you mean?"

Lady Pembroke looked from Cicely to Simon, obviously bewildered.

Simon got swiftly to his feet and came to Cicely's side. He took her hand in his. "Lady Pembroke?"

She exhaled on a deep sigh, and the lines in her face seemed to deepen. "I'm sorry, Cicely. I thought since you came here to ask my husband's permission to wed, that you must know . . ." She hesitated.

"Know? Know what?" Cicely asked breathlessly.

Lady Pembroke sighed again. "Lady Cicely, your father and brother are dead. It happened near three months ago. Some of the king's mercenaries attacked Tathwick when your father refused to pay scutage to the king. They burned part of the village and terrorized the people. Your father and brother tried to stop them. They were both killed."

Cicely felt numb, frozen. "How can this be?" she whispered. "How could the king allow his men to kill my father and brother?"

Lady Pembroke shook her head. "I fear your father angered King John at some time in the past. He refuses to take responsibility for what has happened. Indeed, 'tis said he casts covetous eyes on Tathwick, seeing it as a means to reward one of his supporters by giving him the property, and likely you as well, as heiress of the place."

Cicely bowed her head. Her poor father, after all he had lost . . . to once again be the victim of the king's greed. " 'Tis so unjust, so wicked . . ."

Lady Pembroke nodded. " 'Tis why the rebels rise against John. He has committed many such acts of greed and treachery. Mine own son, William, has vowed to bring the king to heel."

"And your husband, Lady Pembroke?" Simon asked. "What side does he favor?"

A look of grief crossed the countess's face. "He says he is sworn to the king, and he must keep faith with his oath . . . no matter what John does."

Her words hardly reached Cicely. The reality of her father's death was slowly sinking in. When Simon squeezed her hand, she began to weep, silently at first, then as if a dam had burst, she turned into his arms and sobbed harshly against his chest.

The pain welled up inside her, in wave after wave. *He is gone, and I never had a chance to say goodbye . . . to tell him that I loved him! I defied his will and disobeyed him—even as he went to his death!*

"Cicely, sweeting, drink some more hippocras. 'Twill calm you."

The coaxing words reached her from a distance. She shook her head. If she tried to drink, she would vomit. She was sick with guilt, with regret. She wanted to die . . .

"Take her to my chamber. She can rest there."

" 'Tis most kind of you, Lady Pembroke."

Voices swirled around Cicely. She was lifted and carried to a bed. A cup was pressed to her lips, and a warm liquid slid down her throat. She stopped struggling and swallowed, giving in to the oblivion.

"Poor little thing. She took it very hard." Lady Pembroke sat down wearily when they returned to the solar.

Simon sat across from her. He felt very shaken. Cicely's grief over her father's passing reminded him all too keenly of his own fears. If he received word that his parents were dead, would he not know the same terrible loss? The despair . . .

"Mayhap I should have been more tactful, but I thought . . . with you coming so soon after William de Gascon"—Lady Pembroke fidgeted with her rings—"I thought certainly she must know about her father and brother already. I should have waited until she had rested a bit from her travels . . ."

"There was no easy way," Simon reassured her. " 'Tis clear she loved her father, for all their conflicts."

Lady Pembroke's gaze probed him. "I had imagined she had not seen her father for some time, as she was living at Montreau, but I did not know they were estranged."

"The matter of her living at Montreau was the very thing they disagreed over. Cicely was never happy there. She told me that she had made a vow the day her father brought her there that she would one day leave."

Lady Pembroke raised her dark, elegant brows. "That is very bold for a young maid."

"Don't be misled by Cicely's delicate demeanor, when it comes to strength of will, she is a force to be reckoned with."

"And may I presume you are in a position to know something about her 'strength of will'?"

Lady Pembroke's expression was arch, and Simon could not keep back a small smile. "Indeed, I am. I have known her near four months now, and in that time she has managed to sway me to her desired course of action many, many times." He gestured helplessly. "I'm afraid I no longer attempt to oppose her in anything. There is simply no point to it."

"And yet you seem content."

"All men must serve some master. If I must bend my will to someone else's, why should it not be to that of a beautiful young woman?"

"You seem most wise for a man of your years," Lady Pembroke said with a smile.

"I have seen much and done much in my life already."

"I did note that you wear the mark of a crusader."

Simon's amusement faded. "Aye, I took the Cross and traveled as far as Constantinople, where I took ill with a fever. But even though I did not reach the Holy Land, I saw enough to . . ."

"To what?" Lady Pembroke prompted.

Simon shook his head. He could not tell her of the horrors he had seen, the things he was responsible for. His despair must remain his own. "I saw enough to know that kindness and goodness are rare things, and must be valued and protected."

Lady Pembroke nodded fervently. "You certainly speak the truth in that, Sir Simon."

For a moment, her thoughts seemed far away. Then, abruptly, she appeared to shake off the mood. "You've reassured me that Cicely is strong and will recover from her grief. 'Tis a good thing, too, as her situation has become quite complicated. Normally, since Cicely was already dedicated to the church, Robert de Valois would be considered to have died without heirs, and Tathwick would revert to the king. But since she never took vows, Cicely is still in a position to inherit.''

Lady Pembroke steepled her fingers, frowning. "John will probably try to claim the property, especially given that he is in the wrong. To make concessions to the Valois family would be an admission that he was responsible for his mercenaries' outrageous actions.''

"You seem to know much about how the king thinks,'' Simon said.

"Indeed. Having been the victim, and the benefactor, of his ofttimes capricious moods, I have sought to discover a means of predicting them.''

"And knowing what you do of John, what do you advise Cicely?''

Lady Pembroke fixed her gaze on Simon. "If Cicely forsakes her claim to Tathwick, you would be free to wed her, with the approval of her closest kinsman, my husband. Without Tathwick, whom she marries is of little interest to the king.''

"But that seems very unjust. Tathwick belongs to Cicely. Her father and brother died protecting the property!''

"I did not say John would be fair or just. In fact, I suggested otherwise.''

"And if Cicely insists on claiming the property?''

Lady Pembroke shook her head. "The king may favor her cause, but then he will wed her off to a man of his choosing. A man willing to pay a great deal for the privilege, and one who can be counted on to support him if there is war. It would not be you, Sir Simon. I would swear to it.''

"Jesu,'' Simon sighed, "Robert de Valois' death has certainly complicated things. I have sworn to make Cicely my wife, but how am I to do that now?''

"As I've said, if Cicely renounces her claim, which could be easily done based on her years in the priory, she would be free to wed you."

Simon grimaced. "Cicely may have to choose between marrying me or keeping Tathwick."

Lady Pembroke nodded. "Although there is another course. If the rebel barons succeed in coercing the king to agree to their demands, you might appeal to John while he is desperate. In exchange for a hefty relief fee, he might allow you to wed Cicely and keep Tathwick. If that situation should arise, do you have the funds to pay for your heiress?"

"Aye, although I have not spoken of it with Cicely, I am heir to substantial property. I could raise the necessary funds."

Lady Pembroke cocked a brow. "And why, might I ask, have you not revealed your circumstances to Cicely?"

Simon rose. "Since I returned to England, I have not been back to my family's property."

"And you are not certain of what condition it is in? Then, how do you know you can afford to wed Cicely?"

" 'Tis not a matter of whether there is anything to claim, but whether I can bear to go back there. I left under . . . difficult circumstances."

"Go on," she said gently.

Simon paced across the tiled floor. "It fair broke my mother's heart when I left on Crusade. She begged me not to go. She wept and clung to me. And still I went." He turned to face Lady Pembroke. "I have been a coward this past twelvemonth. I have refused to go home, for fear of what I would find."

"What is it you fear?"

"That I will find what Cicely has just discovered, that my loved ones are lost to me."

"You won't go back because you're afraid they're dead?"

He nodded. "Foolish, isn't it? Foolish and childish. I did not realize how much so until I saw Cicely's grief. At that moment, I suddenly knew if there was any chance that they were alive, I must go to them.''

''Your reluctance baffles me. Do you have reason to believe your family has perished? Were they in ill health when you left?''

''Nay. My parents were both fit and healthy, which is all the more reason for my fear. I dread that . . . my mother . . . that she may have died of grief over me—that I . . . I have killed her.'' Simon took a deep breath. Did saying the words aloud make them more likely to be true?

''Forgive me, Sir Simon, but 'foolish and childish' do not begin to cover the matter. If your mother is dead, your going home will neither lessen nor improve the matter. But if she lives, then seeing you would ease her heartache and set her back upon the pathway to health. You have everything to gain by going home, nothing to lose.''

He smiled weakly. ''I was thinking the very same thing but a few moments ago.''

''Where is your home, Simon?''

''In Wiltshire. Near Malmsbury.''

''Why, that is not so far from my dower estates along the Wye! Pray tell, who is your father? Mayhap I have heard of him.''

''Fawkes de Cressy.''

''Fawkes?'' Lady Pembroke's eyes opened wide, then narrowed. ''You do not have the look of him. Not at all.''

Simon smiled ruefully. ''So people have said all my life. Indeed, if my mother did not vouch for the circumstances of my conception, I doubt anyone would believe I was his son.''

''He acknowledges you?''

''Aye, he does. Apparently he recalls the same incident as my mother.''

''Impudent knave,'' Lady Pembroke said, but she returned

his smile. "I have met your father on more than one occasion. A fine, worthy knight he is. Are you his only child?"

"Aye."

"Which makes you heir to considerable property. Enough that you hardly need Tathwick."

"That is true, but the matter is not up to me. 'Tis Cicely's decision whether she wishes to claim her inheritance."

"Do you doubt her love for you, that you think she might desire to keep her birthright rather than wed you?"

"You said there was a possibility she might be able to do both."

"Aye, a small possibility, but I would not advise pursuing it. The risks are great. Lady Cicely might well end up losing both her lands and her choice in a husband."

It was Simon's turn to sigh. "Defying the king is the most dangerous, complicated, and risky course of action. Obviously, that is the one Cicely will choose."

"You have great faith in her determination and resolve."

"Do you know another soul, man or woman, who made a vow as a child and then kept to it ten years later?"

Lady Pembroke shook her head. "I admire your lady's courage, but I also fear for her. As you know, the world is a cruel place for those who cannot back up their ideals with a strong sword arm."

"Then, I will be Cicely's sword arm," Simon said, "even as she inspires me with her undaunted spirit."

CHAPTER 15

The grief overwhelmed Cicely. It carried her away like a raging river, swollen over its banks. Helpless, she floated upon the turbulent force. Down, down into the darkness, a whirlpool of bitter regrets and painful memories.

But when she woke, she was calm, for she knew suddenly what she must do.

Her first vision when she opened her eyes was of Simon leaning over her. His blue gaze was so tender it near made her weep again. But she choked the tears back and sat up, gripping his hand tightly.

"Better?" he asked.

She nodded.

"Would you like something to eat? Your stomach must be unsettled from wine and no food."

"Nay, Simon. I want you to bring me your sword."

His eyes widened in alarm. "Why? What do you mean to do?"

"I mean to swear a vow. A vow to avenge my father's death."

Simon shook his head. "There can be no vengeance against a king. Your father would not want you to risk your life trying."

"But 'tis John's fault! His forces struck my father down. But I must do something. Find some way to atone . . ."

" 'Twas not your fault, Cicely." He took her hands in his. "I know what your thoughts are. You think because you defied your father's wishes, somehow you brought this to pass. But the truth is, he would have died even if you had remained at Montreau. Leaving there changed nothing."

She took a deep breath. "But I . . . I never forgave him." The tears began to flow again. "He came to see me once, nigh on five years ago it was." Her voice broke. "I refused to see him."

She bowed her head and gave vent to her tears. When the racking sobs eased, she continued. "I convinced myself that he did not care for me. But now I wonder. What if he regretted what he did, and I never gave him a chance to tell me?"

Simon pulled her close, cradling her against his breast. Again, the pain seized her. It wrenched her body again and again, until she was limp and weak. And still, Simon held her. She felt his strength, his love, and it was that awareness which finally enabled her to regain control.

Simon handed her a cloth, and she wiped at her face. The subtle sound of a throat being cleared alerted Cicely to Lady Pembroke's presence. She glanced at her, embarrassed to be seen in such *déshabillé*. But Lady Pembroke did not appear discomfited. She gestured for Simon to take away the tear-soaked cloth and said, "Now it is time for you to eat, my dear. No matter what you decide to do, you will need your strength."

Simon helped Cicely to a chair near the hearth and she took a few swallows of warm broth. Then, remembering Lady

Pembroke's words, she asked, "What do you mean, no matter what I decide to do?"

"By rights, you are mistress of Tathwick, but"—Lady Pembroke glanced dubiously at Simon—"to claim the estate, you may well have to forget your plans to wed Sir Simon."

Cicely put down the broth. "I don't understand. Why can't I wed Simon? Do you think the earl will forbid it? Oh, truly, I don't care if Simon doesn't have any property! With Tathwick, I can provide for both of us!"

Lady Pembroke arched a brow. "Even if Sir Simon's dignity is not distressed by such a proposal, 'tis nigh impossible. As you are an heiress, Cicely, the king has a right to decide whom you wed."

Cicely's jaw tensed with her fury. "The king! 'Twas his men who murdered my father!"

Lady Pembroke sighed. "It does not matter. He still has the right to choose your husband."

Fury flooded Cicely's body. "That is so unfair, so vilely unjust!"

"There is another possible course," Simon suggested. "If you decide to use Tathwick's forces in the rebel cause and they succeed, you might be able to force the king to give you Tathwick, as well as the right to marry where you will."

"But that means war. More men will die!"

"It seems likely that war will come at any rate," Lady Pembroke said. "But whether you throw Tathwick's forces in with the rebels, that is up to you. There is grave risk in it. If the rebels should lose, Tathwick would be forfeit and"—she glanced at Simon—"all who are involved with the rebel cause are likely to be punished."

Cicely had a vision of Simon secured with chains, his face a mask of hopelessness. It made her shudder.

But then she remembered the tragic deaths of her father and brother and tears threatened again. *Poor Papa! And poor Hugh!*

The image of her brother's young face filled her mind. Although they were not close, being too different to be compatible, they had shared many of the trials and lessons of growing up. *And now he is gone. I am the only one left!*

"How can I renounce Tathwick?" she demanded. "How can I relinquish the property they gave up their lives for?"

She looked at Simon and contemplated him dead or imprisoned. She shook her head and added, "Then again, how can I not? I have no right to risk men's lives for the sake of my father's dream."

Simon approached her and took her hand in his. "You must do what your heart tells you, Cicely. Don't worry for me."

She met his gaze, stricken. "I must choose, mustn't I? My love, my heart's desire, or . . . duty."

"Only you can know what you must do," he said gently.

She took a shaky breath. "I might have known there would be a price for loving you."

Simon met her gaze, and she could see the turmoil in his eyes, mirroring her own. "There is no need to decide this day, Cicely. You have time to consider your choices and discover which one your conscience demands you take."

She shook her head, already knowing what she would choose. "When I was at Montreau, I wanted to be free, to choose my own destiny. And so, in a bitter twist of fate, I get my wish." She gave him a grim smile. "I am free at last, Simon, and now I find my freedom has become a greater prison than Montreau ever was."

"There may yet be a way to happiness in all of this." Lady Pembroke laid a hand on Cicely's arm. "As I've said, if the rebel forces succeed, 'tis possible you would be able to keep your inheritance and marry Simon."

"Think you that they will?" Cicely asked eagerly. "Has your lord husband told you which side he favors?"

Lady Pembroke shook her head. "The earl is beholden to

King John for everything he possesses, and he will not speak ill of his liege even in private. If you do this thing, Lady Cicely, you must do it upon your own will. I cannot aid you, except to provide you an escort to Tathwick. Your lady mother awaits you there. Mayhap she could advise you in this matter.''

Awareness dawned on Cicely. If she decided to use the forces of Tathwick to fight the king, she would be guilty of treason. She dare not let the taint of that affect her godfather. She must leave Pembroke as soon as possible.

She bowed formally to Lady Pembroke. ''I thank you for your kindness. I will accept your offer of an escort and leave for Tathwick tomorrow.''

Her benefactor frowned. ''Are you certain that is not too soon? You've had a great shock and are already weary from traveling. I would not have you fall ill.''

''I am well enough.'' Cicely tried to smile. ''I have grown used to traveling. 'Tis no longer a hardship.''

Lady Pembroke appeared unconvinced, but she made no protest. Cicely realized suddenly how precarious the house of Pembroke's position was. King John, suspicious and distrustful as he was, might easily misconstrue her visit here and bring his wrath down upon William Marshal.

Lady Pembroke moved to leave the room, and Simon also appeared ready to depart.

''Wait, Simon!'' Cicely called.

Both he and Lady Pembroke paused. Cicely approached Simon. ''I would speak with you in private.''

He glanced uneasily at the bed, but Lady Pembroke made a complacent gesture. ''You have been alone together near the whole journey here. I trust that Sir Simon's honor will withstand this temptation as well. Good even.'' In a swish of skirts, she was gone.

Cicely stared at Simon. There was so much she must say.

Would he hate her for choosing duty over the longings of her heart? "Simon, I—"

He stalled her words with a shake of his head. "There is no need to say it. I know that you must fight for Tathwick. I do not feel bitterness over your choice. I know what pain it costs you."

"Oh, Simon!" She threw herself in his arms. "What am I to do? If I lose you, I will die!"

She began to kiss him, moving her lips tenderly over his beloved face. She pressed herself against his broad chest as if she might never let go.

"Hush," he whispered. "You won't lose me. Somehow we will find a way to be together, I vow it."

She melted into his arms, feeling his strength, inhaling the comforting scent of him. Her kisses became more passionate. She coaxed him to open his mouth, to yield to the heat which rose between them. As she rubbed against him, she could feel the hard ridge of his manhood beneath his chausses. He wanted her as badly as she wanted him.

She pulled on his tunic and edged backward toward the bed. "Please, Simon. This might be the only night we have together. The only night I will have to dream of for the rest of my life."

"Nay," he whispered. "There will be others, I promise. Nights when we are wed and 'tis my right to love you."

"Please, please, don't deny me now!"

"I must. What would happen if I got you with child?"

"Then the king would have to let you wed me," she murmured between kisses. She had worked her hands beneath his tunic, sighing as her fingers found the hard, warm flesh beneath.

"Nay, he would not. He could marry you to anyone he wished, and another man would raise my child." Simon pulled away, and grasping her wrists, held her at arm's length. "I cannot do it. I cannot forget all I believe in for one night of passion."

Tears sprang to Cicely's eyes, but she forced them back. "Oh, Simon, you are the despair of me. I vow, I would ravish you if I could . . ." She turned away and caught her breath. Simon and his cursed honor. But she would not try to suborn his will. She would not hurt him that way.

When she turned to look at him, he was smiling. "Ravish me, would you? No maid but you would say such a silly thing."

She smiled back. " 'Tis true. I even tried such a thing when we were at Montreau. That last night, when I came to your bed. I did not know what I was about. I think I gave you too much poppy. You were"—her gaze skidded to his groin—"you were not capable."

He grinned. "Jesu, you must have rendered me completely senseless. I have been 'capable' almost every waking moment since!"

"I'm sorry, Simon. 'Twas wrong of me to do that. Wrong of me to let you think that you had dishonored me."

"It did not take me long to discover the truth. Indeed, I think I knew almost immediately. My body did not feel as if it had been satisfied."

"But if you knew you did not owe me anything, why did you agree to take me with you?"

He shrugged. "Even then, I was loath to part company with you. You were like a beam of sunshine in my cold, gray life. I could scarce bear to leave you and return to my loneliness."

"That is a relief." Her smile broadened. "I have felt guilty for my deceit ever since."

He rolled his eyes. "Aye, so guilty you have tried a dozen times since to seduce me."

She leaned close to him. "I cannot help myself. I fear I will try again and again on our journey to Tathwick."

He put his hands on either side of her face and tilted it up to his. "I cannot go with you, Cicely. You will be safe enough with an escort."

"Not go with me!" She pulled away. "How can you abandon me now? Is it because . . . because you think I have chosen Tathwick over you?"

"Nay." His blue eyes beseeched her. "I have to go home, Cicely. Back to my own lands, my family."

"But I thought—"

"You thought I was a penniless knight with no place to call home." He sighed heavily. "For a time I convinced myself that my family was lost to me, that I could never return. But on this journey I have discovered that my staying away is cowardly. I must go and face them, and if they are dead and I cannot beg their forgiveness, then I will have to live with that upon my soul. In trying to spare myself, I may have caused them greater grief. 'Tis past time I redeem myself."

"Your parents are living?"

"I know not. I have feared these past five years that I destroyed them with my cold refusal to heed their wishes. Especially my mother. I broke her heart, and I dreaded she died hating me."

"I don't understand. Did you receive news that she was ailing?"

"Nay." He shook his head. "I don't expect you to understand. 'Tis simply that . . . I felt so lost, so damned when I left Constantinople. And I believed I deserved to be punished even more. Though there was no reason to think they were dead, I convinced myself that the responsibility for my parents' deaths rested upon my shoulders, that I could never go back and claim my inheritance."

"Your inheritance?"

"Three castles in Wiltshire."

"You are wealthy! And all this while I have pitied you and worried over you."

"I'm sorry, Cicely. I did not mean to mislead you. I honestly

felt in my heart that everything in my past was lost to me."
He put his hand on her arm. " 'Twas only when I fell in love
with you and my soul began to heal that I realized how foolish
and cruel I had been not to go home. And then, when I discovered that I could not give you up, I began to think of claiming
my birthright. I knew I must have something to offer or your
godfather would never let me have you as my wife." He turned
her to face him. "It does not change anything between us, does
it?"

She saw the fear in his eyes and had to repress a smile. "If
I thought you were rich and found out you were poor, I would
still love you, so why should the other way distress me? Rich
or poor, Simon, you hold my heart."

He exhaled on a sigh. "Then, you understand why I must
go to them, though I dread to be parted from you?"

She nodded. "You have delayed overlong already."

He lifted up her hands and kissed them. "You are an angel,
Cicely."

"Nay, not an angel." She leaned into him and kissed him
long and hard on the mouth. "Angels don't seek to seduce
unwilling men."

For a moment, Simon gave in to the erotic energy moving
between them. Cicely was right. She was not an angel. And
he was not unwilling.

Their mouths melded and mated, and he drank in the scent
and feel of her, committing it to memory. Leaving her would
be the hardest thing he had ever done.

"I will meet you at Tathwick as soon as I am able," he
whispered between kisses. "But for now, I wish you Godspeed."

She clung to him a moment longer, then stepped back, her
face resigned and yearning at the same time. "Godspeed, my
love."

*   *   *

Simon gazed up through the heavy mist, trying to make out the shape of Valmar Castle. A thousand memories washed over him. Home. He had thought never to see it again, had not believed he deserved to look upon its familiar silhouette.

The mist thinned, revealing the high towers, and his stomach clenched. He drew rein and stared. What would he say to her? How could he beg his mother for forgiveness? After all these years of silence.

He closed his eyes and prayed for strength, then opened them and urged the destrier forward.

Market day. The drawbridge was let out, and the traffic across its narrow span was brisk, yet peaceful. King John's war had not touched this place. Or had it? There seemed to be more guards patrolling the walls than he remembered.

His mount fell into step between an ox-drawn wain loaded with barrels and two friars walking side by side, deep in conversation. Simon strained to hear the monks' words, but caught only enough to torment his agitated brain. He wanted to scream, *The lord and lady of Valmar—do they live?* But he did not, merely clutched the reins in a white-knuckled grip and stared fixedly at the open gate ahead.

Inside the keep, he breathed deeply. As if the place would smell the same, conjuring memories of childhood.

And it did. Soldiers. Baking bread. Damp wool. Dogs and horses. The dark miasma of the moat, blown into the bailey by the wind. A rich mixture of scents, as intricate as one of the tapestries on the wall in his mother's solar.

Ah, the tapestries. How many hours as a child had he spent gazing at the scene portraying King Arthur and his knights, imagining himself transported into the magical world of the past?

He would squint at the dense background of green, umber,

tan, and gray until the colored threads blurred to form a real forest. Then, in his mind, he stepped into the lush greenery, and a huge white stallion greeted him, nuzzling his fingers. He mounted the stallion, his golden armor winking in the sunlight, and rode off to fight dragons and rescue fair damsels.

The aching bitterness inside him deepened at the memory. Real knighthood was nothing like his childhood fantasies. It was bloody, disgusting, miserable work. And the causes that real knights fought for were far from exalted. Greed and power, revenge and hatred. Even the holy war had been like a carcass left in the desert sun. On the outside it appeared untainted, but underneath it seethed with maggots and putrefaction.

And that was the dream he had left this place for. A dream of glory and righteousness. That, like King Arthur's knights, he could pursue a holy cause and redeem his sinful soul.

Lies, all of it. He had squandered his youth, his health, his faith, and all for nothing.

But, in truth, he was fortunate. He was alive, while so many of his companions had died. His body was mended, his spirit, too. Cicely had healed him.

He had stood so long in the bailey, people began to give him curious looks. They recognized that he was not some rough mercenary come to offer his sword arm in service to the lord of Valmar. His horse and clothing were too fine. Mayhap they thought he looked familiar, though it had been five long years since he'd left.

Then, one of the knights crossing the yard stopped in his tracks and stared at Simon. A broad grin split the man's weathered face. "Simon," he bellowed. "God's teeth, 'tis the heir! He's come back!"

It seemed that every servant and retainer in the yard turned to gawk at him. Many of them looked doubtful, obviously wondering how dark-haired Fawkes and raven-tressed Lady

Nicola could have a birthed a son so fair. But others nodded and smiled, abruptly recognizing him.

The shout went up. "Fetch the lady!" they cried. "Praise God, Sir Simon has returned."

Simon allowed himself to be borne to the keep, half-carried along on the wave of enthusiastic servants and knights. A sense of unreality crept over him. They were giving him a hero's welcome, but he was not a hero. He had dreaded this reckoning, and like a spineless fool, he had put it off near a twelvemonth since arriving in England.

The great hall looked the same as when he'd left it. Simon blinked in the dim rushlight as, with a sharp pang, he recalled the last time he was here. A child he had been then, a callow, stupid youth.

Yet the servants recognized him. Recognized in the weary man the wistful boy he had once been. His outer appearance must not be so altered.

They dragged the huge, carved lord's chair down from the dais and over near the hearth. There they made him sit, promising to fetch "the lady" as soon as possible.

A serving girl came to offer him wine. She was young and comely, her gold braids swinging as she shyly held out the cup. Her gaze rested on him with a look of awe and adoration, and Simon felt even more a fraud. Did they not know that he returned not as the triumphant victor, but in defeat?

A flush rose to his face, and he grimaced, feeling like a fool. Then he saw her, and all his other turmoil faded in the face of a helpless yearning.

She was smaller than he remembered, her black hair streaked with white near the temples. But she was still beautiful. Her gray eyes shone like opals as she crossed the room to him. The crowd parted and grew silent in her wake. Simon stood, though his legs quivered beneath him.

He could not bear the intensity of her gaze, nor the sight of the tears running down her face. As she neared him, he fell to his knees in the rushes and bowed his head.

She met him there, dropping to her knees and clutching him close. "Oh, my darling, Simon," she moaned. "You've come home."

Simon kept his head bowed, afraid of the tears which threatened to spill from his own eyes. When he finally regained his composure, he raised his head and looked at her. In the croaking voice of a half-grown squire, he said, "My lady mother, I do heartily beg your pardon."

She cuffed him on the shoulder and gave him a girlish, tinkling laugh. Then she hugged him again, even more tightly this time.

She felt fragile and small in his arms, and an overwhelming feeling of protectiveness surged through him. How blessed he was. He had not lost her.

After a time, she stood and urged him to his feet. "What a spectacle we have made," she said breathlessly. "But 'tis not every day that my only son returns from the dead. Where have you been, Simon? The last word we had was that you were terribly ill with a fever. We feared"—her voice trembled—"the worst."

Simon shook his head, stricken with guilt once more. "I'm sorry, Maman, I can only beg your forgiveness for not coming home sooner. I . . . the fever, somehow it seemed to affect my mind. I was prey to strange fancies, terrible thoughts. Somehow, I could not—"

"I don't care what your reasons are, only that you are here." She gave another slightly hysterical laugh. "I told Fawkes that you could not be dead, that I would know if I had lost you."

"Papa—where is he?" Sudden fear afflicted Simon.

"He's gone to the village, but they will have fetched him. Come, we'll await him in the solar." His mother pulled on his arm, and he obediently followed her through the mass of servants and soldiers gathered to witness their reunion. A cheer rose up as they passed by, and as Simon's tension eased, his mood edged toward a giddy euphoria. His mother was alive, and she had forgiven him!

The sights and smells of his mother's solar again brought tears to his eyes. Everything seemed unchanged, as if he had never left. The mixture of herbs his mother used to freshen the room tickled his nostrils, and he remembered the dried clusters of lavender, meadowsweet and rosemary she hung by the window so the sunlight would release their scents.

Her embroidery lay on the arm of the chair with the red velvet cushion—the cushion he had once used as a shield in a mock battle with one of the other squires. The underside would still show the place where his mother had mended it after one of the blunted sticks they'd used as weapons had pierced the fabric. His father had bellowed that he should be whipped for his disgraceful behavior, but his mother would not allow it. She was ever indulgent of him. And so overprotective that he sometimes felt he would suffocate from her attentions.

But now he welcomed her devouring gaze, the tender warmth in her eyes.

She bade him sit and commanded a page to fetch them some wine, then took a seat across from him. For a time she simply stared at him, as if his mere presence was enough to satisfy her.

Simon cleared his throat. "You are looking well, Maman."

She waved away the compliment. "And you, Simon . . . you look different."

"I am a man," he answered simply.

She nodded. "So you are. I vow you are a half handspan taller than when I last saw you. But thinner . . ." Her forehead puckered in a frown.

"I have been traveling and have not had the opportunity to eat well."

"Where . . . where have you been?" The words were spoken carefully, as if she feared he would bolt if she questioned him too closely.

He opened his mouth to answer, but a loud voice from the doorway forestalled his words.

"Aye, where have you been, Simon?"

His father's face was stern, his dark eyes wary. Not quite the ecstatic greeting his mother had given him.

Simon rose as his father entered the room, and found to his surprise that his sire seemed to have shrunk. Simon now stood taller than his father, and was likely broader across the shoulders as well.

Fawkes saw his assessing gaze. "Don't count your victory too quickly, though I might not have your reach or strength, I have cunning and years of experience on my side."

Simon gazed at his father in shock. "You wish to fight me?"

His mother gave a gasp and got to her feet. Abruptly, Fawkes' face relaxed. "Of course not, you foolish pup! You mother would never forgive me if I beat your thick, stubborn head into the ground as I ought to."

He grinned and, holding out his arms, advanced to Simon. "Come here, boy, and greet your father."

They embraced awkwardly, and when Simon pulled back, he was surprised to see tears glinting in his father's eyes. He'd thought Fawkes would hate him for the pain he had caused.

"Does this mean I'm forgiven?" Simon asked.

Fawkes snorted. "Hell, no! I'll have your hide sometime, boy. I'll just have to wait for the right opportunity." He glanced at his wife and then winked at Simon. "She can't hover over you day and night. I'll get my chance eventually."

Simon exhaled a sigh of relief; then they all stood there uncomfortably, as if none of them knew how to begin. The wine arrived, and his mother poured them all goblets and handed them around, then said, "Now, Simon, tell us everything."

Of course, he did not. He spared her the horror of what happened in Constantinople, as well as the gravity of his sickness. Although he thought sometime he would like to speak to his father about the evil he had seen and experienced, he knew it was not fit for his lady mother's ears. For her sake, he dwelled upon the sights he had seen on his journey, the treasures and magnificent buildings of Constantinople.

But when he finished, he sighed and met her gaze. "You were right, Maman. 'Twas all a lie. I should never have gone on Crusade. I never should have hurt you so."

She shook her head, regarding him tenderly. "Nay, I was the one who was wrong. I tried to keep you from becoming a man. 'Twas selfish and weak of me. I feared I would lose you, so I kept you too close and smothered you. You had to go, Simon."

He heaved a sigh. "Mayhap you are right, after all. If I had not gone on Crusade, I would not have contracted the fever. Then, I would not have fallen sick near Montreau Priory and met Cicely."

"You have been sick so recently?" His mother looked alarmed.

"Aye, I had another bout of the fever a few months ago. I was taken to Montreau Priory and there nursed back to health."

"By the nuns?" his father asked.

Simon nodded.

Fawkes frowned severely. "Sweet Jesu, you have not fallen in love with a holy sister, have you?"

"He said naught about love," his mother interjected.

"Nay, but from the look on his face, 'tis plain enough!"

Simon could not help laughing. "Aye, you have guessed aright, Papa. Cicely is my beloved, the woman I wish to wed. But," he added at seeing their stricken looks, "she never took vows, so that is not a difficulty."

He watched his parents visibly relax. "So, where is she?" his father demanded. "Why did you not bring her to meet us?"

"She recently received troubling news. Her father and brother were killed in a skirmish with John's mercenaries. Now, suddenly, she is an heiress. She felt she must go home to her mother, and also"—here Simon hesitated, wondering what his parents would think of Cicely's fierce resolve to hold Tathwick—"she has some notion to join the rebel cause and have what remains of her father's garrison join the fight against John."

"Who will lead them?" Fawkes asked in a deadly quiet voice.

"I will," Simon said.

CHAPTER 16

"Bloody hell!" Fawkes lunged to his feet. "Don't you realize that if the rebel barons lose, you'll be guilty of treason? You might never be allowed to inherit Valmar, Rosebrook—any of your birthright!"

Simon spoke quietly. "I know, Father. But there is no other way. Except for Cicely to renounce all rights to Tathwick, and she feels she cannot do that. It's been in her family for generations, since her great-great-great grandsire himself came over with the Conqueror. Her father died to preserve Tathwick. How can she, in good conscience, let it go?"

"Because she is a maid!" his father exploded. "No one expects a woman to fight for her family property. Especially when she is betrothed to a man as wealthy as you. Tell me, is she so attached to the place that she is willing to risk *your* life to save it? How much does she truly care for you that she would hazard your future for a piece of land?"

His father's caustic words made Simon's stomach clench.

He understood Cicely's decision, but how was he to convince his parents that her determination did not arise out of lack of love for him but, rather, an obligation to her family?

Simon shook his head. "She was estranged from her father. She feels guilt over his death, and she is trying to atone."

"By risking *your* life and future!"

Simon made a helpless gesture. How could he explain Cicely? There was likely no other woman in England like her.

'Twas his mother's turn to speak. Unlike Fawkes, she kept her voice low and calm, "My dear son, are you satisfied that this is the right thing to do? Are you very certain that this Cicely cares for you as much as you do for her?"

"Aye, Mother. I am certain. If you could but meet Cicely . . . behold her sweet, gentle countenance . . . you would not doubt her either."

"Mayhap that is the way of it then. I will have to meet her."

The steely determination in his mother's gray eyes made Simon tense. "Maman, what do you mean?"

"This time when you leave Valmar, I will go with you."

Simon said nothing as his father ranted and raved, forbidding Lady Nicola to even consider doing such a foolish thing. Long ago, he had learned that for all his father's fierce will, his mother's was even stronger. She sat quietly now, her face serene, like a content, self-satisfied cat, while Fawkes' countenance grew flushed and the veins in his temple pulsed.

After a time, Fawkes gave an exhausted sigh. "There is no point to my reasoning with you, is there? You will do what you will, as you always have."

Lady Nicola rose, a fond smile on her lips. " 'Twill be all right, dearest. I will meet Cicely and advise Simon on his strategies. He is a man now, and we must let him go."

Fawkes swore heartily under his breath. Then he went to his wife and kissed her. Simon, who had long ago grown used to his parents' affectionate gestures, felt a warm contentment well

up inside him. 'Twas the greatest blessing of all—to love and
be loved.

Cicely found this journey across England to be much different
than her last one. 'Twas markedly faster as well as more comfortable. She and her escort spent the night at inns and castles
along the way. Many times she and Elgatha, the quiet older
woman whom Lady Pembroke had insisted accompany her as
a bodyservant, enjoyed the luxury of a private chamber where
they could wash the dust of the road from their faces and hands
and eat their evening meal in quiet.

Even so, after days of constant travel, Cicely was so weary
that when they finally arrrived at Tathwick and she beheld the
place of her birth and childhood, she felt little more than relief.
Compared to Pembroke, or even Blackhurst, Tathwick Castle
seemed very small. Cicely wondered at the tricks of memory
which had invested it with such splendor and magnificence.
But she had seen it with a child's eyes then, and now she was
a woman. Now she also faced the grim prospect of going to
war to keep this modest, rather insignificant, fortress in the
hands of her family.

But then they progressed into the yard and she saw a man
running toward them, and she knew suddenly why her resolve
was so strong. His face was lined and grizzled, but she would
have known Sir Henry FitzWilliam anywhere. Her father's
seneschal obviously recognized her as well, for his broken-
toothed smile was radiant.

A lump rose in Cicely's throat as she considered all the years
this man had faithfully served her family. How could she fail
to fight for Tathwick when to fail to do so reduced this man's
whole life to an empty, purposeless thing? She could not desert
Henry FitzWilliam to a new master, one who might well strip
him of his duties and rob him of his honor and pride. 'Twould

be like sending an old hound, who has served well and long, out into the cold to die.

"My Lady Cicely," the seneschal exulted as he dropped to his knees in the muck before her mount. Cicely did not wait for someone to help her down, but slid from her horse and rushed to grasp his hands.

"Get up, Sir Harry. Don't you dare bow before me. 'Tis merely little Cicely, after all. I have not changed so much."

Sir Harry embraced her roughly. "Aye, you have not," he said, still beaming. "You are the same little ray of sunshine you always were."

"Was it not 'devilish imp' you used to call me?" Cicely teased. "I fear your memory has faded greatly if you remember me as always a delight. I caused you more than a little grief, as I recall."

Sir Harry rose stiffly to his feet. He seemed much heavier than she recalled and slower. 'Twas a wonder, and a credit to his excitement, that he had been able to run across the yard to greet her.

"Aye, you did vex me," he said, "but 'twas little things. Enticing my men away from their duties for trivial matters, such as to fetch your pig's-bladder ball from the midden and to dine upon the gooseberry tarts you made 'just yourself.' No harm was done, and in truth, you were the pet of all of us."

Odd, how time changed one's perspective. Cicely smiled at the memory of Sir Harry grumbling and carrying on to her mother about that "little minx of a daughter she had birthed."

Then Sir Harry heaved a sigh and his expression grew solemn. " 'Tis sorry I am about your father and brother, lass."

Cicely nodded as tears threatened. No joyful homecoming this, but a sorrowful reckoning with the harsh responsibilities ahead of her. "I want to know the details of my father's death," she said.

Sir Harry shook his head. "I would spare you that. 'Tis not a fit thing for a young maid to hear of."

"But I will hear it," Cicely pronounced resolutely. "I will also hear of his friends and allies, those men who have not given up their struggle against the king's unlawful dictates."

"But what is the point of that?" Sir Harry asked in dismay. "If you align Tathwick with those who fight the king, you stand to lose everything. As it is now, since you and your mother possess the only strong claim to Tathwick, and you are but helpless women, King John might be moved to let you keep it."

Cicely gritted her teeth at the words "helpless women," and her voice grew grim and bitter. "Aye, John *might* let me keep my inheritance. But you know as well as I what the price will be. He will marry me off to the man willing to pay the most for the privilege of seizing Tathwick's land for his own purposes."

Sir Harry nodded sadly. " 'Tis true, lass. I won't lie to you. And knowing that John can be an avaricious devil, I do fear for you; he might wed you to someone cruel or despicable. Which is why I think the best course for you would be to return to Montreau and renounce your claim to Tathwick. If naught stands between John and Tathwick, I do not think he will deal with us too harshly. Your lady mother ails, and is clearly no threat to anyone. I cannot think even John would let ill befall her. And you would be safe at Montreau. Your vow to God would shield you from the king's designs."

"Nay." Cicely shook her head. "I will not go back to Montreau. I will die first."

"Jesu, I forgot how stubborn you are," Sir Harry complained. "I lay out the best course for you, and you refuse to consider it. Was priory life truly so terrible? You appear well fed and healthy enough; I cannot think you have been mistreated. Now that your father is gone—may God absolve him— can you not accept his will in this? He sent you to Montreau to protect you, and 'tis still the only true refuge you have. A mere woman cannot stand against the king's will. 'Tis madness!''

"I am not a 'mere woman,' " Cicely protested. "And I am betrothed to a brave and mighty knight who has vowed to defend Tathwick and my inheritance!"

"And where is he, this paragon?" Sir Harry made a show of peering around her at the troop of Pembroke knights. "I see no man stepping forward to stretch out his neck on the king's chopping block."

"He will come," Cicely said through clenched teeth. "He was detained by family matters of his own. But he will come."

"We'll speak of this later," Sir Harry said. "For now, you must go to your lady mother."

"You said she was ailing," Cicely said as she and the seneschal fell in step together on the way to the keep. " 'Tis not a serious malady, is it?''

Sir Harry sighed. "I don't know if 'tis grief or age or both, but she has begun to fail these few months past. Mayhap seeing you will revive her."

Cicely felt tension grip her muscles as she entered the great hall and looked around for her mother. Sir Henry shook his head and took her arm to propel her forward. "She does not come to the hall any longer. Nor much to her solar either. Indeed, the Lady Adela spends every waking moment in the chapel, on her knees in prayer."

Cicely tried to swallow down the lump of fear in her throat. She had lost the rest of her family; she could not bear the thought that she might lose her mother as well.

The chapel was located in the uppermost portion of the castle, where, as it had been explained to Cicely as a child, "nothing might come between the petitioner's prayers and heaven."

The first earl of Tathwick, who had built the castle near a century ago, had spared no expense in its construction. Rose-

colored marble, imported from the Continent, had been used
for the altar, and the cross-shaped windows flanking the nave
were glazed with rare colored glass. Finely carved stone effigies
of Cicely's illustrious ancestor and his wife sat in solemn state
behind the rail.

Cicely's father had oft complained about the waste. He said
he would prefer that his great-great grandsire had spent his
fortune fortifying the castle rather than seeking God's favor
with fine adornments to His house.

Outside the chapel door, Sir Harry gave Cicely's arm a gentle
squeeze. "I warn you, say nothing to your mother about your
plans for Tathwick. She has suffered greatly. I would not have
you grieve her."

The seneschal's voice was stern, and Cicely realized how
much he cared for her mother. She nodded dutifully as she
opened the door.

Inside, the small, high-ceilinged space seemed to sing with
light as rainbow hues from the costly windows mingled with
the mellow glow from dozens of beeswax candles lit around
the altar. In the center of the radiance knelt a small figure. Too
small, to be sure, to possibly be Lady Adela.

But it was. Slight as a child, Cicely's mother knelt upon the
cold stone floor before the altar, her head deeply bowed and
her pale, nearly transparent fingers movingly rapidly over the
rosary beads.

Cicely stood a moment, collecting herself, adjusting to the
shock of seeing her once strong and regal mother reduced to
this. Then she called out in a quavering voice, "Maman."

Adela turned her head and her eyes widened. "My darling
Cicely—can it be you?"

" 'Tis I." Cicely rushed to help her mother rise. Adela's
form seemed as frail and insubstantial as a bird's; her grip upon
Cicely's arm was weak and trembling.

"My child, let me look at you," she said. Dark eyes, the

skin beneath hollowed with strain, fixed on her face with an intensity which frightened Cicely.

"Maman, have you eaten today?" she asked.

"Eaten?" Lady Adela shook her head as if the very concept of food was foreign to her.

"Come, Mother," she coaxed. "Join me in the solar, and we will sup."

Her mother glanced worriedly at the crucifix behind the altar, as if she dared not leave her post.

"I'm hungry, Mother. It has been a long journey here, and I am near famished."

The mention of Cicely's needs seemed to jolt her mother out of her trance. "Of course, my dear one." She patted Cicely's hand. "We must have a banquet in honor of your arrival. Let me go down to the kitchen and see what supplies are at hand."

Her mother started to leave her. Cicely put a hand on her arm. "I'm certain Sir Harry can see to the evening meal. Come now, sit in the solar, and I will fetch a servant to bring us wine and bread."

"But you said yourself that you were tired from traveling," her mother protested.

"Nay, not so tired. Please, let me wait upon you, Maman."

Lady Adela smiled tremulously. "You are all grown up." She took a step back and regarded Cicely. "You look like a fine lady"—her smile faded—"not a holy sister."

"I have left Montreau."

"Left?" Doubt darkened Lady Adela's brown eyes.

Cicely nodded. "I always said I would, Mother. I made a vow years ago, and I have kept to it."

"Nay!" Her mother shook her head, and her waxen complexion grew paler still. "Do not leave the sanctuary of God's grace! 'Tis the only place where you are safe!"

Cicely sighed. She had betrayed her promise to Sir Harry and upset her mother. But she could not lie to her parent. At some point her mother must know about Simon and their plans to wed.

"Come, Maman," she urged again. "We will talk of this in the solar."

The private chamber was musty and obviously little used these days. The rushes crunched with brittleness beneath Cicely's feet, and dust motes danced as she plumped the cushions on her mother's favorite chair. She helped Lady Adela sit down, wincing again at how thin and feeble she had become.

Fear that her mother might perish before her eyes made Cicely hurry from the solar and accost the first servant she saw. "I need wine and fresh bread brought for Lady Adela. Hurry now. If you dare to dawdle, I'll box your ears!"

The flaxen-haired girl stared at her dumbly a moment; then the gist of the words and of Cicely's threatening tone sank in. She dropped the broom she was wielding, whirled about, and rushed down the hallway, skirts flying.

Cicely caught her breath and walked slowly back to the solar, trying to decide what to tell her mother. In her current condition, her mother could hardly deal with the prospect of going to war against the king. But somehow Cicely must explain her flight from Montreau and her betrothal to Simon.

Sighing, she went into the solar. Terror gripped her as she saw her mother slumped sideways in the chair, eyes closed and the gold crucifix dangling from her lap. Her mother had refused to release a death grip on the holy object all the way from the chapel.

Cicely approached her mother slowly, dread in every step. Only as she saw the soft rise and fall of Lady Adela's chest did the breath-stealing panic leave her. Her mother was asleep. A blessed, healing sleep, which the deep shadows beneath her eyes made clear she had forgone for days, mayhap weeks.

Cicely sat down in the chair beside her mother's—the one in which her father always sat—and tried to calm her jangled nerves. When she had sworn upon Simon's sword to fight for Tathwick, she had not expected to come home and find that her childhood allies had deserted her. Sir Harry was old and tired and fearful of losing all, and her mother was even worse off. If she meant to do this thing, she likely had no one to aid her except Simon.

"Dear Simon," she whispered. "Please come to me, and soon. I need you."

"Are you certain you aren't tired, Mother?" Simon asked solicitiously. "We need not keep to this grueling pace. Cicely does not expect us for another sennight."

"Hmmmph," his mother said. "You think I am too old for serious riding. I am but two score and one, only a little more than half the age Queen Eleanor was when she crossed the continent to fetch Princess Berengaria to wed King Richard."

"But that was a matter involving the future of a kingdom, Maman."

"Think you that your future with Lady Cicely is less important?" his mother retorted. "I vow, I hope the girl does not realize how little you worry for her welfare."

"Of course, I worry for her welfare!" Simon exploded. "But Cicely is young and strong and, for now, safe within the fortress walls of Tathwick."

"And I am old and feeble, I suppose you think!" His mother fixed him with that disdainful, pale-eyed glare of hers that always tied his tongue in knots.

"Nay, nay, I do not," he said helplessly. "I think you are strong and fearless, and utterly formidable."

"Well, then"—she gave him another cold glance—"if I decide that we can go another few miles ere we stop, you'd be wise to heed me."

Simon clamped his mouth shut, so tight his jaw ached. He

was a little uneasy about what would happen when his mother met Cicely. Heaven forfend that they should take opposite sides in some matter. 'Twould be like the clash of two great natural forces, with him caught in the middle! He suppressed a groan at the thought.

They were not far from Tathwick now. Mayhap his mother was right and they could cover the distance before the sun set.

If she was so determined to press on, why should he rein in his eagerness? He longed to see Cicely again, to gaze upon her sweet angelic face and to hold her in his arms.

The very idea made him sigh with yearning. How long would this battle with the king take? How long before they could be wed and he could explore her beautiful body as he hungered to?

His passion was strong enough that he briefly considered the notion of wedding her without Earl Marshal's permission and with the future of Tathwick unresolved. If they said vows together, he would at last have the right to love her. And not even a king could come between a man and his wife. If John tried, they could escape to France and live there for a time. Simon's father had friends in Angevin and Poitou, knights he had served with when he went on Crusade with Richard. John could not live forever, and in time, he might forget the whole matter of Tathwick.

Glumly, Simon discarded the seemingly idyllic plan. He could not ask Cicely to abandon her home and her inheritance. She had made a vow, and he would not dishonor her by swaying her from her purpose.

"Sir Simon," Girard of Malmsbury, the captain of Lady Nicola's guard, drew his mount next to Lucifer. "One of the men has sighted a castle over the next ridge. Do you think it might be Tathwick?"

Simon stared into the distance, trying to discern if there was a banner flying above the mist-shrouded keep. Cicely had described her father's device as a black fleur-de-lis on a banner of gold. But now that Robert de Valois had fallen, would those left of his garrison dare to fly it?

"We might as well ride closer," he said. "Even if it is not Tathwick, we could still inquire about lodging for the night."

"Milady, if I could speak with you a moment."

Cicely left her mother in the solar and went with Sir Harry to the hallway.

"What is it?" she asked in a quiet voice.

"A large troop approaches, and I do not recognize their banner," Sir Harry shook his head. "I fear the worst, Cicely. What if the king has already sent one of his lords to claim Tathwick?"

Cicely's pulse began to race. "So soon? I thought you said it might be months before the matter of my father's estate came to the king's attention?"

"But who else would come here with a full force of knights?"

Cicely started down the hallway. "Mayhap it is Simon. I pray to God that it is!"

Sir Harry clamped a strong hand on her arm. "Think, Cicely. You left Simon only a fortnight ago and have only been home three days. How is it possible that he could arrive so soon?"

"Mayhap he did not go to his home but hastened here to be with me instead."

"Then, where did he get the knights? My old eyes might fail me, but the man in the watchtower agreed that they rode fine horses and their armor was of the best."

Cicely hesitated. "You think we must be careful about letting them into the keep?"

Sir Harry nodded. "Once they are inside, we are at their mercy, whomever they may be."

"Have you alerted the garrison?"

"Aye. The archers are gathering on the walls."

"If it comes to a siege, how will we fare?"

The seneschal looked grim. "The food supplies run low this time of year, but we won't starve right away. Besides, I doubt that we can hold them off long."

"Mayhap until Simon comes?" Cicely asked hopefully.

"He is but one man, milady. No matter how brilliant a knight he is, he cannot stand against an army."

Cicely released a weary sigh. "Let us go to the ramparts and see what our fate holds."

The cold mist stalking the upper walls of the castle curled clammily around Cicely's thinly garbed body. But as soon as she saw the tall knight seated upon the black destrier, the chill left her. She gave a cry of joy. " 'Tis Simon! He has come!"

"You're certain?" Sir Harry moved closer to the edge of the wall, as if he could not trust Cicely's vision.

"Aye, of course I'm certain. Though he wears a fine new surcote and new armor, my beloved still rides Lucifer. Having seen half of England from the back of that ill-tempered beast, I vow I would recognize him anywhere!"

"But the rest of the soldiers? How comes he to ride in such company?"

"I know not. Nor do I care. Come, Sir Harry, give the order to let them in."

They were standing near the gatetower, almost directly above the castle entrance. Sir Harry shouted down to the soldiers gathered below, "Open the gates! Milady bids us let them in!"

The ancient portcullis, which Sir Harry had ordered let down as soon as he saw the large force approach, was raised with a groaning racket. Cicely gathered up her skirts and ran for the stairs.

As the troop entered the foregate, Cicely dashed to meet

them. She paused when she saw Lucifer; she knew better than to approach the huge warhorse too abruptly.

"Simon!" She held out her arms to him. He wasted no time dismounting and hurrying to meet her. Clasping her to his mailed chest, he held her as if he would never let her go.

She breathed in his familiar scent, discernible even beneath the reek of wet wool and horse. Her eyes closed in bliss, and only when Simon gently set her away from him did the reality of their circumstances intrude.

"Cicely," he said, "there is someone I want you to meet." He left her and returned to where the rest of the knights waited. In the center of the troop was a gray palfrey, and on its back sat a woman warmly garbed in a voluminous mantle of crimson wool trimmed with ermine.

Cicely's eyes widened as Simon helped the woman to the ground. Who was this?

Simon held the woman's arm as she picked her way cautiously across the muddy yard. As they neared the drier ground where Cicely waited, Simon broke into a beaming smile. "My lady Cicely, I would like you to meet . . . my mother, Nicola of Valmar."

The woman approached Cicely and held out her gloved hands. "I am delighted to make your acquaintance."

Stunned, Cicely accepted the woman's proffered hands. Lady Nicola embraced her in a cloud of attar of roses, then drew back. The rich mantle fell away and Cicely caught a glimpse of Simon's mother's face—a perfect oval, set with gray eyes like opals. Her pale skin was flawless. Only the streaks of white hair fanning out from her temples hinted of her age. Cicely decided that if this woman were not Simon's mother, she would be very jealous!

"So petite you are." Lady Nicola's striking gaze perused her with an intensity that unnerved Cicely. "Simon made you sound much more fearsome. He vowed you were bold enough to face down the king himself.''

"I . . . I am pleased to meet you," Cicely mumbled. Did this daunting woman hate her for risking Simon's life and future on behalf of Tathwick's cause?

Lady Nicola smiled. "Your fragile beauty should not surprise me. Simon always favored the cause of the weak over the strong. No doubt you appeal to his tenderhearted nature, as well as his manhood.''

"Mother, you should not speak of me as if I were not here!" Simon chided. "And you've embarrassed poor Cicely!''

"She will survive worse, I'm certain," Lady Nicola said as they all went into the keep.

CHAPTER 17

Cicely led Lady Nicola across the hall, her mind racing with all the things she must do. Her parents' bedchamber must be cleaned and refreshed so that Simon's mother would have a place to sleep . . . water brought for bathing, since they did not have a separate chamber for that purpose . . . the evening meal prepared . . . Thank heavens it was Lent, and Lady Nicola would not expect an extravagant repast . . .

" 'Tis a fine old keep," Lady Nicola said, breaking into Cicely's anxious thoughts. "How long has your family held Tathwick?"

"Since the time of old King Henry." Cicely turned to her guest, once again overawed by the richness of Lady Nicola's garments.

"I can see why you would wish to maintain the property in the family," Lady Nicola said sympathetically. " 'Tis your heritage, something you might pass on to your children's children."

Cicely nodded, wondering if Simon's mother could possibly mean her words. To the de Cressy family, who held not one but three castles, Tathwick must hardly seem worth fighting for. Especially if it meant risking their only son's life.

Cicely quickened her pace, abruptly aware of the inadequacies and shortcomings of her family home, the ancient tapestries on the walls, darkened with years of smoke, the plainly made oak trestle tables scarred with use, the hallway, so dank and gloomy when she compared it to the splendors of Pembroke or even Blackhurst . . .

Lady Nicola interrupted her thoughts. "Goodness, child, can you not slow your pace a little? I'm not as young as I once was."

Cicely jerked to a halt, horrified by her rudeness. "My lady, I do heartily beg you pardon. I did not mean to rush on ahead."

Her guest smiled warmly. "You are young and full of life. You cannot help it, I'm certain."

They continued on at a more sedate pace. Cicely was grateful that the stairway was too narrow for them to walk side by side. She did not want Lady Nicola to see her flaming face and guess her mortification.

They reached the solar, and Cicely resisted the urge to dash in and prepare her mother for their unexpected guest. Lady Adela would be gracious and charming as always; 'twas her daughter who lacked manners!

Her mother sat in a chair by the hearth, praying. Cicely had convinced her that she could not risk her health by kneeling on the cold stone floor of the chapel for more than a few hours a day; still, her mother would not give up her incessant praying. She interrupted it only to eat and sleep, and then only at Cicely's insistence.

"Maman," Cicely said gently, "there is someone here I want you to meet."

Lady Adela looked up, then rose gracefully to her feet. Lady

Nicola went to her and extended her hands. "I am Simon's mother," she said. "But I forgot, you have not yet met him, have you?"

Cicely's mother took the other woman's hands and smiled. "Nay, I have not had that pleasure. But he must be a fine young man, or Cicely would not admire him so. To hear her tell of it, he is the most brave and noble of knights. The very paragon of chivalry."

"Oh, he is, indeed," Lady Nicola said, and Cicely thought there was something dry and ironic in her voice. "And I must tell you, Lady Adela—I may call you that?—I have heard naught but glowing praises of your daughter as well." She glanced at Cicely and laughed gaily. "And those are the only things Simon sees fit to tell his mother. No doubt he expounds on her other virtues to the knights, who might appreciate them."

Cicely flushed. 'Twas hard to grow used to a lady who teased like a bawdy squire, especially when the woman was soon to be her mother-by-marriage!

"Come, sit with me," Lady Adela offered. "Cicely will see that some mulled wine is brought, and you can warm yourself by the fire."

"Ah, that sounds delightful." Lady Nicola sighed and began to remove her mantle. Cicely rushed to help her. The heaviness of the rich garment astonished her. Never had she seen wool so thick and fine, nor an entire cloak lined with costly fur. Anxiety welled up inside her. If she had known how wealthy Simon truly was, would she have dared to fall in love with him?

As soon as she could tactfully leave, Cicely raced down to the kitchen. She arrived so breathless she could barely talk. "Send one of the kitchen boys . . . to the cellar for wine . . . the finest we have. And unlock . . . the spice cabinet." She gasped.

"Sir Harry has already ordered it done," the cook assured

her. "We are making a sauce for the pike and baking the bread with the last of the finely ground wheat flour. 'Twill be a plain meal, milady, but a good one." The plump, round-faced Saxon patted her shoulder. "After days of traveling, they will welcome any hot, satisfying food."

Cicely nodded. She should not worry so much. Lady Nicola appeared to have accepted her, to be pleased with the match.

She continued about her duties, hustling a group of serving women up to the master bedchamber with rags and feather dusters and armloads of fresh rushes and linen bedding. She found men to drag the bathing tub up to the room and fill it with pails of hot water. Other servants carried Lady Nicola's baggage to the chamber. Cicely herself searched for the soap and drying cloths.

In all the turmoil, she completely forgot about Simon. When she met him in one of the hallways, her arms full of supplies, she near dropped everything in surprise. "Simon!" she exclaimed.

"Well, you might welcome me better than that," he said. "Don't I deserve a kiss at least?"

Cicely awkwardly transferred her burdens to one arm and went to embrace him. He held her tightly and gazed down on her. "What is it, Cicely?" he asked, his expression perplexed. "Where is the woman who thought she would die ere she held me in her arms again?"

"I . . . I did not expect your mother to come. I don't want to disappoint her." Cicely started to squirm away. "Her bath is almost ready, and I have the soap."

Simon captured her easily and moved to pin her against the wall. "My mother can wait. I want you to kiss me first. Kiss me as if you mean it."

His mouth came down on hers. So familiar, so enticing, so . . . wonderful. Cicely felt herself melt, and her legs grew as squishy and liquid as the soap she carried. The heat rose up inside her, the yearning fire that Simon ignited. She pressed herself more tightly against him and smelled the scent of soap in his damp hair. His body was warm and solid, the feel of his arms around her like Heaven and Paradise and Perfect Bliss.

His mouth caressed hers, softly, then with more intensity. Her legs wobbled, and he steadied her against himself. With sudden awareness she felt the ridge of his manhood pressed into her belly. For once he did not draw away, but deepened the kiss until Cicely's worries disappeared and the ecstasy sparkled through her like tiny, exquisite stars.

Then the bowl of soap started to slip through her nerveless fingers, and Cicely thrust herself from Simon's arms to catch it. She cradled it against her body and stared at him, her breath still coming in shuddering gasps. Something had changed. This was not her proper, disciplined knight, whom she'd had to coax to kiss her or touch her. This man was alive with passion, as eager for it as she was. Had he missed her so badly, or was something else different?

"Your mother's bath." She gestured helplessly.

He nodded, smiling at her. "Go then. Maman does hate to be kept waiting."

Cicely breathed a sigh of relief. The meal was finished and no disaster had befallen them. The fish had been hot and savory, the bread crusty. The vegetable pottage so expertly seasoned, the lack of meat broth was scarce noticed. The dearth of delicacies could not be helped—'twas impossible to make pudding or pastries without lard, milk or eggs, and all were prohibited during Lent. But there was honey mixed with cinnamon to spread on the bread, and raisins, in case Lady Nicola had a sweet tooth.

In truth, Simon's mother dined sparingly, no doubt the reason for her lithe form, although her slenderness did not reflect the gaunt unhealthiness of deprivation as Cicely's mother's did.

Cicely marveled at Lady Nicola's youthfulness, her remarkable beauty. Had her life been so easeful? It did not seem likely, especially with her beloved son gone for years and no word of him.

But Lady Nicola had always been wealthy and secure in her possessions, unlike Cicely's mother, who had seen her property and her family gradually reduced over the years. All that was left to her now was Cicely and Tathwick.

Cicely could not help pondering the differences between the two women. Nicola so vibrant and fearless, and her mother, a pale, anxious wraith. Was it chance which brought them to such diverse destinies? Or was there something within each of them that made one bend and near break before the winds of fate and the other remain upright and strong?

What stuff was *she* made of? Cicely wondered. If she suffered misfortune and tragedy, if she lost Tathwick and Simon both, would she be able to bear to go on living?

The thought made a shiver of fear travel down her spine. Life was so fragile and fleeting a thing. No wonder some women did not reach out to seize it, but hid away in the safe, quiet world of the priory. Mayhap it truly was better never to love than to love and lose all.

Too late for her, she thought as Simon reached for her hand beneath the table. He was her soul, her other half. If she lost him, there would be a gaping hole inside her.

And here she was, risking his life to save this crumbling fortress. How could she be so foolish?

He squeezed her fingers, and Cicely's heart seemed to be wrenched with a love so intense it was painful. She would tell him, as soon as they were alone, that she'd changed her mind, that Tathwick was not worth risking his life over.

The memory of her father suddenly reproached her. Had she not been raised to do her duty even if it cost her dearly? So often in her life she had failed in that regard. She had been selfish, childish, unworthy. Somehow, in this thing, she must atone for the rest of her failures.

"Come, Cicely." Simon pulled gently on her hand to raise her. "Sir Harry wants to go to the solar to discuss strategy."

Her insides twisting with indecision and turmoil, Cicely stood and followed him from the hall.

She was surprised to find Lady Nicola awaiting them. "I left your mother in the chapel, praying," she said. "I thought she would do well enough alone, at least for a time. Sir Harry warned me that she did not know of your plans, and I daresay she would not approve of them." Lady Nicola frowned. "I'm not certain she has yet accepted the idea of your wedding Simon. She spoke several times of your returning to the priory."

Cicely sighed. "She believes I will be safe there. I cannot convince her that I do not mean to go back."

"Can she not see that Simon will protect you? That you are no longer alone and vulnerable?"

Cicely shook her head. "I fear something happened to her wits when my father and brother died. She no longer seems able to think clearly."

"Great tragedy sometimes disorders the mind, especially in one whose health is tenuous." Lady Nicola reached out to pat Cicely's hand. "Mayhap over time she will heal."

"So do I pray every day," Sir Harry agreed. His aged face looked wearier than ever. Cicely knew that her mother's problems weighed very heavily upon him.

Simon came and sat beside Cicely, taking her hand in his. "We will shield Lady Adela from our plans as much as possible. But we *must* make them. If I am going to carry the Tathwick banner in their midst, I must join the rebels soon."

Cicely opened her mouth to tell Simon of her fears, but Lady Nicola forestalled her. "Aye, you must take only a day or two of rest and then ride with your men, and those Sir Harry can spare, to Stamford."

Cicely rose in agitation. "How can you so easily let him go, now that you have found him again?" she demanded of Simon's mother.

"But I thought this was your wish?" Lady Nicola said, clearly surprised. "I thought you had asked Simon to aid you in retaining Tathwick?"

"I did, but now"—Cicely met Simon's gaze in desperation—"I fear to lose him; I do not think I could bear it."

"You will not lose me," Simon said. "With luck, 'twill not even come to armed conflict. On the way here, I spoke to several lords who favored the rebel cause. They say that the king is weakening, that he may well concede to their complaints."

Sir Harry gave a contemptuous snort. "Concede some points, he might, but then he will go back on his agreement as soon as the balance of power favors him. He is biding time now, so he can bring in mercenaries from the Continent. There will be war, mark my words. If not this year, then the next. King John won't give up a crumb of his power, not while there is breath in his body!"

A muscle in Simon's mouth twitched at these glum words, and Cicely knew a renewal of fear.

Lady Nicola turned her gaze to Cicely, as did Sir Harry. Cicely realized suddenly that it was all up to her. If she said she had changed her mind about joining the rebel cause, no one would attempt to sway her decision.

Except Simon. She saw the confusion and doubt in his eyes, felt the tension in his fingers grasping hers. "I think Simon and I need to be alone," she said quietly.

"Of course." Sir Harry stood.

Lady Nicola rose in her usual dignified, graceful manner. "I will respect whatever decision you make." She glanced from Simon to Cicely. "But I would ask that you not make it in haste. 'Tis often true that people have a lifetime to regret that which they decide too quickly."

When their elders had left them, Simon released Cicely's hand and stood. He went to the window and looked out.

"What think you, Simon?" she asked. "In your heart of hearts, what do you believe we should do?"

He turned to face her. "I would not want you to have a lifetime as my wife, only to regret every day that you did not choose well in this thing." He sighed. "If we could see into the future and guess how this matter will play out. If King John triumphs 'twill go hard with Tathwick, and mayhap with me and my property as well. I do not see how John has the resources or will to ruin all the rebel barons, but he can be a bitter, vindictive man."

"What if we do nothing?" Cicely asked. "Preoccupied as he is with this uprising, John may not have time to look to Tathwick for several years. By then, we could be safely wed."

"He could still strip your family of the property," Simon reminded her. "Can you bear to lose your birthright even then?"

Cicely sighed. "My heart says one thing, my sense of duty, another. Why can it not be simple? Why must I choose?"

Simon approached her and put his arms around her. " 'Tis the way of life. Protected as you were at Montreau, you did not realize how harsh the choices can be. I'm certain your father agonized as you are doing now when he decided to put you in the priory. If he had but known the future, that he and your brother would die, leaving you as heiress, he might well have made a different choice. But he did not, and so he did what he thought best for you. 'Twas an act of love, certes, for all that you resented it.

"And it seems to me that he came to know he was wrong," Simon added, "to understand that you were not meant for priory life. Mayhap that is even what he came to tell you that day when you turned him away. But 'twas late then to undo the mistake."

"As it will be too late for me," Cicely said bitterly, "some years from now when I have lost Tathwick."

"You do not know that will happen."

"But all of you fear 'tis so, am I not right?"

"I would not have you unhappy, regretting your choice for the rest of your life. And so, I would gladly lead my forces and yours to join the barons' cause."

"But what if you die?" Cicely whispered. "I could not bear it."

"A battle in England, even a civil war, is not so dangerous as going on Crusade. I survived that."

"Barely. I saw how weak you were when the fever struck you down."

Simon leaned close and kissed her cheek. "I am not like to catch a fever in the chill of an English spring."

"There are many other dangers in war."

"Aye, and there are many other dangers in life. Remember when you argued that Lady Blackhurst should be allowed to risk her health in childbirth?"

"There is something to be gained when a woman endures the risks of birthing a babe—God willing, her travail brings a new life into the world."

"There is something to be gained in this as well." Simon gestured to the stone walls around them. "Can you agree to give this up without a fight? 'Tis your home, Cicely. The place of your childhood memories and dreams."

"You seek to make it harder for me," she complained.

"Nay, I seek to make certain that you are very *sure* of your decision."

She sighed and laid her head against his shoulder. 'Twas so difficult, so painful. When she had lived in quiet and peace at Montreau, she had not guessed what she might be spared.

"Mayhap it would help you if you knew I have decided we should plight our troth before I go."

"You mean, say vows before God that we mean to wed?"

"Aye."

Excitement stirred in Cicely at the implication of his words. "If we do that, 'twould not be a sin for us to lie together."

Simon smiled. "Nay, it would not."

Cicely took a shaky breath. "What changed your mind?"

"You are not the only one who has faced the prospect of a lifetime of regret. If I plant a babe inside you, the only thing which would keep me from returning to claim it, and you, would be death. And if God decrees such a fate, then it seems a waste not to enjoy these fleeting moments." He tilted up her face so she looked at him. "I love you, Cicely. I would be joined with you. Our bodies and spirits as one."

"Let us go to the chapel," Cicely said breathlessly. "Let us say our vows."

Simon raised a brow. "And what will we tell your lady mother, praying piously before the altar? Do we tell her that we plight our troth so that we can enjoy carnal pleasures this night?"

"I doubt she will notice us. For that matter, mayhap I can coax her to go to bed. I vow, she is ruining her health, spending so much time in that unheated, drafty chamber." Cicely pulled on his hand, urging him toward the door. Suddenly, she paused. "But what will we tell *your* mother?"

"My mother"—Simon hesitated—"I imagine she assumes that we have already taken such steps."

Cicely turned in shock. "She does? Why? Does she believe me a wanton?"

Simon's mouth twisted with amusement. "I rather think it is *my* virtue she questions. I was not always so saintly as when you met me. The trials and horrors of my travels changed me more than you might imagine."

"A pity I did not meet you then, before you became so devout." Cicely smiled provocatively. How delightful to be able to tease him, and know that it would not end in frustration for both of them.

Simon raised his brows in mock surprise. "I thought you admired my honorable nature."

"Aye, I do, but it can also be inconvenient at times." Cicely gave a bubbling laugh and wriggled from his grasp.

What a wicked little minx she was, Simon thought as he followed after her. With every coquettish quirk of her eyebrows and dimpling smile, the blood throbbed in his loins and his shaft grew harder. How could he possibly enter a holy chapel in this appalling condition?

As he neared the chapel doorway, decorated with an embossed gold cross, he paused. "You go ahead," he told her, "and see to your lady mother."

Staring at the gleaming religious symbol, he tried to bring to mind the most sobering, repulsive images he could conjure. Gradually, the recollection of blood and slaughter banished the passion from his body.

Cicely returned a short time later, leading her mother by the arm and speaking soothingly. " 'Twould be impolite to neglect your guests, Mother," she said. "Come, let us go and see if Lady Nicola requires anything else before she seeks her bed."

By the time Cicely accomplished her errand, Simon was suitably composed. He followed her into the chapel. Cicely went quickly to the rail and knelt. Simon approached the altar more slowly, taking time to admire the beauty of the small, exquisitely wrought chamber. He imagined it by day, the light shining through the colored-glass windows and rendering the pale stone walls spectacular, the chapel a vision of light and exaltation.

Simon crossed himself and went to kneel beside Cicely. He joined her in prayer for a time, then turned and took her hands to raise her. Facing each other, the light from the myriad candles trembling and flickering around them, they made their promises.

"I, Simon, take thee, Cicely, to be my wedded wife to have and to hold from this day forward, for better or worse, for richer or poorer, for fairer or fouler, in sickness and in health, to love and to cherish, till death do us part, according to God's holy ordinance; thereunto I plight thee my troth."

"I, Cicely, take thee, Simon, to be my wedded husband, to have and to hold from this day forward, for better or worse, for richer or poorer, in sickness and in health, to love and to cherish, till death do us part, according to God's holy ordinance; thereunto I plight thee my troth."

Death. Could even that destroy their love? Simon pondered as she said the solemn words. Would not their spirits find each other in heaven? They would have no use for earthly love then, for passions of the flesh, but was there not a deeper closeness between them? Something so profound and timeless that it transcended this mortal realm and survived even in eternity?

When he gazed into Cicely's melting brown eyes, he thought that this was so. When he bent his head to seal his promise with a kiss, he knew that if his faith were true, and his soul did not perish, neither would his love for Cicely.

Her face shone with radiance and her smile warmed the final lingering chill in the depths of his soul. "Simon," she whispered. "My beloved, my heart. Give me your love. And, if God wills it, give me your babe."

They walked slowly to Cicely's bedchamber, the quiet of the castle like a magic spell around them. Inside the small chamber, they used a rushlight from the hall to light the brazier and the lone candle on the table.

"We need more light," Simon said. "I want to see you." His eyes narrowed with sexual hunger.

Cicely nodded. "I'll fetch some candles and some wine."

"Do you want me to go with you?"

"Nay, you do not know the castle as well as I. I can creep as quietly as a mouse. As a child, I grew quite skilled at sneaking around the castle."

Simon kissed her lightly on the nose. "Hurry, my little mouse. The cat grows impatient for his prey. Meowww."

Cicely shivered at the hungry growl of his voice and trembled with anticipation. She wanted this sleek, beautiful beast to devour her. Oh, how she wanted it!

She hurried breathlessly on her errand. On the way back, she paused down the hall, relieved to see the glow of candlelight beneath the door of her brother's chamber and to hear the click of the rosary beads. Her mother was safely occupied in her prayers.

Arms full, she used her elbow to knock on the door to her bedchamber, playfully employing the "secret" knock she and her brother had once used. Simon opened the door, wearing nothing but his chausses. Cicely gave a gasp and almost dropped the flagon of wine.

He pulled her into the room, laughing. " 'Tis well I did not have time to take the rest of it off." He quickly took the flagon and candles and set them on the table. "Tell me truly, Cicely, am I really so fearsome?"

"Aye," she whispered. She stared at the hard expanse of his chest, the broad, well-muscled shoulders, the gold hair swirling around his nipples and trailing down to his groin. His mention of a cat was most apt. He was graceful, lithe and beautiful—a magnificent creature. She had desired him so long, the promise of his bare skin and husky voice almost pained her.

He moved nearer. "I would have you naked as well," he whispered, "so I might feast my eyes as you are doing."

She nodded, her hands so weak and trembling she could barely unfasten the girdle from her waist. He did not reach to aid her, but simply watched, his gaze ravishing her. Her nipples peaked and her insides grew hot.

"The candles," she said. She felt as if she would explode with tension if he did not stop looking at her.

"Oh, aye, the candles." He clumsily set them in brackets and began to light them. While he was about this endeavor, Cicely hurried to wriggle her gown over her head. She wore only her shift when he turned back to her.

He shook his head, nostrils flaring and blue eyes hot. "Not enough. I would see all of you."

She took a quick breath and reminded herself that he'd seen her naked before, so why did it seem so intimate and intense? As if her skin were too tight for her, her insides dissolving into fire? She gripped the shift and pulled upward.

The expression on his face near undid her. 'Twas a look of awe, of reverence. He approached her and put his hands on her arms. "Your hair," he whispered silkily.

Before she could reach up to undo it, his big, callused fingers had sent the veil she wore slithering to the ground and had begun to undo the plaits of her braids. He was gentle, careful not to jerk or pull. His tender touch soothed Cicely, and she leaned her head back and savored the feel of his hands gliding through her hair. The strands pulled slightly on her scalp and caused a tingling pleasure to spread down her body.

He smoothed her wavy tresses over her shoulders and followed their spiraling course down her breasts. His palms closed over the aching peaks. He cupped her sensitive flesh, the rough texture of his warrior's hands teasing her skin with exquisite friction. Then, still caressing her, he lowered his head to suckle her swollen nipples.

Cicely moaned and leaned her head back, offering herself to him. He sucked deeply, eliciting tiny pricks of pleasure/pain which pierced throughout her body. He transferred his attentions to the other breast, and Cicely floated in a fevered mist of desire. Her senses seemed heightened, yet the boundaries of her body were blurry and indistinct. She could not tell where her flesh ended and Simon's pulsating warmth began.

Then, slowly, he drew away. Mouth wet, eyes heavy-lidded and dreamy, he regarded her. "I'm going too fast," he murmured. "I will not last this way."

Cicely herself thought things were moving much too slowly. She wanted more. More of his tantalizing mouth and rough fingers. The ache of longing between her legs throbbed incessantly.

He picked her up and carried her the two quick steps to the bed. It was small and narrow, and Cicely wondered how they would ever both fit on it.

Simon leaned over her, his expression rapt. "You are so beautiful. A man could live upon the memory of your splendor for years. I only wish I had known you before I went on Crusade, so I could have conjured your image as a talisman against the ugly things I saw."

"I don't want you to dream of me, Simon. I want you to love me! Love me now!" Her voice was rough with passion and need. She would beg if she had to.

He looked tenderly into her eyes. "Are you very certain? The first time . . ."

"Aye, Simon, I am certain! I don't care if it hurts. It cannot be worse than this unbearable craving!"

He nodded, then removed his chausses. He climbed onto the bed, straddling her. Cicely experienced a twinge of alarm as she beheld his engorged shaft; then he began to move his hands over her, and she closed her eyes and reveled in the skill of his fingers. He shaped her flesh into patterns of ecstasy, wove nets of fire over her skin, opened her secret places like a key fit to a well-oiled lock.

Then, when she thought she could endure no more, he brought his lips to her fiery skin, cooling and soothing her. From wrist to neck, from toe to thigh, nipple to nipple, and lower, he kissed her, tasted her, licked her. She shivered convulsively as his tongue touched her navel, then followed an irresistible downward pathway. Lightly skimming her maidenhair and following her cleft to the mysteries of her womanhood.

Cicely writhed and cried out, giving in to sweet release. But still she wanted more. Completion and joining, the pulse of their bodies as one.

At last, Simon's hard flesh met her slick, yielding opening, and with an agonized groan he thrust into her. She could not help crying out. She felt impaled, penetrated to the edges of her soul, pierced by his lance of flesh.

But the wound their joining made was near painless. A sharp pang, then gone. Her body surrendered with a wet, shimmering sigh. Submission had never felt so delicious.

She enjoyed his conquest of her, exulted in the dazzling rhythms with which he made her part of himself. Together they galloped across a wild, tumultuous sea, floating on waves of ecstatic sensation.

She sensed his tension build, the muscles in his arms and shoulders flex for the final effort, as he took them soaring into the heavens, a midnight blue firmament flecked with twinkling stars.

They floated downward at last. Sweaty and real, bounded again by earthly strictures. He lifted himself off her. "Jesu"— he pushed his damp hair away from his face—"that was good."

"Good?" She sat up, and became aware of a twinge of soreness between her thighs. " 'Twas more than good."

He smiled at her, a sleepy, contented leer. "Aye, but 'tis blasphemy to name it for what it was."

"I cannot think God would have given us this ... this ... marvel if He did not mean for us to enjoy it."

"A marvel, aye, that is a fine way to explain it." He leaned over to kiss her.

He tasted salty with sweat, and wetness was everywhere, as if they had dissolved, transmuting into the sea itself. She sighed and touched his face, wondering, as always, at the differences between them. Roughness against softness. Hard muscles against smooth curves. Opposites, but made for each other. They fit together like halves of a perfect whole.

She slid her fingers over his shoulder and down his arm, feeling the muscles, the scars. His body fascinated her. Drew her like firelight drew a moth. She touched his chest, her fingertips playing in the swirls of damp hair, exploring his nipples, so unlike a women's, yet so similar. Hard muscles in his belly, the sleek skin overlaying them.

He caught her hand as she moved it lower. "Saucy wench, you'll arouse me again if you continue along that course."

She tilted her head and smiled provokingly. "Mayhap that is what I desire."

He raised a brow. "You'll be most sore on the morrow if you tempt me into loving you again."

She drew a fingernail down his torso, pausing mere inches away from his shaft, swelling now before her eyes. "If I cannot walk, I shall keep to my bed and claim a fever. Verily, I am sick, sick with longing for you." She reached lower and touched his shaft. Emboldened by the intimacy they'd already shared, she dared to stroke this strange, magical part of him.

He tensed and groaned, holding himself so rigid Cicely went still. "Am I hurting you?" she asked.

He shook his head, although his features were distorted, his expression like that of a man being tortured.

" 'Tis very big," she said.

He gave a choked laugh. "Should I take that to mean that you are dissatisfied or pleased?"

She thought a moment. "Pleased, I think. Although I should not like you to be any bigger."

" 'Tis you who makes it grow." He ground out the words

as she fondled the silky tip. "Merely the thought of you makes it grow hard, and when you do that . . ." He made a strangled sound and sat up. "If we are to play this game, then I must teach you the rules. You're like to kill me if you keep at that."

He put his hand over hers and guided it in smooth strokes up and down. "If you do that, I will find satisfaction in no time. If you do the other, teasing me to madness, you must be prepared to find yourself on your back with your legs spread wide, experiencing the consequences of your amusement."

Cicely looked at him, then, very deliberately, rubbed the tip of her finger over the tender flesh he had warned her to avoid.

His eyes grew dark and heated, and he leaned over her, transformed into a man she did not know. His hands were rough as he spread her thighs, his kisses harsh and urgent. He stroked her wet, sensitive opening with agonizing delicacy, breaching her defenses and turning her into a gasping, helpless captive of his touch.

Then, he entered her. He did not simply merge himself with her, but possessed her. His hands cupped her buttocks, forcing her to accept more of him. His movements were deep and slow, as his shaft caressed the entrance to her womb. Desperate with sensation, she wrapped her legs around his hips and clasped his shoulders tight.

This journey to the heavens seemed even more splendid than the last, brighter, more intense, more overwhelming. When she came to awareness again, her face was wet with tears.

"Dear Cicely"—Simon sounded worried—"did I hurt you?"

She opened her eyes to look at him and shook her head in wonder. "Nay, nay, 'tis only . . . I did not know it could be like that. I did not know."

He slid her over on the tiny bed, then stretched out and pulled her near so she lay half on top of him, her face against the solid, steady beat of his heart. "There are many kinds of loving,'' he said, ''and all of them sweet. Together, you and I will savor them all, and mayhap discover new ones.''

Cicely raised her head to look at him. ''Do you promise, Simon?''

''Upon my word and honor, I vow it.'' His voice was sleepy, hoarse with contentment. Cicely lay back down upon his cradling form and let her thoughts drift away.

CHAPTER 18

Simon woke in the night, disoriented at first. The small chamber seemed eerie and unfamiliar in the flickering candlelight, reminding him of illness and waking in strange, unknown places where his fevered dreams threatened to drag him into oblivion. But this was no nightmare, and no evil memories clawed at his thoughts. His body felt tired, but at peace. And this odd languor arose from contentment rather than illness.

Silken hair spread over his bare torso; the soft shape of a woman's naked form curved against his side. Cicely. He opened his eyes to look at her, delighted that they had not had the will to quench the candles after their last bout of lovemaking so he could enjoy how sleep enhanced the sweetness of her features and gilded her lovely skin and hair to flawless, honeyed radiance.

As he kissed her softly and inhaled her tantalizing scent, it seemed to him that from the first moment he looked upon her face, he had loved her. Her innocent beauty was forbidden to him then, garbed as she was in a nun's wimple and robe, so he had adored her from afar, as a sainted figure of womanly kindness and healing.

Yet no saint was she, but an earthly, sensual creature. She met his lust with a sexual appetite as intense as his own. No wonder she had not been happy behind the quiet walls of Montreau Priory. Some maids were not meant to remain chaste, but to bloom like the headiest, most voluptuous of roses. And blossom she had. In his arms she had ripened to full-blown womanhood.

He trailed his hand down her body, caressing the delectable buds of her areolas and then the soft down of the dark gold curls between her thighs. The sight of her nakedness aroused him, although he should have been sated long ago. He wanted to plant a babe in her womb, to fulfil the promise of her exquisite femininity.

Mayhap he had this night. Or would on the morrow. He did not have much time, for he knew that unless she bade him otherwise, duty demanded that he go and fight for her, lend his sword arm to her cause. He was her knight, her champion. And he had known that, too, almost from the first time she'd come to him, eyes lowered and voice breathless and shy, and asked him to free her from the prison of her sheltered life.

Desperation had driven him to take up her cause. He had wanted to do one good, true thing before he died, so she had become his purpose, his shining goal. Odd to think that she had caused him to abandon every other vow he had made. He had sworn never to go home, never to entangle his life with another's, to live as a solitary knight doing penance for his sins. He had broken all his promises, yet he had no regrets. She had hacked away at the armor he wore around his wounded, embittered heart and had found her way inside.

He felt her there, a soft, even glow, warming his spirit, banishing his despair. Because of her, he had returned to his home and found he was not lost to those he loved. She had given him resolution and courage, and he must repay her the only way he knew how. He would fight to save her home, her heritage.

To the king, Tathwick was little more than a modest stone fortress and a few dozen hides of land, but to Cicely it was a promise, a link to the father she had lost, and never had a chance to love.

He would save it for her, Simon thought. 'Twould be his gift to repay all she had given him.

He gently disengaged himself from her warmth and climbed from the bed, making plans. First thing, he must find Sir Harry and discuss Tathwick's defenses. Then he would choose men to take with him. Only a small force. 'Twas unlikely to be a battle yet. The king was too shrewd, too cunning, to start a war before he had time to amass an army. And negotiation ofttimes proved more crucial than warfare. If he could combine Tathwick's future with other men's causes, they might all prevail without bloodshed.

He walked restlessly to where his clothes lay, tumbled in a pile upon the floor. Though he longed to linger in bed and love Cicely one more time, he had things to do this morn.

Cicely walked slowly down the stairs to the main hall. She was definitely sore, as well as a bit disheveled. She had dressed without a maid, fearful that anyone seeing her hopelessly snarled hair would guess she had been tumbled, and right well at that! No sensible woman went to bed with her hair unbraided, and even the most harrowing, sleepless night could hardly account for the tangled state of her curls.

She had tried to smooth her hair as best she could, had plaited it unevenly and covered the worst of the damage with a veil. Then she'd washed her face and private parts and donned a clean shift and gown, but still she feared she smelled of the heady musk of sex.

Was her countenance changed in any way? she wondered. Would anyone looking at her guess at the wanton activities she had indulged in the night before? Her mother would not note any change, obsessed as she was with spiritual affairs rather than temporal ones. But Lady Nicola and Sir Harry, they were a different matter.

Simon said that his mother already suspected them of being intimate. Mayhap she did not censure such behavior. But Sir Harry certainly would.

Cicely paused before the door to the hall and tried to calm her nerves. She wished that Simon had stayed with her, to give her courage this morning. Then again, it would be altogether too incriminating if they were seen together soon after rising. That could be the reason he had left the bedchamber without waking her.

But already she hungered for the sight of him, as if they had been long parted. She felt empty and incomplete without him at her side.

In the kitchen, she broke her fast with a hunk of bread, leftover raisins, and some ale. "You look fit and fine this morning, Lady Cicely," the cook remarked. "Having Sir Simon at Tathwick has brought quite a bloom to your cheeks."

The cook winked broadly, and Cicely felt the "bloom" rapidly turning to an embarrassed blush. Blessed Mary, even if Sir Harry didn't guess, he was bound to overhear the servants' gossip! What would he think of her?

She told herself firmly that a vow said before God in the chapel was as binding as a marriage ceremony with a priest. She and Simon were as good as wed now; they had no reason to be ashamed of what they had shared the night before.

But where was he? she wondered as she looked around the

nearly deserted hall. It irritated her a bit that he was too busy to find her and wish her good morning.

Putting on her mantle, she went out into the yard.

"You're satisfied that ten knights will be enough?" Sir Harry asked. "How can you be certain that the conflict won't intensify?"

"I can't be," Simon answered. He gazed out at the rolling hills around the castle, just beginning to green. "Nothing is definite in this matter. Which is why I must go to where the barons gather and learn of their plans firsthand. If it sounds as if there is to be war, I will send someone to Tathwick for the rest of my men. I want you to remain here, in case the castle is attacked, either by the king's forces or some lawless lord who seeks to claim it now and petition the king for the right to it later."

"If that happens, Lady Cicely would be very vulnerable." Sir Harry rubbed his grizzled jaw. He glanced quickly at Simon, then away. "Should some other man take her maidenhead, his claim to Tathwick would be hard to dispute. I will fight to the death to protect her, but I am old, and I well know that fate can deal brutal defeat to even the most determined of warriors."

"Do you suggest I wed her now, before I leave, so my claim could not be contested?"

"Aye."

Simon shook his head. "That was my plan ere I left Valmar, but my father reminded me that if I wed her without permission from the king, and John prevails, I would be considered an outlaw."

"The whole matter is hazardous, indeed, but I thought"— the seneschal met Simon's eyes knowingly—"I thought you might think possessing Cicely to be worth any risk."

"I do." Simon bit off the words. "But my father made me

promise—even as he armed me and furnished me with knights handpicked from his mensie—that I would not take such a step. And so''—Simon walked to the edge of the ramparts and leaned out—''I have said vows with Cicely, vows binding before God, but not before men. And I have taken her maidenhead, and God willing, given her my child.''

Sir Harry did not speak for a time; then he said sneeringly, ''A fine distinction from defying the king. And what happens to milady if you are killed or imprisoned?''

Hearing those threatening words, Simon almost regretted the miraculous night he had spent with Cicely. Then he turned and faced Sir Harry, his eyes blazing with conviction. ''At least now she will have something to remember me by. Life is too short to always be prudent and cautious. I must honor my promise to my father, but I will not cheat Cicely of my love to do so.''

The old warrior's bitter look seemed to ease. ''In truth, I cannot fault you for your lack of forbearance. Cicely has been cheated out of much already.'' He sighed. '' 'Twas not right of Lord Tathwick to put her away. She had not the vocation to be a nun, anyone could see that.''

''Except her father?''

Sir Harry shook his head. ''He knew. 'Twas too late to alter things, but he still grieved over the matter.''

''Cicely said there was a time some years ago when he came to see her. Did he mean to tell her then that he despised what he had done?''

''Aye, but she would not see him. It hurt him that she would not forgive him, and yet, in some perverse way, he was proud of her. 'She has not forgotten her vow,' he said. 'She is as full of spirit as ever.' He would be most gratified to learn that she means to fight for Tathwick.''

''Would he?'' Both men turned as Cicely spoke. In the bluster of the March wind they had not heard her approach.

"Aye, your father, may God assoil him, would be pleased by your decision," Sir Harry told her. "He would think it noble and brave."

Cicely glanced from one man to the other. Her heart sank as she saw the grim determination on their faces. "You're already making plans, aren't you?"

They nodded.

She closed her eyes as the sudden sense of loss lanced through her. "When do you plan to leave, Simon?"

"On the morrow."

" 'Tis not fair," she complained, stroking the soft hair furring his chest as she cuddled, naked, against him. "We've barely had any time together."

He reached up to stroke her cheek. "We've a few hours more," he said huskily.

"Only if we do not sleep."

"Sleep? Sleep is for babes and old men."

"I will feel guilty if you leave here bleary-eyed and fatigued. I know how you push yourself when you travel. I dread that you might fall ill."

He disengaged his arm from beneath her and sat up. He stretched languorously. "I've never felt stronger or more well in life."

Cicely also rose to a sitting position, then leaned back and admired the enticing vision Simon made as he put his hands behind his neck and flexed his upper torso. His glorious muscles rippled, and the tufts of hair beneath his arms glistened tawny gold in the candlelight. A yearning need fired low in her belly. She wanted him as if it had been years since their bodies had been joined, rather than the short while it had taken for them to catch their breath and calm their racing hearts.

She raised her own arms, faintly mimicking him as she thrust her breasts out, the nipples puckering as his gaze fell upon them.

He stared, seemingly entranced, then groaned, "By the Rood, Cicely, do you mean to kill me?"

"But you said only now that you had never felt better." She rose from the bed and shook her head, so that her hair swung in a tangle of wild waves around her. His shaft was rising— she sensed it, though she did not look toward the bed.

She crossed to the trestle table and poured a cup of wine. As she took a long swallow, she imagined in her mind's eye the sight she made with bed-tousled hair and bare buttocks clearly in his view.

Returning to the bed, she climbed on it, then moved to straddle him, knees splayed apart.

"My, you are a determined wench," he whispered, eyes intent, nostrils flared.

"Aye, and this is what encourages me." She glanced at his upthrust shaft, licking her lips with a slow provocative motion.

He gave a growl and lunged. She would have fallen off the narrow bed, but he grabbed her arm and saved her. In a second, he had reversed their positions, deftly pinning her body beneath his. He planted one kiss upon each of her nipples, then spread her thighs and sheathed himself deep.

"Oh, Simon!" she shrieked as his full length impaled her.

He leaned over to kiss her neck and whisper in her ear, "Now you know how I deal with shameless, wicked maids who do entice me."

"I fear I am a maid no longer," she answered breathlessly. Waves of pleasure echoed throughout her body as he began to move in a slow rhythm. She clutched his back, digging her nails into his muscles. The lingering soreness from the last time seemed to heighten her response. Each leisurely thrust of his shaft was like iron striking flint, setting sparks flying inside her.

He stroked the swollen, slippery flesh where they were joined. Cicely screamed her release. Then he lifted himself above her and drove into her with a fury that set her spinning into a violent whirlpool of rapture and left them both panting and gasping when the tumult had passed.

They lay still, cheek to cheek, breast to breast, floating on a quiet river of contentment. Cicely gazed up at the candlelight dancing on the smoke-darkened ceiling and released a sigh of perfect peace.

"The king has broken trust with us!" Robert FitzWalter pounded the table with a meaty fist and sent the cups and wine flagons clattering against the table in the Stamford town hall. "He has defied the charter of liberties set forth by Henry the First and used his royal powers to oppress us. 'Tis our duty as free men and protectors of justice to overthrow him!"

The two dozen barons gathered there met his pronouncement with varying degrees of enthusiasm. Some reacted with violent oaths and cries of "Hear, hear." Others only nodded and lifted their cups in agreement.

Simon, standing in the back of the smoke-blackened, Saxon-built hall wondered if any of the other men gathered there felt as he did, that FitzWalter was a power-mad fool who would use any excuse to march against King John.

No matter what high-minded rhetoric FitzWalter spouted, calling himself "the Marshal of the Army of God and the Holy Church," 'twas clear that he and many of the barons had very selfish, ignoble goals for rising against the king. John had harmed them or their families in some way, and now they sought vengeance. Many also saw the potential for increasing their own power and bringing down their enemies, who were often allies of John.

Simon could easily see why William Marshal had steadfastly condemned the rebels. They were not a very impressive, nor a trustworthy, lot. Although he had come here to Stamford, Lincolnshire, to throw in his own cause with the grievances and complaints of the others, he no longer felt like Cicely's proud champion, nobly pursuing a just calling. There was something underhanded and base about the way the rebels plotted and strategized. He sensed no honor in it, no real courage either.

But it appeared too late to turn back. He had laid out his grievance against the king soon after coming to Stamford, before he knew the nature of the men involved. Now he feared that by revealing Tathwick's vulnerability, he had drawn the avaricious interest of some of the barons and knights. If he was not with them, then he was against them, and they would consider his property fair game.

His turmoil deepened as he suddenly noted a pair of cunning eyes watching him from across the table.

Simon stared, unable to look away. 'Twas him! That murderer, Reginald de Bron!

How could he have become bound up in a cause with the man he despised more than any other?

He fought for control as the memories filled his mind. A dark, cool dwelling. Soft hands tending him. Gentle, musical voices. Then, even as the dizziness of the fever lost some of its power, the knights came. His countrymen, wielding swords and shouting threats.

He dragged himself from his pallet and staggered to his feet. He saw blood spurt and screams of fear turn to cries of anguish. He tried to stop the carnage, but de Bron knocked him down. He lay there, too weak and helpless to rise, listening to the moans and pleas, the haunting cadences of the foreign tongue.

Then, all was silent. The knights, his companions, hoisted

him roughly and carried him from the place. He swooned into blessed oblivion.

When he awoke, de Bron and the others claimed they had thought the Muslim family who took him in had meant to rob and kill him. But he knew better. De Bron and the others had struck down the Saracens not to save him, but to steal the family's treasure. Mingling with images of blood and death were memories of his companions rifling chests and rolling up textiles and rugs.

The recollection still made him want to vomit. For two years, he'd been tortured by the evil his countrymen had done. He'd felt contaminated, unclean. He'd wanted to die, to succumb to the torments of the fever. Only with Cicely's love and faith had he been able to banish those hellish memories. And now he was face-to-face with the cause of his self-doubt and despair.

He wanted to kill de Bron. But how could he? They were allies now. What excuse could he use to strike down a fellow knight?

And there was Cicely's cause to think of. He must concentrate on saving Tathwick for her. De Bron's punishment must come from God, not him.

Simon rose and tried to slip away. A mocking voice sounded behind him as he reached the doorway. "Simon de Cressy, I confess I am surprised to find you in such distinguished company. I thought you had sworn off associating with 'murderers and monsters' as you once referred to your fellow Normans."

Simon turned. Mayhap de Bron would give him some excuse to issue a challenge. 'Twould be sweet to face him, sword in hand, and serve the cause of justice.

"I hear you come here on behalf of a woman. Tell me, de Cressy, is Lady Valois comely, her body lush and sweet?"

Simon reached for the pommel of his sword. "Don't speak of her, you bastard! You're not fit to lick her shoes!"

De Bron laughed harshly. "You always were an idealistic

fool. I recall some idiocy you spouted about the heathen Saracens having souls. That 'twas a sin to kill them.''

Simon clenched his jaw. ''You're a black-hearted fiend, de Bron. A murderer and a thief!''

De Bron smiled. ''And you're a gutless *monk*. A pity that when the Almighty afflicted you with the fever, He did not take the fortuitous step of ridding this earth of your useless carcass altogether.''

Fury flared through Simon, but he turned sharply on his heel and continued down the hall.

Gutless? Monk? Because he found killing women and unarmed men abhorrent? Jesu, he was ashamed that men like de Bron ever bore the title of crusader! 'Twas a blot upon all fighting men, an embarrassment to all who followed Christ's teachings!

Yet he knew that de Bron was not the only man who counted Muslims less than human and did not fear to rob and slaughter them. When he returned to France and complained of de Bron's behavior to some other knights, they had scarce understood his distress. They thought de Bron's behavior more dangerous than heinous. Had there been any reprisals against the Normans? they asked. Had any of their own been called to account for the deaths?

For a time, he had thought the fever must have muddled his wits and rendered him weak and craven. But then he remembered his purpose when he'd taken his crusader's vow. He'd wanted to do something brave and glorious, to find a noble purpose for his life. No matter how he tried, he could not reconcile what he had allowed to happen in Constantinople with the Christian teachings he held in his heart.

So, he had lost faith. In himself, in life itself. The recurrences of the fever he saw as a further sign of the loss of God's grace. He was cursed, tainted by the sins of his companions.

But Cicely had made him believe. In goodness, in beauty and

righteousness. In helping her, he had finally found a purpose, a means of redemption.

Now he was her champion, and he could not fail. Though the rebels' cause be questionable, he had no choice but to embrace it.

For a while he walked in the chill spring night, seeking to clear his head of the gut-wrenching anger. As he left the town to seek his men's camp in the forest, he recognized the wide-eyed, eager countenance of Dewi ab Owain, his new squire. His father said that the Welsh youth showed great promise in handling not only weapons but also difficult horses like Lucifer.

The sight of Dewi's young face caused a wrenching ache of recognition. How much the youth reminded him of himself at that age. The same innocent enthusiasm, the same glowing idealism.

"Sir Simon!" Dewi called breathlessly. "Has it been decided? Do we march on London?"

Simon grimaced at the youth's words. He approached the squire and grabbed him by the sleeve of his tunic. "Hold your tongue, young fool! When men talk of treason, they do it in the shadows. They do not shout it out for all to hear!"

"Jesu, I am sorry! I did not think!"

"Nay, you did not!" Simon growled.

"But truly, I do not see the danger. Are we not all joined in the same cause? Is not the purpose of the gathering to discuss how to confront the king?"

Simon jerked on the youth's tunic, pulling him farther away from the torches which illuminated the area. "Before this thing is over," he said carefully, " 'tis very likely several of these men will betray our cause and go back to supporting the king. Some may even switch allegiance several times. These are not men who lose sleep over such niceties as sworn oaths. Depending upon how the winds of fortune blow, they will choose the course which promises to profit them the most."

''And what of you, milord? Are you fixed in your purpose?''

Simon sighed. How could he explain his doubts? The nagging sense of unease which haunted him? ''When the rebel barons march south, you and I will be arrayed beside them. That is all the answer I can give you.''

CHAPTER 19

"A tournament! Has everyone gone mad?" Simon sat up in his bedroll and rubbed the sleep out of his eyes.

Dewi hastened to hand him his boots. "Well, there's near to two thousand knights gathered here and naught for them to do but drink and brawl. Geoffrey de Mandeville thought that a tournament would make better use of their abilities."

"Count me out," Simon grumbled. "I've no use for such foolery."

"But milord"—the squire's voice rose in dismay—"I've seen you train—you've as good a chance of winning as anyone."

"Not if I don't compete."

Dewi sighed heavily, but did not argue the matter further. Simon finished dressing in silence, then left the tent. Outside in the forest clearing where they were camped, his men were occupied in games of chance and polishing their weapons and armor. Simon found Girard, his captain, squatting down in the grass with a group of knights playing knucklebones. He gestured, and Girard rose, although not without a twinge of reluctance, Simon thought.

"Have you heard word of this tournament?" he asked his captain.

Girard nodded. "The men are excited by the notion, and already laying wagers. They think you will acquit yourself well."

"I can't believe you approve!" Simon exclaimed. "Did not my father charge you with protecting me and seeing that I took no unnecessary risks?"

"Aye, but 'tis only a tournament, not real warfare."

"Men *die* in tournaments! That's why the Church has forbidden them!"

Girard shrugged. "The men need something to think about besides this endless waiting." He shook his head. "I don't see why FitzWalter and Eustace de Vesci won't make their move. All they do is talk and confer, but I sense no real purpose behind their words. They say it is up to John to respond to their demands, but, in truth, he *has* responded. When he circulated the Pope's letters condemning 'all opposition against the king,' 'twas clear enough he means to fight our demands. 'Tis past time to take action. Our leaders may not know it, but the men do. If we wait too long, John will bring in his damned Angevin mercenaries and fortify his castles!"

Simon grimaced. There was some truth in his captain's words. John was a cunning strategist; 'twas unwise to give him time to prepare for war. "I think our leaders are waiting to see whether they can entice any other barons to join us," he said.

Girard gave a derisive snort. "We'll bring no more men to our cause until we have a few victories under our belts. Already, there are those who've been scared away by the news that John has taken the Cross. What a brilliant move that was. He never intends to travel to the Holy Land, but he's gained the protection of the Church and discredited all his enemies in one fell swoop.''

Simon nodded glumly. Although he no longer believed in the sacredness of the crusader's vow, especially when taken up by a man as scheming and immoral as John, he knew there were those men made squeamish by the thought that they defied not only their anointed king, but a man cloaked in the holy grace of a crusader.

''Aye, you are right,'' he told Girard. '' 'Tis past time we marched into battle. I'm going into the town. Mayhap I can learn some news, or even convince some of the others that we must pressure FitzWalter to take action.''

But Simon had no luck in his mission. The talk was all of the tourney. Of how the forces should be divided—northern knights against southern ones—and where the boundaries of the melee should be set. Disgusted by the widespread enthusiasm for such a meaningless activity, Simon had started to leave the castle when he came upon Engelard, the captain of the garrison at Bedford, where Simon had served when he first came back to England.

''By the saints!'' Engelard exclaimed. ''You're alive! I thought certain, when we left you at Montreau, your sickness was mortal.''

''The nuns nursed me back to health. I am as fit as ever.''

''Aye, I see that.'' Engelard still gaped at him. ''What do you here, Sir Simon? What lord do you serve to these days?''

Simon hesitated. Convinced that he could never go home, he had not told Engelard about his inheritance and position at Valmar, but instead had led him to believe he was a penniless itinerant knight. What would Engelard think on learning the truth?

''I serve no man these days,'' Simon said. ''I am betrothed

to the heiress of Tathwick. 'Tis her cause which brings me here. I would force the king to recognize her right to a property which has been in her family for generations.''

"Tathwick?" Engelard looked startled. "I thought Valois and his only heir were dead."

"He had a daughter he placed with the holy order at Montreau because he could not afford to dower her. But she never took vows, so she is free to inherit and to marry."

Engelard's eyes lit up, and he smiled wryly. "You crafty bastard. I did not know you had it in you. To convince a nun to wed you and make you rich."

"That was not the way of it," Simon protested. "I did not know when I met her that her father and brother would die. 'Tis not greed which brings me here, but the desire to see that Lady Cicely keeps what is rightly hers."

Engelard regarded him thoughtfully. "You did your duty when you served in my troop, although your wretched illness delayed us more than once. Mayhap it is admiration for your skill with a sword and your remarkable stoicism which makes me inclined to warn you."

"Warn me?"

Engelard drew near, his countenance wary. "You're not the only one who covets Tathwick. I have heard Reginald de Bron say that 'tis ripe for the taking."

"De Bron!" A sick fury enveloped Simon. He had feared that his presence here would draw attention to Tathwick; how bitter to have his worries confirmed, to learn that the man he loathed above all others conspired to steal Cicely's property.

"Don't shout so," Engelard grumbled, "nor mention to anyone that I told you this. I'd not like to see de Bron set against me."

"Nay, I will not," Simon replied, "but I still mean to confront him with his treachery!"

He went to find his adversary. Stamford was a sizable town,

and with so many men gathered there and so many others camping in the nearby woods, 'twas no easy matter to locate de Bron. At last he tracked him down at the main livery stables, playing draughts with a group of knights, several of whom Simon recognized as fellow crusaders. "De Bron," he said, "I would have a word with you."

De Bron rose. "Well, if it isn't Simon de Cressy." He glanced at his fellows. "I wonder if he's taken sick again. What think you?"

Though fury sang through him, Simon forced himself to say calmly, "I challenge you, de Bron, to fight for the honor of Tathwick."

De Bron grinned. " 'Twould not be well done of us to break the solemn peace of this gathering. Let it be decided upon the tournament field when the melee begins two days hence. If I capture you, Tathwick is mine. If you capture me, I release all claim upon the property, upon my honor as a crusader," he added slyly.

Simon's whole body went rigid, while the group of knights watched expectantly. He dare not refuse to participate in the tourney now. But mayhap 'twas meant to be. This might be his only opportunity to avenge the wrong done in Constantinople.

"So be it," he answered through clenched teeth.

"Try to remain in sight of a herald or some knight who has no interest in the outcome between you and de Bron," Girard warned Simon, as he and Dewi armed him the day of the tournament. "I do not trust that devil to fight fair."

"Nor do I," Simon answered grimly. He ducked his head so they could settle the heavy hauberk on him, then stood still as they fastened the mail coif around his neck and helped him put on his gauntlets and helm. "I believe he means to do more than disarm me and hold me for ransom. I would not be surprised if he carried a real sword instead of a blunted weapon.''

"Mayhap you should also," Dewi suggested. "There is not need to draw it, unless you are in danger of being run through by that devil.''

Simon shook his head. "How can I, in good conscience, defy the rules of tourney custom? Besides, I believe I can take him, blunted weapon or no." His expression grew hard. " 'Tis clear he has spent his days since returning to England drinking, gambling, and swiving. He has grown fat and slow. If I cannot beat him in fair combat, I do not deserve to hold Tathwick.''

"But that is what we fear," Girard said, "that it will not be fair combat, that de Bron will use some sort of trickery to bring you down.''

Simon turned to face Girard, his voice commanding. "If that happens, I want you to ride as fast as possible to Tathwick and escort Cicely and her mother to safety.''

"And your mother?''

"Aye, my mother as well. Take them all to Valmar. My father will see to their safety.''

"Don't speak so," Dewi urged, "you will prevail over that rat-faced sack of filth, I know it!''

Simon closed his eyes and prayed silently. He must defeat de Bron, or poor Cicely would lose her home, her birthright. How could he bear to face her if he failed?

The grinding knot in his stomach did not ease as Simon mounted Lucifer and rode toward the area marked as the tournament ground.

'Twas a cloudy, dreary spring day, though with no rain, for which Simon was grateful. The ground would not be so slippery, nor sighting his opponent so difficult. In a melee the two forces would rush each other, as if in battle, and the conflict might range over a large area as knights took each other captive and then returned to the fray.

The huge lance felt heavy in his hand, and Simon thanked the saints that he had spent much of the winter training at Blackhurst castle. The hours of wielding a broadsword had restored the strength in his arms and shoulder that the fever had taken from him.

Behind him, carrying extra weapons and waterskins for refreshment, rode Dewi. Squires could take the field with their knights, but they did not fight. For safety reasons, they usually ended up in the refuge area where the prisoners where kept. Even as he cantered to join the line of knights from the southern domains, Simon gestured for Dewi to keep well back. He did not want the youth's accidental death or injury on his conscience.

The two rows of knights faced each other across an open area, a hundred yards apart, and the air was thick with the smells of horses and men, the scent of excitement and danger. Fortunes could be won or lost on the tourney field, much as in battle. Simon thought of Cicely's godfather, the earl of Pembroke, who had risen from poor knight to king's man through his daring exploits in tournaments in France. In the ransoming process, horses, coin, and even land changed hands.

With this thought, Simon tried to sight his opponent. He spied him, near the end of the line of knights, wearing a yellow surcote trimmed in green. Simon knew that his own colors, red upon white, made him easy to spot. Had de Bron marked his position? Would he charge directly at him when the signal came?

Knights were still joining the line, while those waiting grew restive. Horses stamped and reared, and men swore. Otherwise, it was surprisingly quiet. Simon could hear the caw of the ravens gathering near the battlefield. They, if no one else, would be disappointed if no blood was spilled.

From the woods came the distinctive call of the cuckoo and the mingled trills of songbirds as they built their nests and fed their young. The meadow where the knights gathered was alive with the signs of spring. Daffodils and bluebells carpeted the ground, and around them the trees budded with tender green leaves and the snowy white blossoms of the blooming hawthorn.

Simon felt a pang inside as he considered the poignant beauty of life and the possibility that he might die. He thought of Cicely, of her face radiant with excitement, her beguiling laugh and glowing brown eyes. Then he adjusted the heavy ashwood lance and prepared to fight for their future together.

The herald gave the signal, and the two lines started forward.

Knowing that de Bron was much too far to the left for them to meet cleanly, Simon headed for a knight across from him, a man who wore a crimson and gold surcote. Their lances clashed, and the knight was unhorsed in the first strike. Simon passed his victim, leaving him to fight on foot, and charged again.

Soon, the meadow was dangerously crowded with knights fighting with broadswords. With no room to manuever, those knights still mounted cantered away from the field and found new combat areas among the woods. Simon continued his success, keeping his seat on Lucifer while downing other men. He bested each knight who challenged him, but did not pursue any man or take him captive. His purpose was fixed on finding de Bron and making an end to things.

Some distance into the wooded area, Simon spotted his adversary. A chill of premonition went through him as he remembered Girard's warning words and realized that de Bron and he were very much alone, screened from sight of the rest of the combatants by a grove of wild cherry trees in full bloom.

De Bron gave a ringing cry, half-taunt, half-mocking laugh, and charged. Simon brought round his destrier and spurred Lucifer straight at his opponent.

It seemed as if minutes passed in the time it took for them to grow close enough that Simon could see de Bron's face clearly. He focused on his enemy's eyes, waiting for de Bron's attention to waver for the split second it took to gain an advantage. In the end, neither man flinched, but their horses turned at the last moment, unwilling to crash headfirst into each other, despite no check from their riders. The knights' lances met with bone-jarring impact.

Lucifer swerved as the force of the collision jerked Simon's body in the opposite direction. Jolted from the horse's back, he instinctively released his weapon and leaned out so that his hauberk would break his fall.

He landed with a crash, a swirl of stars bursting around his vision. Cold fear gave him the presence of mind to get to his feet and assess his opponent's position. For a moment, he could not find de Bron, and he panicked. If the other knight was still mounted, he could ride Simon down and kill him with ease.

Then he saw de Bron's chestnut destrier, wild-eyed and lathered, some distance away. His dread eased. But where was the rider? Had de Bron been knocked unconscious in the fall or struck by his mount's flailing hooves?

Simon drew his blunted sword and started forward in the brush. The gorse and fern reached to his knees, hampering his movements. His breathing echoed harsh and rasping in his helm. As he neared de Bron's mount, some inner sense warned him to turn. He whirled and found de Bron watching him from five paces, his sword also drawn.

"So, it comes down to this." De Bron's helm muffled his voice, but Simon could catch the taunting inflection he gave his words. "What think you, de Cressy, can you take me?"

Simon gritted his teeth. "God willing, I will try."

"Oh, God favors you, does He!" De Bron laughed. "Have you not learned yet, de Cressy? 'Tis not God who determines victory in battle, but might and ruthlessness. Besides, 'twould seem you have fallen from His grace. Why else did He afflict you with that fever, when none of the rest of us suffered? You should have died then, like the pious weakling that you are!"

"But I did not die." Simon's voice rang out, full of defiant fury. "God sent an angel to tend me. And now, now I will fight for *her*."

He rushed forward and engaged with de Bron. The rage seemed to sing through him, strengthening his sword arm, making his movements rapid and sure. He pressed de Bron and forced him backward. Their swords clashed, the blunted metal of Simon's screaming against the edge of his opponent's weapon. The realization that de Bron's weapon was made of sharpened steel infuriated him further. De Bron meant to kill him, else he would not have dared carry an illegal weapon.

Dead men tell no tales . . . but I am not dead yet. With ringing blows, Simon forced de Bron back. He prayed his inferior weapon would bear up and tried to land his blows against de Bron's shield rather than letting him parry. The sweat poured down Simon's face, but his muscles felt fresh and strong. Around him gathered a timeless silence. All fear was gone. There was nothing but the ancient rhythm, check and lunge, swerve and feint.

He heard his enemy's grunts, sensed him tiring. De Bron's lazy habits had caught up with him. Simon drew back to regain his own breath, then swung wide. Too late—too slow—de Bron tried to parry the blow and his sword went flying.

Simon brought the tip of his own weapon to de Bron's neck. "Do you yield?" he demanded.

De Bron laughed. "You cannot hurt me with that child's plaything."

"Yield!" Simon persisted, pushing the blunted point deeper against de Bron's unprotected throat. "I claim you as my prisoner. As your ransom, I demand your horse, twenty marks, and a vow before ten other men that you renounce all claim to Tathwick."

"Fool!" De Bron's voice was low and harsh. "You cannot

win. As soon as you mount your horse, I'll swear that we fought to a stalemate, that neither of us was able to gain the advantage.''

"You would lie?''

"Aye, you miserable dolt, I would *lie*. I will not give up my designs upon Tathwick. Nor will I pay you a penny of ransom.''

Never had Simon been so angry, but he was shocked as well. 'Twas unthinkable that a knight would flaunt the sacred code of chivalry. Even in war, there were rules. Only a monster defied the laws that defined the very meaning of knighthood. But then, he'd known de Bron was a fiend.

For a moment, Simon stood frozen; then he stepped away. With a quick motion, he dropped his sword and lunged for de Bron's.

The bastard did not even move. Indeed, as Simon held out the gleaming, oiled tip of the deadly sharp sword, de Bron laughed again. "And what would you do with that, de Cressy? Impale me with an illegal weapon, and all will know *you* for a cheat and outlaw.''

"If I kill you, then throw your weapon into the nearby stream, no one will know the difference.''

"Ah, but you will know, won't you?'' de Bron taunted. "You will know that you defied your code of honor, and that you are no better than me, whom you despise. Can you live with that, de Cressy?''

The truth of his words struck Simon. He could not kill an unarmed man, no matter the provocation. 'Twould be murder, and his soul would be blackened for all eternity.

With disgust, he flung the weapon down. "Go,'' he told de Bron. "Mount your horse and ride away, out of my sight. We will settle the matter of Tathwick another time. Mayhap on the battlefield where the rules favor the better warrior rather than the better liar.''

He turned and started after Lucifer. The blood pounded in his head, and his stomach churned with frustration. He could not defeat a man so treacherous and deceitful, but he prayed that God would grant him the chance to meet de Bron again in real warfare.

"De Cressy!"

Simon turned around and beheld de Bron fast approaching, sword in hand. "Now *you* will yield," he said.

Simon stared in incredulity as de Bron reached him and pointed the sword at his neck. "You would not dare," he whispered.

"Oh, aye, I would." De Bron's voice rang out gleefully. "Get down on your knees, you bastard, and tell me that you yield to me not only Tathwick, but the little nun who comes with it."

"Do not speak of Cicely!" Simon hissed.

"Have you even bedded her, or are you too much of a monk for that?"

The air seemed to grow thick around Simon, his heart beat much too fast. "I warn you, de Bron, do not speak of such things!"

"Warn me? Am I supposed to be frightened by your threats? Do not forget who holds the sword, and who is ruthless enough to use it."

"If you kill me, you'll be condemned as a murderer. Everyone will know that you carried sharpened steel into a tournament."

De Bron pressed the sword deeper against Simon's neck. "Not if I follow your suggestion and throw the sword away."

"How will you convince them that my wounds were made by a blunted weapon?"

"I will be careful to kill you in a way that makes it plausible you died by accident."

As Simon reacted to these chilling words, de Bron withdrew the sword, then swung it around. Simon tried to duck, but the flat of the blade caught his body and made him stagger. As he struggled to keep his footing, the full weight of de Bron's broadsword crashed into Simon's helm and he went down.

Hampered by the weight of his mail, he struggled to rise. Cold fear beat through him. *He means to make it look as if I was thrown from my horse.* Simon glanced around for his own weapon. Somehow he must retrieve it or de Bron would slowly batter him to death.

The sword was hidden in the tall grass; he'd never find it in time. He must think of something else.

When the next blow came, he did not try to avoid it, but turned his body so that his armor took the impact. He let himself fall back and lay there. Out of the eyeholes of his helm, he kept his enemy in sight as his fingers searched frantically for the misericord fastened to his swordbelt. He found the dagger at the moment de Bron reached him, his sword drawn back for another blow.

Simon rolled so the broadsword only grazed him. As he panted for breath, he realized that even if he got to his feet, he could not fight de Bron with a puny dagger. Somehow he must get his enemy near enough that he could use the misericord at close range.

"De Bron," he called out, trying to make his voice sound weak and pained. "I yield to you. I vow it, on my honor."

"Too late. I think I would as lief kill you," de Bron answered harshly. "Then there will be no challenge to my claim of Tathwick."

"Please," Simon implored, even as he winced at the craven sound of the word.

"Aye, that is it, de Cressy, beg and whimper. 'Twill avail you naught, but still, it gives me pleasure to hear you admit your cowardice."

De Bron struck him another jarring blow and sharp pain shot along Simon's side. This time, he did not have to feign his distress as he said, "Please. If you do not kill me, I will tell you where I hid my treasure."

"Treasure?"

At hearing the greed in de Bron's voice, a plan solidified in Simon's mind. "Aye, the treasure. The Saracen family who cared for me in Constantinople—before you killed them—they gave me gold and precious objects. They wanted me to marry their daughter."

"We saw naught of that when we carried you away," de Bron scoffed.

"I went back for it later. They'd hidden it well, and you were in a hurry." Simon punctuated his words with gasping breaths, then ended with a groan.

"You took their gold!" De Bron gave a crow of delight. "Mayhap you are not quite the fool I thought. Where is it? At Tathwick? Where?"

"I hid it," Simon moaned. "I hid it before I went to Tathwick. Spare my life and I will tell you where."

De Bron struck him another vicious blow, and Simon felt the pain in his side blossom. "Tell me where the treasure is, and I will *think* of sparing you."

Simon gave another shuddering moan and began to breathe in short rasps. "You will . . . kill me . . . anyway. What profit . . . is there . . . in it . . . for . . . me?"

Simon braced himself for another brutal assault. He would feign unconsciousness and hope de Bron would get close enough to grapple with. To his surprise, de Bron did not strike him, but knelt nearby. "If you do not tell me, I will make certain you suffer before you die," he threatened. "I will break your ribs one by one, I will—"

The words ended in a strangled groan as Simon drove the misericord into de Bron's throat. De Bron tried to rise, clutching his neck. Simon twisted away, also struggling to get to his feet.

A sharp blade drove into his side and the pain washed over him like a towering wave.

When consciousness returned, he rose unsteadily to his knees. He tried to turn around to see his opponent, but the pain was unbearable. He sank down again. Gradually, he regained his will and, gritting his teeth, crawled forward. He saw de Bron amid the crushed and ruined vegetation. The knight's eyes stared blindly, and blood oozed in a vivid puddle around his face.

A sense of horror came over Simon, followed quickly by relief. 'Twas de Bron's sword which had sliced open his side. No one would condemn him for fighting for his life.

If he lived. With despair, Simon realized that it might be hours before anyone came looking for him. Even then, the tall brush would hide his prone form all too well. He would likely be dead before they found him, his life's blood pooling on the ground.

A horrible dizziness afflicted him, and he closed his eyes and let his head rest on the ground. If he heard the approach of horses, he would try to sit up or call out so they would see him. He dare not lose consciousness, or they might never find him.

Struggling to maintain awareness, Simon opened his eyes and gazed up at the sky. He summoned the vision of Cicely's sweet face, recalling the first time he had beheld it. His angel. She had saved his life. He could not leave her.

"How could you leave him?" Girard demanded of Dewi. "I told you that I feared treachery. The day is near gone, the tournament finished, and yet there is no sign of Simon. Nor de Bron."

"He would not let me follow after him. He said he feared I would be hurt!"

Dewi looked stricken, and Girard felt a stirring of sympathy for the youth. Tournaments were dangerous business, and for an unmounted squire, even more so. "Did you at least see which way he went?"

"In the woods. To the east."

Girard scarce nodded before spurring his horse in that direction. He told himself he would not panic. Simon was a formidable fighter, unlikely to be bested by anyone, even if he used illegal weapons.

But where was he? Girard had searched the refuge areas on either end of the tournament ground. Neither of the heralds, busily recording captures and ransoms, had seen Simon. Or de Bron.

The twisting anxiety inside him deepened. How could he go back to Valmar Castle and tell Fawkes that his only son, who had survived a Crusade and deadly sickness, had been killed in a tournament? For that matter, how would he face Lady Nicola?

The thought made Girard take a shaky breath and lick his dry lips. Jesu, he could not do it! If Simon were dead, he would have to run away or get killed himself!

He rode among the groves of oak and beech. The place was silent, eerily so. Girard's heartbeat quickened. Had Simon met some awful fate here among the newly budded trees?

There seemed to be a meadow beyond the trees. Girard rode toward it.

He beheld a small clearing broken by a copse of cherry trees in full flower. Their sweet scent came to his nostrils. Gorse and heather bloomed everywhere, and the vegetation was so new and so green it near hurt his eyes.

But where was Simon?

Anxiety nagged at him, forcing him to ride on. On the other side of the cherry grove, he saw Lucifer and his heart leaped into his throat. Simon had been unhorsed.

Girard rode to Lucifer and tried to reach out to grab his bridle. The destrier rolled his eyes and pawed the ground. Girard's dismay deepened. Simon must have been captured.

He left the uneasy horse, deciding he would send Dewi to fetch the animal, then circled the edge of the meadow and started back into the wooded area.

A whinny behind him made him turn his mount. He could see movement near the trees on the other side of the clearing. Girard stared in puzzlement as he spied the second horse. Two warhorses, but no knights anywhere in sight. It did not make sense.

He started toward the chestnut destrier, intending to search for some sign of the owner's device. He was halfway across the meadow when he heard the sound. So soft, barely more than the sigh of the wind through the grass, but it focused his attention on the meadow, and that was when he saw the raven land amidst the brush. He knew immediately what that meant. The birds were drawn by the smell of blood.

Breathlessly, he guided his horse toward where the raven had set down. He moved slowly, carefully, so as not to accidentally step on anything in his path.

He found de Bron, his body twisted gruesomely, the brush around him crushed by his death throes. Girard dismounted and peered at the corpse. A dagger in the throat—an unusual way for a knight to meet his end, especially during a tournament. The misericord was meant for hand-to-hand combat or the final *coup de grâce* when an opponent was too badly injured to live.

The sick, uneasy feeling in Girard's stomach deepened. If Simon had killed de Bron like this, 'twould be hell to pay. It did not look like a fair fight. Had de Bron angered Simon so badly that he'd lost his temper and silenced his opponent by this disreputable method?

But where was Simon? Had he run away after realizing what he had done? He would have taken his horse, Girard decided, so he must still be around somewhere, lurking in the woods, too overcome by anguish to show himself.

For a moment, Girard thought to call out, then decided against it. He did not know what he would say to Simon. His opinion of his liege's son was completely shattered. He had thought Simon the most noble and heroic of knights, but a man like that would never had done this. 'Twas almost murder.

Girard put his foot in the stirrup and prepared to mount. Then he heard that muffled sound again. He froze and waited, straining his ears. The lulling melodies of birdsong. The whisper of the wind in the grass. And far in the distance, men's voices and the thud of hooves.

He shook his head, trying to clear it. He was imagining things. The grisly sight of de Bron's body had rattled him.

He swung a leg over the saddle and went still once more. What was it? What was that noise bedeviling him?

He guided the horse back toward the corpse. Ravens were gathering again. Disgusted by the sight of the birds picking at de Bron's body, he rode nearer, yelling and waving his hands to shoo them away.

Only then did he spy the bit of white fabric fluttering in the breeze and realize that there was another body.

Simon!

He could not get off his horse fast enough, and though 'twas only a dozen paces away, it seemed to take him minutes to reach the prone form. The sight of Simon's deathly pale face and the blood staining one side of his white surcote increased Girard's sense of horror. His lord was injured, and badly.

He bent down beside Simon and removed his helm, then felt for a pulse in his throat. Relief sang through him as he realized his charge still lived. He rushed back to his horse and retrieved his waterskin. Lifting Simon's head, he poured some water on his face to rouse him.

Simon's eyelids fluttered. "Cicely," he whispered through cracked lips.

"Aye, aye, I'll take you to her. But for now you must drink."

Simon obediently swallowed, then groaned.

Girard laid his charge back down. The blood made the location of the wound clear, but he could not tell how bad it was. He rolled Simon to his side and examined the rent in the mail hauberk. The amount of blood made him grimace. Even if the sword thrust had hit no vital organ, 'twas likely that Simon would bleed to death before he could get aid.

Realizing there was no more he could do for the fallen man, Girard quickly remounted and galloped toward the refuge area of the southern contingent. There would be a surgeon there. Mayhap he could save Simon.

CHAPTER 20

'Twas a strange dream. She was watching two knights fighting. At first she thought it was a mock battle; then one man lunged and she saw his weapon pierce the other's hauberk. The wounded man staggered back, then regained his resolve. The swordplay continued. Cicely wanted to cry out, to warn them that they did not have to fight, but no sound came from her mouth.

The knights continued to circle and parry. She could sense their deadly intent, their concentration. With absolute conviction, she knew they would not stop until one had killed the other. She tried to run to them and place her body between their slashing blades. Her feet were frozen in place. She could only watch helplessly.

The terrible sense of dread built inside her. She watched their surcotes grow red with blood, their movements become weak and ineffectual. It seemed they would both fight until they died.

Their swords clashed, locked. She could feel their straining muscles, the frightful resolve which drove them.

Steel grated against steel, then drove into soft flesh. With a scream of agony, they both collapsed.

Her immobilized body was freed. Rushing to the first man, she pulled the helm from his head. He was a stranger; she did not know his face. She hurried to the other man. Even without removing his helm, she knew it was her father.

She bent over him, tears pouring down her face. "Why?" she cried. "Why?"

His eyes were unseeing, empty. Then his face dissolved into nothingness.

Cicely woke to the sound of her own ravaged sobbing. It took awhile to calm herself, to recall that she had already mourned her father's death for over a month. But her grief seemed fresh and raw, the sense of loss unbearable.

She climbed, shaking, from the bed and poured some wine from the flask on the table. After taking a long draught, she went to the window and threw open the shutters. She breathed deeply of the cold, damp air. Almost morning. She could see the lightening of the sky over the far ramparts. No hope of sleeping now. She might as well dress and begin her day.

She meant to know every aspect of Tathwick by the time Simon returned, to impress him with her abilities as chatelaine. In the past few days, she'd gone over the tally accounts with Sir Harry, ridden over nearly every league of land on the property, spoken to villeins and freemen regarding the yield of the last harvest, and spent hours with Lady Nicola, supervising the servants as they scrubbed down the walls, replaced the rushes, and aired the tapestries in the hall. She had vowed that her beloved would return to find that despite her idle years in the priory, she was well capable of learning those things which a wealthy lord's wife should know.

Simon's wife—the thought made a warm glow steal over her

and banished the remnants of her distress. She closed her eyes and savored the memory of their last night together. It had been incredible, every bit as wonderful as she had imagined it would be. And, soon he would return and they would enjoy each other night after night.

She sighed heavily as the familiar throb started between her thighs. Oh, if only he would hurry home; she could scarce think of anything else but being with him, kissing and making love . . . Slowly, she shook herself from her reverie. She would not get anything accomplished if she spent all day indulging in lovesick fantasies.

After closing the shutters, she began to dress. There was a noise in the castle courtyard, the sound of horses. Could it be . . . ? She raced from the room, her belt hanging loose from her fingers, her hair unbraided.

When she reached the hall, there was a man she did not recognize standing by the hearth, talking to Sir Harry. She slowed her approach. Sir Harry glanced in her direction. Her footsteps faltered as she saw the stricken look on his face.

"What's happened?" she asked. "What's wrong?"

Sir Harry shook his head. "Simon's been wounded. He's not expected to live."

She wanted to faint, to let the ground loom up before her and hurl her into blessed unconsciousness, but the anger, the rage, wouldn't allow it. "Nay!" she cried. "I don't believe you!!"

Sir Harry came and held her arm, supporting her. His voice weary, he said, "I'm sorry, child. He was wounded in a tournament. He lost a great deal of blood and now . . . now he is fevered."

Hope glimmered in Cicely's mind. "A fever? I can treat a fever. Clotilde showed me how. I will go to him." She shook off Sir Harry's arm and started for the stairs, her mind on the cache of herbs in her mother's solar. Did they have any meadowsweet, betony, or feverfew? Mayhap the place where Simon was had a healer. There must be a priory nearby. Someone . . .

Cicely's thoughts ran in anxious circles, but as she neared the stairway, she had the sudden worry that the messenger might leave without telling them where Simon was.

She whirled around and hurried back to the hearth. "Where is he? How long ago did you leave him?"

The man shook his head. "He's at Stamford, milady. We took him to the local leech. He's bled him several times, but to no avail. 'Tis not a normal wound-fever which afflicts him, but something fiercer."

"How badly was he wounded?" she demanded. "How did it happen?"

"Somehow he received a deep sword slash in his side, and he was not found for hours. The other man is dead. What transpired between them is unclear."

"This happened in a tournament?" Sir Harry interjected. "I've heard of men being trampled or thrown from their horses. Mishaps with weapons also occur, but this sounds like something much more serious. Why weren't they using blunted weapons? Why wasn't—?"

"It doesn't matter," Cicely interrupted. She brought her trembling hands to her face. " 'Tis my fault . . . all my fault. I should never have insisted that we try to claim Tathwick." She choked back a sob. "I'm going to get the herbs, whatever I can find in the solar. Then we'll go."

"Milady," the messenger cautioned, "there is every chance he will die ere you reach him."

"Then you can bury me with him. I will never forgive myself for what I have done, and I will die of grief without my beloved."

* * *

The ride to Stamford was a nightmare. It rained unceasingly, and Cicely was so tense with worry, she could not get warm. But she forced herself to stay upright on the horse and to keep to the grueling pace she'd urged upon them. The man who'd brought the message, a knight named Thomas FitzWilliam, rode close beside her, as if fearful she might swoon and fall. She was grateful for his steady, solid presence.

They made the journey in two days, but Cicely knew that Thomas had little hope they would arrive in time.

The rain had stopped and a few torchlights could be seen, flickering in the gloom, when they reached the town gates near twilight. Cicely refused Thomas' suggestion that they stop at the inn for refreshment before going on to the barber's house.

When they finally found it, the barber's wife told them that the wounded knight was gone. For one horrible moment, Cicely thought she meant that Simon was dead. Then the leech himself, a slovenly churl with straggly whiskers and a red nose, came out and began complaining about "those wretched knights" who had dared to curse him and threaten him, and then took the sick man away without even paying him.

"Where did they take him?" Cicely demanded.

"To the priory outside the town," the barber said bitterly.

"Thank God they saw fit to get him out of there," Cicely said as they left the barber's house. "Clotilde told me about leeches like that. She said you are better off untended than to fall into their hands."

"It does not solve our dilemma," Thomas reminded her. " 'Tis almost dark. We cannot go to the priory this late. They will not admit us. Please let me escort you to the inn where you can rest."

"While Simon lies dying?" Cicely shook her head. "Nay,

I will go to the priory by myself if I have to. I will create such a commotion at the gates that they will have to let me in.''

Thomas sighed resignedly. "I will accompany you there, milady."

He took her arm and helped her onto her horse.

"Thank you, Sir Thomas." She tried to smile at him. "I don't know what I would have done without you."

"I cannot help but be inspired by your determination, lady. I have also been inspired by your husband's valor. Girard told me that Simon was a crusader. It must be wonderful to have an opportunity to fight for God's holy cause."

"Mayhap you should speak to Simon about that," Cicely said wearily. "He might tell you differently. Come now, let us return to the town gate and ask directions to the priory."

The priory was located at the edge of town, and they reached it without mishap. But, as Thomas had warned, the entrance was locked and there was no porter in sight.

"They'll be at vespers," Cicely said, guessing the time. She turned to Thomas and his squire. "If we all shout at once, they'll have to heed us."

"What should we call out?" Thomas asked.

"Let us yell Simon's name. If Girard and Dewi are watching at his bedside, they might hear us and force the holy brothers to let us in."

They made a fearsome racket. Cicely screamed until she was hoarse. Thomas and his squire shouted and hooted and banged their fists on the gate.

It took a long time before a porter came. He shouted back at them, telling them to go away. "Nay, we will not," Cicely said shrilly, "we will keep this up all night until you let us in. My ... husband, Simon de Cressy, is inside your walls. He may be dying. I will not go until I see him!"

"The sick man is your husband?"

"Aye," Cicely answered, wincing only slightly at the lie.

She feared that "betrothed" did not have the same weight as "wife."

The gate was finally opened and they were led to the infirmary. Simon's young squire met Cicely at the doorway. "Milady!" he cried. "I . . . I am most heartily sorry. I know you must hate us for failing you so. I beg your forgiveness." He sank to his knees in front of her.

"Please get up!" She sounded hysterical even to her own ears. "I only want to see Simon."

Dewi sprang to his feet, still mumbling apologies. He took her arm and led her into the infirmary.

She recognized Simon's tall form stretched out on one of the cots, but for a moment, she was afraid to draw nearer. What if she discovered that it was true—that there truly was no hope for him?

With cautious steps she approached, her heart torn in twain as she looked at him. A part of her soul leaped at the sight of his dear, beloved face. Another part sank into despair. He appeared so wasted, so gaunt. His skin was yellowish, waxen. Sunken shadows surrounded his closed eyes.

"Dear God," she whispered. She went and took his hand, feeling the heat of the fever. "Oh, Simon, oh, my love." She bent over him, weeping.

Someone patted her shoulder. "He won't know you. He's been unaware of anything for the past two days. I fear that his soul has . . . that he is—"

"Nay!" Cicely whirled on Dewi. "I will not give up! I will not. There must be something I can do to save him. I've brought medicines, herbs which will ease his fever and let him heal."

A monk came forward out of the shadows. Cicely realized she had not been aware he was there. The lamplight shone on his tonsured forehead and revealed a lined, sympathetic countenance. "Milady," he said, "we've already tried all that we can. His life is in the hands of God now. Only He can save Sir Simon.''

Cicely nodded jerkily and said, ''Aye, you are right. Where is the chapel? I wish to pray.''

The rows of flickering candles, the solemn chanting of prayers, the luxury and beauty adorning the priory chapel—all of it was familiar to Cicely and helped reinforce her resolve. She had spent ten years of her life in a place very similar to this one. As a child, she had been consecrated to the holy life, but she had defied the calling. Refused it. Now she saw that she had been wrong. Selfish and wicked.

It was not right that Simon should pay the price for her sinfulness. She could not let that happen. She must accept her fate and fulfill the agreement that her father had made with God.

''Cicely? Milady?''

She heard Girard's voice, but she felt too weary to rise and face him.

''Milady, let me get you to bed, ere you sicken as well.''

She allowed Girard to pick her up and carry her. Leaning back against his shoulder, she closed her eyes, utterly at peace. ''I have made a vow,'' she said. ''I'm going to become a nun. Finally, after all these years. And God will save Simon, He will let him live.''

''God may have a hand in it,'' she heard Girard say, ''but I trust that if he does live, 'twill mostly be due to the ministrations of the physician we have brought from the Jewry. The monks are aghast, but this man is our best hope. Samuel ben Ibraham is reputed to know something of Saracen fevers, and that is exactly the knowledge we need.''

"You see," Cicely mumbled, sinking slowly into sleep, "God has answered my prayers. He means to let Simon live."

She slept the deep, dreamless sleep of a child who has handed over her cares to someone older and wiser, someone who will make everything new and right again. And when she woke, the sense of peace remained with her. She rose and washed her face and hands, redid her plaits, smoothed her much rumpled traveling gown and left the guesthouse.

She felt no fear or trepidation as she entered the infirmary, for she knew that Simon would be better. And he was. His breathing was less shallow, his color better, and when she stroked his forehead, she knew the fever had broken at last.

"I think he is on the mend." The man seated on a stool by the cot suddenly rose. He had beautiful dark eyes and a calm, thoughtful manner.

"You must be the physician," she said.

The man nodded.

"What did you give him?"

"Willowbark. He could not chew it, so I made a decoction and forced it down his throat." He shrugged. "There is little enough we can do for this kind of sickness. In truth, 'tis his own strength which will save him or no. He must still recover from the terrible loss of blood and the wound itself. But he has endured much so far, and I am hopeful. His sort are not easy to kill." The physician smiled faintly.

Cicely shook her head. "If he lives, 'twill be because 'tis God's will."

"Mayhap, although myself, I am disinclined to leave such matters completely in His hands." The physician's smile widened. "I think it prudent to use the knowledge and skill of men to aid the sick when possible."

"Oh, I forgot," Cicely said suddenly. "You are a Jew."

The man's calm expression faltered, then returned. "And yet, I do believe in God. My faith is different than yours, but not any less, I think."

Cicely nodded. "Simon would not care. In Constantinople, when he first fell ill, he was tended by Saracens. He said he thought they were as good a people as any Christians."

The physician glanced briefly at Simon. "Mayhap that is Jehovah's purpose in saving this man. He is no common knight."

"Nay," Cicely allowed herself a giddy laugh. "Simon is not common at all."

She went to the cot and leaned over and kissed Simon's fever-parched lips. A terrible pang of regret went through her, but she willed it away. No sacrifice was too great to save Simon's life. She loved him better than herself; his life was far more important than her happiness.

She sat beside him, holding his hand. With each easeful breath he drew, she knew a blessed contentment. Simon would live.

Girard found her there a short time later. He gave her a worried look, then, seeing that she appeared well, took a seat beside her. "Praise God," he said, "it looks as if he mends."

Cicely nodded. "My prayers have been answered."

Girard heaved a harsh sigh of relief. "Milady, I must ask for your forgiveness. 'Twas my failing which caused this. I feared the wretch Reginald de Bron meant to try and harm Simon, but still, I urged milord to fight in the tournament. I should have heeded my instincts."

"But Dewi said you found Simon," Cicely said, "that you saved him from bleeding to death."

Girard sighed again. "If not for my urging, he might have avoided all this suffering and peril."

Cicely shook her head. "Nay, I think 'twas meant to be. How else would I ever have accepted my destiny?"

"What destiny is that, milady?"

Cicely released Simon's hand, which she had been holding. "I'm going back to Montreau. I'm going to take holy vows."

Girard gasped. "But, milady, you're betrothed to Simon! I vow, the only reason he survived this wound and terrible sickness is because he could not bear to be parted from you. The few times he was sensible, he spoke your name over and over."

Cicely bowed her head as the bitter regrets welled up inside her.

Girard touched her arm. "Simon risked his life to save Tathwick for you. He loves you and intends to wed with you. Why would you throw all that away to become a nun?"

Cicely closed her eyes, fighting the tears. "I made a vow, a solemn vow in the chapel last night. I said I would give up Simon if God would save his life."

Girard patted her shoulder. "You were exhausted and near out of your wits with worry. God will understand if you withdraw the pledge."

Cicely shook her head. "Nay, I must honor my vow. 'Tis because I refused my duty and defied God's will that Simon has suffered so."

"Simon suffers because some bastard—excuse the oath—saw fit to stab him when he was already injured! He suffers because he had the misfortune to acquire some wretched Saracen fever which Samuel ben Ibraham tells me is a malady that will linger in his body all his life. Whatever you did or did not do had naught to do with it!"

Cicely shook her head. As much as she wanted to believe Girard's words, she knew better. She had always been a willful, defiant sinner. 'Twas time she repented. "I was raised to honor my pledges," she said stiffly. "I swore to renounce all worldly ties. I swore it upon the surety of my soul. I will not gainsay such a vow and shame my blessed father's memory."

Girard made a helpless gesture. "I've never understood such

things. The oaths I've made have all been to mortal men, not the Almighty. Besides, from what Simon said, you have already plighted troth with him. That vow precedes any that you might have made to God.''

With a surge of embarrassment, Cicely recalled the exchange in the chapel at Tathwick and the night of passion that followed. She'd thought then that it might be wrong to experience such ecstasy; she knew now that her instinct was true. She'd led Simon into sin, and this was her punishment.

She reached out again to touch Simon's face, feeling the roughness of his whiskers. But his skin was cool. He would live. And she would never know if her prayers had brought about his recovery or if the Jewish physician's remedy had done it.

"I will keep to my resolve," she said. "I will do my duty as I have promised."

She heard Girard sigh heavily; then he left her.

Simon woke to burning pain, an unquenchable thirst, and a weakness worse than any he had known. But it all melted away in his joy at seeing Cicely's beautiful face. She was waiting for him to wake, as she had at Montreau. In that moment, the grim, pain-filled struggle back to life, the endless horrifying fever dreams, the agonies of his tortured flesh—'twas all worth it.

She stroked his brow and spoke soft, tender words, and he let himself fall back into the darkness once again, knowing that light awaited him when he woke.

"Cicely." He came to awareness sometime later, and found her holding his hand.

"You seem better this day," she said.

"Thanks to you."

She shook her head. "Nay, God has spared you, as I asked."

That made him smile, to think of Cicely praying for him. Then he felt the grinding pain in his side and grimaced. "I'm not much good to you now," he said.

"Just get well, Simon."

"I defeated de Bron, at least. He will not rob and kill anyone ever again."

She nodded.

"But the future of Tathwick is still uncertain. Can you tell me . . . have the rebels marched yet?"

"Aye, they've gone south to Brackley."

Simon sighed. "I wonder how they will fare, if there is any hope they will prevail over the king."

She said nothing, looking distant.

"I still mean to win you Tathwick," he said. "As soon as I am well, I will join the rebel forces once again."

"Oh, Simon." She shook her head, and he thought he saw a tear trickle down her cheek.

He squeezed her hand. "What's wrong, love?"

"I don't want you to fight anymore. Tathwick doesn't matter."

"Not matter? But what of your heritage? What of your birthright?"

There was no doubt of it now. She was weeping. "What is it?" he whispered. "What's wrong?"

Slowly, she composed herself. When she finally looked at him, her gaze was clear, determined. "Tathwick no longer matters. I'm going back to Montreau. I'm going to dedicate my life to God."

For a time, he simply gaped at her. It must be a jest. She was teasing him. But he had never seen her look so solemn. A cold, harsh fear went through him, penetrating to his very bones. "Why?" was all he could say.

"I made a vow," she said, "a solemn vow to God. I promised if He let you live, I would dedicate my life to His work." She took a deep breath. "He has kept His part, and now . . . now I must keep mine."

"Jesu, I can't believe you mean to do this." Simon stared blindly at the wall of the infirmary. "I swear, 'twas the promise of spending the rest of my life with you which kept me alive these past days." He shook his head. "When my life's blood was trickling away in that meadow . . . 'twas all I could think of. I imagined your face. I held onto that image as if 'twere my only salvation."

He heard the stool creak as she stood. "I'm sorry, Simon. I . . . I have to do this."

He dared to look at her, and what he saw made all his hope ebb away. Her lovely face appeared as cold and controlled-looking as if carved in stone. It was the same look of determination and otherworldliness he'd seen on the marble faces of martyred saints and on the features of men condemned to die. How could he argue with her or try to coax her back to being his playful, impulsive Cicely, the woman he loved?

He turned away and stared at the wall beside the bed. A razor-sharp dagger pierced his heart, and the pain was worse than any sword-thrust could ever bring.

CHAPTER 21

"Do you need to rest?" Girard asked. "There's a sheltered place a short distance ahead."

Simon shook his head. "I'm well enough," he lied, ignoring the stab of pain in his side and the queasiness of his belly. What did it matter if he reopened the wound and bled to death? The gaping hole in his heart was like to kill him anyway.

Cicely rode behind him, the hood of her mantle drawn demurely around her face, her eyes averted, her lips moving in prayer. He could feel her presence there, and he was aware of every breath she took, of the rise and fall of her chest, the flutter of a curl coming loose from its plait and brushing against her silken brow. His senses were concentrated upon her, though his own body raged with discomfort and weakness.

I might as well have died, he thought despairingly. *I am already dead to her, as she is lost to me.*

He choked back a moan, remembering the brutal shock of Cicely's decision.

Somehow he had lived through that agony, despite a fervent wish to succumb to his afflictions. The fever had passed; the wound in his side had mended. It appeared that he was not meant to die, but to endure this endless hell instead. For, having seen paradise and then lost it, his suffering was all the more bitter.

Now, riding through the lush, verdant English countryside, the air alive with birdsong and fragrant with the scents of flowers—buttercups, bluebells, and wild roses—his heart seemed frozen in winter. He rode stolidly toward Tathwick, to confront the final, irrevocable loss of all his hopes. For Tathwick was to be his, not a legacy from his parents, but something he had fought for himself, spilled his blood for the right to own, to walk upon the ramparts and gaze out at lands which were truly his, which would be his son's someday.

A son who even now might be growing in Cicely's womb.

The thought made hope stir within him, but he crushed it quickly. Near a month had passed since he'd bedded Cicely. If she carried his child, she would know it. And then she would not be so muleheadedly certain about God's plan for her life.

Another loss aggrieved him. If only he had started a child inside her. If only . . .

Another failure, another vicious twist of fate. Cicely was very clear about what her destiny held. But he, he could never seem to be so assured. So many times he had been convinced that the hand of God guided him upon a course of action. And so many times he had been proven wrong. The Crusade had been a disaster; it had near destroyed him in body and spirit. His pathetic attempt to do penance had gone equally awry. He'd met Cicely, and she had enticed him back to life, to laughter and passion and hope.

And now, that, too, had crumbled to nothing. Dear God, what was to become of him?

* * *

When they arrived at Tathwick, his mother and Sir Harry met them in the courtyard. Lady Nicola took one look at his face and swooned. Sir Harry caught her, his own expression a mask of worry and puzzlement.

Simon dismounted and went to his mother. "Give her air," he ordered the servants gathered around. He took her limp form from Sir Harry and started to carry her to the keep.

"Here now," Girard protested, "you're in no condition to do that. Jesu, you stupid fool!" he added as Simon walked away from him.

The blood was pounding in his ears, his muscles screaming with exertion when he finally reached the hall. He set his mother gently down on one of the benches, then collapsed beside her. "Are you trying to kill yourself?" Girard berated him. "If you have not opened up that damned wound, then I am a half-witted idiot!"

Simon gave him a quelling look. " 'Tis not like my mother to faint. By God, I don't think she has ever swooned before in her life." He gazed anxiously at her white face. "Has she been ill?"

Sir Harry snorted. "Not so you'd know, although she was frantic with worry when she first learned of your injury."

"Simon . . . Simon . . ." Nicola moaned. Simon leaned over her. "I'm here, Maman. All is well."

She opened her eyes; they looked like gleaming moonstones against the pallor of her skin. "Simon, my darling son," she murmured. She sat up slowly, obviously still dizzy, and reached out for him. "I was so afraid for you," she whispered as she hugged him. "Thank God you are alive."

Simon nodded stiffly and wondered if that fact were not more curse than blessing. He gently helped her to her feet, but remained near in case she faltered. "But what's wrong with you, Maman? Are you ill?"

He could not credit it, but it seemed a blush spread across her face. " 'Tis nothing," she said. "I will be well enough in a moment." She turned toward the doorway. "But where is Cicely? I want to thank her. For surely 'twas her healing skills that saved you. Or was it her love?" She smiled at him.

Simon's face grew stiff; he could not keep the despair at bay. His mother noted it instantly. Her eyes widened, and she put her hand on his shoulder. "What is it, Simon? What's wrong? Why isn't Cicely here, beside you?"

He shook his head, unable to answer. The hall, with a dozen servants and knights gathered around, was not the place to reveal his agony.

"Come, let us go to the solar, and I will have some mulled wine brought. You look half-dead, sweetling." She took his arm and began to lead him toward the stairwell. He could not help looking around for a glimpse of Cicely. With disappointment, he realized that she had not entered the hall.

Following after his mother, he castigated himself for his foolishness. He would have to get used to the empty place Cicely's bright spirit had filled.

"Cicely's decided to return to Montreau?" Lady Nicola looked aghast. "What's wrong with her? Did something happen to addle her wits? Why would she should throw away all hope of happiness for both of you by doing something so stupid?"

"I don't know, Mother." Simon took another swallow of wine and grimaced. "She says she made a vow when I was ill, and now she must keep to it. She prayed that God would spare my life if she returned to Montreau, and since God has seen fit to let me live, she must honor her words."

His mother's eyes narrowed. "A fine time for her to discover her duty—now, when she has already plighted troth with you. What of *those* vows? You could hold her to them, you know. You could insist that she wed you as agreed."

"And endure a wife who's torn by guilt, who might grow to hate me for refusing to allow her to follow her conscience? I think not. I think dying of the fever might come to seem pleasant under those circumstances! Look at Lady Adela, Mother. If you were a man, would you like to be wed to her? Endlessly praying, lost in a dreamworld of saints and Scriptures. That well might be Cicely in a year or two, and I would not want such a holy creature for a wife. Besides it would not be *my* Cicely. *My* Cicely is full of fun and life and spirit. She is lusty and playful and a tiny bit wicked. *That* is the woman I fell in love with—and that is the woman I have apparently lost—forever," he finished glumly.

Lady Nicola sighed. "You are right, of course. One cannot command love from someone who does not feel it. What troubles me is how she could change so much. The young woman you speak of would never willingly enter a priory, renounce marriage and children and all the simple pleasures of womanhood. So, where has *that* Cicely gone, and how can we get her back?"

Simon shook his head. He had pondered the matter for nearly a fortnight, and he had no answer.

"Sir Simon?" A quiet voice interrupted them. Simon started guiltily as he saw Lady Adela standing in the doorway. Had she heard the rather uncomplimentary way he'd referred to her?

"I am delighted to see that you are back." Lady Adela entered the room and came to stand before him. "But you still seem rather gaunt and pale. Mayhap you should seek a bedchamber and lie down."

"An excellent idea." Lady Nicola rose. "Why don't you retire to my chamber. I'll find your squire to help you undress."

Wearily, Simon stood. The miseries of his body could only be ignored for so long.

The two women insisted on escorting him to the bedchamber. After they left him, he heard his mother ask Lady Adela to come with her to the solar. "I have an important matter to discuss with you," she said.

Simon lay down on the bed, boots and all. He had little hope that his mother could solve his dilemma, but he could not help being touched by her concern. He wondered again at why she had fainted, then slowly drifted off to sleep.

Cicely knelt in the chapel and tried to pray, but the words would not come. There seemed to be a painful lump in her throat, which dragged her attention away from pious thoughts and back to her worldly circumstances.

She bowed her head lower and tried to blink the tears away. Sweet Mary, this was the hardest thing she had ever done! She would have to leave for Montreau as soon as possible. To stay here, under the same roof as Simon, 'twas unbearable. No matter how she tried to stop them, her thoughts kept straying to her sinful memories. She had only to close her eyes and the visions would afflict her, tormenting images of Simon's naked body, the recollection of how his skin, his flesh, had felt against hers, inside her . . .

Mother of God, she could not go on this way! Cicely dug her fingernails into the palms of her hands and struggled for control. Now she knew why some monks wore hair shirts. They needed the discomfort, the suffering, to distract them and keep evil thoughts at bay.

But it was not all sin which tormented her. Some of her thoughts were unselfish. She loved Simon, and she could scarce bear to see his pain. He said that she would better have let him die than endure life without her, and she feared he meant it.

Though his body healed, his spirit was grievously wounded. It did not seem right that her decision should cause someone else so much grief.

But what could she do? A vow was a vow. She could not go back on her word. Not only would God not forgive her, but she would not be able to forgive herself. How could she fail to do her duty a second time?

Nay, she would not fail. She would leave for Montreau before first light the next day. She would not see Simon again, even to say good-bye.

"Cicely?"

She jerked upright, realizing that she had dozed off. Stiff with cold, she rose slowly and saw her mother standing behind her.

"Maman." Wordlessly, she embraced the older woman.

"You are cold, child," Lady Adela said. "You should not stay here praying so long. You'll fall ill."

"You do it," Cicely accused.

"Aye, but I am old and do not have much to live for."

With sudden clarity, Cicely realized that she, too, did not have much to live for. Without Simon, the days stretched ahead of her, empty and meaningless.

"Come, love, let us go to the solar, and I will fetch you something hot to drink."

"Nay, I cannot. I do not want to see . . . Simon," she finished lamely.

"He is certainly asleep by now. He looked near dead on his feet when I saw him."

A pang went through Cicely. Poor Simon. He was still so weak. Would he ever be himself again? "I . . . I don't want to see Lady Nicola either," she said.

Her mother nodded. "Aye, she is angry with you, 'tis true."

She sighed. "I cannot say I am pleased with your decision either."

"But I thought you wanted me to return to Montreau!"

Lady Adela shook her head. "That was before I realized how much you loved Simon and he, you. I was afraid, and I thought you would be safe in the priory. But I was wrong. You belong with Simon. Whether you lose Tathwick or no, your place is beside him."

"But I made a vow. I cannot forsake a vow to God!" Cicely closed her eyes. 'Twas hard enough to do this thing, but to have everyone against her, even her mother . . . Would the nuns at Montreau also argue with her decision? Would she have to explain herself a thousand times?

Her mother gently touched her arm. "Aye, a vow is a vow, but sometimes circumstances prevent us from following through on our intentions. I have been thinking, Cicely, mayhap there is a way to fulfill your vow and yet not destroy the lives of everyone involved. What if I took your place at Montreau?"

Cicely's eyes flew open. "You, Mother?"

"Aye, 'twould hardly be a sacrifice. Indeed, the idea appeals to me greatly and makes me wonder why I did not think of it on my own."

"But 'tis not the same. As you said, 'tis no sacrifice for you. And a sacrifice is what my circumstances require. God answered my prayer and let Simon live. I owe Him for that."

"He let Simon live, but what sort of life will Simon have? Without you, I fear he will pine away. He will not be the glorious *parfait* knight he is meant to be. I cannot believe it serves God's will to have two lives ruined, Instead, I will go to Montreau and dedicate the rest of my life to God."

A flicker of hope sprang to life inside Cicely. Could she really have all that she dreamed of? To salve her conscience and also have Simon for a husband and lover?

Her mother put her arms around Cicely. "My dear child,

you have suffered enough. You do not need to bear this burden as well. I will take your place at Montreau, and all will be well.''

''I wish . . . I wish there were someone we could ask, some-one who would know if this is fitting or if I am abandoning my duty to pursue my own selfish goals.''

''There *is* someone.'' Her mother gazed up at the crucifix above the altar. ''Pray to Him, Cicely. He will answer.''

Cicely was doubtful. All those years at Montreau when she had prayed for guidance, she'd never felt certain if the convic-tions which came to her were true ones.

''Come, Cicely,'' her mother coaxed. ''You need to wash the traveling dust from your face. To eat and drink.''

Cicely shook her head. ''I cannot rest until I am clear in this thing. Leave me be. Mayhap when I am alone, I will find the answer I seek.''

Her mother nodded and kissed her cheek. Lady Adela's skirts brushed softly against the paving stones as she took her leave, and Cicely knelt again to pray.

She was interrupted a short time later by the creak of the chapel door. The tread of heavy footsteps behind her made her tense. Had Simon come to argue with her? Or was it Sir Harry?

''Cicely?'' a rough masculine voice called.

She rose as swiftly as her stiff knees would allow. A man loomed behind her, huge and with white hair and a countenance so ancient and craggy that for a moment Cicely thought it might be God Himself come for her. Then he enfolded her in his warm bulk, and the scent of horse and oiled armor made her aware that it was only a mortal man, a grizzled knight who held her. ''My lord!'' She drew back and stared at her godfather. ''What do you here?''

''I bring you news from the king.''

''The king?''

William Marshal nodded. ''I have convinced him to let you

and Sir Simon wed, also to allow you to keep Tathwick. You will have to pay a substantial fine, and Simon must swear to the king, but I believe that would be the prudent course in any event. The rebels are all threats and pompous words. Though they may force John to make some concessions, they'll not overthrow him, not in my lifetime anyway."

"But . . . but how did you know of our plans . . . of Simon and me . . . of Tathwick?"

"My wife wrote me of your circumstances. Since John is depending upon me to pursue his interests and to help guard his kingdom, I thought I could ask a boon of him." His expression grew sorrowful. "I was saddened to learn of your father's and brother's deaths. I convinced the king 'twould be worth his while to make some sort of reparation to you. 'Tis not lost on him that you are to wed a man who is heir to property in Wiltshire."

Cicely shook her head, stunned speechless. Everything was falling into place, her dreams becoming reality. But that did not change the matter of her vow.

"My lord, I must ask your opinion on something."

"Of course," he answered gruffly. "With your father gone— may God assoil him—I am happy to offer you guidance."

"Are there any circumstances under which a vow may be set aside?"

Lord William frowned. "What sort of vow? I would have to know precisely of what you speak."

Head lowered, Cicely told him.

He did not respond for a time; then he said, "A vow made to another man is a matter of honor. I would not forswear my oath to John no matter what he did to injure me, nor whether he was in the wrong. A vow to God is different. 'Tis a matter only between yourself and the Almighty. Only you can decide what is right.

"I can say, though," he added, "that I see precious little

good coming from your returning to Montreau. You were not happy there before, and now you would have many more reasons to despise the life. The truth is, Cicely, I never thought you were meant to be a nun. I think your father knew that as well. But he kept to his vow, and look what came of it? You left Montreau anyway, and he died a troubled man who had lost the chance for many happy years with his daughter.''

"But, if I had not defied him, if I had taken holy vows as he wished, then mayhap God would have spared him." Cicely could scarce speak the words, her guilt was so great. "I was a selfish, wretched sinner, and now my father and brother are dead."

She began to cry, and her godfather gathered her in his arms. "Whist, child. That was no doing of yours. Mercenaries killed your father and brother. Naught you could have done would have saved them."

Gradually, she controlled her tears and drew away.

"If you would honor your father's memory, Cicely," he said, "then consider what he would wish you to do. Do you think he would want you to go to Montreau and live a life of misery? Nay, I do not think so. He would want you to wed Simon and find contentment and happiness."

"But do I have a *right* to be happy? So many others have suffered, their dreams crumbling to dust. My father, my brother . . .''

"That so many suffer means that happiness is an even greater gift. Besides, what of the Valois line? If you do not have children, 'twill die with you. Think you that your father would want that?''

" 'Twas his dream that Hugh's sons would rule Tathwick someday.''

"I think you have your answer, Cicely." The earl moved to leave her. "Mayhap you should pray awhile longer, and consider these things."

Cicely stared after him, then turned back to the rail and knelt wearily. What should she do? How would she know if her decision was right?

With blurry, grit-filled eyes she gazed up at the cross above the altar. She had made a vow to God, just as her father had so many years ago. His vow had brought naught but suffering, for both of them. It appeared her vow would do the same.

She thought of Simon, and the light from the candles blurred as tears again filled her eyes. She had stood in this very spot and promised to love him until death. As part of his pledge, he had placed his mother's ring on her finger. She had worn it until that night at the priory in Stamford when she'd vowed that if Simon lived, she would become a nun.

She could not bear to give the ring back to Simon, and he had not asked for it, so she wore it on a gold chain around her neck. Now, she drew it out and stared at it. The symbol of her pledge. How could she forsake it and hurt Simon? Would that not be a greater sin than renouncing her vow to become a nun?

Simon had suffered much in the past few years, and might suffer more. The Jewish physician said the fever could recur throughout Simon's life. If that happened, he would need someone to care for him. If she were a nun, she would not be able to go to him. How could she abandon her love, her life?

She could not. Her promise to Simon, the pledge she had made to him, was not one she could set aside.

She rose slowly, feeling slightly giddy. Never had she done the dutiful, conventional thing. Why should she begin now? She was probably a hopeless sinner anyway.

A slight smile quirked her lips as she recalled Prioress Elena shaking her head in consternation over some of Cicely's antics when she'd first been at the priory. "Blessed Jesu," the prioress had muttered under her breath, "why did You send me this one? She has no vocation, none at all."

Suddenly, Cicely laughed. How long would she have lasted

as a meek, pious sister? As soon as her grief had worn off, she would have chafed bitterly at the restrictions of the priory and remembered the marvelous enticements of the outside world— fresh air and freedom, life and color.

And Simon. Beautiful, magnificent Simon.

He was waiting for her. Once the fever left him, he had healed rapidly. By now, he might be well enough to . . .

She took a deep breath and left the chapel.

Another dream.

Darkness. Faceless knights loomed over him, their swords dripping with blood. His blood.

He was dying and hell awaited. He could feel it getting closer, hear the screams of the damned.

But it was his own voice screaming, choking in his throat.

"Simon, Simon, I am here."

Soft hands stroked his sweat-soaked brow. Where was he? In hell or . . . heaven.

Cicely. His angel.

He breathed a sigh of relief, then slowly came awake and sat up with a jerk. "What do you here?"

Her soft brown eyes opened wide. "Do you want me to leave?"

"Nay, I . . . I thought . . ."

She shook her head, smiling at him. "I couldn't leave you, Simon. Who else would care for you and love you as I do?"

He reached for her hand and pressed it fervently against his lips. "No one," he said, "no one."

He kissed her fingers tenderly, then stared at her. "Pinch me," he said, "lest this be a dream."

" 'Tis no dream, Simon. I am very real.'' She pulled her hand away and began to unfasten the woven girdle at her waist.

"What are you doing?"

"I'm going to show you that I am flesh and blood." She paused in undressing and smiled wickedly. ''Angels don't have bodies, you know. At least not breasts and quims.''

"Cicely! Where did you learn that word?"

She shrugged. "I must have overheard it. I'm not so innocent as that, Simon. Which is why I am hardly fit to be a nun.''

He shook his head helplessly. "By the saints, you are not. You did not belong at Montreau when I met you, and now you are completely corrupted.''

She drew her kirtle over her head, then gave him a radiant, and utterly provocative, smile. "I was hoping that you felt well enough . . . that is—''

"Jesu, Cicely, when you look like that, you could arouse a dead man!''

She moved nearer to the bed and slowly, seductively, drew her chemise upward and over her head. Standing there in all her naked glory, she said, "You do not appear dead to me, Sir Simon.''

CHAPTER 22

This time when they made love it was different. Slower, rich with tenderness. Their bodies melded and merged as if the boundaries between them no longer existed. Their spirits touched, entwined, mingled.

It felt almost holy, Simon thought.

Cicely fulfilled and perfected his being much as the Holy Grail was said to heal the strife and pain of the world. This was the blessing, the sense of peace he had sought since childhood.

Yet, she was delightfully, wonderfully real. No glowing angel but an earthy, tangible woman. He savored the heady feminine scent of her, the opulent silk of her skin, the exquisite embrace of her warm, lithe body around his flesh.

When they reached their peak, 'twas profound and voluptuous, a memory of earth and sea mating in ancient rhythm.

Afterward, he could not bear to release her, but held her close, his flaccid member cradled against her wet warmth.

"What changed your mind?" he whispered. "Why did you decide to come back to me?"

"I could not leave you," she said. "You are my knight, my rescuer. I do not believe that God would send you to me and then, later, expect me to give you up."

"But what a poor champion I have been. I near got myself killed defending Tathwick, and we still don't know if you will be allowed to keep your home."

"Ah, but we do." Cicely stirred in his arms, stretching languorously. "William Marshal has arranged everything."

Simon sat upright. "What are you talking about?"

Cicely gave him a self-satisfied smile. "He is here, at Tathwick. He came to see me in the chapel and said that he had convinced the king to allow me to keep my inheritance. If the two of us are wed, of course, and you agree to swear to John."

"He wants me to swear to the king?"

Cicely's confidence seemed to fade. Simon decided that she must fear he would be unwilling to swear an oath to John. In truth, a part of him rebelled at the thought of serving such an unscrupulous, impious man. But he had no choice. John was God's anointed king.

He released a long, drawn-out sigh. "Well, if I am ever to inherit Valmar and the rest of it, I would have to swear to him someday. John may not be an honorable man, but I vow he is no worse than most of the rebels."

"So, you will do it?"

Simon nodded. "I must if I wish to keep Tathwick for my son."

"Your son?" Cicely raised her brows. "What is this about a son?"

Simon gave her a wolfish leer. "Well, my little novice, you do know where babies come from, don't you? If we keep at this, I have hopes to have your belly swelling ere next Christmas."

"Aye, we will have to work very hard on this endeavor. Very, very hard." She touched the tip of his rapidly swelling shaft and beamed at him.

Hours later, they went to share their good news. They visited the solar first, and finding it empty, went down to the hall. To their astonishment, they found the place crowded with villagers, villeins, and knights. Lady Nicola, Lady Adela, Sir Harry, and Earl Marshal were all seated at the high table, and the savory smells drifting to their noses made it clear that a banquet was in progress.

Seeing them, Lord William raised his cup and called for a toast. "To the new Lord and Lady of Tathwick!" he boomed out. "May God bless them and keep them!"

The rest of the room were on their feet in seconds, shouting, "Hear, hear. To Simon and Cicely!"

For a moment they paused at the edge of the room, shocked speechless. Then, laughing, Cicely took Simon's hand and led him to the dais. As he neared his mother, Simon hissed, "Pretty certain of yourself, aren't you, Maman? What if Cicely had not relented? You would have felt rather silly if you had planned a banquet *then!*"

"But she did relent." Lady Nicola regarded him with that smug, catlike expression of hers. "Mayhap now you will be forced to admit that your mother does know something of love and life. Mayhap you should remember to listen to her in the future."

Simon rolled his eyes and allowed Cicely to drag him to his place in the lord's chair. He was certainly glad that his betrothed was not as strong willed and stubborn as his mother. Or, mayhap, she was. Did Cicely not always seem to get her way in the end?

He gazed tenderly at her, relishing the innocent charm of

her heart-shaped face and laughing brown eyes. He seemed to drink in life and hope merely from being around her. She had the most remarkable power to heal him, both the ailments of his body and his spirit.

Nearly as soon as they were seated, Cicely picked up her eating knife and began to serve herself from the platter of capon and heron. "Bless the Saints that Lent is over," she said. "I vow I am famished."

Simon watched her pile their trencher high, then stuff a piece of bread into her mouth. "Jesu, you are hungry." He leaned near. " 'Tis hungry work, isn't it?"

"What?" she asked between mouthfuls.

"Lovemaking, my sweet," he whispered in her ear.

She giggled, and everyone at the high table turned to look at them.

Even Lord William raised a snow-white brow, and Simon found himself discomfited by his own jest. He grinned awkwardly at the earl. The stately old man guffawed. " 'Tis well that I was able to square things with the king, isn't it, Simon? I'd not want my beloved goddaughter to give birth to a bastard."

"We did plight troth," Simon said defensively, "and I will marry her properly as soon as the arrangements are made."

"Aye, we must see to those arrangements," said Lady Adela, who was sharing a trencher with the earl.

"I should like to have my father here for the wedding." Simon took a bite of capon. "To show him that things turned out well, despite his misgivings."

"He's already on his way," Lady Nicola said complacently. "I sent him a message near a sennight ago."

"But, why?" Simon demanded. "You could not have known *then* that there was to be a wedding. Neither Cicely nor I knew ourselves."

"I had other reasons for summoning him. Indeed . . ." Lady

Nicola put aside her eating knife. "Mayhap 'tis time I shared my news with all of you."

"News? What news is that, Maman?"

Simon could not credit it, but what seemed very like a blush colored his mother's face. Jesu, she had changed these past years! First, fainting and now blushing. 'Twas nothing like the bold, impervious woman he recalled.

"It seems almost like a miracle," she said. "Indeed, there cannot be any other explanation than 'tis a gift from God. But the fact is"—her gaze met Simon's uneasily—"I'm going to have a baby."

Simon near choked on the swallow of wine he had just taken. The earl reached over and pounded him on the back.

"Now, Simon," his mother exclaimed, "don't be distressed. You are still my heir. Even should the babe prove to be a boy, I vow there is land enough for both of you. And besides, now you have Tathwick."

"By the Saints, Maman, of course I don't begrudge the child a share of its birthright. 'Tis only that I am . . . well, shocked does not even begin to describe it!"

"I'm not *that* old," Lady Nicola said haughtily. "Some women are able to bear up to their forty-fifth year."

"Aye, but they are usually women who have birthed a child a year since they were wed. While you . . ." Simon shook his head. "It's been near ten years since you had the stillborn babe."

Lady Nicola heaved a sigh. "I've a right to hope this time will be different, don't I?"

"Of course, Maman. But . . . are you certain you will be well?" Simon felt the dread rising up inside him.

"I am not so feeble or sickly as you seem to think!" Then her disdainful mood vanished, and she gave him a nervous smile. " 'Tis kind of you to worry for me, son, but you must learn to keep your doubts to yourself. I cannot imagine how Fawkes will ever deal with this.''

"You're right," Simon said. "He'll be mad with worry.''

"Well, I think 'tis wonderful," Cicely said. She patted Simon's arm. "Think of it, if you and I are as fortunate, come next Easter, your new brother or sister might have a niece or nephew who is almost the same age.''

"I think this calls for another toast," Sir Harry stood and raised his cup. "To Lady Nicola!" He turned and gazed fondly at Cicely's mother. "And to Lady Adela and all mothers everywhere!''

The hall resounded with cheers. When the merrymaking died down, Simon turned to Cicely and was shocked to see how pale she'd become. "What's wrong?" he asked.

"I don't know. I think . . . I ate too much.'' She rose unsteadily and hurried from the hall.

"It looks as if you'll get your wish," Simon's mother announced. "The girl's breeding already, I'd wager my best mantle on it. Leave her be," she added to Simon when he started to rise. "No woman wants her beloved to see her crouched on her knees in the privy.''

"If Cicely is already with child, that is all the more reason to plan this wedding immediately," Lord William said. "I would like to stay and give the bride away, but I've delayed too long in returning to the king. The rebels have marched south and are besieging Northampton. I've already sent John a message informing him that the barons have rejected his offer, but he may want me to lead an army to turn them back ere they reach London.''

"So, there will be war," Lady Adela said sadly. "More men will die. More families will suffer.''

"I'm afraid, lady," Lord William said, "that such is the way of life.''

"I refuse to talk about such gloomy matters," Lady Nicola declared. "We are here to plan a wedding."

"I would be delighted to give Cicely away," said Sir Harry. "If you think it appropriate, that is."

"I can think of no one better." Lady Adela regarded the seneschal fondly. "You've been like a father to her these past weeks."

"There are other guests we should invite," Lady Nicola suggested. "Neighboring landowners who will want an opportunity to meet the new lord of Tathwick." She nodded to Simon. "Mayhap some of your father's friends who have property in this part of England."

"I don't want this to become a huge affair, Maman. After all, as Lord William said, the country is virtually at war."

"That does not mean we cannot celebrate with the proper fanfare," Lady Nicola sniffed. "This may be the only wedding I will ever get to plan, and I want it to be perfect."

"You are forgetting the babe you carry," Simon pointed out. "With luck, 'twill be a girl and you will have years to fuss over her and indulge your maternal instincts."

"Jesu, the two of you argue enough." Cicely came and took her seat beside Simon. She still looked pale, but not nearly as sickly. She patted Simon's arm. "Let her have her way, Simon. Since I have you, naught else matters to me. We could be married in the stables, and I would not care. Although, I would like to invite a certain friend," she added shyly.

"Let me guess—Sister Clotilde?"

"Nay, she would never leave the priory. I was thinking of Lady Blackhurst."

Simon groaned. "Of all the meddling, arrogant—"

"Please, Simon? Bella was ever so good to me. And I'm certain she would be respectful and courteous to you now, once she knows that you are not a penniless knight with designs upon me."

"Who is Lady Blackhurst?" asked Lady Adela.

"Our rescuer," Cicely announced brightly. "She helped Simon and me when we were on our way to Pembroke Castle."

Simon clamped his mouth shut until his head hurt, but he did not dispute Cicely's words. How could he begrudge his beloved a chance to repay someone she felt beholden to? Besides, it would be rather satisfying to reveal to that aggravating minx that he was really a man of wealth and substance!

"Whatever you wish, my beloved." Simon drew Cicely's hand to his lips and kissed it. "And you, Maman, I give you free rein to plan the most lavish, ostentatious wedding in creation. But," he added firmly, "don't expect me to do more than show up at the church. I have no patience with gowns and ribbons and fancy victuals. I am a knight, remember?"

"Aye," Cicely said, hugging him close. "My gallant, noble, magical knight."

Simon stood tall in his new crimson surcote trimmed with gold, though the sweat beaded on his skin. Jesu, 'twas hot in the chapel! A pity he was the groom and had to be inside where the June heat was so stifling. His mother had invited so many guests that they spilled out of the village church onto the green. Simon envied them the chance to breathe fresh air and feel the breeze.

But 'twas worth it, he knew, for beside him stood the most beautiful bride in creation. Cicely wore a gown of palest pink trimmed with rose and gold at the neck and on the long, hanging sleeves, and her hair spilled over her shoulders in a cascade of honey gold curls entwined with summer roses. Her face was like a flower itself, glowing brown eyes, flushed cheeks, her mouth like a delicious bloom.

She was summer and sunshine and hope, and she made his

heart soar with happiness. And within her still slender, supple body grew a promise of new life. His child.

The wonder of it left him breathless and helped make the endless kneeling and prayers of the Mass pass quickly. Then it was time to say their vows. Cicely's voice was like a laughing, bubbling stream as she promised, once again, to love and cherish him until death.

His own voice rang clear and proud, for never had he felt anything with such conviction. Cicely was his soul, his life. Naught could part him from her, not even death.

Their kiss was sweet and tender, with the underlying fire which always leaped between them.

They progressed out of the chapel into the sunshine and there endured the felicitations of their many guests. Knights and ladies in bright gowns and rich surcotes mingled on the green beneath festoons of flowers and flapping banners.

Lady Nicola moved through the crowd, greeting guests, radiant in a deep blue kirtle. She looked verily like a girl, Simon thought, with her slim figure barely beginning to swell with the babe and her face flushed and animated. Behind her trailed his father, looking almost as proud and happy as Simon felt. For a moment, Simon caught Fawkes' eye. His father gestured to his wife and shrugged helplessly, then followed her as she approached a group of richly clad nobles.

When Simon turned to speak to Cicely, she was gone. He searched the crowd for her, and finally spied her with Lady Blackhurst. The two embraced, then gestured excitedly. From their exuberant motions, Simon guessed that Lady Blackhurst was also with child.

Indeed, Cicely soon hurried back to him, near dragging Lady Blackhurst behind her. "Bella's going to have a baby, too!" she exulted. "They will both be born soon after Christmas. Isn't that wonderful, Simon?"

Simon looked at Lady Blackhurst, who was smiling at him

with an expression of total bliss, and laughed. "Of course, 'tis wonderful! The more babies, the better."

He stood by indulgently as Cicely and her friend caught up on the happenings of their lives the past winter. Finally, a masculine voice spoke behind him, and he turned in relief to see Girard.

"Damned foolish things, weddings are," the knight said. "I've tried a dozen times to get news of what's happening in London with the king, but the women keep shushing me up. They don't want to hear about matters of State today, they say."

"My father was just in London," Simon said. "He'd have stayed but for the wedding. And many of the barons gathered here are on their way there after this. They say Archbishop Langton has negotiated a charter that John has agreed to sign. They're all gathering at Runnymede to show the king that this agreement has the will of the barons of England behind it."

"So, the rebels have won," Girard said wonderingly. "I would not have thought it."

Simon shook his head. "My father reports that the Earl Marshal thinks otherwise. He believes that although John will sign the charter, he doesn't mean to keep to it. There will be war before the year is out."

Girard nodded grimly. "That sounds like John." He shrugged. "But without war, what would knights like me do to occupy our time?"

"You could sing songs and court ladies," Cicely said gaily, returning to Simon's side. " 'Twould be a much better world, I think, if men would be satisfied with those endeavors."

Girard gave Simon a horrified look, and Simon laughed. Then he turned back to Cicely and bent his head to give her a long, passionate kiss.

Dear Readers,

As the character Girard suspects at the end of *My Gallant Knight,* King John did not submit meekly to the restrictions of the Magna Carta. Within months, he was leading an army to fight the rebel barons and to overturn the limitations they had put on his power. But this time England was saved from serious civil war by John's death in 1216. William Marshal was named regent for the young Henry III, and England entered an era of relative peace.

Although denounced by the Church, tournaments were very popular during this time period, and men did die in them. One of the more prominent of the rebel barons, Geoffrey de Mandeville, was killed in a tournament in 1216 and his death helped to seriously undermine the rebel cause.

In an era of tragic deaths and political turmoil, it is especially gratifying to create a tale of happiness, honor, family, and enduring love. I hope you enjoyed *My Gallant Knight.* It's always a pleasure to hear from readers. Write me at P.O. Box 2052, Cheyenne, WY 82003-2052. A self-addressed stamped envelope is appreciated.

Happy reading,
Tara O'Dell